HEARTS IN MOTION

HEARTS IN MOTION

MIRANDA MACLEOD

Hearts in Motion
Copyright © 2021 Miranda MacLeod

Find out more: www.mirandamacleod.com
Contact the author: miranda@mirandamacleod.com

Cover Design by: Victoria Cooper
Edited by Kelly Hashway

ISBN: 9798508084257
This is a work of fiction. Any resemblance of characters to actual persons, living or dead, is purely coincidental.

ALSO BY MIRANDA MACLEOD

Stand Alone Novels

Telling Lies Online

Holly & Ivy (cowritten with T.B. Markinson)

Heart of Ice (cowritten with T.B. Markinson)

Accidental Honeymoon

Hearts in Motion

Love's Encore Trilogy:

A Road Through Mountains

Your Name in Lights

Fifty Percent Illusion

Americans Abroad Series:

Waltzing on the Danube

Holme for the Holidays

Stockholm Syndrome

Letters to Cupid

London Holiday

Check mirandamacleod.com for more about these titles,
and for other books coming soon!

ABOUT THE AUTHOR

Originally from southern California, Miranda now lives in New England and writes heartfelt romances and romantic comedies featuring witty and charmingly flawed women that you'll want to marry. Or just grab a coffee with, if that's more your thing. She spent way too many years in graduate school, worked in professional theater and film, and held temp jobs in just about every office building in downtown Boston.

To find out about her upcoming releases and take advantage of exclusive sales, be sure to sign up for her newsletter at her website: mirandamacleod.com.

CHAPTER ONE

H adley smelled her next patient before she even laid eyes on him, the stench of cheap alcohol and unwashed human body hanging like a toxic green cloud in the hallway outside exam room three. She grabbed the chart, drawing as deep a breath as she could tolerate as she spied a familiar name printed across the top. *Roger Hart.* "Don't you have anything better to do on a Friday night?" she muttered.

"This is Dr. Cassidy, head of the emergency department at Pioneer Valley Hospital. I'm so sorry to have to tell you, but there's been an accident."

Hadley smoothed her face, allowing her muscles to settle into a well-practiced mask of bland dispassion. The expression was second nature to her by now, a skill honed over years of encountering too many terrible injuries, awful odors, and confounding medical conditions to count. Rule number one was always the same. Maintain composure. Never let on that a situation was anything other than routine and expected. Some women had resting bitch face. After a decade on the job, Hadley had resting doctor face.

"Good evening, Mr. Hart," she chirped, entering the room without looking up from the chart. "I'm Dr. Moore."

The introduction was a formality. Over the past twelve months, this particular man had come through the emergency department doors no less than twenty-seven times, and Hadley had enjoyed the dubious pleasure of being on duty for most of them. Twenty-seven times, and not once had he been sober. Or sick, for that matter.

Like many drifters, Roger would wander into the ER seeking shelter during foul weather, sniffing out the potential to sweet talk his way into a few pills to treat the back pain he claimed to have developed while serving in Afghanistan. As far as Hadley knew, both the injury and the military service that had caused it were unsubstantiated, though the fact he was never without his green ball cap with the crossed swords insignia and the words *10th Mountain Division* embroidered on the bill lent some credence to his claim. He was a nice enough fellow, polite, even funny. Hadley didn't doubt he needed help, but in the form of mental health and addiction treatment, not an emergency room.

"The ambulance arrived minutes ago. They're taking them both to surgery now."

"What seems to be the problem, Mr. Hart?" His chart indicated today's complaint was neck and shoulder discomfort, but Hadley always asked to make sure.

When several seconds ticked by without a response, Hadley looked up. Her patient was stretched out on the bed, lying on one side with his back to her. The matted hair poking out from his cap had left a trail of twigs on the white pillow while his mud-caked boots had formed a dark puddle on the sheets. One toe peeked out from a hole in the worn leather.

Great. Her patient was napping.

"Mr. Hart?" Hadley gave the bed rail a shake, but the man didn't stir. She shook it again, less gently this time. Her patience was running thin. She had other patients to treat. Sick people, injured people, dying people. She didn't have time for this.

Especially not tonight.

Paramedics report extensive internal injuries.

"Come on, Mr. Hart. Time to wake up."

He didn't budge.

Hadley's jaw hardened. This was a hospital, not the fucking Hilton. "Roger!"

There was no movement, no sound, and now a prickle of unease snaked its way through Hadley's belly. Every two weeks for the past year, this man had

3

come to her complaining of lower back pain, but tonight his chart said neck and shoulders.

Shit.

Hadley dashed toward her patient's head, rolling him onto his back as she flipped the red lever on the side of the bed, sending it flat with a bang. She leaned down to study the patient's chest for the telltale rise and fall of breathing.

It didn't move.

Her fingers flew to his neck, checking for a pulse.

Nothing.

"Oh, Jesus, Roger." Hadley slammed her fist into the blue button above the bed. "I need help in room three!"

She'd already begun chest compressions when an automated voice announced, "Code blue, room three," over the emergency room speakers.

Brenda, the charge nurse, skidded into the room, her blonde ponytail flapping. "What's going on?"

"Full code. Get the cart."

Brenda ran into the hallway, returning seconds later holding a white CPR board in one hand and dragging the crash cart with the other. An older nurse, Gracie, followed with a computerized tablet to record notes.

Brenda slid the board between Roger's back and the mattress fast enough that Hadley didn't miss a single compression. "I'll grab the bagger."

Hadley continued what she was doing while the

nurse positioned the purple bag-valve mask over Roger's invisible mouth. It was hiding somewhere beneath his scraggly beard, right?

As she continued to press in a rhythmic motion on Roger's chest, Hadley's fingers detected the crackling of cartilage. This was a good sign. It meant she was doing it hard enough. Her arms and shoulders cried out in exhaustion, which she ignored. She'd allow herself to be tired later, once Roger had rejoined the living.

Relief flooded her as Caleb Lee, one of her favorite third-year residents, came into the room, followed by a young woman she didn't recognize, but whose saucer-like eyes pegged her as one of the first-year residents who was just starting the one-month rotations in the ER.

"Caleb, come take over compressions, and you"— she pointed to the first-year, whose name she would bother to learn later—"stand by to relieve him."

Freed from the backbreaking job of chest compressions, Hadley scanned the room to assess her team. While she'd been preoccupied with keeping the blood circulating through the patient's body, the code team had arrived, consisting of two additional nurses plus Jay, the respiratory technician, who took over ventilation from Brenda.

Hadley pointed to the tall, dark-skinned woman in pink scrubs. "Kim, he doesn't have an IV yet. Get that going and start a one-liter bag of saline." She shifted her finger to the woman with the red curly hair positioned beside the crash cart. "Deb, ready to position the defibrillator pads whenever you are."

In a flash, Deb tore open the buttons of Roger's threadbare flannel shirt to reveal his pale chest and set to work opening the package and removing the paper backing from the two adhesive pads that would soon deliver shocks to his heart. The team assembled, and their roles affirmed, Hadley brought everyone up to speed.

Patient is a twenty-six-year-old female. Shattered pelvis. Extensive chest trauma.

"Patient is Roger Hart, age forty-seven. I'm sure most of you have met him before. He's a regular. I found him unconscious on the bed and started compressions at 23:49." A quick glance at the wall clock told Hadley they were nearing the two-minute mark.

Gracie's stylus tapped furiously at the tablet's dark screen. The murderous look on her face suggested the high-tech contraption was misbehaving again.

"Oh, poor Roger." Kim's expression remained neutral as she slid a large bore IV into his forearm, but compassion filled her eyes. "He's a nice guy. We've chatted lots of times."

With a little growl, Gracie tossed the tablet onto the counter and grabbed hold of the roll of paper towel that was mounted on the wall. She unspooled about a dozen sheets and resumed her note taking on the white paper surface, using a black permanent marker that she always kept at the ready in her breast pocket. "How long has he been down, Dr. Moore?"

"Unknown," Hadley replied. "Anyone remember when he entered the exam room?"

"Just after eleven-thirty," Brenda said. "I brought him in. He said his neck and shoulders were sore."

"So, as long as nineteen minutes." Hadley pressed her lips together, maintaining her calm exterior, even as her brain calculated the terrible odds of survival if he'd been without circulation for that long. "Anyone see him after that?"

"Uh, I think I did." It was the intern, standing behind Caleb like he was a shield and looking even more wide-eyed than before. Crap. Had she never experienced a real code?

"We'll come back to that," Hadley said, switching her attention to the squiggly green lines of the heart monitor. "Let's stop compressions and check his rhythm."

"Looks like v-fib," Deb called out, a conclusion Hadley had reached at the same time.

"Let's defibrillate at 150 joules."

A loud, steady tone filled the room.

"I'm clear. You're clear. Everyone clear," Deb directed, following up a few seconds later with, "Shock delivered at 150 joules."

"You, there." Hadley pointed to the intern.

"A-Amanda."

"Amanda, take over compressions for Dr. Lee. Kim, administer one milligram epinephrine, IV push. Brenda, let me know when two minutes have passed." Hadley called out the familiar instructions, as she had hundreds of times before. The outcomes varied, but the steps were always the same.

"Epi, one milligram, IV in," Kim announced.

Hadley zeroed in on the intern, observing her technique. "Amanda, harder."

"I'm afraid of hurting his ribs," Amanda replied between labored breaths.

"Mr. Hart doesn't have a pulse," Hadley pointed out, her tone firm but not harsh. "That means he's dead. You can't hurt someone who's dead."

The terror in Amanda's eyes increased exponentially, but to her credit, the intern's compressions grew more vigorous. Hadley wondered what specialty the timid woman planned to pursue. Not emergency medicine, that was for sure.

"Let's administer 500 mils normal saline, and prepare 300mg Amiodarone, IV push," Hadley announced, glancing at the clock. Another minute had ticked by. "Caleb, take over compressions. Amanda, what did you mean by you *think* you saw Mr. Hart earlier?"

"I, uh, got turned around and came into room three instead of room seven across the hall." The woman swallowed like she was trying to consume a watermelon without chewing. "There was, um, a homeless looking guy sitting on the bed."

"You're sure he was sitting upright?" A flutter of hope tickled Hadley's chest as the intern nodded. "What time was that?"

"Two or three minutes before the code blue announcement. Not, uh... not more than five minutes, max."

"That's excellent news." Hadley allowed the shadow of a smile to pass her lips. Roger's chances for recovery looked a whole lot brighter, assuming his heart started beating again. Best not to get too far ahead of herself. "How's the pulse looking with compressions?"

"Looking good," Deb answered.

Hadley pressed her lips together, studying the lines around Roger's eyes, which were about all she was able to see of the man at this point. "Amanda, do you remember anything else about the patient from when you entered the room?"

"He said he was dizzy, feeling nauseated. I think he mistook me for a nurse." It was clear from Amanda's tone she hadn't appreciated the mistake.

Hadley frowned. She didn't recall seeing anything about dizziness or nausea when she'd looked at his chart. She was about to pursue this further when Brenda called out, "Two minutes since the last shock."

Hadley nodded. "Let's stop compressions and reassess rhythm."

"Still v-fib," Deb said.

"Defibrillate, 150 joules." Hadley scrutinized her patient's face as the shock fired, as if willing him to rejoin the living through the power of her unblinking stare. Someone had removed his green Army cap, leaving his hair to stick out wildly, like a halo around his head.

Long, dark hair. Her ponytail stuck to a ghost white face, cemented with blood.

Stop, Hadley. Don't try to picture it.

"Shock delivered at 150 joules," Deb announced.

"Kim, administer amiodarone. How's the ventilation going?" Hadley made eye contact with Jay, who wore the intent expression of a man who was struggling.

"Having some trouble."

"We'd better intubate." Hadley reached for the safety glasses and gloves that Deb held out in silent anticipation. "Can I get a laryngoscope handle with a three blade, and a number eight endotracheal tube?"

The team quickly produced these and the rest of the supplies needed.

After moving to the head of the bed, Hadley inserted the laryngoscope blade into the patient's mouth. As she did, her gaze landed on a bright green leaf, the size of a fingernail, that clung to Roger's beard. This was no way for a man to die, caked in dirt and debris. That settled it. He needed to live and make a full recovery so he could take a hot shower and get a good haircut.

Hadley squatted to get a better view as she searched Roger's throat for the white, V-shaped vocal chords. She located her target and slid the endotracheal tube into place, securing the airway. Finally, she straightened up and repositioned herself to place her stethoscope against Roger's chest.

"We have good air entry, bilateral." Hadley informed the team. Before stepping away from the bed, she flicked the leaf out of Roger's beard. It fell to the floor. "What's our oxygen saturation?"

Kim checked the sat monitor. "Ninety-nine percent."

"Good." Hadley made eye contact with Gracie. "How long since the last epinephrine?"

The nurse's eyes scanned the sheets of paper towel. "Five minutes."

"Okay, prepare and administer one milligram epinephrine, IV push," Hadley told Kim. When this was done, she looked at Caleb. "Stop compressions, and let's reassess the rhythm."

"Normal sinus rhythms." As Deb delivered this news, Hadley's own heart leapt.

Hadley almost heard Kim's smile as she called out, "We have a pulse."

There's electrical activity but still no pulse. Start epinephrine.

"Blood pressure?" Hadley demanded.

She's lost so much blood.

Snap out of it, Hadley. You don't know what's going on, so stop imagining and focus on the patient in front of you.

Kim wrapped a maroon cuff around the patient's sinewy arm and took the reading. "Eighty-eight over forty."

"Okay. Thank you, Kim." Hadley let out a breath, the muscles in her shoulders relaxing. "Continue normal saline at 250 mils an hour. I want a chest X-ray, ECG, and CCU blood work. Brenda, call the ICU and arrange a bed. Good job, everyone."

Gracie waved the strip of paper towel, now covered in black ink scribbles, in the air. "I'll get these transferred into the computer, Dr. Moore, so you can sign off."

"Yes, you do that, Gracie." The corners of Hadley's mouth twitched as she admired the seasoned nurse's ingenuity. That woman would never let a technical glitch get in the way of performing her duties. The ER could use a hundred more like her. "Hey, Kim? You mentioned you and Roger had chatted before. Did he ever mention family or anything?"

Kim shook her head. "Not that I can recall. Talked about his army days a lot, though."

"You're on shift until the morning, right?"

"Yeah. Ten o'clock."

Hadley took a long look at the man in the bed. He was so alone. He would wake up in the ICU surrounded by strangers. Or maybe he wouldn't pull through, and he would die without the comfort of even one friendly face. Either way, it was wrong not to have someone by his side.

"I know this isn't in your job description, but do you think you could drop by social work when they get in? They must have contacts at the homeless veterans place downtown. Maybe they can help find someone who remembers him. Tell them he was in the Tenth Mountain Division and served in Afghanistan."

"Will do."

Gracie handed her the resuscitation record, now neatly typed into the tablet, for Hadley's approval. As the rest of the team finished up their tasks, Hadley stepped into the hall, breathing steadily as she waited for Amanda to emerge from the room. Hadley was still on shift, which meant the mask of calm would remain firmly in place, no matter how hard it was to do. She was fairly certain the first-year had screwed up big time, and that was something Hadley had no tolerance for.

Finally, her intended target came into view.

"Can I have a word with you?"

Amanda shot a wary look at Caleb, who raised his eyebrows as he nodded toward Hadley.

"Yes, Dr. Moore?" It was hard to believe this was a grown woman, a full-fledged medical doctor, no less. She sounded like a baby mouse.

"Did you grab Mr. Hart's chart from outside the door before you accidentally went into his room?"

"Yes."

"And you read it?"

"Quickly."

"Enough to know he was complaining of neck and shoulder pain?"

The intern's brow furrowed. "Yes."

"Could you tell me, please, combined with the presence of pain in the neck and shoulders, what condition might dizziness and nausea suggest?"

Amanda was quiet for a moment as she bit her lower lip. "Ven-ventricular tachycardia?"

"That's right." Another long breath. *Keep your cool.* "And what is another sign of v-tach?"

"Abnormal heart rate?"

"Is that a question?" Hadley allowed herself the lukewarm satisfaction of mimicking the young woman's upward lilt. The intern shook her head, not daring to speak. "Right. So, did you check the patient's heart rate or alert anyone else that Mr. Hart felt light-headed and was about to puke?"

"He was drunk," she sputtered as if that excused her from doing her job.

"Yes, he was. But also, his heart was teetering on the edge of calling it quits." Hadley's face turned to stone, and her voice was like ice. "Are you aware that you're a doctor now?"

"Yes," Amanda squeaked.

"That makes it your job to figure out whether your patient's complaints are because of inebriation or a heart attack and then take the appropriate steps. Preferably *before* you have to break a man's ribs with chest compressions and run electrical current through him like he's a stubborn string of Christmas lights."

The young doctor gulped, blinking rapidly as if holding back tears.

"I don't know what specialty you're planning to pursue—"

"Podiatry."

Hadley blinked. She'd meant it rhetorically, but she couldn't help feeling relief at the woman's answer. There weren't a lot of life or death decisions in podiatry. The world would be a safer place, as long as everyone avoided high-heeled shoes.

"One thing I can tell you about the ER, you never know who's coming through the door. And it doesn't matter. Drunk, sober, you treat them all."

"Uh-huh," Amanda barely managed saying by way of agreement.

"Officers at the scene reported the other driver was intoxicated."

"As you might imagine, I've seen a lot of patients who have made very questionable life decisions. It's no more my business to judge *them* for that than it is to tell *you* what type of medicine to practice." *Although, yeah, definitely stick with the feet.* "Some people, like Roger Hart, choose to get wasted on alcohol. Others choose to abuse drugs. I don't know why. What I do know is that no one deserves to lose their life because a doctor writes them off as *just* a drunk who is not worthy of her attention because she was mistaken for a nurse. Do you understand?"

"Yes."

"For as long as you're working in my department, you'll remember that. And whatever else is going on in your life—your personal baggage—stays outside the ER door. When you come in here, it's like flipping a switch. Anything that does not contribute to you being an effective doctor, you shut it down, box it up, put it aside. If you can't manage that while you're in my department, you won't last the month. I'll show you the door myself. And if that happens, you can kiss your career goodbye."

Without waiting for a response, Hadley spun on one heel and strode down the hallway toward her office. She had no doubt as soon as she was out of earshot, Amanda would find someone to complain to about how hard Hadley had been on her. Whatever. She'd heard it all before.

Dr. Moore is so mean.

Dr. Moore doesn't understand how difficult it is.

She understood just fine, which was why she was so hard. Every single day, patients trusted doctors like her with their lives. They didn't need her to be soft and sympathetic. They needed her to get the job done.

Stop the bleeding. Start the heart. Find the problem and fix it.

On those terrible days when she had to look

another human being in the eyes and tell them their loved one had died, she wanted to be damn sure in the depths of her soul there wasn't a single thing she could've done differently to change the outcome. If it meant she didn't win a first-place trophy in the department popularity contest, *that* was something she could live with.

Hadley closed her office door behind her, glancing at the clock as she sank into her desk chair. Twenty-two minutes until the end of her shift. She checked her phone. No missed calls, no text messages.

No news is good news, right?

It was almost as if this thought triggered her phone to ring, the jarring sound causing her to drop it on the desk. She scrambled to pick it up, recognizing the area code of her hometown but not the number.

"This is Hadley Moore."

"Dr. Moore, it's Dr. Cassidy calling again. We spoke—"

"I remember." Hadley swallowed hard, her heart ricocheting in her throat. "How are they?"

"Your brother-in-law's still in surgery."

Alive. At least for now.

Hadley squeezed her eyes shut. "And Kayleigh?"

But in that moment, she already knew. The other doctor's silence had lasted a little too long. Hadley held the phone with both hands so as not to drop it again as her entire body shook.

"I'm so sorry. We did everything we could, but her injuries were too extensive. Your sister has died."

"I'll—" Hadley choked. "I'm on my way."

She set the phone down, staring at it as everything inside of her broke into a million tiny pieces, falling into a heap of dust in the pit of her stomach. Kayleigh was her baby sister, the family surprise. Hadley had been a sophomore in high school when she was born. How could she be dead?

Out of habit, Hadley looked at the clock again. Six minutes until quitting time. She was a stickler about the schedule, never leaving even a minute early.

Box it up, she tried to tell herself. *Flip the switch.*

But there was no box big enough to contain the hurt inside her, no switch capable of turning this off. Not even for six minutes. After alerting Caleb she was leaving, Hadley rose and grabbed her bag from the hook beside her door. She slipped into the hallway, shutting the door behind her, and took slow, steady steps in the direction of the parking garage.

What if someone here needs you? the voice of responsibility demanded. Hadley told it kindly to shut the fuck up.

Two hours away, in the waiting room of the emergency room in the small western Massachusetts town she'd once called home, her parents and her baby nephew, Owen, needed her more.

CHAPTER TWO

Owen let out an ear-piercing squawk.

Tyne tightened her grip on the infant in her arms, pressing him to her chest and swaying back and forth as she whispered nonsense words in a soothing tone. She wished she could tell him everything was going to be all right, but that was a lie. How could anything ever be normal again? He was only ten months old and his mother was dead, while his father was...

Tyne's breath caught in her throat, the terror of not knowing pressing in on her from all around. It was a little after three o'clock in the morning, and her brother Ryan had been at the hospital for almost four hours. Was that a good sign, or was that bad? Tyne had no idea, and there didn't seem to be anyone to ask. The entire Briggs clan—her mother, Michelle, father, Keith, and younger brothers, Evan, Connor, and Mason

—had packed into the small waiting room of the emergency department at Pioneer Valley Hospital, doing exactly that: waiting. It was the loneliest feeling in the world. They were the only ones in the room, and it felt as if they were the only family for miles around going through such a crisis this night.

Except Tyne knew that wasn't the case. Kayleigh's parents, Nancy and Paul, found themselves trapped in an even worse hell. They'd left the hospital maybe an hour before, utterly stricken. Neither had been in any condition to drive, consumed as they were by their grief. A kind neighbor gave them a ride home. The only thing keeping Tyne from collapsing under the weight of her sister-in-law's loss was knowing she had to stay strong for her parents, her brothers, and her baby nephew until Ryan pulled through.

And he had to pull through.

He just had to.

"Tyne?" Her mother rested a hand on Tyne's shoulder. "I can take Owen if you want a break. Your arms must be tired."

They weren't, but the hunger in her mother's eyes to snuggle her pudgy grandson was unmistakable. Tyne held him out, already missing his comforting weight the second he left her arms. "Thanks, Mom."

Her mother peppered the top of Owen's head with kisses before asking, "How much longer do you think it will take before we get an update?"

"I wish I knew." Tyne shot a wary glance at the blue

double doors that led into the ER. If staring at the entrance could've produced information, they would've had answers hours ago. But there was still no sign of a doctor or nurse, and Tyne knew from first-hand experience the guard at the security desk had no insights to share and didn't enjoy being asked. "I'm sure we'll know more soon."

"I hope so." Her mom stifled a yawn, but the dark circles beneath her eyes betrayed her exhaustion.

"Why don't I see if I can wrangle up some coffee?" Tyne offered. "The cafeteria's closed, but there are supposed to be some vending machines down the hall."

"That would be nice." Her distant tone suggested she would've given the same response if Tyne had offered her a puppy or a colonoscopy.

Whether any of them wanted coffee wasn't the point. Tyne needed something to do, a distraction to keep her from bursting out of her own skin. Now to find those machines. She scanned the waiting area, spotting the sign to the vending machines. She'd read the stupid thing at least 726 times since her arrival, but damned if she couldn't remember which way it had said to go.

Left. Got it.

As she angled her body in the correct direction, the automatic doors at the main entrance to the hospital lobby slid open, letting in a draft of chilly air from outside, cold and heavy with dampness. Tyne wrapped her arms across her chest as she shot an annoyed look at the doors. Or maybe it was more the weather beyond them that had provoked her.

April sleet. Poor visibility. Slick roads. A little later in the spring, maybe tonight would never have happened. Then again, drunk assholes weren't confined to a particular season.

Tyne was about to continue toward the vending machines, but a glimpse of the new arrival kept her rooted in place. The woman was tall, with prominent cheekbones and dark brown hair that ended just below chin-length. She wore blue scrubs and a white lab coat, but Tyne knew this wasn't one of the hospital's doctors. It was Hadley Moore, Kayleigh's older sister.

Though Tyne knew Nancy and Paul Moore well, in the five years Ryan and Kayleigh had been together, she'd only met Hadley a handful of times. The woman lived in Boston and was a big shot doctor at one of the city's world class hospitals, the type that attracted Saudi princes and Russian oligarchs as patients because they promised the best of the best in medical care. Hadley rarely made the two-hour trip back home. Despite this, Kayleigh had worshipped the ground her sister walked on and had talked about her so often Tyne felt like she knew her much better than she did.

Had.

Tyne choked up as the past tense struck her like a sucker punch to the kidney. The pain came rushing back with extra intensity, because for the briefest of moments, she'd somehow forgotten why she was there.

How can this be happening?

As Tyne watched, Hadley strode through the lobby and into the waiting room with the supreme confidence of a woman who was completely at home in this environment. The security guard sat up a little straighter in anticipation, and Tyne didn't think he would brush off Hadley's demands for information quite as easily as he had hers. But the woman breezed past the desk without so much as a sideways glance. On a mission, she appeared to be headed directly for the blue double doors.

"They're locked," Tyne muttered under her breath, her eyes stuck to Hadley like a compass needle tracking magnetic north. Almost as soon as she said it, those formidable doors swung open like Hadley had waved a wand or spoken an incantation. A doctor stood on the other side, waving Hadley through. "Well, how do you like that?"

She'd said the words to no one in particular, and luckily, no one overheard. It was a petty response. The woman's sister had died. Still, it didn't completely staunch the resentment. Tyne and her family had been waiting over two hours with no news, yet the moment Hadley walked through the door, they ushered her in like visiting royalty.

Tyne wasn't sure whether she should be angry or impressed.

Now that Hadley had disappeared from sight, the power of motion returned to Tyne's legs, and she set off in search of the vending area once again. It wasn't far, around the corner, in fact. And it took credit cards, which was a real blessing because in her chaotic dash to the hospital after her mother's phone call, she'd grabbed her backpack but left her wallet behind. It was a small stroke of luck that she always kept her license and a single credit card in her phone case, which she gripped in her hand as she assessed her beverage options.

"Coffee for Mom and me, Coke for Dad, Evan, and Connor. Apple juice for Mason."

She slid her card in the reader and punched the numbers for the cold drinks first. One by one, they tumbled down into the collection area with a bang. Tyne retrieved the four plastic bottles, stuffed them into her backpack, and then turned toward the coffee machine. It was one of those single serving types, and to her surprise, a sign above the stack of disposable cups announced it was free for visitors. Another bit of good news, small as it was. Maybe the night was looking up.

Tyne grabbed two cups and lids then paused. What about Hadley? Tyne reached for a third cup. Tyne couldn't forget about Hadley.

This wasn't just because Tyne was a thoughtful person and natural caregiver. The truth was, Hadley Moore was not a woman who was easy to forget, period. Tyne could recall each of the three times they'd met much more vividly than she'd ever admit to anyone else. Their paths had last crossed at Owen's baptism, and though they'd only spoken in passing, the memory of the encounter had lingered for days.

Tyne popped a coffee pod into the appropriate spot, put the first cup into position, and pressed the button. The machine sputtered and whirred. Tyne's attention drifted as she waited for the soul-saving brown liquid to flow.

She could still picture the navy blue pantsuit Hadley had worn to the church. The outfit had looked custom made to fit every curve. It probably had been. Her hair and makeup had been understated but elegant. And she'd carried herself with more poise than anyone, male or female, Tyne had ever met. To say she'd been harboring a secret crush on the Boston doctor for a while now would be putting it mildly. She'd never breathed a word of it, not even to Kayleigh.

The fact Hadley was a lesbian made her even more tantalizing, not that it meant much. Tyne didn't fall into the category of women a sophisticated city doctor like Hadley would go for, not with her thrift shop wardrobe and short, scraggly blonde hair—naturally blonde, anyway, though what color it might be at any given time was anyone's guess. She'd been going through a pink stage over the winter, and it was possible the baptism had occurred during the brief period when she'd been experimenting with two tiny ponytails on the top of her head. They'd stuck out like bizarre alien antennae, and Tyne had quickly abandoned the look. But yeah, that was how she'd appeared the last time Hadley saw her.

Yikes. She'd feel mortified about it, if it weren't for all the much more important things she had to worry about at the moment.

Tyne added cream to two of the coffees before snapping on the lids. She stared at the third with no idea of Hadley's preferences. With a shrug, she stuffed a handful of little creamers and an assortment of sweetener packets in her backpack before putting on the last lid. As she made her way back to the waiting room with three cups balanced in two hands, Tyne felt an unexpected gratitude for those years she'd spent waiting tables at Ned's Diner to supplement the income she earned as an artist.

The waiting room was completely silent when she returned.

"Here you go, Mom."

Tyne held one of the coffee cups out for her mom to grab, trying not to think about how fragile she looked sitting in the vinyl-covered metal chair with her eyes fixed on an invisible spot on the wall. Owen was asleep in her mom's arms, and her dad had dozed off in the chair beside them, his chin resting against his chest. After setting a bottle of Coke on the wide armrest, Tyne waved the other two bottles around until Connor, a senior in high school, and Evan, who had moved back home from Philadelphia while taking a break from what would have been his third year of college, looked up from their phones long enough to notice.

"Thanks," Evan said, his voice sounding distant.

"Sure." Tyne ruffled his mop of dark hair. He was twenty and probably hated her doing it, but as the oldest sibling, she reserved the right to treat her little brothers like children as long as she wanted. "Any updates?"

"Kayleigh's sister is here."

Tyne nodded. "I saw her come in. Is she still back there with the doctor?"

"Yeah, and nobody's been out since she went in."

As Tyne peered through the small windows in the double doors that offered a view of the emergency room's deserted hallway, Hadley came into view. Another doctor walked beside her. They both appeared to be heading toward the waiting room.

Tyne fished the apple juice out of her bag and handed it to Evan. "Can you pour some of this into Mason's cup? I think someone might be coming with an update."

Evan took the juice without a word, his attention already back on his screen even as he followed through with the request by grabbing Mason's special cup with the lid and straw from the table in front of him. Though Mason was fourteen, he had been born with a genetic condition that caused significant intellectual disabilities and developmental delays. He fidgeted, often combined with flapping his hands, so they always gave him drinks in a covered cup to make them harder for him to spill.

Despite the growing lump in her stomach, she couldn't help but smile a little as Mason's face lit up the moment he saw his cup. Tyne thanked the powers that be for the young teen's unusually calm demeanor tonight. With a kid like Mason, who was living with Fragile X syndrome, that was never a given. But despite the long wait, he'd been so engrossed in winding and unwinding a ball of yarn, an activity that soothed him like few others, that Tyne hadn't heard a peep out of him.

His quietness was especially unexpected because new situations and abrupt transitions were a real challenge and could sometimes lead to high anxiety that produced difficult to manage behaviors. Tyne wondered how much he understood about why they were here. Since Mason struggled to express himself through talking, it was sometimes hard to tell, but Tyne suspected he knew more about what was going on than any of them gave him credit for.

Now Tyne could see Hadley and the ER doctor approaching the double doors, and she took a step back as they swung open. A flash of intense pain contorted Hadley's face as their eyes met. It was only there for an instant before dissolving into a mask of calm, but Tyne had seen it. Her heart constricted.

"Hadley, I'm so sorry."

Another glimpse of anguish peeked through the mask. "Thank you, Tina."

Ouch. Not that she'd expected Kayleigh's sister to have been harboring lustful fantasies about her or something, but she had kinda hoped the woman would remember her name. Still, under the circumstances, it didn't seem right to point out the error.

The other doctor, a Black woman in her fifties, held out her hand. "Hi, Tina. I'm Dr. Cassidy. You're Ryan's sister?"

Shaking the doctor's hand, Tyne nodded. "How is he? We haven't heard a thing since we got here."

"I'm very sorry about that. We're understaffed tonight. We've moved your brother to the ICU." Dr. Cassidy's expression remained as neutral as Hadley's, not giving anything away. Was this a skill they learned in medical school? "There's a private room for families on the second floor, and I think you'll all be more comfortable waiting there until one of the ICU doctors can talk to you."

"Okay, but is there anything else you can tell me right now?"

"I think it's best for the doctors up there to explain. Tina, can you point out your parents so I can direct them to the waiting area?"

Crap. It was one thing for Hadley to have gotten

29

her name wrong, but now Dr. Cassidy had called her Tina, twice. She was going to have to say something. "It's not Tina, it's Tyne. And my mom and dad are sitting over there."

As Dr. Cassidy headed off in the direction Tyne was pointing, Hadley cleared her throat. "I'm sorry about that, Tyne. My brain isn't functioning right now."

"I understand. How could it be?" Tyne held up one of the two coffees she was holding. "I got this for you, but I wasn't sure if you take milk or sugar."

"Both." Hadley's neutral expression gave way to a faint smile which didn't quite reach her tired, sad eyes. "You didn't have to get me a coffee."

"I figured you could use it. Plus they were free, so..." Tyne ended her thought with a shrug as she handed both cups to Hadley. She hefted her backpack from her shoulder, unzipped the main compartment, and rummaged for the cream and sugar she'd swiped from the vending area. "Here you go. I've got four creams, two sugars, plus one each of the yellow, pink, and blue sweeteners."

Hadley raised an eyebrow. "Are you always this prepared?"

"Hardly ever," Tyne admitted. "But I'm the one everyone turns to in a crisis."

"I know how that goes."

Tyne took her coffee back and held out her backpack. Hadley plucked out two creams and both sugars. After giving her time to fix her coffee and take a long, slow sip, Tyne put her hand on Hadley's shoulder.

"I am so sorry about Kayleigh. With four brothers in my family, she was like the sister I never had but always wanted."

There was that flicker again, the grief in Hadley's eyes so brief as barely to have existed, but Tyne caught it, and it tore at her heart.

She cast a glance toward her family members, who'd all begun stirring from their seats and gathering their things to head off to the private room Dr. Cassidy had mentioned. Tyne slung her backpack over one shoulder and prepared to follow.

"I know the ICU doctors will probably explain everything, but you're a doctor. Do you have any idea how long Ryan's recovery will take?"

"It's not my area of expertise."

There was that look again. Tyne's body went stiff. "What aren't you telling me?"

Hadley's eyes shifted toward Tyne's family. "They're heading upstairs. You should go with them."

Tyne planted her feet and looked Hadley in the eyes. "I'll catch up in a minute. First, you need to tell me what's going on."

Hadley stared back, unblinking. Then she let out a breath, the lines in her face softening as a new expression transformed her features. No longer raw grief, but compassion.

"While I was with Dr. Cassidy, I had a look at

Ryan's chart. They addressed his injuries in surgery, but his brain activity is concerning. They've called for a neurological consult."

Tyne pressed a hand to her mouth as she absorbed this news. "He might have brain damage?"

Another flicker.

Oh, fuck.

In the distance, an elevator bell dinged. Tyne could hear Owen let out a wail that faded as the doors closed. Hadley put one hand on each of Tyne's shoulders.

"It's more than that. The consult is to determine if there's been a permanent cessation of all brain function."

Tyne's vision spun, the walls of the waiting room seeming to close in on her as she swayed, gulping for air. Only the warm pressure of Hadley's hands on her shoulders kept her upright. "What exactly does that mean?"

"Machines can keep a body going for a long time, but there's nothing they can do if the brain doesn't work."

Tyne closed her eyes. "If it's not working, he's dead?"

"If there's no sign of brain or brain-stem function now, they'll reevaluate in six hours. But, Tyne...?"

Tyne opened her eyes at the sound of her name, nodding almost imperceptibly.

"You need to prepare yourself for the worst."

Tyne's knees wobbled. She pitched forward, collapsing against Hadley's chest. As she sobbed, she was vaguely aware of arms wrapping around her, holding her close. Tyne wondered how, faced with her own staggering loss, Hadley could still provide comfort to someone else, keeping her poise when the world was falling apart.

Was it a sign of incredible inner strength, or was her heart made of ice?

CHAPTER THREE

Hadley was standing in the entryway at her parents' house when she heard the doorbell ring. Should she answer it? There was no one else around, so she reached for the knob.

"Hi," Tyne said when Hadley threw open the door.

"What are you doing here?"

"I couldn't sleep." Tyne pouted, her lips full and glossy. "You're a doctor. Tell me what I should do."

"Start by taking off your shirt," Hadley directed, "so I can have a closer look."

"You're the expert." Without hesitation, Tyne pulled her shirt off to display a thin, pink bra. Hadley's hands cupped the fabric-covered breasts, wanting more.

"This isn't how you do an exam," a voice squawked. It was the voice of Dr. Maddox, her toughest professor in medical school, speaking through a parrot perched on the front porch light.

"I know," she told the bird, "but..." Hadley shrugged then took a step backward as Tyne pushed her across the foyer and into the wall.

"I need you." Tyne kissed her hard, her hand slipping under Hadley's shirt, her fingers digging into the flesh, kicking Hadley's need into an even higher gear. They continued kissing, and fumbling with clothes, limbs, and—

Hadley rolled onto her right side in bed, and her face smacked into something hard and cold.

"What the...?"

She cracked one eye open and met with an endless expanse of pink that looked like it might be a wall.

Who had put a pink wall where the rest of her mattress was supposed to be?

And, why did she have to wake up right when her dream was getting heated?

She groaned as she eased herself onto her back, where muscles she hadn't thought about since her last anatomy class in med school ached. With extreme caution, Hadley spread her arms out on either side of her. They'd hardly made it a foot when her hands hit the edge of the bed. This was definitely not the king-size accommodation she was used to.

As the fog in her brain cleared, the events of the day before rushed back, swamping her under a tidal wave of grief. No, she was not in the bedroom of her

Beacon Hill townhouse in Boston. She was on the twin bed in the guest room at her parents' house.

Because her sister was dead.

So was her brother-in-law.

A memory flashed through her head of accompanying Kayleigh's sister-in-law, the one who'd played the starring role in her highly inappropriate sex dream, to the private waiting area near the ICU reserved for loved ones who needed to be told bad news. Every hospital has a spot like this, a quiet place to stow the bereft so their loss doesn't scare other patients' families. There'd been so many of them. Mom, Dad, three brothers, plus her little nephew. So many lives about to be changed forever.

Shortly after they got there, the neurologist came in and told the rest of the Briggs family the same thing Hadley had explained before leaving the ER. The specialists had found no signs of brain or brainstem function. No gag reflex, no reaction of the pupils to light, no drive to breathe. Although machines were keeping his body going, every sign suggested Ryan was no longer alive.

At ten o'clock in the morning, the tests were run again and the diagnosis of brain death confirmed. Hadley had remained in the waiting room, holding a sleeping Owen while the others said their goodbyes. A representative of the local organ procurement team arrived and confirmed Ryan's status as a registered donor. By noon, there was really nothing left for Hadley to do. Too tired to drive, she'd accepted a ride to her childhood home from a neighbor she didn't recognize. Her parents, just emerging themselves from a pill-induced slumber, had taken one look at her and ordered her directly to bed.

Hadley could only assume she'd looked like hell. Probably still did. She certainly felt like it.

After another stretch, accompanied by a loud groan, Hadley dared to open both eyes and quickly swept the room. It was the same as ever, three walls taken up by plastic shelves that bowed under the weight of a hodgepodge of fabric, crafting supplies, and rolls of wrapping paper—none of which her mother was ever likely to use, but God forbid anyone suggest throwing them away. Lacking space for anything larger, her mom had shoved a twin bed in one corner, topped with what felt like a slab of concrete where a mattress should've been. Having made it through medical school and four years of residency, Hadley couldn't say this was the most uncomfortable place she'd ever slept, but it probably made the top ten.

With an act of sheer willpower, Hadley tossed the covers off herself and swung her legs over the side of the bed. She stared without comprehension at the bare legs sticking out from what appeared to be an ankle-length floral nightgown. Even after blinking several times, the bizarre image didn't disappear like the remnant of a bad dream she'd expected it to be. She actually seemed to be wearing it, for real.

Where the fuck did this come from?

Her eyes darted around the room, but the scrubs she'd come home in were nowhere in sight. There was no change of clothing waiting for her, dug out of some long-forgotten dresser drawer. The only garment, other than the long-sleeved old lady gown she'd somehow been tricked into putting on in her sleep, was a bright magenta velour robe, quilted across the neck and shoulders, that zipped all the way up the front from floor to neck. It was the type of thing her mother loved to order from those catalogs that also sold support stockings and household gadgets that claimed to be *As Seen On TV*. Normally Hadley wouldn't even wear it to win a bet, but given that the fabric of her Victorian-inspired nightie was both impossibly prudish but also half see-through, she had little choice.

Suck it up, buttercup, she told herself as she shrugged the robe over her shoulders. She was here to support her parents, not win a fashion contest. She would call a friend later and have some of her own clothing sent from home.

As she cracked open the bedroom door, Hadley tried to gauge how long she'd slept. Sunlight still filled the bedroom, so it couldn't have been more than a few hours, or it would've gotten dark. Three o'clock, maybe? Hadley shrugged and headed to the kitchen. At least the brief nap had replenished her reserves so she could help her parents navigate this nightmare.

Her mother stood at the sink, her back to Hadley as she filled a glass coffeepot with water. Hadley's heart clenched, and tears pricked her eyes. Her mother was seventy-two, her father seventy-five. How were they going to survive this loss?

Coming up from behind, Hadley wrapped her arms around her mother's shoulders, resting her cheek against the head of short silver hair that turned toward her chest.

"Hi, Mom."

"Hey, sleepyhead."

Her mom shut off the faucet and turned around. The blue eyes that looked up at Hadley were pink and watery, ringed with dark circles. She attempted a smile. "What are you doing up so early?"

"What time is it?" Hadley frowned as she realized the clocks on all the appliances were set to vastly different times. Neither one of her parents had ever really gotten the hang of anything digital.

"A little after six." Her mom gave Hadley a quick hug, headed toward the coffee maker, and began pouring the water from the pot into the top.

Hadley's eyebrows shot up. She'd slept a few hours longer than she'd thought. "I'd hardly consider six to be early."

"I guess you doctors get used to all sorts of strange

hours." Her mom opened the bag of ground coffee next to the machine and pulled out the scoop.

"I hope that's decaf." Though Dr. Cassidy had assured her that both her parents had been prescribed medicine to help them sleep during these first, most arduous nights, Hadley worried all the same. "You don't need to be up all night."

Her mom gave a weak laugh. "I've got plenty of time before bed."

"Mom, you've been in bed with lights out by nine for years. It's very important to stick with your routines right now, and three hours isn't nearly enough time to clear that much caffeine from your system."

"Three hours?" Her mom's head tilted forty-five degrees to the right. "Honey, it's six o'clock in the morning."

"What morning?" Hadley's head whipped toward the nearest window. "Sunday?"

"Of course. When did you think it was?"

"I..." Hadley squinted at the glowing orb in the sky, trying to remember which side of the house the sun rose on. How was this possible? "I thought it was still Saturday night. Are you telling me I slept for almost eighteen hours straight? I'm supposed to be here helping you and Dad. You really should've woken me up."

"We tried. Dad even offered to get you tacos for dinner, but there was no waking you. You must've needed the sleep."

"If I said no to tacos, I must've been—" *Dead*, she'd been about to say, but stopped herself in time. "Really tired. I must've been really tired."

Hadley watched her mom for any sign she'd caught onto the near slip-up, but she was too busy rummaging through one of the cabinets to be policing Hadley's word choice.

"Now, where are they?" Hadley's mom shut the cupboard doors and opened the next set. "I can't seem to remember where I keep them."

"What is it you're trying to find, Mom?"

"My pill organizer's empty. Kayleigh always comes over on Saturdays and refills it for the next week, but..." She drew a ragged breath and squeezed her eyes shut as tears began to flow.

"It's okay, Mom. It's okay." Hadley rushed to her side, pulling her into an embrace. "I'll find them and do it for you."

"What does she need you to do?" Wrapped in a plaid flannel robe, Hadley's father shuffled into the kitchen. He winced with each step, a sign that his diabetes had been causing more trouble with his feet.

"Her pills." Hadley tried not to stare at him as he walked. Her father was a proud man and hated to be reminded of his weaknesses. "She can't remember where they are."

Her dad pressed his lips together, his expression

grim as he muttered, "I keep telling her they're over there, but her memory..."

He hobbled to a cabinet on the opposite side of the kitchen from where her mom had been looking. When he opened the door, it looked like a mini pharmacy stocked with dozens of amber plastic prescription bottles. Were those all for her mom?

When did my parents get this old?

The air seemed to be sucked from the room as the reality of it hit her full force. Kayleigh had been the caregiver, the one who stayed close to home and made sure Mom and Dad were okay. Her sister had never asked for help, and honestly, Hadley had never offered. She'd never realized how things were getting with them. What was going to happen now?

"Your sister would always come over with Owen on Saturdays..." The rest of her father's words disappeared in a gulp, followed by a low, mournful sob.

Panic stabbed at Hadley's gut. Her father, a retired police chief and former marine, was crying. In all her forty-one years, she'd never seen him do this before. Not when the Red Sox lost the playoffs in '03, or when he'd had to take their old golden retriever, Bartley, to be put to sleep when his kidneys failed. He hadn't even cried when her grandparents had died, at least not so anyone could see him do it.

Hadley's first impulse was to run screaming from the house, but her limbs didn't respond. She stood frozen in place, her mother sniffling against her chest.

For a woman who dealt with death nearly every single day at work, Hadley had no idea what to do for her own mom and dad. Losing Kayleigh had turned everything she knew on its head.

You've got to pull yourself together.

"How about some TV?" Hadley suggested, unable to think of a single other activity she had the mental energy for.

This was an easy sell, as the television was rarely off in her parents' house. Soon, her dad was in his favorite recliner, and her mom was on the couch with her knitting bag beside her. After topping off her coffee mug, Hadley sank into the love seat's well-worn upholstery. Her dad had already switched on the set and held the remote hostage in his hand. A competition involving four adults, an obstacle course, and several pools of green slime flashed on the screen. The show's host spoke a language Hadley didn't recognize, and the subtitles were of little help as they were written in Japanese.

"Dad, what is this?" How had her foolproof suggestion taken such a wrong turn so quickly?

Without answering, he pressed a button on the remote, tilted his head back, and shut his eyes. The new selection, which featured a woman extolling the virtues of a blender like it would cure cancer, wasn't much better, but Hadley didn't care enough to complain. It didn't matter what was on as long as she didn't have to think. She sipped her coffee and stared as the morning crawled by.

The sound of the front doorbell yanked Hadley out of her trance. "Who could that be at this hour?"

The cable box said it was a quarter to nine. Hadley was shocked to discover so much time had passed, but unlike the appliance clocks, the cable box set itself automatically, so she assumed it was accurate.

"Probably Tyne." Her mother's hands were buried in yarn, knitting needles clicking. "She's supposed to come by this morning with some questions before going to talk to Roy about planning the services."

Hadley's cheeks burned as the snatches of her dream drifted in front of her like particles of dust floating on sunbeams. *Tuck them away, right now!*

The doorbell rang again. Her mother tried to set her project down, but it was tangled all around her.

"Why don't I go get it?" Hadley offered, catching on to her mom's flustered look. She was happy for an excuse to get out of the living room and away from the woman with blonde curls on the TV screen who was dressed like Goldilocks as she hocked the perfect mattress. Anything had to be better than that.

It was only when Hadley reached for the doorknob that she remembered the dream. Vividly. Every detail rushed back with images so graphically realistic she might as well have been watching her own private porno. She squeezed her legs together in a desperate attempt to hold herself in check down there. She had no idea what expression she wore, except to know it was *not* her well-practiced mask of bland dispassion.

I bet I look like a sex-starved lunatic.

"Hi," Tyne said when Hadley threw open the door.

Just like in the dream.

The woman's deep blue eyes flicked downward for the briefest moment, and when she met Hadley's gaze, her expression made it clear there was something she was trying to suppress. But it wasn't unbridled lust, and contrary to expectation, she did not toss Hadley against the wall and have her way with her.

No, the look on Tyne's face was more like shock or amusement.

"Good morning." Hadley was still trying to work out the reason for Tyne's strange expression when it hit her. She'd answered the door wearing lingerie that was less Victoria's Secret and more Queen Victoria's high-necked nightie. Her cheeks kicked up so many levels they probably appeared to be on fire. No wonder Tyne was looking at her like that. Why had she volunteered to open the door? Under the circumstances, she knew she shouldn't care what she was wearing, but that didn't mean she didn't. Especially after the dream.

Stop thinking about the dream.

Tyne, dressed in a sensible pair of dark jeans and a loose, long-sleeved top made of a sky-blue linen that highlighted her eyes, held up a dark green folder. The gold lettering across the front spelled out the name of the local funeral home. "I brought these by for Paul and Nancy to look over. May I come in?"

"Uh, of course." Hadley stepped aside to allow the willowy blonde-haired woman through the door. Had she always been blonde? Not that it didn't look natural, but Hadley couldn't shake the thought it used to be something else. Pink, maybe?

Hadley knew they'd met a few times before, but somehow it hadn't left an impression on her. Not when conscious. Dream world was an entirely different matter. She'd called Tyne the wrong name at the hospital. Yet her appearance was as striking as her personality was caring. She'd even thought to bring Hadley a coffee the other night. How was it Hadley had never paid closer attention to this woman in the past?

Uh-oh. Tyne was staring at her in that way people do when they're waiting for a reply to something.

"Sorry, what?" The tingling in Hadley's cheeks intensified. "I must not have been paying attention."

Oh, she'd been paying attention. Just not to what Tyne was saying. Seeing the woman in the flesh, so to speak, while trying not to picture her that way was hard enough. Tyne's visit was also a brutal reminder of what had brought Hadley back home. Her jumbled thoughts and emotions threatened to do her head in. This was possibly the worst time to lose her sanity, and Hadley dug deep to search for her steely doctor persona. It had to be in there somewhere. Where was that blasted off-switch in her head?

"I said, thank you again for staying with us as long as you did yesterday. I hate hospitals," Tyne added sheepishly.

"I guess I'm used to them," Hadley said with a shrug. "But you're welcome."

She closed the front door and started back toward the kitchen, noting that Tyne walked in front of her and clearly knew her way around like she'd been here before. With a pang of guilt, it occurred to her that the younger woman had probably seen her parents more often than Hadley had over the last few years.

As soon as they entered the kitchen, Tyne gave each of her parents a big hug before settling down at the table and opening up the folder she'd brought. It was as thick as a school binder—stuffed full of color brochures for caskets, prayer cards, and other products no one ever wanted to have to contemplate. One look at her parents told Hadley the task at hand already overwhelmed them.

"I went over to see Roy yesterday, and he had some very helpful suggestions." Tyne's tone was soothing as she plucked a few sheets from the daunting stack before closing the folder and setting it aside. "Why don't you join me, and I'll walk you through them?"

Hadley watched in silent appreciation as Tyne did just that, turning a terrible task that could have taken days into a straightforward conversation that was over in less than fifteen minutes. When Tyne had said she was good in an emergency, she hadn't been joking. She had worked out every detail for the joint memorial service on her own before arriving, leaving nothing more for Hadley or her parents to do.

"Thank you," Hadley said as she walked with Tyne back to the front door. "I'm not sure we could've gotten through that without you."

"We're in this together."

Somehow, hearing this and knowing someone as competent as Tyne was on her side gave Hadley's spirits a boost.

"Do you know if Roy will be in later today? I'll need to stop by and make sure I give him my credit card. On top of everything else, I won't have my parents worrying about how to pay for this. Or yours, either," she added on impulse.

Tyne's eyes widened. "You don't mean you're planning to cover the whole thing, do you?"

"I do." Now that she'd set her mind to it, Hadley was firm in the decision. "Please, don't argue. It's one of the few things I can do."

Tyne hesitated a moment then nodded. "But if there's any way I can help, you'll let me know?"

"Actually, there is." Hadley glanced down at her ugly velour robe, biting her lip. "Can you tell me if Graham's department store is still open downtown?"

"It is, but not on Sundays." Tyne's eyes drifted to Hadley's ensemble. "Also, if you don't want to find pretty much more of what you've got on, you might look elsewhere. I'm not sure Graham's carries anything that doesn't have an elastic waistband or a kitten embroidered on it."

Hadley chuckled, well aware the town's only clothing store catered to the retirement crowd. "I don't think I have a choice. I drove straight here from work and didn't stop to pack. I was planning to ask a neighbor to send me some essentials by courier, but if I don't go shopping, it's either this or my scrubs until tomorrow night."

Tyne's eyes swept over her again, raising the hairs on Hadley's arms and sending a little shiver down her back, almost as if the woman had touched her physically. "I think I have a few things at home that might work. I'll bring them by later."

"You're a real lifesaver." Hadley smiled crookedly, still off balance from the effects of Tyne's eyes and the memory of the dream, wishing she'd been able to see more of the woman than the snatches of her fading memory.

Seriously, stop focusing on that! she scolded herself.

When Hadley returned to the kitchen, she poured a cup of coffee and joined her mother at the table. "You doing okay, Mom?"

Her mom nodded. "I am for now. It was so nice of Tyne to help with the planning like she did."

"It was," Hadley agreed. She stared into her cup, watching the cream swirl around like clouds as she tried to piece together the little snippets she knew of the woman. "It's funny. I remember babysitting for

49

Ryan once or twice when he was little, but I can't remember Tyne being there."

Recalling those earlier chills, Hadley wrinkled her nose, not liking the idea that someone she could've babysat for could make her body respond in that way.

"No, Tyne didn't come to live with Michelle and Keith until well after you would've left for school."

"What do you mean by that?" Hadley took a sip of coffee, enjoying the feel of the fiery liquid on her throat. "Is she adopted?"

"Keith is Tyne's uncle," her mom explained. "I gather her mom has substance abuse problems, and Tyne was in and out of foster homes. Then she ended up with one of those ultra conservative families who thought they could pray the gay away."

"Oh?" *Pray the gay away.* Had she heard that right?

"As soon as they heard what was going on, Keith and Michelle had to step in. I think Tyne was in middle school, maybe twelve or thirteen, at the time." Hadley's mom shook her head sadly. "She dotes on the whole family, but she and Ryan, who was only two years younger, were particularly close, the poor dear."

"Yes, poor Tyne." Hadley's heart was thudding like she'd finished a sprint.

She frowned into her half-empty mug. Her mother's revelation about Tyne's sexuality had been unexpected, but it really made no difference. Just because she hadn't technically been the younger woman's babysitter didn't mean she was any less off-limits.

Besides, Hadley had too many family issues to deal with as it was without adding any other complications to her life. Best to cram it into the mental vault never to be reopened. When Hadley chose medicine, she understood on all levels she'd be forever married to the job and nothing else. Like a nun, but without the vow of celibacy.

Hadley took another sip of coffee, recalling the cup Tyne had brought her in the ER, along with every variety of sugar and creamer known to humankind. And the reassuring warmth of Tyne's hand on her shoulder that had accompanied it. Her kindness and quiet confidence as she cared for everyone around her. The humor that sparkled in her eyes, even in the darkest of times.

Put all of that into the vault this instant.

Yeah, sure. Hadley would get right on that. If only she knew how.

CHAPTER FOUR

"Thank you, Mrs. Reed." Tyne clutched the foil-wrapped bundle her neighbor held out to her with both hands, raising her voice to be heard above the crowd. More than half the town had turned out for the joint memorial service for her brother and his wife. Now that it was over, they all packed the church hall for the reception. Even with everyone speaking in reverent, hushed tones, it was getting loud.

The elderly woman, who had once been the middle school English teacher, gave Tyne's hand a pat. "It's a tuna casserole."

"Yum. Thank you so much for coming."

Tyne did a quick mental calculation. This made four tuna casseroles plus seven lasagnas just today, not to mention all the food people had been dropping off throughout the past week as word of the accident spread across town. She'd be lucky to find enough room for it all in her parents' chest freezer and had no idea when they would ever eat even half of it. Regardless, she was grateful for the excuse to slip away for a few minutes to find a temporary home for the meal in the hall's industrial refrigerator.

As Tyne made her way to the kitchen, she spotted Hadley coming from the other side of the room. She, too, was holding a foil-wrapped rectangle and eyeing the door with obvious relief.

"Tuna casserole or lasagna?" Tyne asked when she was close enough for Hadley to hear.

"Neither. It's American chop suey."

"Seriously?" Tyne pretended jealousy over the quintessential New England dish of ground beef, macaroni, and tomatoes. "I'll trade you."

"No way." Hadley held the pan protectively to her chest. "I haven't had this stuff since the elementary school cafeteria."

Tyne opened the refrigerator door, added her pan to a stack, and reached for Hadley's. "Here, let me put it away for you. I promise I won't steal it."

Hadley handed hers over. "I was joking. The neighbors have given us enough variations on noodle dishes to last six months."

"Us, too." Tyne shut the stainless-steel door but was in no hurry to head back to the hall. "People want to help, you know? At least it's keeping my brothers from going hungry. I haven't had much of an appetite."

"Me neither. I've had to add a reminder on my

phone to make sure my parents get three squares. Between the lack of appetite and my mom's poor memory, I don't know what they'll do when I'm not here." Hadley cast a wary glance toward the door that led back to the hall. "There are so many people."

"That's small-town life. You can't sneeze without the news making the rounds."

"They all certainly seem to remember me. But, can I confess something?" When Hadley paused, Tyne raised her eyebrows in silent encouragement to continue. "I hardly recognize a soul, and I can't remember anyone's name. It's so stressful that every time I see someone headed toward me, I want to duck under a table."

Tyne couldn't help but laugh at the thought of this woman who appeared so cool and collected doing something so ridiculous. "That may be the case, but your nervousness doesn't show, if that helps."

"Are you sure?" Hadley shifted her weight like a child who had to pee.

Tyne allowed herself a closer look, taking her time to evaluate Hadley's silky smooth hair, tasteful makeup, and perfectly fitted pantsuit. It was similar to the one she'd worn to Owen's baptism but black instead of dark blue. "I know one thing. There's no way you found this outfit at Graham's."

"You got that right. Thanks for loaning me those jeans and tops, by the way. I was able to get enough clothing delivered from home yesterday to last me a week or two."

"Is that how long you'll be in town?" A prick of disappointment tickled down Tyne's body at the reminder Hadley's stay was only temporary. Her presence had added a touch of excitement in what had otherwise been nearly unbearable days.

"I'm not sure yet. Michael, my hospital's new chief of staff, is an ass who tried to tell me I needed to be back in two weeks, but legally I'm entitled to twelve. According to the head of HR, the official policy is I can apply for an unpaid leave of absence of up to a year if I need it, not that I can even imagine being here that long." Hadley's eyes flicked toward the crowded hall again. "I need to see how my parents are doing before making a decision."

They inched closer to the main room, lingering in the hallway beyond view from most eyes in the room. Tyne spotted her parents conversing with a neighbor on the other side of the space, and Hadley's parents similarly engaged nearby. "You may not remember everyone, but your parents have a lot of friends, and people around here take care of their own. They'll be in excellent hands."

Hadley opened her mouth to respond but was interrupted when a woman about her age bounded toward her. Tyne recognized her as Rebecca Porter, a local real estate agent who regularly handed out pads of notepaper with her photo on the pages to every house in town.

"Hadley," Rebecca said, wearing the look of earnest concern Tyne had grown accustomed to seeing on everyone's faces. "It's so nice to see you, even if it is under such terrible circumstances. Everyone missed you at the twenty-year reunion a few years back."

"Yes, thank you," Hadley mumbled, and Tyne knew she couldn't remember the woman at all.

"Rebecca, it's so kind of you to come today," Tyne interjected, earning her a grateful look from Hadley for supplying the classmate's name. "How's the real estate business these days?"

Rebecca perked up visibly at the conversation's turn. "Things are really hopping. I haven't seen a spring like this in years. I was talking to your brother about a condo that's coming on the market soon. That was before, well, you know..."

As the real estate agent's smile evaporated, Tyne did her best to smooth over the faux pas. "He'd mentioned he and Kayleigh were hoping to buy something soon."

"Such a shame." Rebecca's eyes shifted, avoiding eye contact. Tyne was getting used to it. Since the accident, a lot of people struggled to look at her directly when they spoke about her brother. "I don't suppose you're in the market for a condo? It's a great find."

"Afraid not, but if I ever am, you'll be the first to

hear." Inwardly, Tyne was marveling at the balls it took to try to sell a condo at a funeral.

Rebecca nodded, possibly looking sadder now at the prospect of a lost commission than she had when offering her condolences. She turned to speak to Hadley, who looked as blown away by the woman's bravado as Tyne was. "And how about you?"

"I have a condo already." Hadley blinked then added, "In Boston."

"Oh, I assumed, what with your parents..." Rebecca's voice trailed off in a way that seemed to imply she knew more than she wanted to say. "I must've heard wrong."

"Heard what?" Hadley's eyes narrowed, and Tyne could tell she was on edge.

"It's just... my mom has been trying to get your parents to check out the new assisted living facility where she works."

"She has?" Hadley glanced toward her parents.

"Yeah, only your sister always said with her nearby, they didn't need to." Rebecca shrugged. "If you're not going to be moving closer, I should tell Mom to start sending those brochures over again."

While Tyne was silently wondering who was more opportunistic, Rebecca or her mother, Hadley seemed too stunned to respond. Tyne swooped in for the rescue. "Hadley, I think my mom needs us. Rebecca, if you'll excuse us."

"Oh, of course." Rebecca started digging purposefully in her handbag, quickly producing a business card. "If you change your mind, call me."

Tyne hooked her arm through Hadley's and pulled her away from the real estate agent before the woman could do something even more gauche. Not that Tyne could think of many actions that would qualify. As soon as they were far enough away, she stopped and let out a sigh. "Wow."

Hadley's head swiveled like she was searching the room. "I don't see your mom. What do you think she needed?"

"Oh, I made that up. It didn't seem like you were enjoying the conversation."

Hadley grimaced. "Not at all. I don't even remember that woman from high school."

"That might be because she looks a little different now." Tyne gestured toward her own face and then her chest to provide some clues as to what she meant. "She won't admit it, of course, but everyone in town knows she had some work done after her divorce settlement a few years back."

Hadley covered her mouth to hide her laughter. "I'd forgotten how quickly rumors spread around here."

"Everybody knows everybody's business; that's for sure." Tyne scanned the room, which was possibly even more crowded than it had been when the reception started an hour before. "However, no one seems to be paying any attention to us right now. Wanna make a break for it?"

"What? You mean leave?" Hadley's eyebrows shot up at the unorthodox suggestion, but it was clear by the hopefulness in those dark eyes it tempted her.

"I don't think either of us is enjoying being here. At least, I know I'm only here to support my parents, and they seem to have plenty of other people showering them with attention right now." Tyne gestured to where her parents, along with Hadley's, stood surrounded by at least a dozen friends. "I doubt anyone would miss us if we slipped out."

"You make a good point." A slow smile spread across Tyne's face. She held out her elbow toward Hadley. "Shall we?"

Once again, Hadley hooked her arm through Tyne's, but after taking a step, she hesitated. "Should we interrupt long enough to let our parents know we're going?"

Tyne's face fell. "Then they might ask us to stay. How about we send a text? But *after* we get outside."

Tyne started walking again, thrilled when Hadley came along without another hesitation. She felt like a kid playing hooky from school and had zero regrets.

-ⱽ\/\/\⸜-

"THANKS again for springing me from in there." Hadley pulled a set of keys from her jacket pocket, jingling them in her hand.

"Where are you going?" Disappointment tugged

the corners of Tyne's mouth into a frown. "I thought you might like to go for a walk by the falls or something."

Hadley's face registered surprise. "Oh. I was under the impression you wanted to leave because you had something else to do."

"Not at all." Tyne started to bristle but forced a calmness to ease her hackles. "It was stifling in there, with so many people feeling sorry for me and asking how I'm doing. I…" Tyne's shoulders heaved.

Hadley sighed. "I know exactly what you mean."

Tyne studied Hadley's face thoughtfully before saying, "You're probably the only one who really does. What do you say about that walk?"

Hadley looked down at her feet. "Will we be okay dressed like this?"

Tyne glanced at Hadley's shoes, noting the sensible flats with satisfaction. "We should be fine as long as we stick to the paved rail trail. Come on; I'll drive."

They walked side by side through the church parking lot, stopping when they reached Tyne's forest green station wagon. She opened the dented passenger door, quickly tossing an assortment of blank canvases, brushes, and bottles of paint into the back seat. As she stepped aside so Hadley could get in, Tyne cast an embarrassed glance at her dilapidated ride. She wasn't sure what kind of car Hadley drove but was willing to bet it was a lot nicer than this.

"Sorry about the mess. All of this is headed for my

art studio, but I've been staying with my parents since the accident, so I haven't had a chance to drop it off."

"It's not a problem." Hadley's foot connected with a stray bottle of paint on the floor, causing it to bounce out of the car and onto the pavement. "I guess I do remember Kayleigh mentioning you were an artist. You have your own studio?"

Tyne lunged for the paint, retrieving it before it could roll underneath the car. "Yeah. The studio is in one of the storefronts downtown, and my apartment is just above it."

"A storefront. Do you have an art gallery, as well?"

"Not exactly." Tyne clutched the bottle of cheap acrylic paint, suddenly overcome with self-consciousness. "It's, um, one of those paint and sip places."

Tyne closed Hadley's door before the woman had a chance to ask any questions. She should've guessed a sophisticated city doctor like Hadley would immediately assume she ran a gallery instead of a kitschy destination for a girls' night out.

"What is a paint and sip place?" Hadley asked as soon as Tyne opened the driver's side door.

"It's where people come to learn how to do a simple painting while drinking wine with their friends." Tyne had worked hard to build the business, and she was proud of what she'd accomplished, but hearing herself explain it to the likes of Hadley, it sounded kind of silly.

"You own the business yourself?" To Tyne's

surprise, far from judging her for a frivolous occupation, the woman who saved lives for a living sounded impressed.

"I do." Tyne turned the key in the ignition, thankful that even though her car didn't look the greatest, the engine was solid thanks to her dad's tinkering. "I thought about buying into a national franchise, but in the end, it turned out to be more profitable to do it on my own. Plus, I get more creative license over what I get to teach."

"It sounds like you've found a smart way to make money doing something you love."

"Yeah. I never thought of it like that, but I like the way you put it." She wasn't sure why, but Hadley's admiration made Tyne glow inside. "You should take a class sometime."

Hadley chortled like Tyne had told a hilarious joke. "Trust me; I don't have an artistic bone in my body."

"You might be surprised," Tyne pressed. "I'm a very good teacher." Her breath caught as she realized her words had sounded way more suggestive than she'd intended. She couldn't help it. Every time Hadley was around, Tyne ended up with sex on the brain. Maybe Hadley could suggest a decent head doctor, because there had to be something wrong with her for thinking about sex when they'd literally just buried their siblings. Was she a deviant or something?

"I have no doubt." A half-smirk said Hadley had caught the unintended innuendo. "But I'm a very poor student. In art, at least. Even my stick figures are less than convincing."

As Tyne turned onto the road that led to the rail trail, her determination to get Hadley into the studio grew. She'd get a paintbrush into that woman's hand if it was the last thing she did. Of course, if she could convince Hadley to do other things with her hands, that would be a delightful bonus.

"Here we are." Tyne pulled the car into the empty lot, shut off the engine, and opened her door. It didn't come as a surprise they were the only ones there. It was a Friday, and anyone who hadn't taken off to attend the memorial service would be at work. "I hold most of my classes on Wednesday through Friday nights and on weekends. One of the best parts about having an unusual schedule is I get to enjoy places like this without the crowds spoiling it."

"We've got that in common." Hadley climbed out of the car, shutting her door. "At this point, I have enough seniority that I can get almost any shift I want at the hospital, but I mostly like to stick with the night and weekend shifts for exactly that reason. I don't like crowds."

Tyne led the way to the paved path that ran along the river's edge, smiling at the odd realization that an artist and a doctor could have anything in common. She inhaled deeply, taking a moment to close her eyes and enjoy the warmth of the sun on her face. Then she opened them again and watched the water gathering speed as it raced toward the falls in the distance.

"It's a beautiful day," she commented, wondering if she ought to feel guilty for saying it. The memorial had been emotionally draining. Losing her brother and sister-in-law left her so raw that every thought of them hurt, but maybe that was all the more reason to stop and enjoy the simple pleasures of life. The look of peaceful satisfaction on Hadley's face suggested she was of the same mind.

"This is the one part of living here I miss," Hadley said as they began walking side by side along the path. "I remember as a kid I would get excited every time we were driving home because we'd have to take the bridge over the falls."

"I love that bridge," Tyne agreed. "Given your dislike of crowds, I'm surprised you ever left. What made you move to Boston?"

"Medical school, and then work," Hadley answered, "but even if that hadn't been the case, there was no way I would've stayed. I always knew as soon as I graduated from high school, I was outta here."

"Why?" Moving here had probably saved Tyne's life. She couldn't imagine how anyone could want so badly to leave.

"It was pretty obvious early on that I wasn't like the other girls. I hated Barbie dolls and dresses when I was little. I never had crushes on any of the boys." Hadley made a circular motion with her hand as if to say the list of reasons went on and on, but the general theme was clear. "People's attitudes have evolved a lot since then, but growing up queer in the nineties was not great, and especially not in a small town where you were the only one. At least the only one out of the closet in high school."

"I understand; believe me." Tyne added this experience to the growing list of unexpected commonalities. "Until I was twelve, I lived in West Virginia, mostly with foster families. I'm not sure if they'd ever heard the term pansexual before, but let's just say their attitudes on the subject were *far* from evolved."

"I'm sorry," Hadley murmured. "But it's been better for you here?"

"So much. My parents—well, technically they're my aunt and uncle, but I think of them as Mom and Dad—they've been so supportive. Not only of my sexuality, but my art, my business, everything. The church they belong to is very progressive and welcoming. Plus, I think if anyone had ever tried to give me shit, Ryan would've—" Tyne choked on the last of her sentence, the mention of her brother hitting her like a kick to the gut. "I'm sorry. I—"

"I know." Hadley reached across Tyne's back, resting a hand on her shoulder and pulling her into a gentle sideways hug.

"The worst part is"—Tyne paused to clear her throat, which had become thick with emotion— "sometimes, for a little while, I forget. It's like I've been keeping myself busy with all these checklists. Talk to the cemetery people, order the flowers, choose the hymns. And then I'm okay getting things done, as long as I don't stop and think about why I'm doing them."

"It's surreal." As they walked, Hadley continued to hold on to Tyne's shoulder. "Since I was so much older than Kayleigh and haven't lived near her since she was a little girl, it's easy to think of her as still being out there, living her life like always. It's been a struggle to remind myself every day."

"Do you think it will ever seem real, that any of this will ever feel normal?"

"Normal, no, but real?" Hadley withdrew her hand and shrugged. "I imagine it will, eventually."

They came to where the path ended at a stone wall that overlooked the crashing, white foamed falls. The river was swollen from snow melt and early April rains, and Tyne watched as the fast-moving water swirled, the spray of mist dampening her face, obscuring the tears that trickled from the corners of her eyes. She snuck a glance at Hadley, remembering her touch so vividly she could almost still feel the imprint of Hadley's long slender fingers on her back. The only thing that made any of this at all tolerable was knowing she wasn't completely alone.

"I guess we should head back," Tyne said when they'd both been watching the falls for so long she'd lost track of time. "I'll take you to your car, but would you mind if we stopped by my studio first? We'll be going right past it, and I really should bring those art supplies inside."

"Sure. I'd love to see it."

The way Hadley smiled, that slight upturn of her lips and softening of her eyes, made Tyne's tummy flutter. The prospect of showing her studio to this woman was both exhilarating and a bit terrifying, like she was sharing a part of herself she wasn't sure she was ready to reveal. Someone as worldly and important as Hadley would probably think her business was a dumb kid's hobby.

"Okay." Tyne swallowed. "Let's roll."

CHAPTER FIVE

The downtown area looked more vibrant than Hadley remembered. An antique store displayed a grand opening banner in its front window, and there was a trendy tavern with an outdoor seating area she didn't recall seeing before. What had once been a dilapidated brick building with broken windows was now a performing arts center, and all along the street, colorful window displays promised a wide variety of unique shops.

Though it was nearing evening, the sun was still high in the sky as Hadley stepped onto the sidewalk, arms loaded with canvases, and followed Tyne in the direction of her studio. It was disorienting how much sunlight she'd experienced over the past several days. The truth was, Hadley couldn't remember the last time she'd gone so long without working a night shift. Or without working at all, for that matter. If only she weren't too emotionally exhausted to benefit from the rest.

They stopped in front of a shop with tall windows filled with colorful canvases of varying degrees of artistic ability, clearly done by students. As Tyne dug for her keys, Hadley studied the artwork on display. They were all overwhelmingly bright and cheery, with subjects ranging from tropical sunsets to vases of flowers adorned with inspirational sayings like *Dream Big*, or *Home is Where the Heart is*. Not exactly what you'd call fine art, but there was no way Hadley could do any of them, so she wasn't about to start throwing stones.

"This is it." Tyne opened the door and snapped on the overhead lights. "The canvases go on the back counter."

Hadley picked her way along the narrow aisle between two long, paint-splattered tables. A dozen round, backless stools surrounded each one, with a small, portable easel set up at every space. They were angled toward a full-size, professional-looking easel in the front, where presumably Tyne stood while demonstrating techniques for the class.

Was she a good teacher? Hadley assumed so. Something about the young woman's presence was very calming, her voice soft and smooth as butter. Though Hadley doubted she could learn to paint a single stroke, she didn't think she would mind listening to Tyne trying to teach her for hours on end.

Was that the only thing she could picture doing for hours with Tyne? If she were completely honest, no. Walking with her along the trail, there'd been a current of electricity that pulsed through her when her fingers touched Tyne's shoulders. And the times the younger woman had gotten ahead of her, it was safe to say the river wasn't the only enjoyable view. But there were limits on how far Hadley would allow her imagination to wander when it came to someone who had been learning her ABCs from Elmo the same year Hadley was heading off to college.

At least, there *should* be limits, she reminded herself as the hem of Tyne's black skirt rode up several inches on her thigh when she bent over to put the paint bottles in a bin under the counter. She really needed to stop looking. Digging her nails into the palms of her hands, Hadley tore her eyes away.

"Oh, look here!" Tyne cried out.

Hadley immediately did as she was told, her eyes flying back and landing right where they'd been before. On Tyne's perfectly rounded rump.

God dammit.

This was not Hadley's fault. She'd tried to look away and had taken pains to remind herself how much younger Tyne was. Except, from where Hadley was standing, admiring the woman's scrumptious curves, it was evident that regardless of the difference in their ages, Tyne was every bit a full-grown woman now.

Be real, she chided herself. *This woman is way too young and hot to be interested in some middle-aged workaholic.*

As Tyne straightened up, Hadley scrambled to return her face muscles to their well-practiced, neutral mask. For the first time in as long as she could remember, she was pretty sure she had failed, and that she might as well have written her less than pure thoughts in red ink across her forehead. She froze, not daring to breathe.

"I found wine." Tyne hoisted two bottles in the air, one in each hand, with a look of triumph.

Hadley let out a puff of breath. Against all odds, it appeared Tyne had not caught on to the way Hadley had been mentally undressing her while she was busy rummaging in the cabinets. "You said this is a paint and sip. Don't you always have wine?"

"Actually, no. Funny story, but because of some sort of blue laws put in place by the Puritans, it is illegal in this state for me to serve wine to my students. It's strictly B.Y.O.B. I provide the corkscrew and glasses, but some students left these bottles behind, unopened, after one of my classes."

"So, what you're saying is we have wine, glasses, *and* a way to open the bottle?"

Tyne grinned. "That's exactly right. Shall we?"

"God, yes." All at once, the overwhelming stress of

the past several days hit Hadley like she'd slammed into a brick wall. She'd never needed a glass of wine so badly in her life.

Tyne opened a cabinet above the sink, pulling out two bulbous, oversized wineglasses and a device shaped like rabbit ears. Hadley watched as Tyne expertly popped out the cork. Then she filled each glass well past where a bartender would stop and handed one to Hadley. When Tyne set the bottle on the counter, Hadley noted it was empty.

"I don't think I've ever seen someone fit half a bottle of wine into a single glass before," she remarked as she lifted the dark red liquid to her lips.

"A little trick I learned from some of my regulars," Tyne said with a chuckle. "When it comes to the sipping portion of the paint and sips, they can get pretty hard-core."

"Impressive." Hadley closed her eyes, giving herself over to the experience of velvety wine rushing across her tongue. It was the way she liked it, full-bodied and dry, but not so acidic as to make her mouth pucker. As she swallowed, a flush of warmth flowed through her veins like a meandering brook. "This is good."

"Like I said, my students don't mess around." Tyne took a few sips, paused, and pressed a hand to her temple. "I, however, am a lightweight, and I realized I haven't eaten since breakfast. This is going to go right to my head."

"Come to think of it, even with all those casseroles people brought, I didn't have a single bite." Hadley looked longingly at the sizable portion of wine left in her glass, knowing there was no way she could finish it on an empty stomach without passing out. She was a doctor. As much as she'd love to lie to herself, that was science.

Tyne pressed her lips together, seeming to consider for a moment before speaking. "We could head upstairs to my apartment."

Hadley cocked one eyebrow, appraising the glass again. "For?"

Recalling Tyne's enticing ass, Hadley could think of any number of things she might *like* to do if they found themselves alone in an apartment. But surely that wasn't what the woman had in mind.

"Food."

Damn.

It had been a long shot, but you couldn't blame a girl for hoping.

Except...

Maybe she was crazy, but the way Tyne's cheeks flushed pink, it was possible that, for a moment, her mind had gone to the same place as Hadley's.

Interesting.

"I've got a few types of cheese, salami, some crackers." Tyne continued. "I mean, it's not a tuna casserole, but it might sop up enough wine that we don't have to let our glasses go to waste."

Hadley laughed. "Brilliant idea. I'll take cheese and crackers over casserole any day."

"It would worry me if you felt otherwise."

Grabbing her wineglass in one hand and the unopened bottle in the other, Tyne winked. A shiver traveled from Hadley's scalp to her toes. Maybe going upstairs wasn't such a good idea. Unfortunately, now that she remembered she hadn't eaten, Hadley's stomach had started gnawing a hole through her belly button. As she followed Tyne to a door that led to a back stairwell, Hadley eyed the wine sloshing in her glass. When had her mouth become so dry?

The apartment on the second floor was smaller than Hadley had pictured, a single room with a small kitchen in one corner, a dining nook with a table and two chairs that had probably come from a yard sale, and a futon that, judging by the stack of blankets beside it and lack of anything resembling a second room, must serve as both a couch and bed. Opposite the futon were two mismatched bookcases filled with a jumble of well-worn paperbacks, flanking a stand that held a television. A colorful rug covered much of the wood floor. Though the space was tiny and cluttered, the ceilings were high, and there were five enormous windows along the brick exterior wall that allowed in plenty of sun. It surprised Hadley that it was so cozy, despite the chaos.

"I'll go get the food," Tyne said, already halfway to

the refrigerator after only a few steps into the room. "Make yourself comfortable."

"It's nice," Hadley said, being sincere.

"I think the word you're looking for is miniscule," Tyne countered with a laugh. "It was all I could manage a few years ago when I first started my business. I've thought about getting a bigger place now that I can afford to, but it's so convenient for work, and after all, how much space does one person need?"

A little more than this was Hadley's first response as she eyed the futon, unable to remember the last time she'd sat on one. Medical school, maybe? When she'd finally made it through her residency and started earning a doctor's salary, she'd purchased her Beacon Hill townhouse, thrown away her crappy furniture, and paid a decorator to make the place look good. Of course, with as much time as she spent working and as infrequently as she saw it in daylight, Hadley could as easily live in an apartment like Tyne's and never know the difference. Maybe the woman had a point.

She wandered to the bookcases, her eyes landing on a grouping of framed photos, informal snapshots from family gatherings. There was one of Ryan and Kayleigh from when she'd been pregnant with Owen, and another of the young couple with their new baby, still wrapped in the pink and blue striped blanket, the day they'd left the hospital. Gently, Hadley took the frame from the shelf, brushing a fingertip along the frame as she studied every detail. They were so happy. So young.

"Hadley?"

She jumped at Tyne's voice behind her and quickly swiped her fingers along her cheeks as she realized they were wet with tears. All those years spent perfecting the control of her emotions, and when she needed it most, the skill had deserted her completely. She turned around anyway. Somehow it didn't seem to matter too much if Tyne saw her cry. She didn't need to keep her feelings in check here.

Hadley sniffled. "Yeah?"

"Dinner's served, such as it is." Setting a wooden cutting board with an array of snacks on the coffee table, Tyne's eyes flitted to the frame in Hadley's hand. The subtle shift in her expression said she understood exactly what Hadley was experiencing at that moment but wouldn't make a big deal of it unless Hadley wanted to.

Hadley really didn't want to.

Instead, she set the picture back in its place and chose another. This one was of Owen at Christmas, wearing a big silver bow on his head from the package he was opening. Hadley smiled. "I love this. I don't think I've seen it before."

"Oh, I took that picture. It was at my parents' house on Christmas morning."

Hadley's smile faded. She'd been working this past Christmas, as she always did. She'd sent a giant stuffed giraffe for Owen, which her sister had scolded her for but seemed to love, and Hadley had talked with her family on a video call after her shift. It had seemed like enough at the time, with infinite Christmases they could spend together in the future.

"Do you think Owen looks like Kayleigh in that photo?" Tyne asked.

Hadley squinted at it and shook her head. "No. He looks like your brother did when he was little, don't you think?"

Tyne's shoulders drooped slightly. "I never saw Ryan at that age. He was already ten when I came here."

They made their way to the futon, with Hadley taking a spot on one end and Tyne on the other, leaving plenty of empty space in between.

"I remember babysitting for him once. I think he was three. All I know is he was potty-trained during the day, but apparently not overnight. Which I did not know at the time." Hadley grimaced. "So, he's getting ready for bed and tells me he needs his diaper, and being a stupid know-it-all teenager, I was like no, buddy, you're a big boy now, remember?

"Oh no."

"Oh, yeah. I was sitting down on the couch with a couple slices of the pizza your mom had ordered for me, which was definitely the biggest incentive to babysit as far as I was concerned. And I hear this little voice calling me from down the hall. I go in to see what's going on, and I swear to you, it was like he'd gone over Niagara Falls on his mattress. And then while he was trying to explain, he started peeing again, all over the floor."

"So much for pizza and a movie." Tyne's mouth puckered as she tried not to laugh.

"It was so embarrassing, because of course your mom had put the part about the bedtime diaper right on the instructions she'd left, and I hadn't read them all the way through. I managed to get it all cleaned up, even got the sheets washed, dried, and back on the bed before your parents got home. I don't think they ever found out, but I'm pretty sure that was the day I realized kids were *not* in my future."

"Aw, that kind of thing can happen to anyone." The way Tyne's cheeks and mouth continued to twitch in amusement, Hadley had a feeling she said that to be nice. "Trust me. I may not have been there when Ryan was little, but I was for my other three brothers. I don't even have kids yet, and I've probably washed enough pee-soaked sheets to last a lifetime."

Yet, huh? Clearly, she and Tyne had processed these formative interactions with children very differently from one another for the younger woman to still be set on having children of her own.

"Your parents are brave to have taken on such a big family. That's all I have to say."

"Brave or crazy. And now they'll have Owen, too."

Hadley nodded, donning a slight frown as she

thought of her nephew's future. Though her sister and brother-in-law hadn't left a will, and the courts had not yet granted permanent guardianship, the assumption on everyone's part was Michelle and Keith would raise Owen. She would do whatever she could to help financially, but it was a huge undertaking, and she marveled at their stamina.

Hadley stacked a piece of cheese onto a cracker, popping it into her mouth and chasing it down with a big swig of wine, leaving only a few drops in her glass. "Do you have any other pictures of Owen?"

"Tons. My mom might be the last person in America who gets prints of all her photos." Tyne drained her own glass and set it down. "I'll go find them if you crack open the other bottle and get us a refill."

"Will do," Hadley replied, even though the way the room wobbled a little when she stood was a good indicator she should ease up on the vino.

Entering the kitchen area, she glanced at the clock on the microwave. It said it was a little after seven, a claim supported by the fact the sun had dipped low and was now sending out a glow of fiery orange along the horizon. It was later than she'd thought, but not so late that they didn't still have plenty of time to sober up before heading home. She adjusted the weird bunny-eared device on top of the bottle, easily removing the cork and carrying it back to where the glasses waited on the coffee table.

Tyne was sitting just off the center of the futon, flipping through a shoebox of photos. Hadley added a splash of wine to each of their glasses. Then a little more. It was best not to overindulge.

Oh, who am I kidding?

She tilted the bottle and filled both glasses as full as before. She hesitated for a second before taking a seat beside Tyne. They were so close now that their legs nearly touched, and as Hadley breathed in, the scent of apricot tickled her nose. Tyne's shampoo? Whatever it was, it smelled like heaven.

"Oh, look at this one." Tyne held up a photo, angling it slightly. It was a picture of Hadley holding a tiny, smiling Owen in a red, white, and blue sun hat. "He'd just turned two months old."

"That must have been the Labor Day barbecue," Hadley commented.

"No," Tyne corrected matter-of-factly. "It was a couple days before, at the lake."

"Are you sure?" Hadley squinted at the photo, trying to recall any details of the day.

"Positive. You wore that blue V-neck tank top at the barbecue." As soon as the words had left Tyne's mouth, her eyes widened. "I mean, uh…"

Hadley raised an eyebrow. "You remember what I was wearing?"

"No," Tyne denied a tad too vehemently to be believed. "Just the color. I'm an artist. I notice colors."

Yeah, right, Hadley barely stopped herself from

crowing in response. Tyne had definitely been checking her out that day, even if Hadley had been entirely unaware of it. The realization filled her body to the brim with a sensation akin to warm honey. Could she really have a chance with someone like Tyne?

Not that she wanted that, of course. She was married to her job, which was demanding and required constant sacrifice. Everything else in her life came second and had since the day she'd donned her white coat.

Wow. If her job was a human spouse, she might want a divorce.

"You know what I notice?" Hadley's voice sounded strange to her own ears, low and gravelly. She swallowed, not exactly sure how she'd come to lean so close that her shoulder pressed against Tyne's, erasing all distance between them. "Sitting with you right now is like finding the calm at the center of a storm."

"It's impossible to feel good, but I think I feel better than I would if you weren't here." With a sigh, Tyne rested her head against Hadley's shoulder. "Will it ever hurt less?"

"When patients' families ask me, I always tell them that someday it will get easier and that the mention of their loved one will bring a smile to their faces before it brings tears to their eyes. I really hope it's true."

Hadley closed her eyes, resting her cheek against the top of Tyne's head, her hair tickling Hadley's cheek. She felt Tyne's arm slide across her back, hooking at her waist. It felt so good to sit close like this, so healing. Hadley put her own arm behind Tyne, resting her hand on her shoulder, shifting slightly so she could wrap her other arm around the front, holding Tyne in a sideways embrace.

They sat silently, their breathing in sync, their bodies gently swaying like a boat bobbing on a quiet pond. They drifted closer, so slowly the movement was barely perceptible, until Hadley became aware that they were front to front, and that somehow both Tyne's arms were around her, holding her tightly.

She felt warm. Safe. There was the faintest glimmer of hope that maybe, someday, life could be normal again. With the wine buzzing through her and the scent of apricot surrounding her, Hadley felt hypnotized, like she was under a spell. Nothing else mattered except holding onto this feeling as long as she could. She couldn't bear for it to end.

Not loosening her grasp, Hadley leaned backward onto a pile of pillows that were propped against the arm of the futon. Tyne shifted, too, a comforting weight pressing against her belly and chest. Still not letting go, Hadley maneuvered her legs to stretch out along the length of the futon, Tyne's hip resting between her legs. Eyes still closed, she stroked Tyne's hair, curling the short locks around her fingers. Tyne nuzzled against her neck, hot breath puffing against Hadley's skin, melting her deeper into the pillows like a wax crayon in the summer sun.

Still playing with Tyne's hair with one hand, her other hand drifted along the length of Tyne's back. She arrived at the waistband of Tyne's skirt, dipping her fingers beneath as they continued to travel along the silky fabric of Tyne's blouse. The fabric ended at a neatly rolled hem. Hadley ran one finger along it lazily.

Tyne shifted, and the sudden pressure of her hip against Hadley's crotch sent a jolt coursing through her. Hadley's back arched as she dug her fingers into the small of Tyne's back. At the sound of Tyne's gentle moan, Hadley's eyes flew open. Her heart raced as she suddenly realized where her hands were.

Tyne's face hovered just a few inches above hers, Tyne's eyes staring down at her. Even in the dim light, the smoldering intensity of Tyne's gaze singed her. Hadley's breath caught in her throat, and she was vaguely aware of a voice in her head telling her she should put a stop to whatever this was that was happening between them.

With every muscle frozen in place, she waited for the voice to tell her why, but it was unable to present a single good reason. Hadley's body, on the other hand, presented all sorts of compelling evidence to spur her on.

Every nerve ending sizzled. Every inch of skin strained to be touched. After seemingly endless days of more pain and loss than she could stand, was it really so wrong to want to lose herself for a while?

She tilted her chin, parting her lips. Who would

blame her—or either of them really—for seeking comfort in something that felt so good? It didn't have to mean anything, right?

And then Tyne's mouth was on hers, the world around her dissolving in a burst of craving that left no room for thinking.

CHAPTER SIX

Tyne floated in a sea of sensation, lost in the taste of luscious lips, surrounded by the faint smell of spice and fabric softener, as the body beneath hers bobbed and rolled. She wasn't sure how she'd gotten here and didn't really care. All that mattered was the frenzied euphoria of physical desire had banished the dark emptiness that had consumed her for days.

Two hands burrowed beneath her blouse, fingertips trailing along her bare sides, stopping at her bra band. After a brief pause, blunt nails raked their way back down, shooting pulses of electricity to her core. Tyne disengaged her mouth long enough to glide her tongue from jawline to ear, sinking her teeth playfully into one plump lobe before working her way slowly toward the collarbone.

Long legs beneath her spread wider, wrapping

around her knees, pressed to her waist while heels dug firmly into her ass. Tyne rocked her pelvis with a rhythmic motion, sinking deeper into the roaring furnace that awaited her between two shapely thighs. Tyne couldn't count how many times she had fantasized about exactly this, kissing Hadley Moore.

Wait. Tyne's brain reengaged with a click. *I'm kissing Hadley Moore?*

Tyne's body tensed.

Here they were, both still dressed in black clothing from the funeral, and somehow, she'd decided *this* was the appropriate moment to act on her fantasies and kiss an emotionally vulnerable woman who'd just lost her sister?

What the fuck is wrong with me?

Tyne dug her knees into the futon, pushing up with one arm to put some much-needed distance between her and the amazingly tempting body beneath her. She was grateful for how dim the light had become, as it meant Hadley was less likely to notice how Tyne's cheeks burned with shame.

"Oh, God. I can't believe I..."

With hands still burrowed into Tyne's waistband but suddenly still, Hadley frowned. "Can't believe what?"

"This. I..." Buying herself a few moments to compose her thoughts, Tyne hoisted herself into a sitting position. Her entire front felt cold, like someone had turned off the sun. "This is wrong. I'm sorry."

Hadley sat up as well and attempted to straighten herself out. It was a losing battle. Her usually smooth hair stuck out at odd angles, her shirt was untucked, and the top half of its buttons gaped open to reveal a nude tone bra beneath. The well-tailored jacket that had completed the outfit was missing entirely, and Tyne vaguely recalled it being flung to the ground. Had she done that, or had Hadley? Tyne couldn't remember, but it must have been her. She was the one who had lost control of herself, not Hadley.

Hadley rubbed her temples. Her face wore that neutral expression that made it impossible for Tyne to guess what she was thinking. "The wine must've gone to my head." Even her tone was devoid of emotion.

"Yes, exactly. Way too much wine." Tyne let out a relieved sigh.

For a moment, she'd been afraid Hadley would be angry with her. She had every right to be. After all, the whole kissing thing was completely Tyne's fault. Of course, it had kinda *seemed* like Hadley was enjoying the kiss, too. But probably only because Tyne sprang it on her so suddenly that she didn't have time to react properly. Look how quickly she'd cooled off after taking a moment to process what was happening.

"It's probably best if we call it an evening," Hadley said. "My parents will worry if I don't get back before they go to bed."

Tyne attempted to get to her feet but sat down again almost immediately as the room started to spin. "Just one problem. There's no way I can drive you."

"I have no business driving either," Hadley said, "even if I had my car with me, which I don't. I guess I'll get an Uber."

Tyne laughed but tried to stop when she realized Hadley had been serious. "We don't really have that out here."

"Oh, come on. It's not that rural. There's gotta be at least one driver."

"There is. Dave Neumeyer."

Hadley's eyebrows shot up. "Mr. Neumeyer, the driver's ed teacher? He's gotta be ninety years old by now. He was already ancient when I was in high school, and that was a million years ago."

Tyne nodded, not in agreement with Hadley's estimate of how long it had been since she'd graduated, but because Mr. Neumeyer really was close to ninety. "I'm afraid he's the only driver I know of in town, and he likes to be in bed by eight."

"Shit."

Tyne was so frustrated with herself she could scream. First, she'd thrown herself at Hadley, now she'd made it impossible for Hadley to get away. The woman was going to think she was some kind of lunatic stalker. "I could call my parents. One of them can come get you."

"No. Today had to have been one of the worst days

of their lives. I'm not going to trouble them." Hadley patted the back of the futon. "I assume this folds down flat."

"Yeah." Tyne swallowed hard, nearly choking as she realized where this was headed. "I usually sleep on it the way it is, but it folds out to a full-size bed."

"Not a queen?" From the look on Hadley's face, Tyne could've told her the mattress was filled with nails.

"No, just a full. I don't have much room. Plus, the bigger one cost more, and it's not like I ever bring anyone back here, um, to... What I mean is, I, um..." *What I mean is I am babbling, and if I don't stop talking right now, I might die.* "You know what? I'll be perfectly fine on the floor."

"Don't be silly. I'm sure we're both adult enough to handle the situation without getting into any more trouble."

Ouch.

On the inside, Tyne flinched at what had to have been a dig at her immature behavior earlier. Well, she'd show Hadley how much of an adult she was. She was going to sleep on that futon all night without so much as brushing a single hair on Hadley's head. Assuming she could remember where she put the extra pillows. And the sheets.

Crappers.

Why did being an adult have to be so complicated?

"I'm going to give my parents a call. I assume you'll

be able to drive me back home first thing in the morning." Hadley bit down on her lower lip, and her expression grew uncertain. "Unless it would be better if I take an Uber."

"Of course not," Tyne replied, but inside her head, she was berating herself for complicating what had been turning into a nice friendship, all because of one brief kiss.

Only it hadn't been a *brief* kiss at all. It had been a full-on make-out session that had lasted who knows how long, and it almost definitely would've gone a whole hell of a lot further than it did if they hadn't both been so nicely dressed. Or maybe Tyne was the only one who had been on the verge of ripping all their clothes off.

Uh, yeah, stupid. You pretty much were.

Tyne studied the back of Hadley's head as she crossed to the far side of the room to place her call. That was the whole problem, wasn't it? Hadley had never given the slightest indication over the years of being interested in her. She hadn't even remembered Tyne's name, for Christ's sake. And now Tyne had acted on impulse and made it all weird between them.

All the while she was berating herself, Tyne scoured the closet, finally locating the plastic bin with the extra bedding, along with an old T-shirt and yoga pants for Hadley to sleep in. She slipped into the bathroom and changed into her own pajamas, thankful on the one hand she never slept in anything too sexy, but also cringing that her best option that night was a shorts set printed with SpongeBob characters. Hadley was going to think she was twelve.

Tyne had folded down the futon and was smoothing out the top blanket when Hadley finished her call.

"Everything okay?" Tyne asked, noting the cloud that had come to rest over the woman's face.

"Fine." At first it seemed like that was all she was going to say, but then Hadley sighed and added, "I feel guilty, not being home with them."

"I'm so sorry." Tyne had really screwed up. "I never should've brought up that second bottle of wine."

"No, it's not that." Hadley hesitated as if weighing her words. "I feel guilty because part of me is kind of glad to get a break. I mean, I want to be there for them, but it's draining. And being back in the house where I grew up doesn't help. I'm forty-one years old, but the minute I walk through those doors, it's like I'm a teenager again. And not in a good way."

"Can I confess something? I kind of feel the same way." Saying it out loud made Tyne feel a little lighter. "Staying with Mom and Dad this week in a house with three brothers and a baby has been like living in a zoo. I can't even hear myself think, let alone take care of my own needs. I'm running on fumes."

"Listen to us." Hadley shook her head, letting out a short, humorless laugh. "No wonder we went through two bottles of wine tonight."

"I do feel bad about that." Tyne stared at the ground, kicking the edge of the rug with her toe.

"It's not your fault."

"I'm usually not so out of control with alcohol. And other things." She glanced up and saw Hadley's gaze had shifted away, her cheeks tinged with pink. "Look, Hadley, I don't want what happened earlier between us to make things strange. Do you think we can kind of hit the reset button and pretend it didn't happen?"

"Done." Hadley scooped up the nightclothes Tyne had set out for her. "It's completely forgotten."

As Hadley went toward the bathroom to change, Tyne eyed the bed, her belly clenching. It really *was* small. She climbed under the covers, scooting as far as she could toward the edge and trying not to think about what it had felt like to have Hadley's body under hers, their mouths pressed together and tongues intertwined.

The more she tried not to think of it, the more vivid the memory became. Tyne's body tingled, her core heating up like she was an electric teakettle as she teetered on the verge of a full-blown fantasy about what might happen later that night, if only...

Nope. Terrible idea.

Tyne shut her eyes and imagined unplugging the teakettle and tossing it into a twenty-foot snowbank. How nice for Hadley that she'd found their kiss so completely unmemorable that she'd already put it out of her mind and moved on.

If only Tyne could do the same.

She groaned and pulled the blanket up to her chin. It was going to be a long night.

SOMETHING WAS BUZZING in Tyne's ear. It wasn't her alarm, which usually woke her with the soothing sounds of a meditation chime. Whatever this was, it was harsh, grating. Why wouldn't it stop?

"Will someone please answer that fucking phone," a woman's voice groaned beside her, "before I find it and throw it against the wall?"

Tyne's eyes flew open as memories of the night before came flooding back. She turned gingerly, both because she didn't want to accidentally roll on top of Hadley and also because her head was pounding like someone was trying to hammer their way out from inside her skull. Thankfully, it was not a bright and sunny day, but there was enough light to signal it was indeed morning and to make Tyne wish she could shut her eyelids permanently and lock herself inside a cave.

Please, God, if you make this hangover go away, I promise I will never drink wine again.

After a few moments of bumping and scraping, a cold, flat rectangle smacked against Tyne's palm. As she searched for the green answer button, her mother's face on the screen told her who was calling and caused a prickle of unease that traveled from her neck to her shoulder blades. It was a quarter to six, way too early for a casual phone call.

"Mom, what's wrong?" Tyne held her breath, scared to hear the answer. She knew all too well how bad an unexpected phone call could be.

"No, honey, it's Dad. I'm using your mom's phone."

This did nothing to ease Tyne's mind. "Is Mom okay?"

"Yes. Well, no. There's nothing to worry about, but your mother and I need some help."

Tyne had become completely lost in the conversation but clung to the part where her dad had said there was nothing to worry about. "Okay, when do you need me to come over?"

"Um, now."

Nothing to worry about, my ass.

"On my way." Hangover forgotten, Tyne sprang from under the covers, causing the futon to shake.

Hadley let out what could only be described as a murderous groan as she propped herself up on her elbows. Her hair stuck out like a bird had built its nest on top of her head while she slept. Only her left eye was fully open. The right eye was more of a slit that gave her face the look of a clay sculpture that someone had smooshed on one side.

It was absolutely the most fucking adorable thing Tyne had ever seen.

"What the hell is going on? Where am I?" An octave lower than usual, Hadley's voice was pure sex.

It took Tyne a moment to tear her attention away from the sudden throbbing between her legs long enough to remember the answer to the question. "My apartment, remember?"

"It's starting to come back to me." Hadley blinked slowly, giving her head a little shake as if attempting to clear it. "I woke up thinking I was in the on-call room at the hospital. Was someone on the phone?"

"My parents. They need my help for something." Tyne rummaged through a pile of clothing in the corner near her closet to find whatever looked the cleanest. She grabbed a pair of jeans and a flannel shirt and prayed they wouldn't smell bad because there weren't many other options.

"This early on a Saturday morning?" Hadley rubbed her eyes as her mouth stretched open in a yawn. "Is that normal?"

"No. It isn't." Tyne couldn't keep the worry out of her words, and Hadley seemed to pick up on it, looking instantly more alert as she rallied herself to get out of bed.

"Okay, let me find my shoes, and I'll be ready to go. I can wear what I've got on and change at home."

Tyne's eyes landed on Hadley's head, and she couldn't help snorting. "I appreciate your sense of urgency, but I think we can spare a minute for you to brush your hair. There's one in the top drawer in the bathroom."

As soon as she switched on the bathroom light, Hadley laughed. "Good call on the hair. I'll be ready in a sec."

In under five minutes, Tyne and Hadley were out on the sidewalk, walking at a fast clip toward the car. Tyne tried to tamp down the nervousness that was growing inside her, but by the time she was in the driver's seat, her hands were shaking so much she could barely get the key into the ignition. Whatever was going on with her parents, it probably wasn't good.

On her third try, she managed to turn the key and get the engine going. "I'll drop you off at home and circle back to my parents' after that."

"Tyne, no. I remember where your parents live, and I know it's out of the way for you to take me home first. We'll go straight there." Hadley's expression radiated a calming compassion that helped settle Tyne's nerves. "Besides, depending on the emergency, maybe there's something I can do to help."

Tyne nodded silently, grateful for the offer even if she didn't want to think about the types of situations that required a doctor's expertise. She was anything but reassured on this front several minutes later when she walked into her parents' living room to find her mother stretched out on the floor, her eyes squeezed shut as pain contorted her expression.

"Mom, are you okay?" Tyne rushed to her mother's side, kneeling on the beige Berber rug. "What happened?"

"It's my back," her mom replied through gritted teeth, each word punctuated by a gasp.

"Hey there, Michelle. It's Hadley." As she knelt on the other side of Tyne's mom, Hadley's tone had become both professional and soothing. "Do you have a history of back problems?"

"Herniated disc," Tyne's mom said with a groan.

"All right. Let me take a little look here, okay?"

As Hadley gently rolled Tyne's mom to one side and began examining the injured spot, Tyne rose and took a few steps back to get out of the way. Her dad came in from the kitchen with a bottle of pain relievers in one hand and a glass of water in the other. As soon as he saw Tyne and Hadley, the relief on his face was evident.

"I brought her pills," he said, setting the prescription bottle and the glass down on an end table. "The doctor prescribed them last time she had a flare-up."

Hadley nodded without looking up from her exam.

Tyne stood next to her dad, asking in a low voice, "What brought this on? What are you guys even doing out of bed so early?"

"Owen's on his own clock. Your mom had gone into the kitchen to heat a bottle." Her dad wrung his hands as he spoke. "There was only one clean one left. I'd loaded them into the dishwasher last night but forgot to start the wash cycle. When she bent down to put the detergent in, she said she felt something pop, and she couldn't straighten up."

At the mention of her nephew, Tyne's head swiveled. "Where's Owen now?"

"He's in with Evan, finishing off his bottle."

"Maybe I should go check on them." Tyne could only imagine how grumpy her brother must be over being dragged out of bed at dawn on a Saturday.

"In a minute." Her father's face was pinched and deep lines creased his brow. "There's something we need to talk about first."

Tyne swallowed. Even without knowing the topic, her dad's tone had caused a lump to form in her throat. She followed him into the kitchen, out of sight of her mom and Hadley. "What is it?"

"You know the doctor said if she had another episode, your mom was probably going to need surgery." Her dad's face crumpled, and he looked like he was about to cry. "I don't think we can do this."

"I know Mom was hoping it wouldn't come to this, but if surgery is her best option, I'm sure she can do it. She'll get through it fine."

"I wasn't talking about the surgery." His jaw tensed. "I was talking about Owen."

"Oh my God, of course, Dad." Tyne gave her head a little shake. How could she have overlooked something so obvious? "I know I said I wanted to move back to my apartment, but forget all about that right now. I'm happy to stay here and help with Owen for as long as it takes Mom's back to heal."

"Honey, I wasn't talking about temporarily." Her dad's eyes shifted to the floor, like he couldn't bear to look directly at her. "Your mom will need time to recover if she has surgery, but that isn't my only concern. You know as soon as I go back to work, the trucking business keeps me on the road several days at a stretch. I depended on Ryan's help with the business. Conner's trying to step up, but he doesn't have a license yet." He wrung his hands, his eyes laser-focused on them. "I think it's time we spoke with the social worker about finding Owen a more suitable home."

Tyne's eyes widened. "A foster home?"

"It might be for the best." Still her dad avoided looking directly at Tyne.

Her heart pounded in her ears. For the best? She'd been in enough foster homes to know they were *never* for the best. "No. You can't do that. We'll figure it out. I'll work out a schedule, put Evan and Connor on baby duty along with me. I could probably even come up with a way for Mason to help."

"That's another thing." Her father's voice cracked. "Since losing Ryan, Mason's going through some setbacks. He's started biting his hands again, and if his episodes of aggression start up—"

Tyne's heart clenched. "That hasn't happened, has it?"

"Not like before, but if it happens even once, someone could get hurt. Including Owen."

"You're blowing it out of proportion," Tyne said accusingly, even though part of her knew her dad was right. It wasn't Mason's fault, but with this much upheaval in his life right now, it wouldn't be surprising for his behavior to regress and for him to lash out against uncomfortable feelings he couldn't fully verbalize. "It's nothing we haven't handled before."

"When he was little," her dad pointed out, his tone firm. "Your brother's fourteen now, and as tall as your mom."

"Dad—"

"Don't you think Owen deserves the very best?" he snapped.

"Of course, I do. Family is what's best." Tyne stood her ground.

"With an open adoption, we'd still be involved with his life." Tyne's dad paused a moment, pressing his lips together as if considering what he was about to say. "There's something else. I'm turning fifty-six this year…"

His voice trailed off, the number hanging in the air. He didn't need to explain. Tyne knew what he meant by it. His own father and grandfather had died of heart attacks shortly after they turned fifty-six. Despite doctors reassuring him he was in good health, it was clear he feared a similar fate.

Before Tyne could formulate a response that might

ease her father's mind, Hadley came into the kitchen. She held out the pill bottle and a now-empty water glass.

"I had Michelle take two of these and helped her to bed. She should get an appointment with her regular doctor as soon as she can, but until then, I recommend bed rest and absolutely no lifting anything over twenty pounds."

"You see?" Tyne's father gave her a significant look. "Owen was twenty-two pounds at his last checkup."

A slight frown wrinkled Hadley's forehead as she turned to look at Tyne. "What's going on?"

Tyne started to shake. "My parents are going to send Owen away."

"Tyne—" her father began, but Hadley interrupted.

"At the moment, your mom really can't look after a baby," Hadley said. Her tone, while still soothing, grated on Tyne's raw nerves, perhaps because the words weren't at all what she wanted to hear.

"Not temporarily." Tyne balled her fists. "For good."

"Oh." This revelation seemed to have left Hadley at a loss for words as she took a step back.

"It's the responsible thing to do," her father said, sounding like he was pleading for someone to tell him he was right. "There's no other option."

Tyne's brain spun. She couldn't let her little nephew go to a foster home. She just couldn't. There was only one option. It was time for her to step up and take responsibility. "Dad, there *is* another thing we could do."

"Tyne's right." Hadley's face was a picture of determination, and Tyne was suddenly very grateful to know they were both on the same side.

"I'm listening," her dad said.

Tyne took a deep breath. She hadn't planned on becoming a mother so soon, but she was almost thirty, old enough to handle raising Owen on her own. She had to. "Dad, I think—"

"I'm obviously the only one who can do it. I'll take Owen." Hadley edged forward.

Tyne choked on the rest of her sentence as she stared, dumbfounded, at Hadley. Had she heard that correctly? This woman who had admitted to never wanting kids, who was such a workaholic she missed every holiday, thought *she* was the best choice to raise their precious baby nephew?

Was she insane?

Tyne crossed her arms, jutting out her chin, and said the first thing that popped into her head. "Absolutely not."

CHAPTER SEVEN

"What do you mean, absolutely not?" Hadley scowled at Tyne, dumbfounded at the young woman's angry expression and defiant tone. Hadley was trying to do the right thing here, which was hard enough, considering she'd had no time to prepare herself mentally for this type of lifelong commitment. The last thing she needed was an argument.

"What I mean is you live in Boston, you work all the time, and you said yourself you never wanted to have kids." Tyne's nostrils flared. "You can't possibly give Owen the kind of home he deserves."

Hadley threw her hands in the air. "Well, what do you suggest?"

"That *I* take him, obviously."

Before she could think better of it, Hadley burst out laughing.

"You live in a shoebox apartment over an art studio

that smells like paint, and your couch is also your bed. Where would you even put him?" As soon as she saw the stricken look on Tyne's face and the obvious disapproval on Keith's, Hadley regretted her words, but it was too late to take them back. The best she could do was try to soften the blow. "I'm not saying you wouldn't make a great mom; I swear. It's just that you're not really at the stage in life where it would be easy for you to take on the responsibility of a baby."

"Is that so?" From another flash of anger in Tyne's eyes and the redness of her cheeks, it was clear Hadley's reassurances had done nothing to smooth things over. "First of all, I don't really know where you get off thinking you know what life stage I'm in, considering a week ago you couldn't even remember my name. But second, just because you're older doesn't make you more qualified. You hardly know Owen, whereas I've been in his life constantly from day one. Do you even know how to change a diaper?"

Hadley's eyes narrowed as her temper rose. Had Tyne called her *old*? So much for being gentle. Tyne certainly wasn't pulling any punches with *her* words. "I'm a doctor. I think I can manage a diaper."

There were YouTube videos on that, right?

"Ladies," Keith said, looking a little anxious and very much outside his comfort zone, "I'm sure we can come to some sort of agreement. It won't do any good to argue."

"You're right." Hadley reached for her phone.

"There's no sense bickering when what we really need is an expert opinion."

Tyne's face scrunched into a look that was half worry and half distrust. "Who are you calling?"

"My lawyer."

Technically, Marcy Wang was employed by the hospital and specialized in fending off malpractice suits, but Hadley didn't feel compelled to share those details. Marcy was a talented lawyer, and besides, she was the only person Hadley could think of to ask for advice in the heat of the moment. Fortunately, the woman's number was in Hadley's phone from the last time there'd been a legal dustup in the ER.

"Dr. Moore," a woman's sleepy voice answered, obviously having seen Hadley's name come up on caller ID, "haven't I asked you and your colleagues to try to refrain from maiming or killing any of your patients on the weekend?"

Hadley chuckled at what she knew was the lawyer's dry sense of humor, even as she cringed at having forgotten how early it still was. The day already seemed a decade long.

"I promise I have done neither, but I do need your help on a different sort of legal matter." She cast a glance at Tyne and Keith, who were both observing her call with more intensity than if she were trying to tame a wild tiger. Cupping her hand over her mouth to muffle her voice, Hadley retreated to the living room.

"I don't know if you've heard, but my sister and brother-in-law recently passed away."

"Oh, I'm so sorry." Marcy paused. "But you know I'm not a probate lawyer. I can't help you with their will."

"No, it's not that. In fact, that's part of the problem. You see, they didn't have a will, and they left behind a ten-month-old son. We all thought his grandparents—not my parents, but on his father's side—were going to take him, but now it seems like that won't be possible. I'd like to know what I need to do to gain custody."

"Where is your nephew right now?"

"Still with his grandparents. A judge granted them temporary guardianship right after the accident. The thing is, his other aunt, their daughter, wants him, too." Hadley stepped into the mudroom. "But she's much too young and not at all in a suitable position financially to take care of him. My parents are too elderly. I'm really the only reasonable choice."

"Oookay... This aunt, though. She's over eighteen?"

Hadley's nose wrinkled as she made a sour face at the phone. The way Marcy had drawn out the word *okay* as if it had a hundred syllables did not inspire confidence that the woman fully grasped what Hadley was saying. "Yes. But she's only twenty-nine."

"And she has a job?"

"Well, I mean, technically." Hadley's frustration

was rising. It didn't seem like she and Marcy were on the same page at all. "She owns one of those paint and sip places here in town."

"Oh, I love those. I go with my sister and mom all the time." Again, not exactly what Hadley wanted to hear. "And she owns it, huh? I'd say being a small business owner counts as being employed. A judge won't expect her to be a millionaire, just to have a steady paycheck, which it sounds like she has."

"Right, now that we've established that, are you going to tell me how to get custody of my nephew, or...?" Hadley let her words trail off, not really knowing what the alternative would be.

"This isn't my area of expertise, so I don't feel comfortable representing you in an official capacity. But as long as you understand I'm not giving you advice as your lawyer but as a friend, I do have a little bit of information that might clarify things."

"I'm all ears, and I promise not to sue you if I don't like what you have to say."

"Good, because you might not. The truth is, the other aunt probably has as strong a claim as you do. It will not be clear cut, especially since it sounds like she lives in the same community as your nephew's other family members."

"Yeah, she does." Hadley let out a breath like someone had punched her in the gut. "So, what do I do?"

"First, you prepare for a long, drawn-out battle. If

all parties come to an agreement, it's possible for something like this to get resolved fairly quickly, but as soon as you hand it over to a judge, it's a whole other issue. A *guardian ad litem* will need to be appointed. There will be home studies. Background checks. And I can tell you right now, family courts are notorious for their backlog of cases. Nothing moves quickly. Are you sure you're up for that?"

"Absolutely." Hadley's tone proved to herself she meant it. Did what Marcy had described terrify her? Yes. But after all her prior failings as a big sister, she couldn't let Kayleigh down. She had to give Owen the life he deserved. "So, do I need to fill out some paperwork?"

"So much paperwork you might go blind. A petition for guardianship is a good place to start, but I'm not at all convinced the court will sign off on you temporarily taking an infant all the way back to Boston and away from the rest of his family and familiar surroundings."

"You mean I'd have to stay here?" Hadley's pulse increased. She hadn't been planning to extend her stay past another week or two at most. "For how long?"

"From start to finish, you're looking at months. How much of that time you choose to spend out there is up to you. It's not like you'd be under house arrest, so no one can make you stay. What a judge *can* stop you from doing is taking the baby with you, which means if you don't agree to remain local, the other aunt would likely get guardianship, at least temporarily."

"Which would torpedo my standing in the court's eyes, I'm sure." Hadley's stomach dropped. This was getting more complicated by the second. "Let's say I decide to take a sabbatical from work and stay here for a few months. I could get Owen?"

"You could. But most likely this other aunt is going to file a petition for guardianship as well. In that case, it wouldn't surprise me if the court reviews them both and opts for a co-guardianship arrangement."

"We'd have to share?" Hadley tried to keep the whine out of her tone, not wanting to come across as a toddler hoarding her toys.

"You'd have to share," Marcy confirmed. "Probably fifty-fifty."

As she hung up the call, Hadley cursed her role as a responsible adult. Sure, being a doctor was a tremendous responsibility, too, but this was different. Taking on a child would be an enormous burden. And yet, if she was really going to take on the role of Owen's mom, she'd better get used to thankless tasks. From what she understood, motherhood was full of them.

As soon as Hadley re-entered the kitchen, Tyne fixed her with a steady stare.

"What did your lawyer say?" The way Tyne emphasized the word lawyer made it obvious how she felt about Hadley making the call.

"I might as well tell you." Hadley swallowed, her

throat scratchy. "I've decided to extend my time here indefinitely."

Tyne's eyes widened. "You're moving back home?"

"God, no." Hadley shuddered at the prospect of spending months in her mother's craft room. "I plan to rent someplace in town for as long as it takes for me to win guardianship of Owen."

"For you to win?" Tyne crossed her arms. "We'll see about that."

"I should head home. Where did I put my keys?" Hadley patted her hips at the standard position for pants pockets and found she didn't seem to have any pockets at all. With a sinking feeling, she looked down and saw the T-shirt and yoga pants she'd slept in the night before.

"Shit."

"What's wrong?" Tyne smirked. "Oh, that's right. You didn't drive."

Hadley's jaw tightened. "I guess I'd better see if Mr. Neumeyer's hit the roads yet so I can get a ride home."

Tyne rolled her eyes and gave her head a slight shake. "Come on. I may be mad as hell over this guardianship stunt you're trying to pull, but I'm not so petty as to leave you stranded."

For a moment, Hadley considered calling for an Uber anyway, but then she sighed. Given the choice between getting in the car with a woman who hated her guts right now or her ancient driver's ed teacher, Tyne was the better choice. Barely.

"Fine," she muttered, her cheeks growing hot. "Thank you."

AFTER CHECKING ON MICHELLE, who had fallen asleep once the pain pills kicked in, and saying goodbye to Keith, Hadley followed Tyne out to her car. From the murderous look in Tyne's eyes, Hadley half wondered if she'd made the right choice. Her parents were only about five miles away. Maybe it would've been better to walk.

When Tyne started the car without so much as a word, Hadley pulled out her phone. "It's a good thing Rebecca gave me her card yesterday. I wonder if it's too early to call."

"Please." Tyne snorted. "Considering the way she behaved after the memorial, it serves her right to be dragged out of bed early."

Hadley laughed, the unexpected burst of humor making her forget for a moment that she and Tyne suddenly found themselves on opposing sides. Her smile faded as she dialed the number on Rebecca's card. After bonding so quickly over their losses, it was disconcerting to Hadley being at odds with Tyne, the one person who really understood what she was experiencing at this terrible time. Hadley had to put the awkwardness of their kiss in the rearview mirror and move on, despite how much it had stung to be rejected. Why couldn't the younger woman see reason and get over this newest bump in the road so they could go back to being friends?

"Hello, Rebecca?" Hadley said when her call was answered. "This is Hadley Moore. I hope I didn't wake you."

"Oh, I've been up for hours. I'm a real morning person. What can I help you with?" The realtor's cheerfulness, despite it being before eight on a week-end, told Hadley that she and Rebecca could never be close friends. Sure, Hadley had gotten used to putting in all sorts of bizarre hours in the ER and had learned to live with it, but she would *never* refer to herself as a morning person. The very concept made her shudder.

"It turns out I might be able to use your services after all."

"You're interested in the condo? It'll be competitive, but there's still time to get in a bid."

"No, I'm not looking to buy," Hadley corrected quickly. "As it turns out, I'll be sticking around longer than I'd planned, and I need to find a rental. Furnished, if possible, and preferably month to month."

"I don't do many rentals, and it's a really tough market to find apartments right now." Rebecca's tone was no longer nearly so upbeat. Apparently being denied a condo sale put a much bigger dent in her attitude than being up at the crack of dawn. "Couldn't you extend the lease on your sister's place?"

Hadley hadn't even considered the possibility. She was fairly certain they had already assured management they would clear the apartment out by the end of the month. Even if that decision could be reversed, now that she thought about it, the idea of living in what had been Kayleigh's private space made her feel queasy. "I'd rather not. Don't you have anything at all?"

"There may be a house or two, if you don't mind something bigger."

"It's worth a try."

Rebecca sighed. Hadley heard the rapid clicking of a keyboard, followed by another sigh. "Twelve-month lease... twelve-month—wait, no, that one's gone. Oh, here we go. There's exactly one listing that might work. Twenty-seven-hundred square feet, three bed, three bath, post and beam Cape on four acres, with a two-story artist studio and a barn for horses. You know what? I'm going to text you a link to the listing so you can see the photos."

Hadley made appropriate noises as Rebecca reeled off the stats so that it would seem like she'd understood all that realtor mumbo-jumbo. She heard the ding that accompanied an incoming text, but she didn't bother to check the pictures. Given this was temporary, there was really only one detail she needed to know. "How much?"

There was more clicking. Then the sound of Rebecca letting out a low whistle echoed in Hadley's ear. "Man, that's... wow."

Hadley tensed, but when Rebecca told her the amount, she nearly laughed in relief. The rent was a fraction of what she would pay in the city for a place that was nowhere near the same size. For the amount of time she would need it, the cost was well within her budget. "I'll take it."

"That's splendid news! Let me get in touch with the owners to see what needs to happen next, and I'll call you back."

"You found a place?" Tyne's words were clipped, and Hadley could feel the tension she was trying to hide.

"Fingers crossed." Hadley left it at that. There was no sense going into details she was sure Tyne had no desire to hear.

They drove the next few minutes in silence. When Tyne pulled into the driveway at Hadley's parents' house, she put the car in park but didn't turn off the engine. "Here you go."

"Thanks." Hadley unbuckled and paused with her hand on the unopened door. She wanted to say something but wasn't sure what. All she knew was leaving things like this was wrong on so many levels. As she opened her mouth to speak, her phone rang. "Hold on. It's Rebecca."

"Hadley?" Either Hadley was nuts, or Rebecca

didn't sound nearly as happy as before. "There's a problem."

Hadley's entire body clenched. "What problem?"

"The owners, they're an older couple. Retirement age. In fact, they just moved to North Carolina. This is their first time renting a property, and they're only doing it because their kids insisted they didn't sell the house until they were certain they liked it down south and wouldn't want to move back. They've heard one too many tenant horror stories from friends, and they're anxious about damage."

"What does that mean for me, an extra security deposit or something?" Whatever she needed to do to ease their minds, Hadley was happy to comply. She wanted to get things settled so she could turn her full attention to Owen.

"The thing is," Rebecca's voice sounded even more tense than before, "they're saying they won't rent the house to a single person. I explained you're a respected doctor and very trustworthy, but all their friends told them never to rent to single people. Couples only."

"Are you serious?"

"Afraid so. They're adamant about it. I'm so sorry. I know it's ridiculous, but they won't budge. Please don't worry. I'll keep looking. Maybe we can find something else next month when a new batch of rentals comes in."

Next month? No way. Hadley couldn't stay with

her parents that long. She'd go out of her mind, and besides which, she'd never get temporary guardianship of Owen if she didn't have an appropriate place for him to live. Her head was spinning.

"What's wrong?" Tyne asked in a hoarse whisper.

Hadley's eyes landed on Tyne, the woman coming into sharp focus as an idea exploded in her brain. "Rebecca, did they say what kind of couple? Like, did it have to be a married husband and wife, or would a nice lesbian couple be okay with them?"

"They didn't say, but I think that would be fine," Rebecca answered. "Do you have a girlfriend who will be joining you out here?"

"Maybe. Let me call you right back." Hadley hung up and looked squarely at Tyne. What she was about to do was crazy, but it might be her best option. "I have a proposition for you."

Confusion was written all over Tyne's face, but there was more than a hint of interest, too. "What's going on?"

"That place Rebecca found, I can't rent it by myself. But I could with your help."

"Too expensive? Because I don't have any spare cash lying around to help pay your rent."

"Money's not the issue. In fact, I wouldn't take a dime. It's… something else."

Tyne arched an eyebrow, which even under these less than ideal circumstances Hadley couldn't help but find excruciatingly sexy. "Intriguing. But you're, like, the enemy or something now. Why would I want to help you?"

"Because I think you'll benefit, too." Hadley paused, letting her jumbled thoughts fall into place. "Here's the deal. According to my attorney, neither one of us is likely to get Owen outright. The court will probably want to grant a co-guardianship. Make us share. Only let's face it; neither one of us has an appropriate place in town for Owen to live right now."

Tyne nodded slowly, not exactly in agreement, but at least in acknowledgement that she was listening and maybe keeping an open mind. "Keep going."

"I don't mean to be rude, but you said your studio is—what was the word you used, minuscule? And according to Rebecca, the apartment market is tight. I, on the other hand, can afford to rent an entire house, but the owners won't let a single woman live there."

"You want me to pretend to be your girlfriend?" Tyne's eyes widened with shocked understanding.

"No, of course not. I want you to agree to live in the house with me so they'll be okay with renting it out. There's plenty of space from what Rebecca said. Three bedrooms, something about posts and beams..." From the expression on Tyne's face, Hadley feared she was losing her, but then she remembered another key detail and blurted, "There's an art studio!"

"What?" Tyne leaned forward, the doubt in her eyes transforming to a look of near-rapture. "A studio. You're sure?"

Hadley was almost certain she'd hooked Tyne, but to be sure, she pulled up the listing on her phone and scrolled through the photos until she reached one of a large, two-story outbuilding with cedar shingles and huge windows all around. "See? This is it right here."

Tyne stared at the photo without blinking, her mouth slightly open. Finally, she swallowed and blinked. "If I moved in, you'd be paying the rent? Because while I have the income to cover a slightly bigger place for myself and Owen, no way can I afford to keep my current apartment while paying for half of what sounds like a mansion at the same time."

"No worries. I'll pay the deposit and rent, plus all the utilities. And one thing more. I promise to agree to a temporary co-guardianship with you."

"Are you serious?" Tyne regarded her with suspicion. "I thought you were planning to have your high-priced city lawyer swoop in here and pull out all the stops to get what you want."

"Look, we're both going to need legal representation, but let's make a deal. No dirty tricks. We'll each get to say why we would be best for Owen, and then we'll let the courts decide."

Tyne blew out a breath. "I guess they're the experts, after all. And in the meantime, we'll both get to be with Owen without him having to go back and forth."

"Exactly. He'll even have his own room." Hadley held out her hand. "I'm willing to shake on it. Let's agree right now not to let this get unfriendly or out of hand."

Tyne pressed her lips together, her eyes studying Hadley's hand.

Hadley held her breath and listened to her heart pound.

Tyne looked up, took Hadley's hand, and gave it a firm shake. "Okay. Go ahead and tell Rebecca the deal's on."

"You'll do it?" A smile spread across Hadley's lips as Tyne nodded. She slapped her hands together, and the smile became a grin. "Thank you. You won't regret it."

As Hadley waited for Rebecca to answer her call, she felt like she was floating. She and Tyne were going to live together and take care of Owen. She was vaguely aware of being quite a bit more pleased by this turn of events than she had any business being, but it was a lot easier to pretend it wasn't the case than to sort out what it could mean. So, she did what she always did each time she started a fresh shift in the ER. She flipped the switch in her head, shut it down, boxed it up, and put it aside for another time.

CHAPTER EIGHT

Tyne felt a sense of wonderment as she stood in the living room of her new abode, taking in the soaring cathedral ceiling with its honey-colored exposed wood beams. It had only been a week since she'd agreed to the move, but since the house came furnished, relocating had been a cinch. She could hardly believe this was really her home. Well, not exactly. Not permanently, anyway. Given that, she planned to appreciate the view of the woods from the wide picture windows and the crackle of a fire in the cozy brick fireplace every chance she could while she was here.

How long that would be, Tyne wasn't sure. She was guessing three months if there were no delays with the court, and even less if her instincts about Hadley were on target. Despite what some people had thought when she'd agreed to this living arrangement, Tyne wasn't a fool. If she hadn't believed she would benefit from it to come out on top, she never would've agreed to it.

To begin with, Tyne hadn't sat idly by in the kitchen that day while Hadley was calling her attorney. She might not have a lawyer of her own, but she did have the home number of the social worker who had helped her parents with the emergency guardianship petition. She didn't know the going rate for a fancy Boston lawyer, but Tyne had managed to find out for free pretty much the same thing Hadley had. Given the situation, a co-guardianship was the most likely outcome in the short term.

Since there was no way around it, Tyne figured she could at least make the best of things by getting a nice place to live out of it and more time with Owen. And the promise of a fair fight was huge, because Tyne knew she could never afford a good enough lawyer if Hadley let things get ugly. And, of course, this arrangement gave her a front-row seat for watching Hadley find out exactly how much was involved in being a parent. Tyne had a sudden desire to make some popcorn to go along with what was sure to be a hilarious show.

"Ahhhhhh!" came a high-pitched screech from somewhere down the hall.

Tyne held back a chuckle even as she continued at a

leisurely pace toward the bedroom she and Hadley had set up earlier that day to be Owen's nursery. A baby's cry had not followed the scream, so Tyne knew Owen was fine. Honestly, in the case of bodily harm, he would be in much better hands with Hadley to tend to him than Tyne. But what he actually needed right now was a diaper change, and letting the good doctor deal with it on her own was all part of Tyne's master plan.

The infuriating thing was Tyne knew Hadley meant well. She was a decent person who truly cared about giving their nephew the best life possible. The problem was she had a blind spot when it came to deciding what constituted the "best life," not to mention her own ability to provide it. Hadley had spent a lot of time weighing the importance of top-notch schools and big houses, the things a doctor's salary put within easy reach. But as far as Tyne could tell, she'd never actually taken care of a real human baby before.

Hadley was in for an eye-opening experience.

"Oh my God, Owen. Stop!" Hadley spluttered as Tyne peered in through the open bedroom door.

"Problem?" She didn't really need an answer. The arching stream coming from the changing table, coupled with Hadley's dripping chin and soaked shirt, told Tyne all she needed to know.

"I've got it under control," Hadley said, clearly determined to pretend her struggles weren't obvious. As if to increase the challenge, Owen let loose with a fresh spray. "For the love of Pete!"

With a snort, Tyne lunged for a fresh diaper. Unfolding it with a practiced hand, she slipped it into position like a pro. "One thing you learn by growing up with brothers is boys pee up. Never leave them uncovered."

"Yeah, I..." Hadley shook her head rapidly, her hands flying up toward her chest like she wanted to clean herself off but didn't know where to begin.

One hand still holding the diaper in place, Tyne used the other to grab a few wipes out of the plastic container. "Here. Start with these."

While Hadley wiped everything she could, Tyne quickly completed the diaper change. Fortunately, while he'd made a total mess out of his aunt, Owen had kept himself nice and dry. *Good job, little buddy,* Tyne thought, winking at her nephew as she buttoned his onesie.

"I'm not usually squeamish about bodily fluids," Hadley said, her expression somewhat sheepish as she tossed the wipes in the trash. "I guess I wasn't expecting it like I am when I'm at work."

"To be fair, he got you pretty good." Tyne allowed herself a chuckle as she took in the usually put-together doctor's bedraggled appearance. Lifting Owen from the changing table, Tyne snuggled his pudgy body against her chest. "I can watch him if you want to jump in the shower."

"Really?" Hadley's tense expression melted into one of relief. "Thank you."

"Sure." Tyne gave a little shrug. She didn't mind lending a hand. In the coming days, she was certain Hadley would find taking care of an infant over-whelming enough on its own that Tyne didn't have to be cruel about it.

She bounced Owen gently in her arms as she watched Hadley retreat toward the master bedroom suite, where an oversized tub and luxurious walk-in shower awaited. Not that she was jealous. Her own bedroom at this house was bigger than her entire apartment, and the bathroom down the hall from it was almost as amazing as Hadley's.

"It is a delightful house," Tyne murmured, planting a kiss on the top of Owen's head.

Owen made a gurgling sound that Tyne decided to interpret as agreement.

"Look at this beautiful peace lily Uncle Mason grew. He wanted you to have it because it's supposed to bring good luck." Tyne poked Owen's belly, eliciting that giggle that always made her heart quadruple in size.

Her eyes moved from the dark blue pad on the changing table to the white slats of the crib. They had brought all of Owen's furniture over from Ryan and Kayleigh's old apartment, which her dad had finished clearing out during the past week. There was a rocking chair, too, the stuffed giraffe Owen loved, and a fluffy rug that softened the hardwood floor. Tyne had swapped out the plain curtains that had come with the room for the ones with little moons and stars that had hung in his old nursery, but that was the extent of decorating she'd been able to do, not wanting to put holes in the wall or change the paint color for their very temporary stay.

She inhaled deeply, savoring the delicious baby scent that clung to his mostly bald head. "We don't need to live in a mansion to be happy, do we?"

Saying the words out loud eased some of the tightness in Tyne's belly that had started the moment she thought about setting up house with her nephew for real. Some, but by no means all. Hadley had been right about one thing. Tyne's current apartment would never do. Still, once the court gave her permanent custody of Owen, she would have access to the insurance money his parents had left behind. It wasn't a lot but enough to make sure he was comfortable.

Tyne sighed, her breath moving Owen's blond wisps like a breeze through tall grass. He'd have his own room, but he'd never have a barn for horses or a three-acre backyard to play in like he would if he lived with Hadley.

Am I doing the right thing? Tyne's insides twisted into knots again. *Yes,* she assured herself, recalling the disastrous diaper change. His other aunt might have more money, but she didn't have a single maternal bone in her entire body. Not like Tyne, who for all intents and purposes had been practicing her whole life for exactly this. She and Owen belonged together, and this little experiment of theirs would prove it.

As she turned to leave the room, Tyne heard the buzzing of a phone coming from the vicinity of the changing table. Tyne patted her pocket, feeling the rectangular outline of her own phone inside. Hadley must have left hers there when she went to change Owen. Tyne left it but made a mental note of its whereabouts for when Hadley started tearing up the house to find it, as she almost inevitably would. Tyne had already witnessed the woman misplace her keys at least a dozen times. It was a good thing Hadley wasn't a surgeon, or goodness knew what she might leave inside some unfortunate patient.

The phone vibrated a few more times then stopped. As Tyne stepped into the hallway, her own phone began to ring. She swung Owen onto one hip and pulled it out. A picture of Hadley's mom, Nancy, appeared on the screen. Well, now she knew who'd been calling a moment ago.

As Owen tried to reach for it, Tyne pressed the phone to her ear. "Hello?"

"Tyne, dear, do you know where Hadley is?" There was a quiver in Nancy's voice that pierced Tyne's heart with how sad it made her sound.

"She's in the shower," Tyne explained. "There was a little diaper incident. Isn't that right, Owen?"

Owen gurgled and cooed, evidently pleased with himself over the whole thing.

"Aw, how is my precious grand baby?"

"He's doing just fine," Tyne assured her, bouncing Owen on her hip as she swayed from side to side in that way that never failed to keep a little one calm and content. "We're settling in nicely, and his room is all set for his first night here with us."

"I don't suppose..." Nancy hesitated. "I wonder if maybe you could send me some pictures of your place when you get a chance? I'd love to see it, and I'd ask Hadley to, but you know how she can be with little details like that."

"Yeah." Tyne made a sound that was half laugh and half groan. Tyne had definitely noticed that Hadley had a memory like a steel trap for anything she found important, and a memory like a leaky sieve for anything she did not. "I'd be happy to send some photos, but you and Paul should plan to swing by and see it for yourselves."

"Really?" At the obvious elation in Nancy's tone, Tyne bit into her lower lip. Had her daughter not already invited the woman? It kind of sounded like she hadn't, in which case Tyne was afraid she may have made a major mistake.

"Um, you know, I've gotta run. Owen's starting to fuss," she added, even though he was busy chewing on his fist, slobber running down his arm, without a care in the world. "Let me have Hadley give you a call back when she's out of the shower, okay?"

"Thank you, dear."

After she'd ended the call and shoved the phone back into her pocket, Tyne looked at Owen and made a face. "Uh-oh, buddy. I may have gotten myself into hot water with your auntie."

So that he wouldn't end up eating his hand down to a tiny nub, Tyne carried Owen downstairs and into the kitchen in search of the container of puffy treats he loved to nibble on. Like the other rooms in the house, the kitchen was a dream, with top-of-the-line appliances and solid wood cabinets that glowed in the afternoon sun that streamed in through the windows. Tyne pulled one of the cabinet doors open and rummaged around until she found the shelf with Owen's food.

"Banana pumpkin," she read out loud to Owen as she squinted at the picture on the label that showed a small pile of cereal in the shape of lopsided ovals. She'd given him strawberry flavored ones before, but this was something new and kind of strange sounding. "Seems like a weird combo, kiddo. Do you like this one?"

She shifted him back to her hip and popped off the lid of the container, reflecting that it was possible to do just about anything one-handed if you really put your mind to it. Not quite sure where Owen's plastic dishes had ended up, Tyne shook out a pile of the treats directly onto the counter, plucked one up, and held it so her nephew could see. He responded by opening his mouth wide, like a baby bird. Tyne placed the puff between his lips, and he chomped on it happily.

"That answers it. You're a huge fan."

Tyne looked at the pile of puffs with growing curiosity. The potent smell of banana tickled her nose. Finally, she couldn't resist. Tyne picked up a puff and stuck it on her tongue.

"Huh. Not too bad." It melted away almost instantly, leaving Tyne with an odd craving for more. "You want another one? Me, too."

Spotting the high chair, Tyne set Owen down in the seat, buckled the strap, and sprinkled about a dozen of the little treats onto the tray. Owen slapped his hands jubilantly on the white plastic, sending the Os bouncing around as he chased them down and wrangled them into his mouth. Drool drenched the front of his onesie, but he looked like he was in heaven.

"We definitely found a winner." Tyne dipped her fingers into the container, plucking out several pieces and putting them into her mouth with a shrug. "They're kinda tasty. And it says they're organic, so that's pretty good, right?"

"Oh, is that how it works?"

Tyne jumped at the sound of Hadley's voice. She whirled around to find the woman leaning against the doorframe, dressed in a clean set of clothes and wearing a turban-style towel over her hair.

"You startled me."

"You mean I caught you red-handed." Hadley

arched an eyebrow as she pointed to the container of banana pumpkin puffs. "Are you stealing food from a baby?"

"Of course not. He offered me some. Didn't you, little guy?" Tyne dropped a few more puffs on the tray, and her nephew let out a delighted squeal. "See? He says yes."

"No fair," Hadley protested. "You're tampering with the witness."

"I thought you were a doctor. Since when did you become a legal expert?" Tyne regretted the words as soon as she said them. She and Hadley had negotiated a truce over the past week that included an unspoken agreement, not to mention their legal dispute. The last thing Tyne needed was to upset the delicate balance that made the prospect of living together for the next several weeks bearable and maybe even a little bit fun. She searched for a change of subject. "Did you get your phone from upstairs? You left it in Owen's room."

Hadley patted her pockets with a frown. "Oh. I forgot I set it down. I'll have to go get it."

"Actually, your mom called while you were in the shower. She called your phone first, I think, and when you didn't answer, she called me."

Hadley tilted her head. "You talked to my mom?"

"Yeah, for a few minutes." Tyne shifted uneasily from one foot to the other. "I sort of suggested she and your dad should stop by soon to see the house."

Hadley's expression clouded. "What did she say?"

"She sounded excited by the idea." Tyne could tell something was off with Hadley, and for some reason, she couldn't let it go. "You've barely spent any time with them this past week, between driving into Boston for your stuff and then getting things settled here. Your mom sounds really lonely."

Hadley closed her eyes and let out a low groan. "I know. I'm really not sure what's wrong with me, except..."

"Except?" Tyne prompted after a few seconds had passed and Hadley hadn't finished her thought.

"Between my mom's memory and my dad's diabetes..." Hadley gave a helpless shrug. "When did my parents get so old?"

Tyne tilted her head, trying for perhaps the hundredth time to figure out what made Hadley tick. "You're a doctor. You know all about those conditions."

"As a doctor, yes. As a daughter, not so much." Hadley came into the kitchen, pulled out a chair from the table, and sat down with a thump. "You know what I like best about working in the ER?"

"The adrenaline rush?" In the past few weeks, she'd hardly seen Hadley slow down, constantly itching to do something and stay busy. Tyne assumed boredom was half the reason the woman had been so eager to leave their small town years before.

"That might factor into the whole equation,"

Hadley admitted with a half-smile. "But the thing I found so appealing was the simplicity."

Tyne crossed her arms and shot Hadley a disbelieving look. "You're saying it's easy?"

"Not easy," Hadley corrected. "Simple. My patients are guaranteed to have one of three outcomes. Either I fix the problem and discharge them, they need more care and I admit them, or they can't be fixed and they die. It's very straightforward. Any way you look at it, at the end of the day, my part is done."

Tyne nodded slowly, a slight frown on her face. "What does that have to do with your parents?"

"Every time I see them and spend time with them, it's a reminder that nothing with them is simple. They are in a slow but steady decline. It could last years, and there's not much I can do for them." Hadley propped one elbow on the table and rested her head against her palm. "When I came into town before, Kayleigh used to be the buffer. I am not good at feeling helpless. I've been kind of avoiding spending time with them because without my sister, it's all too real. Geez, that must sound pretty bad."

"Not really." Tyne pulled out a chair across from Hadley and sat down, giving Owen a bonus handful of puffs to keep him occupied for a few more minutes. "It sounds honest, and I can appreciate that. I know what it's like to realize your parents aren't invincible like you once thought. I mean, my mom is in physical therapy and may still need surgery, and my dad's worried about heart attacks. When did that happen?"

"But somehow you've seemed to manage it better than I am."

"You said you like fixing things," Tyne said. "This thing with your parents is nothing you can't fix. Not their aging, of course, but how you relate to them."

Hadley leaned forward slightly. "What are you suggesting?"

"Call your mom. Invite your parents to the house." Tyne smiled encouragingly as she saw the doubt darken Hadley's eyes. "There's a grill on the deck. We can have a cookout."

"You mean you'll stay here when they come to visit?" A spark of light returned to Hadley's eyes.

"Of course, I will." Tyne's smile widened. "You never know. It might even be fun. Now, go give your mom a call before she has to hunt me down again."

After Hadley left the kitchen, Tyne continued looking at the recently vacated chair, lost in thought. Just when it seemed she had the woman figured out, she learned something new. Who would have thought the fierce, capable doctor was so vulnerable? Perhaps the only thing more surprising was that she was willing to let down her guard so Tyne could see. Hadley's honesty about her fears had touched Tyne deeply.

Owen's fist hit the high chair, snapping Tyne back to earth. His pile of snacks was gone, and he demanded her full attention. Tyne obliged, rising from the table and unbuckling him from his seat. She felt unsettled, shaken. When it came to their nephew, she and Hadley were rivals. Tyne should have been happy for this new insight into Hadley's weaknesses. Just about anybody would probably encourage her to take advantage of the situation however she could. Instead, the only thing Tyne wanted was to figure out some way to help.

CHAPTER NINE

The screen door squeaked to a close behind her as Hadley made her way onto the front porch. Tyne looked up from the rocking chair where she sat with a book in hand, wearing a sundress and sandals, enjoying the pleasantly warm spring day. "Did you get him to go down?"

Hadley smiled. "Piece of cake."

She cast a sidelong glance at the baby monitor that sat on the glass topped wicker table, hoping the sound was switched off. If Tyne had overheard what was going on upstairs a few minutes ago, she would know Hadley was stretching the truth about her nap time prowess. But after twenty minutes of begging and pleading, and finally offering him a pony if he cooperated, Owen had gone down for his morning nap. Who knew it could be so hard to get a baby to go to sleep? Seriously, other than eating and pooping, sleeping was pretty much all they did at this age. She hoped her nephew wouldn't remember the part about the pony and hold her to it later on.

"Good news." Tyne's smile stopped before it reached her eyes.

That Tyne's expression didn't match her words wasn't a surprise to Hadley. She'd had an inkling since the moment Tyne agreed to this plan to take care of Owen together that she was counting on Hadley becoming overwhelmed and giving up. Of course, Hadley had no intention of quitting. If she could make it through medical school, Hadley had no doubt she would make it through this, too.

Or die trying.

"By the way, thanks for getting up for his early feeding this morning," Tyne said, and from the crinkles next to her eyes, this time the sentiment appeared to be genuine. "I appreciated the extra time in bed."

Hadley sank into the other rocking chair, resisting the urge to groan like an old lady as her joints creaked and popped. "I was up anyway."

Actually, Hadley had never really slept. Insomnia had been a recurring problem since moving into the new house. No matter what she did, her brain refused to shut down. It didn't help that she had so little to keep her occupied other than taking care of Owen, which was an exhausting job but not in the way Hadley needed to help her sleep at night.

Tyne, on the other hand, had been sleeping so

soundly that even the ruckus of Owen's insistent fussing barely caused her to stir. Hadley knew this because Tyne had left her door open last night, and she'd taken a quick peek in passing to find the younger woman sleeping so peacefully she'd never have the heart to wake her. Hadley couldn't recall the last time she'd slept like that.

"Still, that makes three in a row," Tyne pointed out. "I promise to do it tomorrow."

"I thought you were going back to work tomorrow night. Won't you need the sleep?"

"It's something I'll have to get used to," Tyne said with a shrug. She left the *when I get custody of Owen* part unsaid, but Hadley knew that was what she was thinking.

"Speaking of work, have you had a chance to check out the art studio yet?"

"I have!" Tyne set her book down on the little table beside her and turned to Hadley with excitement radiating from her face. "It's amazing. There's so much natural light, and the view of the brook is stunning. I'm planning to bring back some supplies after class is over tomorrow night so I can start something new. I'm not sure what yet, but it would be a shame to let a space like that go to waste. My creative juices are whirring."

"I envy you." Hadley stretched her arms above her head, sending the rocking chair into a backward tilt. "I miss working. I can't believe I haven't worked a single shift in over two weeks."

"Think of it as a vacation," Tyne suggested.

"Vacation?" Hadley chuckled. "What's that?"

"Come on now," Tyne challenged. "You must have taken a vacation or two in your time."

"Honestly, no." Hadley wrinkled her nose as she tried to remember the last time she'd taken so much as a day off for fun. "That's not entirely true. I did take an extra day a few years back when I was attending a conference in Puerto Rico. I wanted to see the rainforest."

"A whole extra day, huh? You sure know how to party." Tyne let out a low whistle. "No romantic getaways?"

"Nope."

Hadley cleared her throat, making a little hacking sound that she hoped would discourage Tyne from continuing down that path. Of course, when it came to her romantic history, there wasn't much to explore. Her love life over the years was hardly like a well-marked and bustling bike trail and more of a meandering set of footprints in the woods, long since abandoned and mostly grown over with vines. Had she meant for that to happen?

"Is it typical for doctors to work so much?"

Hadley's shoulders relaxed as it became clear Tyne had taken the hint and planned to leave the topic of her past girlfriends alone. "It varies. Believe it or not, the emergency room can be pretty flexible. Our shifts are long, but it means working fewer days each week. A lot of people take advantage of the ability to arrange their schedule to have a lot of days off while still technically working full-time."

"But not you?"

"I like my work," Hadley said in a clipped tone. It was hard to tell if Tyne's question was intended to convey mild reproach, but that was certainly how Hadley interpreted it. Would this be an issue for the custody battle? Hadley was already researching full-time nannies.

"You have an important job," Tyne said quickly, sounding apologetic. "It's good that you enjoy doing it. I didn't mean it to sound otherwise."

"Sorry. It's a sore subject, I guess. I've had exactly one serious relationship in my life, back when I was a resident and didn't enjoy the luxury of flexibility in my schedule. It was... an issue." Hadley snapped her mouth shut as she realized she'd shared the one thing she'd been determined not to mention. How was it that when she was around Tyne, things she usually kept hidden seemed to come tumbling out?

"What are you going to do with all this time off?"

Hadley shrugged. "I have no idea. This house is great, but it's so quiet out here I might lose my mind. I heard a siren go by yesterday evening, and I could tell it was an ambulance. In my mind, I could picture exactly what would happen when it arrived at the hospital, the team jumping into action. My heart started to race, and I seriously considered running down the road after it."

"Here I thought *ambulance chaser* was something people said in jest." Tyne studied Hadley with obvious amusement. "You sound like an addict jonesing for a fix."

"I might be," Hadley agreed, still remembering the buzz of excitement in her veins. "I've been thinking I should pay a visit to Dr. Cassidy and see if I could pick up some shifts in the Pioneer Valley ER. Small hospitals like that are almost always understaffed."

"It's not a bad idea." Tyne said this slowly, in the way people do when they believe your idea actually is bad but are trying to be diplomatic. "But I have another suggestion for something you could try."

"What's that?"

"You could learn to relax." Tyne's blue eyes focused on Hadley's as she brushed a few strands of blonde hair from her face. "Like, do you even know how?"

Know how to what? Hadley thought, so transfixed by Tyne's eyes that for a moment she'd lost track of the conversation. She shook herself back to attention. It was bad enough the way she'd been lusting after the woman before, but now that the situation between them was so precarious, Hadley couldn't allow her mind to wander. Not even a little. Besides, the last time she'd dipped even a little toe into that water, Tyne had swatted her down instantly. There was no sense letting herself become infatuated with someone who would never feel the same way. The day of the funeral had been emotional, and Tyne had given in to it. That was all there was.

"I suppose I really don't know how," Hadley admitted, remembering what they'd been discussing at the last possible second before Tyne would have been sure to notice her awkward silence.

"It's a skill worth learning, and I think I know how to teach you." Tyne's lips curled upward, and Hadley's tummy did a flip-flop. "You're coming with me to the studio tomorrow night. I'm going to teach you how to paint."

"Me? Oh, no." Hadley waved her hands from side to side as if to say *no deal*. "I told you before I don't have an ounce of artistic talent."

"You're telling me you can wield a scalpel, but you're afraid of a paintbrush?" Tyne teased. "I don't believe it."

"I didn't say I was afraid." At that moment, Owen must have made a noise in his room because, though the sound was off, a row of lights on the monitor lit up red then went off to show he was quiet once again. Hadley pointed to it triumphantly. "Much as I'd love to join you, if you're going to be gone, I have to stay here with Owen."

"We'll have my parents watch him. Mom's back is doing a little better thanks to the physical therapy, and

Dad and Evan are perfectly capable of taking care of him for one night."

Hadley shook her head. "We can't ask them to do that. The whole reason he's here is because they needed relief. Now you're suggesting we should hand him back when he's only been here less than a week?"

"For one evening." Tyne gave a slight roll of her eyes, her tone making it clear she thought Hadley was being overly dramatic. And maybe she was. "My mom's already missing him so bad she can hardly stand it, and Owen loves getting attention from all the family. She'll jump at the chance to watch him for a few hours. You're just looking for an excuse not to paint."

Hadley let out a sigh. Tyne was right on all counts. Michelle and Keith had been crystal clear that even though Owen would be living with his aunts, they still wanted to be involved as much as possible. And Hadley hated making a total fool of herself by being spectacularly bad at something in front of a room full of strangers.

"Fine, but only if your mom and dad are up to it." Hadley crossed her fingers they would decline. Her hopes were quickly dashed if the sheepish expression on Tyne's face was any indication.

"They are. I may have kinda already asked."

Hadley's mouth fell open. "You've been planning this all along?"

"You seemed stressed," Tyne countered. "And in my

defense, it's not like it was some big revelation that you don't know how to relax. I knew I had an open seat, and I thought it would do you some good."

"I feel like I've been set up," Hadley said with a huff, but it was only pretend. Even though Tyne's scheming should have upset her, somehow the only feeling she could muster was amusement. Well, that plus something deeper down that was a little more tender. Hadley couldn't put a name to it and sensed it was probably better that she didn't.

THE STUDIO LOOKED different from the last time Hadley had been there. All the lights were on, and the air buzzed with the energy of a dozen or more students, all of whom were women ranging in age from early twenties to late fifties. With a few minutes to go before the class began, they were milling around and chatting while sipping frequently from the glasses of wine grasped in their hands.

Hadley stayed separate from the crowd, occupying a stool at the back of the room and hoping to remain invisible. While there were one or two women who looked to be around her age, she didn't think she knew any of them, and so far, no one seemed to recognize her, either.

Not that she was usually a wallflower, but Hadley was just as happy tonight to sit by herself and drink the sparkling water she'd poured into a tall, clear glass. No wine for her, not this time. She, and her libido, remembered all too well what had happened before when she'd overindulged in the vino at this place. Her terrible painting skills were already destined to make her the laughingstock of the room. She didn't need to get tipsy on top of it and make even more of a fool of herself by coming onto the teacher. Especially considering Tyne had already made it clear it had been a terrible mistake the last time that had happened.

Probably because Tyne remembered she was an old lady.

"Class starts in five minutes," Tyne called out from the raised platform in the front of the room. "Please find your seat, and make sure you have water, two brushes, some paper towels, and a palette of paint next to your canvas."

Hadley watched as Tyne slipped a hands-free device over her head, adjusting it before checking the sound. She projected the cool confidence of a professional, proving to Hadley what a sophisticated operation this was. The studio wasn't just some artist's hobby but a legitimate business, and one Tyne had built all by herself at not quite thirty years of age. It was impressive as hell and surely every bit as challenging in its own way as medical school had been for Hadley.

Right before they'd left the house, Tyne had painted a fresh streak of hot pink in her platinum hair. It should've made her look less mature, but it seemed to have the opposite effect. With the slender microphone at her mouth, she looked like a rock star getting ready for a sold-out concert, and the way the room responded to her instructions with giddy enthusiasm added to the impression. Even Hadley's body seemed to thrum with anticipation. Did that make her a groupie?

As everyone headed for their places, a woman in her late twenties, or maybe early thirties, settled onto the stool next to Hadley. She turned and stuck out a hand. "Robin Fowler. First time here?"

"Hadley Moore." Hadley shook the woman's hand. "And, yes. Is it that obvious?"

Hadley caught the flicker of recognition on Robin's face as she realized who Hadley was. "You're Kayleigh's sister, aren't you? I was a couple years ahead of her in school, but I sat next to her several times when she came here for the paint and sips. She was such a lovely person, and I'm so very sorry for your loss."

"Thanks," Hadley mumbled, longing for the anonymity that came with city living. Even though she didn't know a soul in the room, they would all know her, just like at the memorial service. As much as she appreciated knowing how many lives her sister had touched, each mention of Kayleigh tore a fresh hole in Hadley's heart no matter how many invisible stitches she'd sewn to get through each day for Owen's and her parents' sakes.

145

"As for this being your first class, don't be nervous. I didn't know a thing about art when I started, but I'm totally hooked. Tyne's a brilliant teacher. You're in expert hands."

An unexpected pang of jealousy made Hadley's eyes twitch. Maybe she was imagining it, but there'd been something about Robin's expression when she talked about Tyne that made Hadley think learning how to paint wasn't the woman's primary motivation for taking this class. As for any mention of Tyne's hands, that topic was strictly off-limits tonight. Hadley remembered all too well how good Tyne's hands were, how the touch of them on her bare skin made everything in her upside-down world feel suddenly right again. Just knowing Tyne's apartment was upstairs, and remembering kissing her there, was enough to drive Hadley to distraction.

"Welcome, everybody. Let's get started." Tyne's voice sounded through the speakers, filling the room and bringing the chatter amongst the students to a halt.

A picture flashed onto the wall behind Tyne's head. The canvas had been painted to look like wooden slats with the words *Just Be You* written across in swirly handwriting, but instead of the word *be*, there was a plump bumble bee sitting in the middle of a yellow sunflower. Tyne had positioned a blank white canvas on the easel beside her, which Hadley assumed she would use to demonstrate each step to the class.

"You should have a big brush and a little brush," Tyne explained. She held up a brush with wide bristles. "We're going to start with this one. I like to call her Big Bertha. Find that one, swish it around in your water cup, and blot it off on your paper towel."

Hadley did as Tyne instructed. So far, so good. If only all the steps were this easy.

Tyne explained how to mix the paint to get the colors they needed for the background and then demonstrated making bold brush strokes to cover the canvas. Hadley followed along but was only halfway through the first step when Tyne announced it was time to move on.

"Oh, sh—shooot," Hadley muttered, editing her word choice from one of the more colorful exclamations that had been her first instinct. Now that she had Owen to think about, Hadley was making an effort to watch her language.

"What's the matter?" Robin leaned in to examine Hadley's canvas. "You're doing okay. Just keep painting while she does the next step, and I can help you with it after you catch up."

Hadley did as Robin suggested, her body growing more tense with each brush stroke. This was going even worse than she'd expected. Even after her neighbor showed her how to paint the petals of the sunflower three times, Hadley might as well have been trying to master Chinese calligraphy. Her painting was a disaster, and the more she worked on it, the worse it became.

"I'll be coming around to look at your progress," Tyne announced toward the end of the class, "so if you need any help, just flag me down. When we're all done, we'll take a group photo of everyone holding their masterpieces so I can post it on the studio website."

While the rest of the class laughed nervously, Hadley stifled a groan. As Tyne started walking down between the tables, stopping to critique or offer advice, Hadley's embarrassment intensified to the point her head wanted to burst.

Robin gave Hadley a nudge with her elbow. "I need to get a refill on my paints, but make sure Tyne knows you need help if she comes by."

"Uh, yeah, I will," Hadley said, while inside her head, she screamed, *Uh, no I won't*. The thought of Tyne finding out how bad she really was made her cheeks kick to three-alarm fire level.

As soon as Robin got up, Hadley tilted her canvas to make it harder for anyone to see, slumping lower in her seat the closer Tyne came to her row.

Tyne grinned eagerly as she approached Hadley's table. "How's it going?"

"Great," Hadley lied, forcing her voice to sound bubbly with the right amount of confidence. "Nearly done."

"Do you need any pointers or have any questions

you want to ask?" As Tyne started to come around for a closer look at the painting, Hadley swiveled it even more, blocking her view.

"Nope." Even as she said it, Hadley was calculating the best way to get her canvas from the table to the trash when Tyne had her back turned.

"Okay." Tyne looked quizzically from Hadley to the painting she was clearly trying to hide but didn't press the issue as she moved on to the next student.

There was no denying it. Hadley's painting was terrible. Instead of resembling wood grain on boards, her background looked like a pig had wallowed in mud. Her sunflower might have been growing next to a leaky nuclear reactor, as that was the best explanation for its mutant appearance. And what was a jolly bumble bee on Tyne's example glared menacingly from Hadley's canvas, an angry insect with murderous intent. As for the whimsical lettering, well, there was a reason doctors seldom received praise for their handwriting.

"It's time to wrap up," Tyne said, once again standing at the front of the room. "Everyone, pick up your canvases, and let's get that group picture."

Robin, whose efforts had produced something nearly indistinguishable from Tyne's, was quick to hop up. Hadley's eyes narrowed as the woman brought her canvas to Tyne, who examined it with an approving expression. Then Tyne put her hand on Robin's arm, and Hadley's temperature spiked. That decided it.

Hadley did not like Robin. Not one bit. As all the other students made their way to the front, Hadley grabbed her monstrosity off the easel and slipped away in search of the trash can at the back.

Damn it. The canvas was too big to fit in the skinny bin.

Eyes darting to the front, Hadley did the next best thing to throwing it away and stowed the painting in the narrow space between the edge of the cabinets and the wall. Like a lost letter she'd recently read about that had slipped into a crevice at the post office in the 1920s, Hadley felt confident no one would find the awful thing for at least another hundred years. To further escape Tyne's detection, Hadley ducked into the bathroom, counting on her absence going unnoticed in the mayhem of much better artists jostling for position in the class photo.

After a few minutes, the noise from the studio died down, and Hadley cautiously reemerged from her hiding place with as innocent an expression as she could muster. The first thing she saw was Tyne, who was standing in front of the bathroom door, holding Hadley's discarded canvas and wearing a *gotcha* expression.

"Really?" Tyne gave the canvas a wiggle.

Hadley fought the urge to step back into the bathroom and shut the door. There was no reason to act even more childish than she already had. "I told you I'm no good at art."

"Which is why you were taking the class, and why I made sure you were sitting next to one of the most experienced students, so she could help you out."

At the mention of Robin, Hadley crossed her arms. "We didn't really hit it off."

"You didn't get along with Robin?" Tyne's eyebrows shot up. "She and her boyfriend, Dave, are like the nicest two people on earth."

Boyfriend? Perhaps Hadley had judged the woman too quickly.

"The fact remains I know nothing about painting, as you can clearly see." Hadley gestured at the canvas in Tyne's hands.

"You don't know anything about babies either, but you've been learning." Tyne flashed a mischievous grin. "Or do I need to worry you're going to hide Owen behind a cabinet the next time you have trouble with a diaper change?"

Even as her face scrunched up in embarrassment, Hadley couldn't help laughing at her own ridiculousness. "I've always been competitive, and it's possible when there's something I'm not good at, I don't always handle it very well."

"You think?" Tyne held Hadley's canvas at arm's length. "You know, it's really not as bad as you think. Do you want me to show you how to fix it, or will that damage your pride?"

"Yes, it will, but"—Hadley put her hand over her

mouth to muffle her response, mortified to be asking —"I would still like your help fixing it."

Tyne carried the canvas to the big easel in the front of the room while Hadley followed. Once it was in place, Tyne handed Hadley a paint palette and a brush.

"Let's start with the background. Your woodgrain doesn't show up because you need to use a lighter shade of brown. See that creamy beige?" She pointed to one color on the palette. "Put some of that on the brush and make those swirls like I taught in class."

Hadley did as instructed, her hand trembling under the pressure of having Tyne standing behind her to watch every move. "Uh, I'm not sure I remember how to do it."

Tyne stepped closer, resting her left hand on Hadley's back as she reached from behind to guide Hadley's right arm with her own. Hadley shivered as soft breasts pressed against her back. It took every ounce of concentration she possessed not to drop the brush onto the floor as Tyne's fingers closed around her hand, moving it, and the brush, in gentle circles.

"Wow." Hadley swallowed. Between the feeling of amazement that her painting no longer looked terrible and the sudden rush of adrenaline from Tyne's touch, she was a little light-headed. "It looks more like it's supposed to already."

Tyne's face was only inches from Hadley's head, so that when she laughed softly, it tickled Hadley's ear. "You'll do better if you're not so tense. This is supposed to relax you, but your shoulders are stiff as bricks."

Sure, Hadley thought, *you try relaxing with a beautiful woman's breasts against your back.* She doubled her efforts to focus and continued making the swirls Tyne had shown her, but this quickly became impossible as Tyne's thumbs dug into the tender shoulder muscles. It felt so good it nearly reduced Hadley to a heap on the floor.

"There. That's a little better," Tyne said, kneading Hadley's shoulders and apparently oblivious to the effects she was causing beyond simply helping the muscles relax.

Almost without realizing it, Hadley leaned into the massage. The paint brush in her hand drifted downward as her arms went limp by her sides. She was in heaven and hell simultaneously, caught up in the most rapturous physical sensations while being aware enough to know she couldn't give into them. Was Tyne trying to kill her? It might not be such a bad way to go.

Hadley closed her eyes. A tiny moan escaped her. Moments later, hot breath blew across the nape of her neck, followed by the brush of moist lips. Her eyes flew open, but the kiss did not evaporate. This wasn't a dream. Tyne's lips were still against her skin, trailing along the contours of her neck. What was going on?

Completely shocked, Hadley pulled away.

CHAPTER TEN

"Tyne, what are you doing?" Hadley sounded stern.

Tyne's insides grew cold. "Getting the wrong idea, apparently."

Hadley's face displayed such intense yet inscrutable emotion that it was impossible to understand what was going on with her. Talk about mixed signals. Their connection had seemed so strong Tyne had been certain they were both on the same page, but she was mistaken.

"What are you talking about?" Hadley's mouth settled into a deep frown. "You were the one who said this was a bad idea."

"I did not."

It was starting to feel like they'd experienced two entirely different realities. Try as she might, Tyne couldn't remember a single thing she'd said that

Hadley could've construed in that way, yet she seemed adamant.

"You certainly did. I remember it clearly." The sting of rejection seemed heavy in her tone, which Tyne couldn't understand. Hadley was the one who had pulled away, not Tyne.

"When?" Tyne ran through their conversation and couldn't pinpoint where anything remotely like *this is a bad idea* was said or even hinted at by either of them.

"That night in your apartment, when you realized how repulsive it was to be making out with a woman who's much too old for you just because you felt sorry for her. You said it was wrong."

Tyne took a step back to see Hadley's face more clearly. "Is *that* what you think happened that night?"

"You're denying you said that?" Hadley threaded her arms protectively over her chest.

Tyne searched her whirling brain for the right way to answer, feeling like a city slicker on a dude ranch trying to approach a horse who was known to buck off even the most experienced rider. "I don't deny saying what I was doing was wrong, but it had nothing to do with age or feeling sorry for anyone."

Hadley's arms moved from her chest to her hips as she fixed Tyne with an *I don't believe you* stare. "Then what *did* it have to do with?"

Tyne kept her hands close to her sides to prevent herself from throwing them in the air in exasperation. "For one thing, I knew it was unforgivable of me to take advantage of the situation when you'd obviously had too much to drink."

Hadley did not appear swayed by Tyne's logic. "We'd both had a lot to drink."

"Yeah, but I knew you wouldn't have been into me if you were sober," Tyne blurted out, cringing at the raw truth. It hurt, but she couldn't deny it.

"Why would you think that?" It was Hadley's turn to sound confused and exasperated.

"Oh, come on. Look at you." Tyne gestured with one hand, encompassing the entirety of Hadley's body as if presenting it to a jury as exhibit A. "You're so perfectly put together. Your hair is always smooth and shiny. Even for a painting class, you put on designer jeans and a nice top. And underneath it, I'll bet you have on really expensive underwear. That *matches*. Not red, though. That would be too common. It's probably a sophisticated color like plum, with a tasteful hint of lace around the edge and maybe a floral pattern woven into it in that tone on tone thing they sometimes do."

The corner of Hadley's mouth twitched. "You've put a lot of thought into this."

Tyne lifted her chin as if daring Hadley to say whatever she was going to say. Not that she had any clue what it would be. The woman was a fucking enigma. "Into what?"

"Into what underwear I'm wearing." She was capable of stopping herself from laughing out loud, but mirth danced in Hadley's eyes and popped Tyne's frustration bubble in a way that left her teetering on the verge of collapsing into a giggling heap.

"Yeah, kinda." Talk about showing all her cards. Then again, hiding them hadn't exactly been working for her, so she had little to lose. "Can you blame me? You're like the sexiest human in at least a hundred miles, and we live in the same house. It's a distraction."

"You want to talk distraction? Try being a chronically single woman who is rapidly approaching middle age and suspecting her best days are behind her, and then start sharing a house with a young, vibrant, gorgeous artist and discovering that even the scent of her apricot shampoo gets your libido revving."

"Peach." Out of everything Hadley had said, there were other things Tyne might have addressed, but her choice of shampoo variety seemed safest.

"Peach." Hadley tilted her head a few inches to one side. "Are you sure? I could've sworn it was apricot."

"No, it's peach. It's a shampoo bar I get from the farmer's market. Very environmentally friendly."

"Fascinating." Hadley paused, her lips curled in a half smile like she couldn't quite believe she was standing here discussing underwear and shampoo. "I really thought you slammed on the brakes the other night because of my age."

Tyne swallowed, her pulse racing. She'd half expected Hadley to leave that topic where they'd dropped it. Since she hadn't, Tyne needed to make the most of the situation. "What does this mean for tonight, now that you know you were so very wrong?"

"I don't know."

Well, it wasn't a flat-out refusal, anyway. "Knowing isn't everything. What do you *feel*?"

"Conflicted." Hadley wrung her hands together and began counting off the reasons with her fingers, one by one. "First, we're in the middle of fighting over Owen's custody, so that could get ugly. Plus, there's the whole family angle. I mean, what would any of them think if they found out? Also, with the trauma we've experienced from our losses, neither one of us is emotionally stable right now."

"All good points."

Yet something in the woman's eyes was nearly begging Tyne to refute each one. Closing the distance between them, Tyne wrapped her hand around the three fingers Hadley held up. They could stand here debating every obstacle all night, or Tyne could try taking a different tack. Drawing the hand she was holding to her mouth, Tyne pressed her lips against the inside of Hadley's wrist. Beneath the smooth skin, Hadley's pulse fluttered like the wings of a hummingbird, delicate but also exuding strength.

"And now?" Looking into her eyes and holding her gaze, Tyne sensed the reservations falling away. But not quite enough. There was only one argument left to make, if she dared.

Go big or go home.

Tyne edged closer still. Hadley's breath rippled against Tyne's cheek with the warmth of a light summer breeze. Hadley's chest expanded as she inhaled, first shakily and then with a sharp intake of air the instant Tyne captured Hadley's lips with her own. The kiss was light and sweet but held for long enough that it hinted at how much more there could be, if Hadley wanted it to happen.

"How do you feel now?" Tyne asked, her words a breathy whisper against Hadley's neck, laced with anticipation.

"Like I never have before," came the strangled reply.

Tyne moved back only as much as she needed to see Hadley's face, which instead of being closed off and neutral as was so often the case with her, appeared awhirl with too many emotions for Tyne to decipher.

Hadley closed her eyes. "If there were rules for this kind of thing, we'd be breaking every single one."

"But there isn't. And even if there were, rules are meant to be broken."

"In my line of work, breaking rules gets people killed." Even so, Hadley inched closer to Tyne, like maybe even she wasn't swayed by her own arguments anymore.

"This isn't work."

"Really?" Hadley let out a faint laugh. "You seem to be working awfully hard to get what you want right now."

"I suppose I am." Tyne rested a hand on each of Hadley's shoulders, and when there was no protest, she slid them around to Hadley's back, pressing their bodies together. "I want to be close to you. And as much as you're looking for every reason not to, from the intensity of your stare, I have no doubt you want the same. Or, am I wrong?"

They were nearly nose to nose. Hadley swallowed. "You're not wrong."

"This has been building so much these past weeks I don't think it's something that will go away simply by saying we shouldn't. And one thing we both know too well is life can be so very short. Sometimes you have to take a little pleasure where you can find it."

"What do you suggest?"

"My apartment *happens* to be right upstairs." Tyne's mouth formed a wicked grin. "And you know what they say. What happens there, stays there."

"You're thinking of Las Vegas."

"Either way, I'm wagering on getting lucky."

Hadley snorted a laugh, leaning backward, but not so much that she slipped from Tyne's embrace. "What would this be? A one-time thing?"

"Do you really need a firm answer to that, or can we leave it open to future negotiation?"

"That's a possibility." Hadley's shoulders relaxed, a sure sign that she'd decided in the affirmative and was becoming increasingly comfortable with her decision. "So, how does this work? Do we go upstairs and like, ya know?" Hadley made some sort of cryptic hand gesture Tyne could only assume was intended to mime having sex. Either that or a complicated gymnastics maneuver.

"What is that supposed to be?" Tyne burst out laughing. "And why are you looking at me like I'm supposed to be an expert on how this plays out?"

"You're a millennial. Didn't your generation basically invent hookup culture?"

"Pretty sure that's been around since at least the seventies."

"Just like me," Hadley quipped.

Unable to restrain herself any longer, Tyne leaned in for a kiss. Hadley's arms closed around her, welcoming her with eagerness in a tight embrace. The kiss soon deepened. Tyne was convinced Hadley was the instigator, not that she was going to complain.

Because there were kisses, and then there was this.

Hot, sensuous, and filled with need.

Before Tyne could act on a similar impulse, Hadley wound her fingers through Tyne's short locks, pulling both of them even more into the moment. All of Tyne's body heat traveled to her core, which came alive with possibility.

Without having to speak, they moved as one toward the stairs, never breaking contact. Not until they reached the first step did Tyne loosen her grasp so she could take Hadley by the hand and lead the way. Fortunately, it was a private staircase, because once they reached the top,

Tyne couldn't wait another second to resume her frenzied exploration of Hadley's mouth with her tongue.

It was impossible to hold back. Even if Hadley hadn't noticed her existence until recently, Tyne's vivid imagination might have played out scenarios like this one a few times before.

Or maybe more than a few times.

Way more.

And now it was happening for real.

Somehow Tyne managed to find the doorknob, and she thanked every lucky star in the galaxy that she'd left her door unlocked when she'd run upstairs for a few things before class. If she'd had to find her keys, not to mention remember how keys are supposed to work, she might have died. As it was, a quick turn of the knob sent the door flying open and the two of them stumbling inside.

While her teeth nibbled Hadley's ear, Tyne's fingers worked with record speed to unfasten the buttons of her shirt. She'd been truthful earlier about how nice it was, and as much as part of her wanted to rip the garment from Hadley's chest and send buttons flying across the room, she doubted that would go over very well. Instead, when she'd undone the last one, she eased it from Hadley's shoulders, carefully removing a sleeve from one arm and then from the other, but she did give herself the satisfaction of tossing it aside without a single thought to where it landed.

An excited shudder worked through Tyne as she took in the elegantly simple bra with its tasteful hint of lace. The color was more orchid than plum, but otherwise, her prediction was spot-on. Tyne gave the waistband of Hadley's jeans a playful downward tug, revealing a matching strip of orchid beneath. Laughing, she pulled Hadley close to her chest.

"I knew it," she whispered in Hadley's ear. "I knew they would match."

Since she was already almost there, Tyne's mouth sought the crook of Hadley's neck, tracing a path from there to the earlobe with the tip of her tongue, which she used to circle the outline of the ear, stopping to give the plump lobe a little nip before plunging her tongue inside. Hadley moaned with abandon, a sensuous sound that unleashed a flood of wetness between Tyne's legs.

As Tyne struggled to retain enough control of her limbs to remain upright, Hadley rallied, taking advantage of the moment to strip off Tyne's shirt and flinging it aside with absolutely no caution whatsoever.

"Pink polka dots?" Hadley flashed a wolfish smile as she slipped both bra straps from Tyne's shoulders simultaneously. "Adorable."

But not so adorable that it didn't find itself a moment later sailing across the room in search of its cast-off companions. "That was quick." Tyne glanced from Hadley's still bra-clad breasts to her own bare ones. "You've managed to pull ahead of me."

"Is this a race?" Hadley cupped Tyne's breasts, holding their weight in her palms then easing them back into place as she allowed her hands to return to her sides. "I really hope it isn't. I don't like to rush."

Hadley touched her tongue to her lower lip in a way that seemed to telegraph every single thought that was running through her head. Much to Tyne's delight, all of them were naughty. While the good doctor had mastered the art of keeping her feelings bottled up most of the time, the bedroom seemed an exception to her rule. Tyne's body zinged in anticipation, even as she reminded herself to slow down.

It really wasn't a race, and she would make sure Hadley knew it.

With that in mind, her fingers traveled up and down Hadley's sides so excruciatingly slowly she was sure Hadley already regretted her comment. Inch by tantalizing inch, both hands worked their way around to the hooks on the back of the orchid bra. Tyne slid the first bra strap off at a glacial pace, her lips trailing right behind to pepper the path with kisses. As she moved to repeat the process on the other side, Hadley rolled her eyes and made short work of the thing before Tyne could torture her some more.

"No fair. You're interfering with my method."

"And you're trying to make a point at the expense of my sanity."

Without a word to either confirm or deny the accusation, Tyne lunged forward, sucking Hadley's pink nipple into her mouth. She worked her tongue against it, gently at first, increasing the pressure as it hardened, and only boosting it up to the maximum level after Hadley dug her fingers into Tyne's shoulders to urge her on.

"How's your sanity now?" Tyne asked sweetly when her mouth was once again free for talking.

"Balancing on the brink," Hadley admitted, swiveling her torso as if to remind Tyne she had two breasts, not just the one.

Ignoring the hint for the time being, Tyne's fingers worked on undoing Hadley's jeans. She lowered the denim at a leisurely pace, bending at her knees like a ballerina performing a slow, deep plié. Tyne brushed her cheek along the newly freed skin, so creamy and soft, moving from high up on Hadley's thigh all the way down to right below her knees.

Straightening up, Tyne plucked at the orchid panties, the only item left of Hadley's evening ensemble. "I don't want you to think I lack appreciation for the effort you took in selecting these, but since they lost their matching top some time ago, I really don't think you need them anymore."

"You might be right." Before Tyne could reach for them, Hadley hooked her own fingers into the slim elastic at the waist and guided them downward, every bit as slowly as Tyne had done before. "I hope you don't mind if I take my sweet time with this, too."

"Touché," Tyne squeaked, unable to tear her eyes away as she gained a new appreciation for exactly what torment she'd been putting Hadley through.

Finally, the task was complete, and Tyne took a moment to appreciate the view, her eyes drinking in the result of her handiwork.

Then she took another moment.

And another.

"What?" Doubt flickered in Hadley's eyes, as if she was afraid Tyne didn't like what she saw.

Nothing could be further from the truth.

"You're stunning. Even more so than I imagined."

Heat replaced insecurity as Hadley arched a brow. "Did you imagine it a lot?"

Oops. Busted.

"I think it's in my best interest not to answer that." Tyne took a step forward, nudging her toward the futon, which was still folded out into a bed from the last time they'd slept here. How convenient, not to mention a great argument for skipping housework if there ever was one. Tyne almost wished she could travel back in time to tell her then-self the encouraging news of their good fortune to come. "Shall we?"

Hadley didn't budge, and Tyne feared she may have been hasty in declaring that good fortune after all.

"What is it?" she asked, urging herself to sound calm and not give in to the sudden panic Hadley's hesitation sparked. In the back of her mind, the phrase *please don't change your mind* was playing on a loop.

"You're still dressed," Hadley pointed to Tyne's jeans.

Oh, thank God.

"That can be fixed." At record speed, Tyne stripped off her remaining clothes. She was no longer in the mood for teasing. "Better?"

"Much." They explored each other's skin with eager hands. Then Hadley pulled free and lowered herself onto the bed, reclining onto her elbows. "You going to join me?"

Realizing she'd frozen in place like a tin man in the rain, Tyne scrambled to get onto the bed with some measure of grace. Or at least without being so clumsy they both ended up on the floor. Once Hadley sat down, she beckoned Tyne to come closer still. Tyne happily did as she was told, lowering until they were both fully prone. Relishing the view from on top, Tyne straddled one of Hadley's thighs, supporting her weight with hands planted beside Hadley's shoulders.

Amazing.

That a take-charge woman like Hadley would allow herself to be dominated in bed was a surprising development, and one Tyne wouldn't let go to waste. "I like this side of you."

Without waiting for a reply, Tyne dove for Hadley's lips. They devoured each other, their mouths fused, tongues tangled in an epic battle that neither would concede.

With a rocking motion, Tyne glided back and forth across Hadley, who bucked and wrapped her legs around Tyne's hips. Each thrust pressed Tyne deeper into the V between Hadley's legs, the evidence of her arousal leaving a trail of wetness on Tyne's thigh.

Hadley shuddered, letting out a primal moan.

She was close to the edge. Too close.

Tyne slowed. She pulled back and straightened until she was on her knees and looking down at Hadley's flushed face and lust-darkened eyes. A thrill surged through her at the power she held in that moment, to be in control of where they were going and how long it would take to arrive.

She locked eyes with Hadley, and a slow smile spread across Tyne's lips. Triumph shone in Hadley's eyes, making it obvious to Tyne that she'd guessed correctly. Slowing down was what Hadley wanted, too.

With only the tips of her fingers, Tyne traced lazy spirals around Hadley's breasts. She would reach the pink buds in the center, eventually. When she felt like it. As the one in charge of their adventure, Tyne was taking the scenic route.

Scooting forward on her knees and straddling Hadley's hips, Tyne dipped her head until she could place a light kiss on a single dark freckle in the middle of Hadley's snow-white chest. She gathered plump breasts with her palms, pushing them together so she could move her mouth from one nipple to the other with ease. Then she turned her exclusive attention to the mound on her left, sucking it into her mouth and teasing the rock-hard nipple with her teeth.

Hadley writhed.

Tyne lost herself in her task, oblivious to everything surrounding her. She plotted the path she would take: first the other nipple then down Hadley's belly. Tyne's mouth watered as she imagined arriving at her destination at last. The faint, musky whiff of intimate scent. The tickle of downy hair against her nose.

Tyne imagined the taste of Hadley's sweet juices against her tongue as she took the first lick.

And then she gasped.

The sudden presence of a hand between her legs, of fingers spreading her folds and stroking the sensitive flesh hidden therein took Tyne completely by surprise. Her head bobbed up, her mouth open and jaw slack. Just as her eyes met Hadley's, the thrust of a finger inside her turned whatever words Tyne might have planned to say into an incoherent cry. Her thighs stiffened as her insides quivered.

A second finger joined the first, a thumb strumming her clit with a relentless rhythm.

Once. Twice. Three times.

Only moments before, Tyne's single focus had been bringing Hadley to climax, but now the tables were turned.

And how.

Tyne clenched around Hadley's fingers as they stroked her deep inside. Panting. Grinding.

Her body shook. Her heels pressed into Hadley's legs, as if anchoring her so she wouldn't accidentally fly into orbit.

How was she already this close? It would take next to nothing to send her over the edge completely.

Hadley's mouth claimed her breast, ravishing it with an exquisite skill that was too much to bear. Wave after wave of unrelenting ecstasy wracked Tyne's body until finally she collapsed against Hadley's chest, a spent and useless heap of quaking flesh.

"That wasn't fair," Tyne said sometime later when she found the energy to speak. "You tricked me. I thought I was calling the shots."

"I'm sure you did." There was humor in Hadley's tone as she stroked her fingers through Tyne's hair. "I couldn't have gotten as far as I have in life without learning to get what I want when other people think they're in control. As a woman working in a man's world, it's not a trick. It's how I survive."

"Sounds like a useful skill."

"It certainly is, but don't let my secret out. I always play to win."

CHAPTER ELEVEN

Heavy rain drenched the pavement, the double yellow lines barely visible. Headlights swerved. The crunch of metal and shattering glass. Blinding flashes of red light, followed by the flurry of action as the paramedics brought a gurney out of the back.

Kayleigh.

"I can save her," Hadley tried to scream, but no sound came out of her mouth.

She tried to run after them through the emergency room doors, but her feet were as heavy as lead. Nothing would move. When she finally managed a step, the white-tiled hallway stretched like taffy. The distance between her and her sister grew longer, an unending tunnel growing darker by the second. Everyone disappeared.

She was alone.

She had failed.

"Hadley," a sweet voice called her name. It sounded familiar, but Hadley's foggy brain couldn't make out who it was. "Hadley? You're okay. Wake up."

"Wh-what?" Hadley struggled against the sheets that wrapped around her naked body like an Amazonian snake.

The voice spoke again. "You were kicking and flailing. I think you were having a bad dream."

Hadley forced her crusted eyelids to open. It took her a second to place where she was and why she wasn't wearing any clothes.

Tyne.

All at once, images of the previous night flooded Hadley's memory. Her hands roaming across silken skin. The crush of Tyne's velvet mouth against hers. That look approaching pure devotion as Tyne had eased her body between Hadley's legs.

That look was a problem.

That look said there was more to Tyne than the superficial encounter she'd claimed it would be. But more troubling had been the jolt of longing Hadley had experienced at the same moment, that no matter how much she denied it, the connection they shared was deeper than anything she'd experienced before.

This was everything it wasn't supposed to be, and someone was going to get hurt.

"It was nothing," Hadley lied. Her eyes darted around in search of a sheet or blanket to cover herself with. She felt cold, exposed. "Actually, it was silly. You know that dream where you're back in school and you walk into a class you didn't know you were taking to find out it's the final exam?"

Yeah. There was no way Hadley was going to confess what had really been going on. Her fingers closed around the edge of the blanket she'd finally latched on to, and she tugged it up to her chin.

"Oh, I've had that dream." Tyne stretched her arms overhead, yawning. "What time is it?"

Hadley squinted at the closest clock. "A little after eight. I never sleep this late."

"That's what happens when you stay up half the night." Tyne jostled Hadley's side with an elbow.

This was a mistake. A huge mistake.

Hadley bolted upright. "We should get going."

"I'm barely awake."

"Aren't your parents dropping off Owen at nine?"

"That's an hour from now."

It was obvious Tyne considered this to be plenty of time. And it was. But this wasn't about Owen. It was about getting out of this studio apartment—the scene of the crime—which seemed to shrink around Hadley by the minute. With everything going on, starting a relationship couldn't be the right decision. Could it? Hadley's brain and heart were on different trajectories, and Hadley leaned on her brain to determine the right path forward.

"Then I think it wise we should actually be there."

Her tone was no nonsense, her legs already swinging out from beneath the sheet.

"Okay, fine. I wouldn't want you to have to give back your Miss Punctuality trophy." While Tyne didn't sound thrilled about getting up, she seemed to have bought Hadley's reason, flimsy as it was.

Hadley contemplated wrapping herself in the covers while she went in search of her discarded clothing. But was that too ridiculous? It wasn't like Tyne hadn't seen it all, and more. But Hadley also didn't want to encourage anything. Paralyzed with indecision, she remained perched on the edge of the futon until a soft bit of terry cloth plopped into her lap.

"Here, you can wear this." The terry cloth turned out to be a robe, which meant on top of everything else, Tyne could apparently read Hadley's mind.

Hopefully, not all of it.

Much to Hadley's relief, Tyne was already donning something similar. The thought of watching Tyne strut around naked for the next fifteen minutes was enough to drive Hadley to the brink of insanity, because now it wasn't just her heart betraying her steadfastness but every part of her aside from her brain. Truth be told, even that part was wavering with thoughts like, "Why can't it work?"

Tyne grinned as Hadley tied the belt at her waist. "It's not as fancy as your orchid lingerie, but it's the best I could find on short notice."

Hadley nodded dumbly, all the while cursing herself for her choice of underwear. Oh, Tyne had been right on the money. That bra and matching panties she'd chosen to wear last night—to a casual paint and sip, mind you —was one of her best sets. Why had she worn it?

Because you wanted this to happen.

Hadley spotted the bra on one side of the room and the underwear on the other. Jeans. A top. All were accounted for. She scooped them up and got dressed with the speed of a firefighter. As she closed the last button on her shirt, the one all the way at her throat that made her feel like she would choke but assured there would be no accidental flashing of cleavage, Hadley noted Tyne had only gotten as far as gathering up clothes from the floor.

"Aren't you ready yet?" Hadley demanded in a half growl then immediately apologized for her unwarranted tone.

What was wrong with her? Nothing in Hadley's mind was making sense. All she knew was she needed space to think. At least back at the house she had her own bedroom. She could hide in there until she'd figured things out. Last night was a big mistake. One she couldn't repeat again. Not ever.

What had Hadley been thinking? She was a doctor, not a slave to her impulses. Put it aside, box it up, flip the switch. How many times had she taught that to her residents? It was to the point she sounded like a street corner preacher yelling for everyone to repent because the end was near.

Stupid. Stupid. Stupid.

"Okay, I'm ready." Tyne, gorgeously rumpled in yesterday's clothes, her hair mussed, was in a cheery mood. The woman looked like she was walking on clouds while sunshine and rainbows beamed from her head.

Hadley's phone buzzed.

It was a text from a lawyer in Boston, the one Marcy had recommended. She would be passing through town later that morning on her way to the Berkshires and wanted to meet for coffee to discuss the case.

Hadley's chest constricted. She could barely breathe.

As if she needed another reminder that the previous night had been a terrible mistake.

"Is everything all right?" Tyne's million-watt expression had dimmed, and Hadley feared she was catching on that the two of them were no longer on the same page.

"Yeah, fine." Hadley forced her lips into something approximating a smile. "Actually, I got a text from Dr. Cassidy at Pioneer Valley hospital."

Which was technically true. Dr. Cassidy had sent a text. Yesterday.

"Is that who that was?" Tyne gestured toward

Hadley's phone. "Does she want you to come in for an interview or something?"

"She does. I'm thinking I should go over there later this morning. If you don't mind watching Owen, that is."

"Not at all. I'm sure Owen doesn't want Aunt Hadley to get so restless she literally starts chasing after ambulances." Tyne flashed a sly smile. "Although if you decide to give painting another try, I might be persuaded to arrange some private lessons."

There came that jolt again.

Damn it.

What use was it to train your mind to stuff everything inside and seal the lid when your body was intent on betraying you? All it took was a smile, a joke, an arch of the eyebrow, to rip open the box and send the contents scattering all over the place. Keeping herself under control with Tyne was going to be significantly harder than Hadley had thought. Maybe harder than anything she'd ever done before.

WITH EACH LUNGFUL of hospital air, Hadley's anxiety dissipated, floating away from her like dandelion seeds on the wind. No doubt most people would think she was crazy for feeling that way, but there was no place in the world where Hadley felt more at home. She hadn't realized how deeply she'd missed it until she'd taken the first step through the doors at Pioneer Valley Hospital.

Hadley checked the time. She'd told Dr. Cassidy she would drop by at ten o'clock, which gave her over an hour before Brandy Swanson of Swanson, Howe, and Mathis, LLC, the heavy hitting Boston law firm in custody cases, expected to meet with her in the hospital cafeteria. The location was an unorthodox choice and certain to be a far cry from whatever swanky coffee places the lawyer frequented, but it suited Hadley's needs just fine. No one who knew her was likely to wander by and start asking questions.

Dr. Cassidy's office door was open, so Hadley tapped on the doorframe to announce her arrival. When she looked up, the doctor broke into a smile. "Dr. Moore, thank you so much for coming in. I have to admit even after you texted, I wasn't convinced you were serious. It's unusual for a small hospital like PVH to attract the interest of a doctor with your reputation, even on a temporary basis."

The doctor motioned to a chair, and Hadley took a seat. "Trust me; giving me something to do would be a huge favor. It turns out I'm one of those people who doesn't know how to relax. The prospect of several more months without work is more than I can bear."

"You're on a leave of absence at the moment, is that correct?" Dr. Cassidy opened a folder and glanced at the contents.

"Yes. I will be, anyway. I'm actually on family leave

right now, so I need to fill out some paperwork to make the longer leave of absence official, but my family situation has become complicated enough that I can't see a way around it."

"I'm so sorry." The doctor's words were heartfelt, her expression full of compassion. Hadley felt sure they would get along well for as long as she was there.

"It will be a relief when I have something to take my mind off it all. I miss working."

"I wouldn't be able to guarantee a set schedule, as I never know from week to week which shifts will need coverage."

"That's totally fine. I'm more than happy to take on day or night shifts, weekends, whatever you need. Any idea when I could start?"

"Considering our chronic staffing shortage, how about yesterday?" Dr. Cassidy gave a wry laugh. "Given all your qualifications, I don't see any reason I can't push this through the proper channels right away. Although, you know we won't be able to pay you what you were earning in Boston."

"No worries there," Hadley said quickly. "I'm sure whatever you offer will be fair. I'll be looking forward to hearing when I should report for my first shift."

She and Dr. Cassidy shook hands, and Hadley's spirits were decidedly lighter as she ambled toward the cafeteria for her meeting. With a job on the horizon, the only thing that would improve her mood even more was a cup of really terrible hospital coffee. It was the little things about her normal life she missed most. Owen was doing his part to make sure she still enjoyed her share of sleepless nights, but the coffee Tyne made every morning tasted way too good.

Hadley's heart twisted into a knot.

Stop thinking about her, and it will go away.

Hadley had never met Brandy Swanson and hadn't a clue what she looked like, but the minute Hadley entered the cafeteria, she knew the take-charge type in the expensive suit who was sitting by herself and scrolling on her phone with a look that practically screamed *I'm more important than you* had to be her. Hadley walked right up to her and put out her hand.

"Hi, I'm Hadley."

The woman shook Hadley's hand but didn't bother introducing herself. "Thanks for making time today. I really didn't want to make a separate trip."

"I should thank you. Marcy says you're the best." Hadley glanced down at the table, noting it was empty. "Can I get you a cup of coffee before we get started, or maybe a muffin?"

Brandy's nose wrinkled. "Is it safe to drink?"

"Probably. If not, there are half a dozen medical professionals in the room who would be happy to revive you." Hadley laughed at her own joke. The lawyer did not.

"Coffee. Black." Having placed her order as though Hadley were a barista, Brandy pulled a yellow legal pad out of her bag.

"Right. Got it."

If this had been a blind date, Hadley would've walked, but no one said she had to fall in love with the woman. Hell, she didn't even have to like her. She just needed her to win. Fairly, yes. She'd promised that much to Tyne. But win, nonetheless. And according to Marcy, winning was Brandy Swanson's middle name.

Because of that, Hadley dutifully fetched two coffees and threw in two blueberry muffins. She suspected Brandy didn't consume carbs. It was possible the lawyer feasted mainly on human blood, but then again, wasn't that a selling point when choosing legal representation? Besides, Hadley loved these prepackaged, preservative-packed blueberry muffins to a degree that she, as a doctor, probably shouldn't admit publicly. If Brandy didn't want hers, Hadley would eat two.

When Hadley returned with the coffees, Brandy set hers aside without a second glance and picked up her pen. "In order to get everything started, I need to ask some questions."

"Sure." Hadley wrapped her fingers around her coffee and took a sip. Even with copious amounts of milk and sugar, it was every bit as bitter and tepid as any hospital coffee she'd ever had. It tasted like home.

"Now, this other woman—"

"Tyne."

Brandy's brow furrowed. "Like the things on a fork?"

"No. It's spelled T-Y- N-E."

"That's *different*." The word different in Brandy's dictionary definitely meant bad. "Tell me why this Tyne woman won't be a good mother."

"I, uh…" How was she supposed to answer that? Was this a trick? "I don't think she'd make a bad mother. In fact, she's wonderful with Owen. I just believe he'd have better opportunities living with me."

"Sure," she said as if it were obvious. "Private schooling, a college fund, trips to Disneyworld. The whole nine yards."

Disneyworld? Hadley smiled as she pictured Owen wearing a tiny mouse ear hat. Tyne would get such a kick out of that.

You can't invite Tyne, Hadley reminded herself. *You're trying to take Owen from her, remember?*

Hadley shifted uncomfortably in her chair. She had a sour taste in her mouth, and she was pretty sure it wasn't because of the terrible coffee.

"Owen is all I have left of my sister. I can't leave his happiness to chance."

"I couldn't agree more, which is why I'm going to need you to dig a little deeper here. I already know you're a successful and well-respected doctor. What does this Tyne woman do for a living?"

"She's an artist." Hadley hadn't liked the way Brandy referred to Tyne, intentionally being combative, but it was best not to point that out and to get through the appointment unscathed. Perhaps that was how the lawyer separated her humanity to do the job to the best of her capability. As someone whose job made similar demands, Hadley could respect that. Doctors weren't the only professionals equipped with an emotional kill switch.

"Really?" The woman leaned back with a Cheshire Cat grin. "That's great news for us. Please tell me she lives an open lifestyle."

"Uh…" Hadley knew exactly what the lawyer was implying, but that didn't ensure how best to react. Blurting out, *I don't know, but we slept together last night,* didn't seem like the wisest choice. "I'm not sure I feel comfortable bringing that type of angle into this."

"Never mind. Artists are flaky. That's a given, and judges hate flaky."

This characterization of Tyne didn't sit well with Hadley. "I'm not sure that's accurate. She owns her own business."

Brandy arched an eyebrow. "How much money does she earn?"

"I have no idea."

"Interesting." Brandy tapped her pen against the tablet. "And how old is she?"

"Twenty-nine." Hadley was grateful for a straight-forward question.

Brandy made a low whistling sound. "Young. Anything under thirty is way too young for a baby as far as I'm concerned."

"Exactly." Hadley bit her lip. "Although, come to

think of it, my mom was twenty-nine when I was born. And Kayleigh was younger than that, so it might be more common outside the city."

"Kayleigh who?"

Hadley sucked in a breath. "My sister. Owen's mom."

The one who died, you cold-hearted bitch, she wanted to add but didn't.

"Well, look. They might call this place Pioneer Valley, but it's not *Little House on the Prairie* days anymore. Twenty-nine is young." There was furious scribbling on the yellow notepad, followed by a quick rereading of her notes. When Brandy looked up, she appeared satisfied. "I'm loving this so far. Young, an artist, self-employed. The financial angle is obviously our best bet. What do her parents do for a living?"

"Well, her birth mom's not in the picture anymore, but her adoptive parents, Owen's paternal grandparents, have a trucking business."

"She's adopted?" Brandy laughed, though the sound was utterly devoid of humor. "This keeps getting better. If the other stuff doesn't work, we can always make the argument you're Owen's blood relative."

"She's still related that way, too, but a cousin, I think." Hadley tried to conjure up the family tree, but her brain sputtered.

"But not actually his aunt, like you are."

Hadley frowned. As a lawyer who specialized in this kind of thing, shouldn't she be more open-minded about adopted kids being real family? The way she'd made it sound, a lack of blood ties made Tyne little better than a complete stranger to Owen. It didn't seem fair.

Brandy tucked her notebook back in her bag. "My first step will be to request every scrap of financial paperwork from both Tyne's business and her parents."

"Her parents? Is that really necessary? It sounds a bit over-the-top."

"It's all part of the process. Trust me, if they've ever been through an IRS audit, this will be ten times worse." The woman sounded gleeful, like she took particular pride in being worse than the IRS. Was that normal? "We want to make them jump through so many burning hoops they give up."

"Tyne's not the quitting type." It was one of the qualities Hadley admired most about her.

"She hasn't met the likes of me, yet. When I get done with her, she'll be begging for mercy. Trust me."

Hadley didn't, and this wasn't the way she'd pictured the case going at all.

After a moment to find her words, Hadley said, "Hold on, now—" She stopped herself from calling the woman Atilla the Hun, or whatever the female equivalent was. "I don't want to run roughshod over Tyne and her parents. I gave her my word I wouldn't play

185

any tricks to win this thing. It comes down to my belief that Owen will be better off with me."

"I completely understand your impulses." To Hadley's relief, the woman softened her expression and now looked mostly human instead of like a shark who smelled blood in the water. "These battles are not for the faint of heart. But neither is parenthood. Or did you think raising a baby was going to be a walk in the park?"

Hadley swallowed. "No, of course not."

"No. You're a woman of the world. You know what it takes to survive." As Brandy spoke, Hadley nodded at the description of herself. "I do, too. This is my job. I'm as good at it as you are at fixing broken bones. If you want to give your sister's baby the very best life he can have, you need to leave everything with me. That's what you want, right? Owen to have a great life?"

"Of course." Hadley closed her eyes. She was doing this for her nephew and for the sister she'd lost. She had to stay focused on that. "You promise you won't do anything that isn't absolutely necessary?"

"The strategy I'm suggesting is all standard stuff. I've done it a hundred times."

"That doesn't mean it isn't nasty and underhand-ed," Hadley shot back, not caring at this point if the lawyer knew exactly what she thought of her.

"I get it. I do." The woman placed a hand to her chest. "You're a good person. To me, that's the best reason of all that your nephew should be with you. If you let me do my job, I assure you of this: when everything is said and done, that's exactly where he will end up." Brandy rose from the table, holding out her hand. "Do we have a deal?"

Hadley pressed her lips together. She still wasn't completely sold on this woman or her tactics, but it was probably true that what was being suggested was commonplace. Technically, that wouldn't count as letting things get nasty, right? Because what else could she do? If she wanted to win, this was the only way forward.

This is for Owen.

After taking a breath, Hadley reached out to shake Brandy's hand. "We have a deal."

CHAPTER TWELVE

"**D**id you fill the chip dish?" Tyne breezed past Hadley, who was putting the finishing touches on the snack table to prepare for their first official family get-together at the new house.

Not that we're a family, Tyne reminded herself. *And this isn't really our house.*

But they were expecting company, and that meant food.

"I set out everything you mentioned." Hadley gestured to the heavily laden kitchen island like a game show hostess revealing an exciting bonus prize. "I even filled the salsa and guacamole bowls, even though you didn't ask."

"That was going to be my next request." Tyne appraised the doctor, trying not to laugh at how pleased she looked with herself, as if with her brilliant addition of salsa and guac she had single-handedly revolutionized tortilla chips. But Tyne had to admit a smug Hadley was sorta cute. "Let's see. What's missing?"

Hadley scratched her head as she examined the massive spread. "How many people are we expecting?"

"Your parents, plus mine, and all my brothers."

No, not all. A stab tore through Tyne's gut. It had been three weeks since the accident, and she still never knew when some small reminder of her loss would tear open the wounds afresh.

"There's enough food here for at least twenty people."

"You think?" Tyne scanned the assortment of offerings with uncertainty. "I've never hosted a party before, not on my own as an adult. This is the first time I've lived someplace large enough to invite more than one person at a time."

Hadley rubbed her chin, also studying the food. "Come to think of it, I never have, either."

"Your place in the city is too small?" Tyne asked.

"The space is all right. Three bedrooms and a patio. It's the guest list that's too small. Anyway"—Hadley gave a mock salute—"what's next, Boss?"

"I don't know," Tyne teased. "Are you sure you can handle it?"

Hadley swallowed, her smugness giving way to confusion, perhaps tipping into full-on fear. "Depends."

Tyne laughed. "I need you to chop the cilantro."

"Fortunately for you, chopping is my specialty." Hadley wiggled her fingers. "I basically wield a knife for a living, you know."

"That's terrifying, considering your job is supposed to be stitching people back up."

"Most of the time, but I've performed a pretty mean appendectomy when the situation called for it. I considered becoming a surgeon at one point."

"Why'd you change your mind?"

"I wasn't arrogant enough." Hadley snickered.

Tyne raised an eyebrow. "I find that hard to believe. At least if the cilantro has a bad appendix, I'm relieved to know it will be in good hands."

Hadley did an impressive eye roll but got to work.

"I came across a closet with some games the other day." Tyne said. "Do you think I should put a few out in case everyone wants to play?"

"What kind? Lawn games?"

"No, it's already getting hot and humid out there. We might need a break from it. There's rain in the forecast later, too." Tyne cast a glance out the window to where dark clouds were gathering on the horizon. "Can you believe this house has central air-conditioning?"

"Yeah, it's great."

The offhanded way Hadley said this made it obvious it had never occurred to her a house wouldn't have such a basic amenity. As she opened the closet to search for games, Tyne's cheeks burned. How stupid her enthusiasm must've sounded to a woman who usually lived in what Tyne imagined qualified as a luxury condo. "How about Pictionary? There's even a white board and an easel in here."

"Yes! I'm a whiz at Pictionary. Er, probably not as good as you, since you're an actual artist, but I do okay."

"Watch your back because my brothers are cutthroat at this game." Tyne grabbed the box and other supplies before shutting the closet door. "Will your parents enjoy it?"

Hadley shrugged. "No idea. I can't remember the last time we played, if ever."

The doorbell rang, and Tyne clapped her hands giddily. "The first guests have arrived!" She swept Owen up from his bouncy chair. "Come on, little man. Be a good host."

Through the peephole, Tyne saw her mom and dad looking around the entrance, clearly impressed. Meanwhile, Evan and Connor looked bored, which was to be expected since boys at their ages always looked that way. Mason had positioned himself behind their mom, hunching like he didn't want to be seen, which made Tyne's spirits fall a notch. He'd gotten really good about going to new places since hitting his teen years, and to see him so anxious about the new house that he needed to hide behind an adult made it clear how much Ryan's death was impacting him.

She flung open the door, announcing, "Welcome to Owen's Castle!"

As if on cue, Owen giggled, waving his hands up and down in the air.

"Hand him over!" Tyne's mom demanded.

Tyne hesitated briefly, eyeing the black strap of her mom's back brace warily. When her dad gave a go-ahead nod, she relented, noting how he positioned himself to help hold the baby, offsetting the weight so as not to trigger a back spasm. The subtlety of his maneuver impressed her. It was possible her mom wasn't even aware he was doing it.

Wasn't that the definition of a perfect relationship? Seeing what needed doing and stepping in to get it done?

Like how Hadley had filled the salsa and guacamole bowls without being asked, Tyne thought and then froze in horror. That wasn't the same thing at all. They weren't a couple, and she needed to stop thinking like they were.

But it was hard.

The trouble was, ever since they'd slept together, things had been strained. Not terrible, or even unfriendly, just weird. They were cordial to one another, but almost too much so sometimes. And though Tyne was as attracted to Hadley as ever, the other woman hadn't experienced that spark even once since then, or at least if she had, Tyne hadn't caught onto it.

Which, of course, had been the whole argument for sleeping together in the first place. Get it out of their system so they could move on like rational adults. And it had worked. For Hadley.

Which was disconcerting, not to mention deflating.

Even as Tyne had suggested the plan, she'd known it was absurd. People always said stuff like that, as if you could funnel attraction through a garden hose to turn on and off at will. Despite it being a persuasive argument, it hardly ever worked, because sex was like dessert. If it was any good at all, you immediately wanted more.

And the sex had been good. Mind blowing. Magical, even. At least for Tyne. Based on the shift in Hadley's behavior, it had simply been a roll in the hay for her. And now it was over. Out of her system. Mission accomplished.

Which was fine, Tyne reminded herself for the millionth time. That had been the whole point, after all.

Careful what you wish for, right?

As soon as everyone was inside, Tyne showed her parents around while her brothers made a beeline for the food. As they dove into it like three starving castaways newly rescued from a deserted island, Tyne caught Hadley's eye and gave her an *I told you so* look. Hadley grinned with an expression of disbelief that seemed to say she had never seen humans consume so much, so quickly. Tyne shrugged. That was life growing up with boys.

The house soon filled with excited chatter. It was like so many other family get-togethers they'd had over the years, but it was difficult to block out the missing pieces: Ryan and Kayleigh. They were all trying, but Tyne could see it in a certain look her mom had as she waited for Ryan to pop in with one of his classic jokes at exactly the right time in the conversation, or when Owen made an excited squeal, but it wasn't Kayleigh who held him in her arms.

"Iced tea?" Tyne offered after one such moment, as an excuse to retreat to the kitchen and collect her emotions so no one would see her cry. "It's a special spicy kind, guaranteed to make your tongue dance with delight."

"Hard to say no to that." Tyne's dad cleared his throat, and she knew he, too, was trying to cover his momentary wave of grief.

Not long after Tyne returned with the pitcher of tea, the doorbell rang again.

Hadley leapt to her feet. "Got it!"

That was new. Usually, she avoided seeing her parents, and now she was dashing to the door to let them in. Tyne smiled to see the happiness on Hadley's face as she led her mom and dad into the room. She seemed more at ease with them than she had before.

"Paul. Nancy. It's so lovely to see you again." Tyne hugged each one. "Iced tea?"

"Please." Nancy fanned her face with her hand. "It's quite warm today, isn't it?"

"Can't recall it being so warm this early in the season in at least ten years," Paul added.

"And the winter was unseasonably cold," Tyne's dad chimed in.

Tyne shook her head in amusement as she poured two more glasses of tea. If there was one thing you could count on in New England, it was bonding over a lively discussion of the weather as if it'd never happened before.

"Here you go, Nancy." Tyne handed her the glass.

After everyone had a glass in hand, Tyne's dad got to his feet and raised his arm. "I'd like to make a toast. To Ryan and Kayleigh. While they're not physically here, they'll always be in our hearts and in their beautiful baby boy."

"Hear, hear," Paul said, his eyes misty, and everyone else murmured in agreement.

Owen, seeming to know he was the center of attention, did his adorable baby jig, which involved raising his arms in the air coupled with blowing excited bubbles. This brought a peel of laughter from everyone in the room, and Tyne wondered if this roller coaster of emotions was their new norm.

When Nancy took a sip of tea, her eyes lit up. "My goodness, this is wonderful."

"Thank you," Tyne replied, grateful for a distraction to keep herself from slipping into melancholy. "It's my favorite blend from the tea section at Big Y. I brewed it myself this morning."

"Wait until you taste my tacos!" Hadley crowed.

Tyne nearly dropped the iced tea pitcher onto the floor, her imagination plummeting to the depths of the gutter like someone had cut the elevator cables. Had anyone else caught how crudely suggestive that declaration was? Her eyes darted around the room, but no one else seemed fazed. Even Connor, whom she could usually count on in such situations to act like a total ass, kept his eyes glued to the game console he was sharing with Mason.

Right. Apparently, Tyne was the only one with the X-rated brain. Not a single other person had picked up on what, given Hadley's innocent expression, had surely been a completely unintended innuendo. Or maybe Tyne was still so fixated on their night together that almost anything would bring it rushing back.

Seriously, she urged herself, *stop thinking about that night right this second.*

Tyne chugged the rest of her tea, wishing it was something stronger, and set her glass down on the table with a bang. "So, Hadley here claims she's a rock star at Pictionary. What do you think, fam? Shall we put that statement to the test?"

"Are you kidding?" Evan jeered. "Connor and I can wipe the floor with you."

"Me, too," Mason added, his hands flapping. It was

good to see him settling in enough to get excited, and it gave Tyne hope his grief was starting to heal.

"You bet, bud," Connor said, giving his brother a nudge. "The three of us will be a team like the old days."

There was that reminder again, that nothing would ever truly be the same.

"For the rest of us, let's make it a battle of the couples," Tyne's mom declared, doing her best to stay the happy course. "Me and Keith, Paul and Nancy, and Tyne and Hadley."

"Hadley and I aren't a couple, Mom." Tyne's face burned so hot she feared it might soon melt right off her skull.

"What?" Her mom cocked her head, befuddled, and waved her hand dismissively. "Oh, you know what I mean."

Tyne's dad set up the whiteboard, testing a handful of dry erase markers Tyne had dug up before he settled on one he found acceptable. Tyne couldn't help noticing that although her family was brimming with enthusiasm, Paul and Nancy wore uncomfortable expressions like they hoped no one would notice them if they sat quietly and didn't make any sudden moves.

"Let the games begin!" Evan cried with the exaggerated tone of a sports announcer. The other boys cheered and high-fived each other, ready for battle.

"Battle of the couples! Woot!" Hadley cheered,

rubbing her hands together like a crazy person. "Who goes first?"

"What?" Tyne gave her head a slight shake. She'd never seen Hadley so relaxed and carefree, but what was throwing her off even more was the way Hadley had thrown the word couple out there without a moment's hesitation.

"Why don't you two go first?" Tyne's mom suggested.

Tyne could only nod. Her brain was still caught up in a loop. Yes, she and Hadley were sharing a house and taking care of Owen together, but did their families think that made them an instant couple? Of course, they'd also slept together, but thank God none of them knew about that. Or did they? Were Tyne and Hadley putting off some *we slept together* vibes?

"Do you want to draw first?" Hadley handed Tyne the black marker with a look that implied if she didn't snap out of whatever weirdness was going on soon, Hadley was going to evaluate her for signs of a stroke.

"Uh... uh-huh." Yeah, good. Perfect. Tyne was well on the path to acting totally normal again with *that* response.

When she drew the first card and flipped it over, she nearly laughed out loud. "Okay, let's see if you can get this one. It might be a stretch."

"Hit me with it, babe." Hadley clapped again. "Woot!"

Did she just call me... oh, never mind.

Casting her artistic nature aside, Tyne scribbled a basic stick figure on the whiteboard, adding a hat with a cross on it and sticking a huge knife in one hand.

"Surgeon!" Hadley shouted.

Tyne waved for her to keep going on that path.

"ER! Doctor!"

"Ding, ding, ding!" Tyne screamed, jumping up and down. "Got it in record time."

Hadley shrugged with mock humility. "Would've been faster, but I thought maybe you were drawing a chef chopping cilantro."

Tyne and Hadley both laughed uproariously at the inside joke while their parents exchanged baffled glances. Tyne squeezed the cap back onto the marker until it made that satisfying clicking sound. "Who's next?"

Evan bounded off the couch. "That was cheating, but watch us."

"How was that cheating?" Tyne demanded, crossing her arms.

"You two are all..." He waved his hand around in lieu of actually finishing his thought. "Whatever. It just is."

Tyne laughed off whatever her brother was implying, but way down deep, she was pleased. She and Hadley made a good team. At Pictionary... and maybe at other things, too. They were doing a good job with Owen. Maybe there was some way to work out a compromise so they could both continue doing the things they did best, together.

Her brother waved a hand in her face, snapping her back to attention.

"Card?" he demanded.

"Sorry." She handed him the box.

He chose one, and as soon as he looked at it, his face paled. "How do you even *draw* that?"

Beside her, Hadley snickered. Tyne felt a slight glow at how well the game was going. She'd missed these family gatherings, and they were all getting along so perfectly. Hadley especially was fitting in like she'd been doing this her whole life, and it was hard to believe this was the first time she'd joined one of the informal parties the Briggs family was known for. It felt like she'd been one of them forever.

Still muttering, Evan started drawing random lines, and then some circles.

His brothers shouted guesses.

"Rotary!"

"Wedding rings!"

"Infinity symbol!"

"No." Frustrated, Evan wiped away some of his drawing with the side of his fist and used the pen to add more circles.

"Dude," Connor said. "What's up with the circles?"

Evan grasped a handful of his hair and yanked. "I can't remember the number."

"Crop circles?" Connor sounded as if he knew it was completely off base.

"Aliens?" Mason slanted his head, either to get a different perspective or because he was completely confused.

"No talking," Hadley chided, inching to the edge of the seat as she watched Evan struggle and the boys shouting.

"Time!" Tyne's dad said.

"The word was Olympics!" Evan pounded the pen into each circle. "They're all connected, like the rings?"

"That's bad," Mason said.

"Yeah, thanks," Evan huffed.

"Better luck next time." Tyne took the pen from the red-faced Evan, who was still scowling as he reclaimed his seat.

It was her parents turn, and her dad happily strode to the board. Ever since Tyne could remember, game nights were the Briggs family specialty. Whether it be poker nights, Pictionary, or an epic Go Fish battle, this was how they dealt with everything.

Her dad stretched out his hand, pointing to his wife with the pen and then tapping it to his forehead. "Let's show these youngsters how it's done."

He glanced at the word on his card, and his lips tugged upward. As he sketched out an animal—a dog, perhaps? Tyne's mom called out an entire zoo full of guesses. But, when he added a horn to the head, she shouted, "Unicorn!"

He did a celebratory dance and handed the pen back to Tyne.

"That's the worse unicorn I've ever seen," she teased her father with a dramatic *pffft*.

"It's not about the form but getting it right."

"Don't get cocky, Keith," Hadley said boldly, drawing a surprised look from Tyne. "We're tied, and I always play to win. Right, Tyne?"

"You bet!" Tyne loved this competitive side of Hadley and was ready to annihilate the competition, but as she was about to ask who's turn it was next, she turned to Hadley's parents, who were seated on one of the love seats off to the side. It couldn't have been more obvious that neither of them really wanted to play, and they were dreading being called up. Immediately, Tyne's bloodlust fizzled. "Maybe we should have a snack first."

"What?" Hadley whined. "We're on a roll!"

"Well, I'm hungry. How about you, Mason? I got your favorite juice boxes."

Mason, who was always up for a snack, agreed with enthusiasm. Was it unfair to use her little brother with special needs to influence the outcome of the debate in her favor? Maybe. But she was doing it for a good cause. Already Paul and Nancy looked much more at ease.

"What gives?" Hadley asked in a low voice as the rest of the group made their way to the table.

"Your parents were up next, and they looked miserable."

Hadley's features softened with understanding.

"Right." Then she announced loudly, "I'm starved. You coming?"

There was a creak of hinges and the solid thunk of mail being dropped through the slot onto the entryway tile. "Yeah. I'll be there in a minute. Save me some of your special guac."

Tyne headed to the front door. A chunky white envelope lay on the rug. She picked it up and noted it had an official feel to it. Her mouth settled into a frown at the unfamiliar Boston return address, which deepened as she discovered it was addressed to her.

"That's odd." Tyne hadn't changed her mailing address, since she had to go to her place for work, so she never received mail at this house. Tensing a little, Tyne slid her finger under the lip of the envelope, and pulled out the contents. Scanning past the fancy letter-head, it quickly became apparent this was an official communication from Hadley's lawyer. As she continued to read, her breath hitched. Was this for real?

Tucking the letter back into the envelope, Tyne tiptoed back toward the kitchen. She stood at the edge of the room until she made eye contact with her mom and gestured for her to come closer. When she did,

Tyne took a step into the other room, moving out of Hadley's sight.

"Mom?" Tyne's volume was barely above a whisper.

"What's wrong?" her mom asked.

"I just got this—" Tyne couldn't put it into words and simply handed the letter to her mom.

"Oh."

"It's asking for every financial document, tax filing, bank statement, and God knows what else for my business and personal accounts for the past ten years." Tyne squinted at a list of forms she hadn't known existed until now. She'd need a dictionary to understand some of the technical jargon.

"I know. We got one, too."

Tyne's jaw dropped. "Why didn't you tell me?"

"It only arrived yesterday. We haven't had a chance to look it over thoroughly."

Tyne could practically taste blood. "Why are they requesting all of your financial details. You're not the one trying to get Owen."

"It's probably routine in these cases."

"You think so?" Tyne wasn't so sure. Though she hadn't consulted an attorney yet, the social worker hadn't mentioned anything like this when she'd walked her through the process. "It doesn't sit right with me."

"I'm sure there's a simple explanation, honey. Don't worry about it today. Come on. Don't you want to enjoy Hadley's tacos?"

Tyne snorted. Her imagination may have gone somewhere else entirely when Hadley had made a similar suggestion earlier, but right now all she could picture was giving that scheming, no good, duplicitous doctor a firm, swift kick in her... tacos.

Hadley's own words replayed in Tyne's head: *I always play to win.*

How could she have been such a fool, thinking she and Hadley had some sort of special connection? Hadley had been lulling Tyne into a stupor—even playing Pictionary with her family—and all the while plotting war.

Well, two could play at that game, and Tyne was kicking herself for falling for Hadley's routine. Tyne knew firsthand Hadley didn't relax. The woman admitted as much. No, Hadley Moore only knew one thing: winning at all costs.

Tyne had some money put aside. It wasn't much, but she'd been saving it to open a second paint and sip studio next year. That would have to wait. If Hadley could find some fancy, big city lawyer, so could Tyne. Right then and there, she vowed to spend every last penny she had fighting for sole custody, because the thought of her nephew being raised by the likes of two-faced Hadley was too terrible to ponder.

No. That woman was rotten to the core.

Tyne owed it to her brother and Kayleigh to keep Hadley far away from that sweet baby boy.

CHAPTER THIRTEEN

It was Thursday afternoon, and Hadley was returning home from a meeting with the Pioneer Valley Hospital human resources department. She walked into the kitchen, whistling a cheerful tune. Her interview had gone swimmingly, and with a little luck, she was a mere pile of paperwork away from being assigned to her first shift. It would feel so amazing to get back to work after almost a month off. In the meantime, as the baby monitor on the counter sprang to life and sent her racing up the stairs, she was reminded she had a different job to keep her on her toes.

"Come on, buddy." Hadley scooped the bundle of joy up from his crib and into her arms. "Did you have a nice nap?"

Owen, warm and cuddly in his cotton footed sleeper, cooed in her ear.

She changed his diaper without much fuss, quite pleased with her newfound efficiency, not to mention how adept she'd become at avoiding any additional shots to the face. This whole baby thing wasn't nearly as daunting as it had been in the beginning.

On her way downstairs, Hadley heard the plop of mail arriving through the slot in the door. Her heart beat a little faster.

"Shall we see what we got?" she asked Owen in a singsong voice that masked her apprehension. She studied the stack of junk mail, unable to decide if she should feel relieved. "Nothing yet."

Which was strange. Brandy Swanson's assistant had sworn she was mailing the letter requesting Tyne's detailed financial reports last Thursday. It was Wednesday now, and still, it hadn't arrived. At least Hadley hadn't seen it, and Tyne hadn't mentioned it.

If Tyne had already opened it, there was no way she would've kept quiet. Tyne would've read Hadley the riot act, and she probably would've deserved it, too. Did it break the letter of the law of their agreement? Maybe not. But it was getting harder for Hadley to remain convinced it didn't break the spirit. If she were in Tyne's shoes, Hadley would be royally pissed.

Hadley left the supermarket flyers and credit card offers where they'd landed, bouncing Owen on her hip. "Let's go get you some lunch. How about bananas? You like those."

She put Owen in his chair and pulled a banana and

zucchini baby food pouch from the cupboard, along with the largest bib she could find. Meal time with Owen was a full body experience, especially when bananas were on offer.

When they'd first cleaned out Kayleigh and Ryan's apartment, there had been a few dozen pouches of homemade food in the freezer. When they'd run out, Tyne had wanted to make more, but Hadley talked her out of it, buying an assortment of these fancy ones from the organic market instead. What she hadn't said was when Owen came to live with her in Boston, he'd have to get used to store-bought food, anyway. She had neither the time nor the inclination to boil and mush it herself.

Hadley refused to feel guilty about it.

Unfortunately, guilt didn't work that way.

As it turned out, stomping your foot and declaring your refusal to feel bad about something didn't magically fix everything when you knew what you'd done was wrong. Or in this case, when you'd given the go-ahead for someone else to do it. As each day passed and Hadley grew more tense about the lawyer's letter arriving, Hadley had become increasingly more convinced she'd made a horrific choice. She dreaded its arrival. Maybe it had gotten lost in the mail.

Sitting in the chair next to Owen, Hadley squeezed a dollop of food onto a brightly colored plastic spoon. He giggled and smacked his lips as he got his first taste, gobbling down as much as he could. After every few bites, Hadley used the spoon's edge to swipe the mess from his lips and face, funneling it back into his mouth where it belonged. It was a neat trick she'd learned from watching Tyne, who was the source of just about everything Hadley now knew about babies.

There was that guilty sensation again. The one that made her turn ice-cold all the while bursting into a sweat.

"What should we do this afternoon?" Hadley asked Owen after he finished his lunch. She knew he didn't understand a word, but she'd been reading a parenting blog Tyne had recommended and discovered it was important to speak to babies as often as possible to give them a head start on their vocabulary building. "I know. What if we take a walk out to the art studio and see if Aunt Tyne will let us check out her latest masterpiece?"

When she wasn't on baby duty or teaching classes, Tyne spent most of her time working in the studio. Hadley couldn't blame her. The one-room building with its big windows and ample natural light was an ideal place for painting, and the fact the rental house had such an amazing structure had probably been what won Tyne over to Hadley's scheme of living together more than any other argument Hadley could've made.

For the most part, Hadley had left Tyne alone whenever she'd ventured out there. As someone who understood the value of work, Hadley didn't want to interrupt or get in the way. On the other hand, Hadley had seen little of Tyne since the party, despite them living under the same roof. She missed the woman's company. Bringing Owen for a visit was a perfect way to check in on her without it seeming weird. Or desperate.

The temperature had been approaching summer highs for the past week, though today there was a delightful breeze that chased the humidity away. Hadley welcomed it, feeling it was unfair for Mother Nature to skip past spring the way she'd been doing when it was one of New England's best seasons.

"We need rain, don't we, Owen? The grass is so brown." Hadley shielded the baby's eyes with her hand as they stepped from the sliding patio door into the blistering sun. "Once we're back home, and you get a little bigger, I'll take you to the Frog Pond in Boston Common so you can splash around in the fountains. Would you like that?"

Owen grabbed a fistful of Hadley's shirt and stuck it into his mouth by way of answering.

"I'll take that as a yes. I bet if I look into it, I'll find all sorts of things for a little tyke like you to do around Beacon Hill."

When they'd made it the few hundred yards across the parched grass to the little studio, Hadley found the door open, but the artist was nowhere in sight, which made sense because come to think of it, Tyne wouldn't put Owen down for a nap and head to the studio. It was too far for the monitor to get good reception. That meant Tyne was in the house but avoiding Hadley. If that was the case now, wait until the financial disclosure letter arrived.

Not wanting to dwell too much on that, Hadley's eyes wandered to the easel with a large canvas occupying the middle of the room, angled in such a way that Hadley could only see the back from where she stood.

Hadley couldn't tear her eyes away from it, her curiosity burning to see the work that had consumed Tyne for so many days. "Do you think we should take a peek?"

Owen giggled.

"Me, too. Glad we agree."

Holding Owen close, Hadley threaded her way around the extra canvases and boxes of art supplies that littered the floor. When she made it to the front of the canvas, it was nothing like she'd expected based on the cutesy projects from Tyne's paint and sip classes. All Hadley could do was stare, slack-jawed, as Tyne's creation washed over her in a crash of riotous color and bold brush strokes. As if they breathed life into the feeling of anger.

That was an emotion Hadley knew well. It had consumed her since the accident, not only because of the deaths but because they'd died in such a heinous way. As a doctor, she valued the life of each patient equally. As a grieving sister, she was of the opinion drunk drivers should be shot on the spot, if they survived.

There were times Hadley didn't recognize the dark thoughts in her head as her own. She'd been afraid to give them voice, convinced no one would understand. But Tyne knew that same darkness, the constant battle that raged between moral decency and soul-crushing rage. The proof was right in front of Hadley's eyes. Tyne had captured it in paint, transforming the grotesque into a thing of beauty.

After several seconds passed without so much as blinking, Hadley let out a low whistle. "I've never seen anything like this, have you?"

Owen babbled incoherently, and Hadley laughed as she spied the playpen Tyne had set up nearby. The little guy had been a frequent guest in his aunt's studio. "I suppose you have, which makes me the only clueless one in the house."

Though Hadley was no expert on the subject, she'd seen a rotation of work from up-and-coming artists on display in the windows of a high-end gallery on Charles Street that she passed on her way to and from work. She'd been tempted to go inside once or twice when a piece caught her eye, but nothing had ever quite moved her to the point of shelling out what she assumed would be an exorbitant price to acquire any of them.

This one was different.

Even in its unfinished state, Hadley felt she was

looking at something extraordinary. If she'd ever seen a painting like this in the gallery window, she'd have handed over her credit card without bothering to ask how much. If that was true for her untrained eye, she imagined people who actually knew what they were talking about would get into bidding wars for the honor of acquiring a painting like this for their collection.

Brimming with a deep sense of pride, Hadley kissed the top of Owen's downy head. "I have a feeling your auntie won't be a small-town artist for much longer."

"There you are!"

Hadley jumped at the sound of Tyne's voice, her heart practically bursting from her chest when she turned to see the woman coming toward her with excitement sparkling in her eyes. Her spirits deflated almost instantly, though, when Tyne held her arms out in a way that made it obvious her expression was all about Owen.

"Did you have a good nap, little sweetums?" Tyne wiggled her fingers until Hadley reluctantly relinquished the baby. "Is that some food I see on your ear?"

"Oops." Removing all evidence of her nephew's mealtime adventures was one skill Hadley hadn't quite mastered yet.

Tyne licked her finger and swiped it along the side of the baby's face in the way mothers had probably done since the dawn of time. "All better, handsome fella."

"Sorry about that." While it wasn't the type of infraction that required an apology, Hadley did so anyway. Tyne had yet to make eye contact with her, or talk to her, since returning to the studio, and Hadley found herself desperate to make her do so. "He woke up half an hour ago, and I gave him some banana and zucchini for lunch."

"I saw."

As responses went, it wasn't much, and Tyne still didn't meet Hadley's eyes. Hadley fidgeted with the edge of her shirt, her nerves jangling. Something felt off. Hadley had worried things would be awkward between them after she'd shown the incredibly poor judgement of not resisting sleeping together, but the party over the weekend had made it feel like they had swerved past it without too many bumps and bruises.

So, what was going on? Was Tyne upset Hadley had come into the studio uninvited and invaded her private space?

"I'm sorry for peeking at your painting. I should have asked before barging in."

Tyne shrugged. "You pay the rent, so it's technically your space."

That was a dagger to the heart.

"No, Tyne. This is your workspace, and I had no right."

Tyne took a breath. When she looked up, the half-smile on her lips suggested she hadn't entirely forgiven Hadley, but maybe she was considering it. "Do you need a change?"

Of scenery?

Hadley paused a beat, and realized she was referring to Owen. "No, I already did that when I got him up. He's fed, but I'll get him a bottle in a little bit, and it's my night to bathe him before bed."

It struck Hadley that all of their conversations for the past several days had revolved around Owen and nothing more. Sure, he was their primary focus, but it wasn't like that was all they had in common. Were they becoming that couple who got so preoccupied with being parents they forgot how to interact with each other like people?

Not that they were a couple.

But they *had* started in friend territory before this custody stuff reared its ugly head. And they'd been managing so well living together and taking care of Owen until now. It was important for that to continue. Children needed a lot of love and support, probably more than either of them could manage on their own. Hadley wasn't about to ruin everything by taking Tyne for granted the way she knew so many of her male colleagues seemed to with their wives. She could do better, starting now.

"I have an idea." Hadley looked into Tyne's eyes, wanting her to see she wasn't ignoring her. "You know I need to head to Boston tomorrow to finalize my leave of absence paperwork with the hospital, and it's supposed to be a beautiful day. What about a family outing?"

"You want to take your parents into the city?" Tyne's brow scrunched. "You don't need my permission for that."

Hadley swallowed. Clearly, she hadn't phrased that quite right. "Uh, no. I meant, you, me, and Owen."

"Tomorrow's Friday," Tyne pointed out. "Since you were already planning to be away, my parents had asked to have Owen overnight, remember?"

"Oh, that's right." Hadley's shoulders slumped. "Shoot. I don't want to mess up their plans, but I can't put off signing the paperwork."

"Another time, maybe."

"Yeah. Unless…" Hadley hesitated, not sure if the idea she'd just had was appropriate or crossed a line. Only one way to find out. "Would you like to come into Boston with me?"

"Tomorrow?"

"Yeah. You aren't teaching a class, are you?"

"No, but—"

"We can stay at my condo—totally on the up and up, I promise. I have a guest room you can stay in. But it would be nice to have company on the drive, and besides, there's something in my neighborhood I want to show you. I think you'll like it."

The prospect of introducing Tyne to the art gallery on Charles Street made Hadley's insides dance. It was too perfect. Seeing what Tyne was capable of had convinced Hadley the woman's art career would take off like a rocket, if only she could make the right connections. Boston was the perfect place for that to happen.

For a moment, it seemed Tyne was going to say no, but then her expression shifted. "Actually, I've always wanted to check out the Freedom Trail."

Hadley's heart thumped. Tyne was close to giving in. There had to be something she could say to push her over the edge. "It would be good for us to have a break. It's been chaotic this past month, and Owen deserves for both of us to keep bringing our A game. Isn't that right, little fella?"

Owen blew spit bubbles, and Tyne laughed. "I can't really argue with that."

"In that case, let's plan to head out after lunch tomorrow." Hadley quickly added, "If that works for you."

"It does, thank you." Tyne rested Owen on her hip while she rummaged through a container of paint tubes.

"Do you want me to take him back to the house so you can work?" Hadley offered.

"No, leave him with me, if you don't mind. He helps me stay focused on what's really important." She must've been onto something with that, because Tyne looked a lot less stressed now than she had the past few days. Or maybe it was the prospect of their trip that was making her appear that way. Regardless, it made Hadley happy to see.

"Will do. Don't forget to come in for dinner."

As she walked back to the house, Hadley barely refrained from pumping her fist in the air. It wasn't like she had a master plan when it came to Tyne. Hell, she didn't even know her destination, much less how to get there—but if she *had* been planning to make progress with her on almost any front, a getaway to Boston and a visit to an art gallery would've been the first steps in putting that plan into motion.

Make that step two.

Step one was calling off the attack dog that was Brandy Swanson, Esquire. No way did Hadley want to bury Tyne and her family under a mountain of legal and financial paperwork that would make their lives impossible. Especially not after the lovely get-together they'd had over the weekend.

Hadley had been stupid for agreeing to the tactic.

Cruel, even.

Winning was one thing, but Hadley was coming to realize how much she'd been missing by skipping so many family events over the years. Yes, work was important, but so were loved ones. She still wanted to take Owen to live with her in Boston, of course. She knew she could give him the best life, and nothing had changed her mind about it. But she had to do it the right way. Nothing nefarious.

She would make her best case for Owen, and let

Tyne do the same, like they'd promised. The Briggs family deserved that much, most of all Tyne, who'd been in Owen's life right from the start while Hadley had been too busy playing the role of big shot Boston doctor.

And maybe, just possibly, they could come up with a compromise. After all, she and Tyne were doing such an outstanding job working together with Owen right now that it was almost a shame it couldn't continue. Hadley needed to put her brain to work on finding a way for that to happen.

If Tyne made some connections at the art gallery, perhaps she'd have a reason to spend more time in the city. She could stay in Hadley's guest room, even. They could take Owen to the Frog Pond together and watch him play in the fountain in the summer, or go ice skating in the winter when he was old enough.

While she was at it, Hadley might ask Rebecca Porter if that condo she'd been trying to sell her was still available. Hadley's mom and dad were getting older, and they would need her around more often as time went by. She would bring Owen out here on weekends and for a month in the summer. Tyne would end up seeing the little guy so much it would almost feel like joint custody.

Grinning with satisfaction at how perfect her vision of the future seemed, Hadley typed a quick email to Brandy, letting her know the change in plans. No more jumping through flaming hoops. No more driving Tyne to the point of exhaustion so she would quit. Hadley would win this thing the right way, fair and square.

Walking through the entryway, Hadley scooped up the junk mail and tossed it in the recycling bin. What a wonderful stroke of good luck that her lawyer's letter had never arrived.

CHAPTER FOURTEEN

"Okay, Miss Briggs." The attorney stretched his arm across the table to point to the dotted line. "I need one final John Hancock here, and we'll get the ball rolling."

Robert Atkinson was number one in family law, at least according to the Google search that had led Tyne to his office. He certainly looked the part. It struck Tyne that the man's crisp striped shirt and silver cufflinks probably cost the same as her rent. Not to mention the pen he'd handed her. It was gold, very heavy, and most likely required a special ink cartridge that was sold only at Neiman Marcus.

But it meant he'd won enough cases to afford it. And Tyne needed to win.

"So, once I sign this, you'll officially represent me?" Her fingers gripped the cold pen.

"That's right. It's all spelled out in the contract,

which as your lawyer I urge you to read. Of course, I've also read it, and as your lawyer I can advise you to go ahead and sign it." He gave a hyena laugh at his own clever joke. "To sum up what it says, I have a few policies. First, I always insist on meeting with a prospective client in person, but we're all set there. Thanks for coming in."

"I appreciate you fitting me in on short notice." Tyne felt compelled to say something, and that was all she could come up with.

"Of course. Clients always come first. Second, the retainer, which is due today, is nonrefundable. And finally, while I will take your views and preferences into account, ultimately, any final decisions on legal strategy are mine. That's just how I operate. If you disagree, we cancel the contract and go our separate ways. Otherwise, I'm the boss." He hooked a thumb toward his chest.

Tyne bristled at his controlling tone. Then again, he was far from the only man who liked to be in the driver's seat. It seemed to run in their DNA. She forced a smile. "I guess that's fair. You're the expert, right?"

"That's the spirit. And yes, I *am* the expert. You leave things to me, and you'll get what you want. If that sounds good to you, all you need to do is sign." His smile could only be described as smarmy, but that was typical for a lawyer, right?

Tyne winced as the nib scratched across the paper,

feeling almost as if she was literally carving into Hadley's flesh.

She started it, Tyne reminded herself. *All I'm doing is protecting myself and my family.*

"There's the minor matter of the retainer…"

Swallowing hard, Tyne used the lawyer's fancy schmancy pen to write out a check that would come within a few bucks of draining back down to zero all the money she'd socked away over the past few years to open a second paint and sip studio. As she slid the contract and retainer across the table, what she really wanted to do was grab the closest wastebasket and throw up.

"That's it!" He smacked his hands together like he'd watched the Red Sox score a run. Tyne wondered why so many testosterone-fueled men treated every little thing like they'd smacked the winning homerun in the World Series. "Trust me. I've gone head-to-head with Swanson, Howe, and Mathis plenty of times. You have nothing to worry about. They're tough, but they don't think outside of the box."

As soon as the deal was done, Tyne wasted no time in finding the elevator. When the doors slid closed, she let out a breath, watching the number display as it counted down the floors to the lobby. Tyne's skin was clammy, but she felt flushed at the same time.

She needed to get out of this building, away from its marble veneers and slick lawyers. She needed sunshine and fresh air in her lungs, because she was on the verge of hyperventilating. At least, she thought that was what was going on. She'd never experienced anything like this before. Then again, she'd never watched all her hard-earned savings disappear in a puff of smoke before, either.

How about stabbing a friend in the back? the meddlesome voice in her head pressed. *When was the last time you did that?*

Yes, Tyne had told herself a million times that Hadley had started this, that she was bringing it on herself, but the guilt wouldn't fade away. None of this made sense. On the surface, everything between them was fine. Better than fine. They took care of Owen together like a well-oiled machine, and ever since they'd started living together, Tyne had found more time for her painting, and experienced a greater rush of creativity, than she ever had when living alone.

If she hadn't seen that letter from Hadley's attorney with her own eyes, and therefore knew beyond a shadow of a doubt Hadley was more than willing to play any and every dirty trick behind her back, she never would've believed it. Now here Tyne was, doing the same thing. How did that make her any better?

The hardest thing was her brain playing tricks on her. Even with a court order looming over her head that had her scurrying to dig up receipts for every pack of chewing gum she'd bought since high school, Tyne found herself forgetting about it until she consulted her to-do list, outlining the next piece of information she needed to track down. In between those times and reality, she would laugh over one of Hadley's jokes or chat with her about something cute Owen had done, and she could hardly believe they weren't the best of friends.

Sometimes it was so hard not to wish they could be more.

But it was like there were two of Hadley, existing side by side. One was the sweetest, caring woman you could imagine, and the other one attacked like a lion pouncing on an injured gazelle. If only she knew which one was the real Hadley, because it was impossible for her to be both. Not that it mattered. Tyne's decision to visit Robert Atkinson's office—not walk along the Freedom Trail as she'd said she was going to do while Hadley went to her meeting at the hospital—had sunk any remaining hope where she and Hadley were concerned. The betrayal on both sides went too deep for that now.

Crossing Boylston Street, Tyne spotted an entrance to the Public Garden and seized the opportunity to duck away from the late afternoon crowds that clogged the red brick sidewalk as workers left their offices and streamed toward the trains and busses that would carry them home. She wasn't accustomed to all this hustle and bustle, and hard as it might be for a city dweller to believe, she'd only made it into Boston a handful of times in her life. Any other time she might find the change of pace exciting, but the way her brain was swirling with so much anxiety and doubt, all she wanted was a bit of peace.

According to the map on her phone, the spot where she was meeting Hadley was off Charles Street, a diagonal line from where she was now, though the large pond in the middle of the garden kept it from being a straight shot. It was okay with her, though. A long stroll was exactly what she needed to clear her head.

It was still early May, but everywhere her eyes landed, she saw vivid summer colors. Even the grass was lush and green in this mid-city oasis. Remarkable, considering how parched and brown it was in their yard back home. Except it wasn't home. The house with the welcoming deck, the art studio, and the gorgeous view of the woods was only temporary. Tyne needed to remember that. This loud, scary city was Hadley's home, and she wanted to take Owen away from his family and bring him to live here instead. The fact Boston had one nice garden to walk through hardly redeemed the situation.

Tyne strode past the pond, watching one of the iconic swan boats make its lazy way through the water. Well, lazy for the passengers, though not for the worker who pedaled furiously to keep the thing moving. A little boy waved from his mother's lap. He was maybe a year older than Owen, and Tyne imagined how much her little tyke would love taking a ride when he was that age.

Tyne could see him now, reaching his hands in the air and then clutching hers with one and Hadley's with the other. That had been his thing recently when Tyne and Hadley were in close proximity. He'd hold on to both of them, with that big goofy, innocent smile, and pull himself up, eagerly preparing for that moment in the not-too-distant future when he'd take his first step. By next summer he'd be running all over the place, harder to catch than a greased pig. She and Hadley would be begging him to hold their hands then, probably wondering why on earth they'd ever looked forward to him learning to walk.

Only it wouldn't be the three of them next summer. Just two.

Tyne realized a tear was rolling down her cheek. She flicked it away.

It's not like they'd never see the woman again. Once she got permanent custody of Owen, Tyne would insist his other aunt got to see him. Tyne wasn't a monster. In fact, in this fight, she was the little guy, the David against Hadley's Goliath. She couldn't afford to shed tears.

Toward the middle of the garden, a statue of George Washington stood out against the deep azure sky. Tyne paused when she reached it. Now, there was a person who had known what it was like to be the underdog. He'd fought against a rich and powerful tyrant and come out on top. No way had Washington cried into his hankie because he was going to miss having tea with King George. She needed to be more like him.

Of course, George Washington had owned slaves, which made him a bit of a tyrant himself. All that talk about freedom was a little ironic, given the circumstances. Kind of like Tyne calling herself an underdog when she'd secured the services of a lawyer every inch as cutthroat as Hadley's.

Maybe she was more like George Washington than she'd thought.

After exiting the garden, Tyne waited for the light to turn green so she could cross to the other side of Beacon Street. This turned out to be pointless. Eventually, even though the light was still very much red, enough pedestrians congregated at the corner that they outnumbered the cars. As soon as this magical tipping point was reached, it was as if someone blew a whistle and everyone stepped off the curb and into the street with zero regard for traffic safety. Tyne went along with the crowd. By the time the light turned green, there was no one left waiting to cross. What a strange city.

The moment she started down Charles Street, Tyne felt like she'd stepped into a different world. Gone were the towering glass buildings of downtown. Here it was all old brick, and the street lamps were powered by gas. To say Beacon Hill looked like a high rent area didn't begin to describe it.

While the rest of the state leaned toward good ol'

blue collar Dunkin Donuts as the coffee of choice, a massive Starbucks stood guard on the corner as if to proclaim exactly what this neighborhood was all about. The clientele on their laptops appeared so high-brow Tyne doubted they allowed aspiring authors through the doors. You probably had to produce a publishing contract before they would give you the Wi-Fi password.

A little way down at a table for two on the sidewalk outside a chic restaurant, a couple took slices from a pizza topped with prosciutto and asparagus. They had a preschooler with them, who eagerly bit into a slice of her own, and Tyne realized with a profound sense of wonder that there existed in the upper echelon of society some number of children who thought those toppings on a pizza were normal.

The street Hadley had told her to turn down was quiet, with leafy trees and cobblestones. Tyne rechecked the address on her phone to ensure this was indeed the right place. She had a moment of panic, wondering if someone was going to stop her and ask to see a copy of her bank statement before letting her continue. With a sinking feeling, the full weight of what she was up against pressed down on her like a hand from the heavens.

If the judge decided where Owen should live based on neighborhood alone, Hadley would win, hands down. Setting aside for a moment the fact Tyne didn't even have a permanent home for him yet, no matter what she found would be nothing like this. Was she insane for thinking she would win? Perhaps. But even more important, was she wrong to try?

Boston was an amazing city, full of culture and opportunity, and Owen had a chance to live in the heart of it. He would attend the best schools. He'd live next door to doctors and lawyers. Hell, from the looks of it, he'd probably go to school with future ambassadors, too. Maybe she was being selfish, denying Owen these opportunities.

But raising a child was about more than a house or a school. If he grew up in Boston, Owen would be hours away from his family. He'd miss out on time with his grandparents, game nights, and backyard barbecues. Worst of all, he'd become one of those kids who thought it was okay to put asparagus on pizza.

If only she knew for certain the right thing to do.

At the deafening gong of a bell directly above her, Tyne's feet ground to a halt. She stood in front of a magnificent church. The doors were open, and if she hadn't already done so, the glow of the stained glass inside would've stopped her in her tracks. An other-worldly aroma of spicy incense wafted on the air, because around here, even the churches tried a little harder to impress.

"You found it!"

"Oh, good God," Tyne yelped, placing a hand on her heart, now busy clobbering her rib cage. Hadley appeared from around the corner, her voice even more startling than the bell.

"You found God? Well, this is the place for it," Hadley teased. "I was afraid you couldn't follow my directions and got lost."

"If I had, would that count as losing my religion?" Tyne grinned at her corny joke.

"An R.E.M. reference? Wow, what was that, 1991? I think I was in Miss Jones's fourth grade class when that song came out. How about you?" When Tyne remained silent, Hadley's eyes widened. "Holy shit, you weren't alive yet, were you?"

"Technically, I was alive," Tyne replied, dodging as best as she could. "And it's a great song."

"Admit it." Hadley crossed her arms. "You were a fetus."

"It still counts. Go in and ask." Tyne jerked a thumb toward the church. "I'm sure they'd agree."

"Thanks, but that's a can of worms I'd rather not open." Hadley let out a slight laugh. "I can't believe I forgot."

"Forgot what?"

"How young you are."

Tyne thought for a moment. "You could just as easily have said how *old* I am, you know. It means the same thing. Depends what you want to focus on."

"I suppose you're right." Hadley drew a deep breath. "Before we go to dinner, I want to show you something. It's right around the block. We can head to the restaurant from there."

Tyne looked down at her Capri pants and peasant blouse. "Will I need to change first?"

"Change? Of course not." Hadley held Tyne's gaze long enough that Tyne felt a tingling down her spine. "You're absolutely perfect."

Did Hadley mean Tyne's clothes were perfect for the restaurant, or had she been speaking more broadly? Tyne cast a wary glance at the open church door, knowing how far from an angel she really was. Her stomach knotted. When Robert Atkinson got ahold of Hadley, she would know it, too.

-᠕᠕᠕᠊-

TYNE FOLLOWED Hadley back to Charles Street and down a block in the opposite direction from where she'd come earlier. They stopped in front of a shop window, and Hadley made a ta-da motion with her arms. "What do you think?"

Tyne's breath caught as she took in the paintings on display in the storefront. "It's an art gallery."

"I pass it every time I walk to work. After I saw what you were working on in the studio at home the other day, I knew I had to bring you here." Hadley swung the door open.

An older woman with gray hair pulled into a severe bun stood toward the back of the gallery, speaking with exasperation into the landline telephone she held to her ear. "What do you mean they're held up in customs? Damn it, Greg. I've got a buyer lined up for one of the pieces, and he's going to walk if he can't have it by the end of June. Not to mention the big blank spot on the wall I'm going to have all summer where the other one's supposed to be." She held up a hand, making a welcome gesture to Hadley and Tyne. "I don't need excuses. I need you to fix it." She slammed the receiver back into its cradle and smiled. "Sorry about that, but there is something so satisfying about a phone that slams. It's one thing we're missing in this digital age."

"I hope we didn't come at a bad time," Hadley said. "I've walked past this place on my way to work so many times and have always wanted to stop."

"Where do you work?" The woman asked.

"The hospital," Hadley answered.

"A doctor?" When Hadley nodded, the gallery owner's eyes lit up, probably seeing dollar signs in her future. "I'm glad you came in this time. You ladies look around, and don't mind me and my temper. The downside of working with artists. Most unreliable people in the world. Whatever you do, avoid artists."

Tyne stifled a giggle, but not thoroughly enough to escape the woman's attention.

"What is it?"

"Nothing." Tyne waved her hand, almost shaking now from the laughter she was holding in.

"She's an artist," Hadley said.

The woman burst out in a hearty laugh of her own. "Of course. Wouldn't you know? I do beg your pardon. Clearly, I'm off my game today."

"It's okay," Tyne said. "I'm a business owner as well, so I know how frustrating it can be when shipments run late."

"That explains why I didn't get an artist vibe from you," the woman said. "Well, that, and you didn't come in here clutching a portfolio and begging me to hang your painting in the front window."

"People do that?" Tyne was horrified. It would never have occurred to her to do something so tactless.

"You wouldn't believe some of the things I've seen in the thirty years since I opened this place." The woman stuck out her hand. "I'm Sheila, by the way."

"Tyne." She shook the woman's hand. "And this is Hadley."

"Nice to meet you both. So, Tyne, what type of business do you run? An art gallery?"

"Nothing so glamorous," Tyne replied. "I have a paint and sip studio out west where I teach classes several nights a week. Kind of silly compared to..." Tyne let her sentence die as her eyes took in her surroundings.

"Honey, running a gallery is anything but glamorous, and I don't think yours sounds silly at all. I've seen those places. Lots of rich ladies with money to spend, looking for a way to unwind. It seems like a solid business model to me, and better than the idiots I have to deal with sometimes." Sheila made a face that revealed exactly what she thought of her job after three decades. "I'm about at my breaking point today, though."

"What happened?" Hadley asked.

"What happened is my assistant, Greg, forgot to file the appropriate customs forms. Again. And now I'm short several paintings, and he's trying to blame it on bureaucratic red tape, like I don't know any better." Sheila let out a sigh as she rolled her eyes. "I don't suppose you brought any paintings with you. This is the one time I might've welcomed an artist coming in with a portfolio, because it sure looks like I'll have unexpected space to fill."

Tyne pointed to her outfit. "Afraid I didn't have room in my pockets tonight for any paintings."

"I did," Hadley said, causing both Tyne and Sheila to whip their heads in her direction. She pulled out her phone and held it up. "Well, sort of. I snapped a couple pictures of your work in progress, Tyne. If you don't mind me sharing."

Tyne's heart skipped a beat even as her cheeks flushed at the prospect of showing a stranger her unfinished work. "I don't know. It's not done yet."

"Oh, come on," Sheila urged. "You've got me curious now. I'd love to see it."

"Okay, fine." Tyne covered her eyes with her hands. "You can show her, but I can't watch."

It was silent for several seconds, and Tyne thought she might keel over and die. Then Sheila spoke. "This is really your work?"

Tyne separated her fingers wide enough to have a peek at Hadley's screen. She nodded. That was her painting all right. Sheila probably thought it looked totally amateur and was searching for the right words to let her down gently.

"How big is it?"

Since Tyne was still mostly hiding behind her hands, Hadley held out her arms, giving a general indication of the canvas size.

"Is it available?" Sheila asked.

Tyne's fingers fell away from her face. "For what?"

"Display," Sheila said. "Purchase?"

"Well, it's..." Tyne's mind raced. "As I said, it's not quite finished, but, uh, I guess so."

"When do you think you'll finish it? Because that shipment Greg bungled was supposed to be here at the end of June. Could you have it ready before then?"

"I..." This turn of events left Tyne stunned, and she could barely get her mouth to move. "Uh-huh."

"Great." Sheila handed over a business card. "Give me a call as soon as it's done, and I'll arrange for someone to go pick it up. You're out in western Massachusetts, you say?"

"Yes, we are," Hadley said when Tyne was still too shocked to speak. "It's a tiny town no one's ever heard of, about half an hour from Amherst."

Her wits returning to her, Tyne found a scrap of paper and scribbled the address of her studio. "Afraid I don't have any business cards with me, but this is the address of my place. Unless, should I give her our house address, too? That's where the painting is."

Tyne asked this of Hadley, who quickly rattled off the address.

Sheila wrote it down and smiled at Hadley. "What a stroke of good luck for me you and the missus decided to come in today. You two have a lovely evening."

Tyne nearly floated out the door, barely registering that the gallery owner had assumed she and Hadley were a couple, and certainly not occurring to her to set the woman straight on the matter.

CHAPTER FIFTEEN

The restaurant Hadley had chosen was in the Seaport District, and though its exterior was the glass and chrome typical of so many Boston establishments that catered mostly to the financial district's executive lunch crowd, the inside was far from humdrum. Three walls were painted in shades of cream, with tablecloths and chairs in similar hues, but at that hour, as the sun was setting, the dining room's dominant color was purple. This was due to the spectacular evening sky that appeared to form the building's fourth wall, which was actually composed of floor to ceiling windows that afforded an expansive view of the harbor.

As soon as they stepped inside where Tyne could see, the artist gave a tiny gasp. Hadley smiled. She'd chosen well.

Tyne whispered, "I don't think I'm dressed up enough for this—"

"Don't be silly." Hadley assured her. "I've come here in my scrubs."

Tyne shot her a dubious look. "Totally not buying that, just so you know."

"Okay, maybe not scrubs, but the dress code for dinner is business casual at best. I promise." Hadley pointed to a man at a nearby table who was wearing shorts and a shirt with rolled-up sleeves. "See? Now, if this were lunchtime, executives would probably be in suits, but with as hot as it was today, even city dwellers know how to dress for comfort."

Tyne's body visibly relaxed as they followed the host to their table, and from the many tables they passed, it became clear their clothing blended in fine. When the host pulled out Tyne's seat, a momentary return of self-consciousness flickered across her face. It relieved Hadley to see that by the time he'd handed Tyne a napkin, her confidence had returned. This was supposed to be a fun evening, and the last thing she wanted was for Tyne to feel uncomfortable with Hadley's restaurant choice.

"Adam will be your server tonight," the host announced, presenting them each with their own menu encased in a thick leather binder. "And the special of the evening is a surf and turf combo of baked lobster tail with a delicate drizzle of brandy mustard, paired with our braised beef short ribs au poivre in a sherry wine reduction."

Hadley set her menu aside and wiggled in her seat. "I think I know what I'm having."

As the host departed, Tyne bit her lower lip. "What did he say? He lost me at the brandy mustard part."

"Basically, it's steak and lobster with some fancy sauces on the side," Hadley translated then tensed as she realized Tyne, being a sensitive artistic type, might have moral qualms about the meal. "Are you okay with lobster? I should have asked your preference. It's not a whole one, so no eyes or anything, but I don't have to order it if it bothers you."

"Who in their right mind doesn't like lobster?" Tyne looked at her like she'd grown a second head. "I've been eating it ever since my first vacation to Maine the summer after I came to live with my family."

At ease once more, Hadley laughed. "Phew. My mouth was so set for lobster I might've cried if you asked me to order something else."

"I wouldn't want that." Tyne toyed with the edge of her menu. "Have you ever been to the lobster shack at the Cape Elizabeth Lighthouse, outside Portland?"

Hadley shook her head.

"It's a hole in the wall kind of place, but their lobster rolls are to die for. The problem is all of their sides are equally as divine. Before you know it, the bill's as high as a five-star restaurant, yet you're sitting outside at a picnic table, eating with a plastic fork."

Tyne licked her lips as if reliving the experience. It was a totally innocent action that nonetheless triggered a forceful zing that made Hadley shift in her chair. There would be none of *that* this evening. This was not a date, and even if it might be nice to fantasize that it was, Hadley couldn't afford to give into the temptation considering how much their last slipup had derailed their blossoming friendship.

"Do you know when they open for the season?" Hadley asked, because talking about something safe was her best option for keeping her libido under control.

"Early May, I think." Tyne's face brightened. "We could take Owen. It would be like a family vacation."

"He can't eat lobster." But even as she laughed off the suggestion, Hadley's heart beat faster at the word *family*. Could that magical word apply to them?

Of course, it can, Hadley reminded herself sternly. They were both Owen's aunts, which made them family to him. That was certainly all Tyne had meant, even if Hadley's brain liked to torture her by reading more meaning into it than she should.

"Oh, I don't know. He's got quite a few teeth now, and it's best to start him young. We can't raise a child who doesn't know how to eat lobster."

We? As in together? The little pitter-patter her heart had been doing before turned into the entire percussion section of a marching band. With talk like this, not to mention the offer Tyne had gotten from Sheila at the art gallery earlier, could it be they were closer to a compromise on the Owen situation than Hadley had dared hope?

A server came to the table, placing a water bottle in between them, along with a basket of bread that tickled Hadley's nose with a delightful, *right out of the oven* smell. "My name's Adam, and it will be my pleasure to serve you this evening. Would you like to see the wine list?"

"Yes, please," Hadley responded, taking the list from the server's hand.

"Water's fine with me," Tyne said, looking a little fidgety. She could definitely use a glass of wine as much as Hadley could.

"Nonsense. It's always a better deal to get a half bottle." Hadley scanned the menu. "Here we go. How about the 2016 Poliziano Vino Nobile di Montalcino?"

The space between Tyne's brow creased. "Is that white or red?"

"Red." When her dinner companion didn't react with an immediate no, Hadley turned to the server. "We'll take that one and two glasses, please."

"Certainly. And have you decided what you'll be having tonight?"

"I think so," Hadley said.

At the same time Tyne answered, "Actually, I haven't looked at the menu."

"Not a problem," Adam said with a little bow. "I'll be back in a few minutes."

"I'm sorry," Hadley said after he left. "I thought we were on the same page with the surf and turf."

"I should take a quick look. See what they have." Tyne cracked open the menu. As her eyes scanned the page, she swallowed, her face turning a little green. "Where... uh, where is the surf and turf listed? I don't see it, or a price, or anything."

"Oh, it's the evening special. It won't be on there."

Tyne pressed her lips together as she checked the menu again. "How do you know what it costs?"

"I don't know." Hadley shrugged. "I'm sure it's fair, whatever it is."

Tyne nodded but didn't seem convinced. She flipped the page. "You know, this roasted beet salad with goat cheese sounds fantastic."

"It does," Hadley agreed. "Are you going to get that, too? Because if you do, I might have to steal a bite."

"No, I meant instead of the other one."

"Instead?" Hadley frowned. "I thought you said you love lobster. This place is famous for it."

"I'm not sure I have much of an appetite."

Hadley opened her own menu, searching until she found the salad Tyne had mentioned. When she read the description, she shook her head. It was going to be tiny. If that was all she ordered, Tyne was going to starve.

"Honey, that's not even meant to be an entrée. You can tell by the—" She'd been about to say the word *price* when it clicked. How could she have been so dumb and insensitive? Tyne had tried to pass up the wine and was forgoing the meal she wanted because of how much it all cost. "Please, order anything you want, and don't give it a second thought. Dinner's my treat."

"But—"

"No buts. It's a simple rule of hospitality. You're my house guest, and I'm the one who was too lazy to cook you a proper dinner."

"I can't let you do that. Aren't you the one who quit your job today?"

"I asked for a leave of absence. It's not the same thing. Granted, the way Michael reacted, you'd think I asked for time off to go club baby seals."

"Michael's the asshole Chief of Staff?"

"That's the one. He hates my guts at the moment, but rest assured I'm still gainfully employed for the foreseeable future and perfectly capable of paying for dinner."

"Even so, I didn't expect—"

Hadley held up a hand to stop her.

"I picked the restaurant and didn't even run it past you. I'm not taking no for an answer. You might as well give up because I never compromise." A fleeting look of hurt passed over Tyne's face, stabbing Hadley in the gut as she remembered the much larger battle they were in the middle of. No wonder her word choice hadn't landed well. "I'm not going to compromise about this."

They placed their orders when Adam returned, and though Tyne joined her in getting the special and didn't put up a fuss when Hadley added not only the beet salad but also smoked gouda and bacon au gratin potatoes, roasted shaved Brussels sprouts, and sautéed mushrooms to top both the steaks, Hadley couldn't decide if she should be glad.

The reminder of the custody dispute was still painfully fresh, piled on top of all the conflicting emotions she experienced whenever she and Tyne were together. Hadley's head was spinning. Until a month ago, work had been Hadley's sole focus. Then, in the midst of grief and loss, she'd found Owen. And Tyne. Now everything was so confusing, to the point she barely knew which end was up or who she was half the time.

For instance, when Hadley had proposed this trip to Boston, she had no idea what she'd been thinking. Or rather, she knew all sorts of things she'd been thinking, and all of them conflicted. There'd been guilt over the demands her lawyer had talked her into making, and shame at having given in because she hated to lose. But there had been excitement, too. And wild daydreams about the future she barely dared acknowledge.

Showing Tyne her neighborhood and introducing

her to the art gallery down the street had been the highlight of the trip. After fantasizing about it so much, the actual visit couldn't have gone better. It had felt like fate was moving all the chess pieces around for the perfect win. But was Hadley fooling herself?

Here she was, sitting back and enjoying the moment, letting life wash over her, in a way she never had before. She could barely remember the last time she'd gone out to a nice restaurant with someone who wasn't a colleague from work. She'd almost forgotten that was a thing. But here she was, treating Tyne to a night out on the town and soaking in the pleasure of knowing the most beautiful person in the entire restaurant was hers.

At least for the night.

The pain of loss was still there, never far from the surface, but when she and Tyne were together, Hadley felt hope. She didn't know how she would cope if that went away. But she didn't know what to do to make it stay.

The server returned with the bottle of wine and went through the whole routine that they always do in top-quality restaurants, like they're pouring water from the Fountain of Youth into the Holy Grail. When he splashed some ruby red liquid into the glass for Hadley to test, she pointed to Tyne.

"Why don't you taste it? See if you approve."

Tyne's face turned a beautiful shade of strawberry, but she took the tiniest of sips. "Perfect."

Hadley couldn't have said it better herself, though she wasn't thinking about wine.

Hadley looked out the window at one of the Boston Harbor cruise ships doing its thing. "I've missed the ocean. That's one of the many drawbacks to life in western Mass."

Tyne swept her wineglass to her lips, taking a sip before speaking. "I try to get to the ocean as much as possible, but you're right. It can be a challenge."

"Do you go to paint?" Hadley could picture her standing on the sand with an easel, the breeze blowing her hair.

"Landscapes aren't really my style, although I've done a few. But mostly my work is more abstract." Tyne gave a slight eye roll. "Unless we're talking about the paintings I do in class. There's nothing abstract about an owl wearing a Gryffindor-colored scarf."

"I kinda liked that one," Hadley admitted with a laugh. "I was sorry that wasn't the one we did the night I went."

"I'll keep that in mind the next time I convince you to come to the studio with me."

Hadley's throat constricted as she met Tyne's unwavering gaze and recalled in vivid detail what had happened the last time they'd been in the studio together. Hadley reached for a glass, skipping her wine and opting for ice water. Was it getting warm in here?

"How do you get your inspiration?" Hadley asked

once the cold drink had brought her temperature down.

"Oh, gosh, I'm not sure I can explain it. People always ask artists that question, but I bet no one asks you how you decide what treatment to give a patient."

"Honestly? I toss a dart at the symptom board I keep on the back of the exam room door and hope it won't let me down." Hadley crossed the fingers on both hands like she'd thrown the dice at a Vegas craps table. "Come on, penicillin!"

Tyne's eyes were wide as saucers. "Really?"

"No!" Hadley dissolved into a fit of laughter. "Most cases are pretty straightforward in the ER. I do a lot of setting broken bones and sewing stitches. But, there are some that are harder, like solving a riddle. Those are the most rewarding."

Then there were the hopeless ones, where there were no answers because nothing would make it right. Those were the ones that ripped a doctor's heart out. Like Kayleigh and Ryan. Those were the ones that extinguished your faith, leaving you cold and dark inside.

She reached for her wine, needing to lock up that memory. Not tonight, of all nights. It was four weeks ago exactly that Hadley had received that terrible call.

"Riddles. I can relate to that," Tyne said.

From her chipper tone, Tyne hadn't noticed the change in Hadley's demeanor. Or perhaps she had and was doing her part to give Hadley the time needed to regroup. Knowing Tyne, that was the more likely explanation.

"How so?" Hadley encouraged, desperately craving the soothing sound of Tyne's voice as she struggled to put herself back together.

"The actual answer to your question about how creatives find that spark is it comes from all over." Tyne turned her head toward the window. "Like, I'll see the way the moonlight is bouncing along the water. Or the way a beam of light can practically pierce an object. I get these visions—like bursts—and then I do my best to capture them on the canvas."

"But not the actual scene, like a landscape?"

"No, more like the essence." Ever so briefly, Tyne's eyes shone with something so beautiful it defied description. Hadley's heart stood still. But then Tyne's cheeks tinged pink. "I really can't explain it, and I probably sound insane right now."

"Not at all. You sound passionate. That's a trait I admire." Hadley lifted her glass in the air. "To passion."

-\/\/\/\-

AS THE UBER pulled up outside of Hadley's apartment, she feared it would take Herculean effort to hoist herself, and her overstuffed belly, out of the back seat. She managed it, barely, then stuck her hand out for Tyne. A swift electric zap zinged through

Hadley's body at the touch, which she vowed to ignore.

"I can't believe we ordered dessert." Tyne seemed unsteady on her feet, not as a result of wine since they had kept that to a minimum but from a similar overindulgence to Hadley. "I just felt so bad that Adam had to wheel the dessert cart all the way out from the kitchen. It took so much effort that it felt rude saying no."

"And it was impossible to decide between vanilla bean panna cotta or the homemade salted caramel gelato," Hadley added, punching in the security code to open the main door to her building. "We had to get both."

"Exactly. But now—flat." Tyne made an adorable motion with her hand, indicating she needed to lie down right then and there.

"My condo's all the way on the third floor," Hadley joked. "Do you think you can make it?"

"Are you offering to carry me?" Bemusement danced in Tyne's eyes.

"I guess we'll find out." Hadley crouched down as if to let Tyne hop onto her back. "Come on; up you go. I'll try not to fall down the stairs and break both our necks."

"On second thought, maybe I should try on my own. A broken neck sounds bad."

"As a doctor, I can assure you it's not recommended."

"Thank heaven for an expert opinion," Tyne teased. "Otherwise, I wouldn't have been sure."

When they reached her landing, Hadley spotted a bright yellow note taped to her door. "Huh. Let's see what happened this time."

"What is it?" Tyne asked.

"Maintenance. Any time they enter a unit when you're not home, they leave a bright and cheerful note to let you know they were here and what they had to do." Hadley looked over the chicken scratch that passed for an explanation. Frowning, she handed it to Tyne. "Any idea?"

Tyne shook her head. "Didn't they teach you to decipher terrible handwriting in medical school?"

"No, only how to write in it." Hadley unlocked her front door and gestured for Tyne to step inside. "Normally, I'd give you the grand tour, but I think you mentioned something about needing to be flat."

"Please. Before my stomach explodes, which I've heard is also high on the *not very good* list, medically speaking."

"Definitely in the top ten."

Hadley quickly led Tyne through the living room and down a staircase that connected her main floor with the lower level where the bedrooms and office were located. The guest room door was the first one on the right. Just beyond it, she glimpsed her own bedroom door, which provoked a twinge of sadness since they wouldn't both be staying there. She'd lost track of how many times that night she'd had to remind herself she wasn't on a date, and she needed to keep herself under control. Hadley opened the guest room door and flipped on the switch without looking inside. Having to look at the spot Tyne would actually spend the night—alone—felt like unnecessarily pouring salt into her wound. "Here you go."

"Uh, Hadley?" Tyne's confused tone verged on frantic.

"What?" As soon as she turned and got a look at the room, she knew exactly what had made Tyne sound that way. "Oh, fuck."

Usually pristine, bordering on clinical, Hadley's guest room currently looked more like a war zone. Tarps were draped over every surface, an open tool box sat on the floor, and where one wall and part of a ceiling had been, there was now a gaping hole that exposed all the plumbing belonging to the adjacent guest bath. From the look of things, there'd been a sizable leak from the unit above in her absence.

"I think I know what that maintenance note was all about," Tyne said, attempting a weak but unconvincing laugh.

"Oh my God, I am so sorry." Hadley shut off the light and closed the door with a shudder. "My bedroom is right over here. My housekeeper's been by since I left, so the sheets are clean, and there should be fresh towels in the master bathroom. I just need a minute to grab a couple blankets and a pillow."

"For what?"

"To bring to the living room sofa."

"I can't make you sleep on the couch in your own house," Tyne argued.

"Well, I can't make a guest sleep on the couch, and it's my house, so I make the rules."

Tyne locked eyes on Hadley. "Stop being so fucking bossy and trying to control everything. We're rational adults. We're perfectly capable of sharing a bed without any shenanigans."

Hadley arched an eyebrow. "Are we?"

Tyne's expression grew more sheepish. "In theory."

A wave of exhaustion overtaking her, Hadley couldn't suppress a loud yawn. "I'm too tired to argue. You win."

"Is that all it takes?" Tyne laughed. "Filing that discovery away for later."

Hadley donned a silky nightshirt while Tyne went into the bathroom to change, emerging wearing a pair of loose sleeping shorts and T-shirt with an illustration of a kitten holding a cup of coffee.

"Cute," Hadley said with a gesture toward the shirt when she realized she'd been staring.

"What, no floor-length flannel?" Tyne grinned, and Hadley laughed at the reminder of the terrible night-gown Tyne had seen her in at her parents' house.

After brushing their teeth, they slid under the covers of Hadley's thankfully very large bed, each one careful not to touch the other or encroach on foreign territory on the opposite side of the mattress. In what seemed like seconds after the lights were off, Tyne had drifted to sleep. Hadley laid on her back, staring at the ceiling, enjoying the sound of Tyne's even breathing. After a while, Hadley counted the seconds between each breath, as if in a trance.

Under the circumstances, sleep was going to be impossible, but she tried shutting her eyes anyway, hoping for at least a small bit of rest.

The next thing she knew, Hadley was answering her phone. "This is Dr. Moore."

"There's been an accident. If you don't come now, Kayleigh will die."

Hadley was in the ER. Kayleigh's broken and bloody body rushed past her on the gurney.

Hadley snapped to attention, opening her mouth to shout for someone to start chest compressions. No sound came out. Her mouth filled with a thick, clear gelatin. It surrounded her. She kicked her legs, trying to swim through it, but she was sinking. Drowning.

"We're losing her!" a voice shouted. "Why didn't you save her?"

"No!" Hadley's chest burned as she struggled to breathe. She kicked at the blankets that were wrapped around her legs, gasping as she gulped in air.

"Hadley?"

"No," she whimpered. Where was she? Where was her sister?

"Hadley, it's okay." The nightlight on the bedside

table came on with a click, and Hadley could sense the dim glow through her closed lids. A warm body pressed against her back. An arm held onto Hadley, making soothing sounds in her ear. "It's okay. I've got you."

"Don't let go." Hadley was awake now, mostly, but she didn't want to open her eyes, didn't want to move. She wanted to stay this way, safe, forever.

"It's all right, Hadley." Tyne's voice was soft and calm. "You're okay. Everything's okay."

But it's not, a voice in Hadley's head cried. *Nothing is okay.*

"They're gone." Hadley's shoulders shook, and she couldn't stop the sobs.

"I know." Tyne held her tighter. "Shhhh, I know."

And she did. Hadley knew Tyne was the one person who did. Having Tyne hold her when she cried was better than any medicine, stronger than any drug she could find. But it was so impossible. Why did it have to feel so good?

Tyne nestled her face into Hadley's hair, her arm tightening around her just under Hadley's breasts. Close enough to be provocative but far enough away to be safe. Which somehow felt about as safe as standing in a room with a hungry tiger on a chain and being assured it *probably* wasn't long enough to reach you.

Hadley would rather risk being eaten alive than push Tyne away.

The fiery sensation of Tyne's closeness, which

hovered somewhere between pouring liquid sunshine or hot lava through her veins, consumed her. Her crying subsided, the sting of grief fading, but as it did, every other emotion she'd been tamping down since the very first time she and Tyne kissed swamped her.

All at once, she knew what had been missing from all those daydreams, all those master plans she'd been cooking up for her and Owen's future. Tyne. Not as an occasional visitor in their lives, in *her* life, but a permanent fixture. She hadn't let her heart hope for it, but she didn't think she could stop it now if she tried. She wanted Tyne beside her like this always, during the good times and bad.

But especially now. She needed her so badly right now.

As if Tyne understood her unspoken thoughts, Hadley felt her place a light kiss on the back of her head. As Hadley sank into her, Tyne shifted, and Hadley rolled onto her back. Tyne placed a hand on Hadley's cheek, soft fingers flicking away the remnants of tears.

Hadley gazed up into Tyne's eyes. So gentle and full of comfort but maybe something else lurking deeper. It was the same look of heartbreaking, indescribable beauty she'd had when she'd spoken to Hadley about the essence of her creativity. The embodiment of passion.

Unless Hadley was imagining it.

Tyne bent nearer, as if to kiss her, but Hadley put up her hand to hold her back.

"Is this you feeling sorry for me?"

Tyne's face clouded with confusion. "Why would I feel sorry for you?"

"I'm crying. You want me to feel better."

"I was planning to make you feel *good*. Actually, both of us." Tyne's eyes twinkled with mischief. "It's not quite the same thing as better. Don't you want that?"

Damn. Hadley had never wanted anything so badly. But she had to know one thing first.

"Is that all this is, making ourselves feel good? Is that what it is to you?"

If she says yes, you have to say no.

No matter how good it might feel in the moment, the pain later on would be unbearable because Hadley wanted so much more.

"No." There was enough fear in Tyne's eyes that Hadley knew she was telling the truth. "That's not all it is. Do you trust me?"

"Yes."

Hadley trembled wildly as Tyne took the hand that had held her at arm's length and raised it to her lips, kissing it. Tyne stared down at Hadley for an unbelievably long time before her mouth found Hadley's. The dam broke, and neither of them could deny what was right in front of their eyes, let alone hold it back any longer.

A knee separated Hadley's legs. Tyne climbed on top. She shoved Hadley's nightshirt up, baring her breasts and giving access to a nipple. Tyne giggled as she chose a side and playfully allowed her teeth to sink in.

Hadley let out a gasp.

As Tyne's hands roamed freely, Hadley tried to reach between Tyne's legs. This time her way was blocked. When she tried again, she met with the same result. Hadley let out a low growl.

Letting go of her nipple, Tyne sat up enough so Hadley could see her flash a triumphant grin. "Nope. You've tried that trick before."

Hadley frowned. She liked to be in charge. She needed it.

But it was possible she needed Tyne more, so she tried a softer approach.

"Please?"

"No."

"Pretty please?" This time she batted her eyelashes.

Tyne gave her a *quit goofing off* look. "You know, if you stop trying to control everything all the time, you might end up winning anyway. We both might."

It went against her nature, but suddenly Hadley wanted Tyne to possess her body tonight with more urgency than she'd ever experienced before. She needed the woman's touch. Craved it. Every caress and kiss seemed to hold the power to heal her soul, sealing the promise of more.

With a slight nod, Hadley put her hands above her head and lay still.

Waiting.

Tyne stripped her nightshirt the rest of the way off. Then her hands were on Hadley's underwear, not wasting a moment before tugging them down. Keeping her hands behind her head, Hadley shifted, her legs falling open as she surrendered herself completely to Tyne's control.

Each kiss sent delicious shivers through her as Tyne worked her way downward, mouth and tongue forging a bold path. Hadley's aching need intensified with every inch.

"Oh, God," Hadley cried out when she thought she couldn't stand it anymore.

Tyne didn't stop.

Closer and closer.

The gentle prodding of a finger at her opening gave way to the most satisfying fullness as Tyne entered her. She let out an excited noise, halfway between a whimper and scream.

She needed more.

And then it happened. Tyne's mouth was on her, claiming her. A tongue circled Hadley's clit, teasing then intensifying. Hadley fought her urge to direct, to take control, letting herself be swept away to whatever destination Tyne had in store for her.

Holy fuck.

It was so amazing.

How long had it been since she'd felt this?

Had she ever?

She couldn't recall. It didn't matter. There was no past, only the present.

Just here and now, the plunging of fingers and stroke of a tongue, driving everything else out of existence.

Only Tyne's touch could make her feel this way, as if everything in the world would be okay.

As long as they were together.

The beginning of an orgasm started to swell, rapidly reaching its crest.

Another finger joined the first, sliding in and out with ever-increasing speed.

She bucked off the bed, cradling Tyne's head, calling out her name as she came.

After the strongest waves had passed, Tyne's tongue continued lapping slowly, sending new bolts of ecstasy through her, finally bringing Hadley home.

Home.

The word echoed in her mind as if she'd said it out loud.

It was what Hadley had been searching for, what she'd been lacking without ever knowing it. But now she knew. She wanted a home with Tyne. She never wanted to be apart.

She felt good.

And Tyne had been right.

Everything was okay.

CHAPTER SIXTEEN

What the hell have I done?

Tyne rolled an inch at a time as she tried to get from her side to her back, holding her breath and praying not to wake Hadley. The mattress was deep and fluffy, one of those expensive brands with a pillow top and special springs that promised to absorb all movement. However much it had cost, it didn't live up to the hype. Tyne felt the shift and braced herself.

A moment later, Hadley's hand smashed into Tyne's face. Tyne sniffed, sensing a trickle of blood. It wasn't Hadley's fault. It's not like she'd meant to hurt her. The woman was sound asleep and, apparently, not nearly as graceful with her body parts when comatose as she was during waking hours. It was the third time Tyne's escape attempt had been thwarted in such a manner, though the other two times had not drawn blood.

Fuck.

The trickle was turning into a drip. Tyne really needed to get out of bed immediately. The urgency was no longer just because the litany of self-recrimination and regret racing through her head had her on high alert status and unable to sleep. She desperately required a tissue before she bled all over Hadley's extremely high thread count sheets.

This is what you get, her brain informed her as she made a mad dash for the edge of the bed and slid out from under the covers, her bare feet hitting the cold floor. She could see clearly, like a giant subway map, how every one of her life choices had sent her barreling down a track to this exact moment in time, where the woman she had both betrayed and then seduced within less than twenty-four hours would inevitably smack her in the face while unconscious and give her a bloody nose. It was the obvious outcome, the culmination of twenty-nine years, as unavoidable as adding one plus one and always coming up with two.

What in God's name was I thinking?

Like God had anything to do with this mess.

Tyne tried to snort at this profound observation of hers, but since she was pinching her nostrils shut at the moment, the result was not a sound but a painful popping in her ears. Which she definitely deserved, along with any other punishment the universe could throw her way.

I am not a good person.

What was Hadley going to think once she found out the woman she had trusted so thoroughly with her body tonight, not to mention her heart, had signed on the dotted line to rake Hadley's life over the coals? The ink was barely dry.

What in God's name had she been thinking? No. She didn't get to blame God when she'd willingly entered into a contract with the Devil.

She retraced her steps through the darkness to find the bathroom, but since it was connected to the bedroom, Tyne couldn't risk turning on the light. Finding a box of tissues proved impossible, but Tyne managed to find the toilet paper roll and spin off a fistful. A few dabs revealed the wound was much less serious than she had feared, which was a lucky break.

Of course, if she had to choose, Tyne would have braved a busted nose and saved her luck for something she really needed. Like, what were the chances Robert Atkinson's office would burst into flames in the middle of the night and turn their contract into a handful of ashes?

A stray moonbeam filtered through a crack in the curtains that shaded a set of patio doors beside the bed. Still pressing the makeshift handkerchief to her nose, Tyne paused to watch the sleeping Hadley, her face looking so calm and beautiful. In the month since the accident, she'd rarely looked at peace. Grief wasn't the only source of her distress. Her return home had made her parents' decline real to her and highlighted how many unpleasant choices she would be forced to confront in the near future. Then there was Owen.

Though she hadn't wanted to believe it at first, seeing Hadley with their nephew left Tyne with no doubt that the woman loved him completely. Now that she'd glimpsed the life Hadley could offer him, it was impossible not to feel conflicted. But Tyne loved him, too. Otherwise, she wouldn't be fighting so hard to win. But had she been fighting too hard and lost sight of what was right?

With sleep nowhere on the horizon, Tyne padded up the stairs to the main floor. She'd hardly noticed anything on their way in, but now she took the opportunity to study her surroundings more closely. She could sum up her overall impression in two words: white and clean.

The kitchen cabinets and countertops were the color of pure snow, as were the chairs surrounding a dark dining room table. The walls were shades of light cream and taupe, and except for one that featured a large, rectangular, built-in glass fireplace, they were sparsely hung with paintings that were pleasant enough to look at but in no way spectacular. Aside from the art, a sofa of deep blue velvet and a dove gray armchair in the living room provided the only relief from the designer's thoroughly neutral palette.

That a professional designer was responsible was a given. The space was as impeccable as it was impersonal, like the condo had been staged for use as a model home. There wasn't a single trace of Hadley's personality to be seen.

It was only when she opened the kitchen cabinets in search of a water glass that Tyne got a sense of the woman who lived here. Hadley's very ordered mind made for an extremely logical arrangement of dishes, pots, and pans. Everything had a place. But instead of even more white, the plates were surprisingly whimsical, featuring deep shades of teal and sweet songbirds. Pint size glass tumblers were stamped with raised honeybees. When she spotted a stacked set of measuring cups shaped like brightly colored owls, Tyne couldn't help but smile.

No way had a designer chosen these things. Hadley Moore had been located at last.

But a single cupboard of cute kitchenware could hardly dispel the reality that Tyne and Hadley were as different as night and day. Tyne thrived in artistic chaos, while aside from the unfortunate construction zone that was the spare bedroom, there wasn't a speck of dust in Hadley's place.

Tyne chuckled to herself as she wondered what thoughts had raced through Hadley's mind the moment she'd taken in the mess downstairs. Tyne would pay money to listen in on that internal dialogue. She'd probably learn some swear words she'd never known existed. Poor Hadley. Of all the ways to end the evening.

Only that hadn't been the end of their evening, not by a long shot. Tyne had assured her they were grown-ups who could handle sleeping in close proximity without anyone's virtue being at stake. Had Tyne really believed her own words? Had Hadley?

Impossible. Neither one of them was stupid.

Although the way they were behaving, they both must be fools.

Why couldn't I keep my hands to myself tonight?

Tyne didn't need words to answer the question. Her body told her everything she needed to know. As cold as it was, standing barefoot in the kitchen wearing nothing but some skimpy nightclothes, the embers still smoldered in her core. The slightest thought of Hadley's scent, her taste, her touch, threatened to bring the flames roaring back to life.

Is that all this is, making ourselves feel good? Hadley's voice echoed in her head.

Tyne could see her face as she'd asked; Hadley's vulnerability had pierced straight through the middle of Tyne's heart. She'd sworn it wasn't. No matter what else she'd done to betray Hadley, that answer had been honest and true, God help her.

Sure, try to pin this on God again.

That she found Hadley attractive was a given. Tyne had known that for years, longer than the good doctor had even known her name. But there were plenty of attractive people in the world. Tyne had spent nights of passion with more than a few. But nothing in her life had ever felt like this. She and Hadley clicked in a way that defied explanation. How could they be so entirely different, yet fit together like two pieces of a puzzle?

But did they?

When everything felt so good and right, it was easy to forget that beneath the surface they were locked in a bloody battle over their nephew, both playing dirty. How could they be so hot and cold, and would they ever manage to meet in the middle? If they couldn't, everyone was going to get hurt.

Her throat tickled, and with a start, Tyne realized she was holding a water glass and still standing in front of an open cupboard. Closing it, she searched for the refrigerator and wasn't the least bit surprised to find the appliance was more hi-tech than Hadley's car. The dispenser in the door didn't just have a button for water and ice. It was Wi-Fi enabled, and the choices for ice included cubed, crushed, and craft.

What the hell was craft?

Tyne put her glass underneath and pressed the appropriate button to find out. Three of the most perfectly formed spheres of ice Tyne had ever seen dropped into the glass.

Are you fucking kidding me?

To top it all off, the door on the refrigerator side had a clear glass insert, with subtle back lighting. Hadley had filled this compartment with an assortment of things, like Icelandic yogurt and Italian sparkling water, that made it look like a display in an upscale supermarket. But in Tyne's imagination, dinosaur yogurt tubes and apple juice boxes lined the shelves.

Owen could grow up like this, if you step back and let him.

"No kid needs craft ice," she muttered to herself, knowing that was beside the point. What all kids needed was love, from as many people as possible.

Owen needed them both. And what Tyne felt in the depths of her soul, even if she couldn't quite say it in words, was that she and Hadley needed each other, too.

Right now, somewhere in an office high above the city of Boston, a contract with her signature on it threatened to destroy everything.

What am I going to do?

A door in the corner of the kitchen led to a small patio. Tyne opened it and stepped outside, oblivious to the chilly air. The sun hadn't made an appearance yet, but a faint blush of pink at the edge of the horizon told her it was on its way. She took a seat at the bistro table, big enough for two, and stared at a pointed steeple that must have belonged to the church where she'd met Hadley yesterday afternoon.

Why was being an adult filled with so many dangerous pitfalls that threatened one's sense of right and wrong? On the one hand, Hadley had broken their agreement, escalating things by hiring a cutthroat lawyer who was clearly willing to win at any cost. Surely Tyne deserved to have one, too. But Robert

Atkinson was a creep and a bully, the type of man who made her skin crawl. He was on her side, though, so maybe that made it okay.

Or maybe it made Tyne a creep and a bully, too.

She looked at the serene brick church, the tulips and daffodils starting to give way to summer flowers. That was the way of life, moving on. But moving on was hard when she wasn't sure what direction to take.

She didn't expect any answers from God, but it was someone else's opinion Tyne really wished she could seek. She closed her eyes.

"Ryan," she whispered, "I think I've made a huge mistake."

The one person who had always been her lodestar, who had walked with her through some of the hardest decisions in her life, was her brother Ryan. He'd never let her down. Now that he was gone, she couldn't afford to let him down when it came to raising his beautiful son.

"Please, Ryan, tell me what to do."

The church bell tolled loudly, causing Tyne to jump several inches from her seat. It sounded again and again. Her heart rate returned to normal as she realized it must be marking the hour. She counted the bells, six in all.

It was morning, a new day.

As the final bell echoed, peace washed over her, and Tyne knew what she had to do.

Maybe it had been a message from Ryan or from

God. Maybe her own conscience had finally managed to speak out over all the internal noise.

Whoever was responsible, they were right.

Tyne crept inside, finding her bag hanging on a hook next to the front door. She pulled out her phone and returned to her post on the patio.

She searched for Robert Atkinson's number in her contacts and dialed it. Though it was Saturday morning and too early for a law firm to open even on a weekday, attorneys were odd creatures, and it was likely the man would monitor his voice mail all weekend. When prompted to leave a message, she cleared her throat and started to speak.

"Hi, Robert. It's Tyne Briggs?"

Damn it, why was her voice so shaky, and how come she'd made her name sound like a question? *Focus.*

"Uh, we met earlier today, or I guess it was yesterday..." She was babbling and close to tears.

Oh, for fuck's sake, pull yourself together, and start sounding like the adult Owen needs you to be.

"Look, I don't think this is how I want to proceed. I just can't do it. It's not right. I need to do things a different way. So, uh... I'll be back in touch when I have a court date, and we can talk about how to do things in a more civilized way. So, I guess I'm saying, stand down. Thanks. Bye."

Tyne hit the red phone image on the screen, feeling a weight lift from her shoulders. Behind the church spire, the sky was turning a lovely shade of purple as the first fingers of sun embraced the new day.

A day she could face holding her head high.

"Thank you, Ryan," she whispered, in case he could hear her wherever he happened to be. "I promise to make you proud, and I won't let you or Owen down again."

CHAPTER SEVENTEEN

It was only as Hadley shifted the car to park in front of Tyne's parents' house that she realized her hand had been resting on Tyne's knee for most of the drive back from Boston. Tyne hadn't raised an objection. In fact, Tyne had laced her fingers through Hadley's without a word, as though it were the most natural thing to do.

It had been. But what did it mean? That answer eluded Hadley. Neither of them had mentioned the fact they'd slept together. Again. There'd been no awkwardness between them, but it was more like they'd come to an unspoken agreement to, well, not speak about it.

They got out of the car and walked to the front door. Tyne paused with her hand on the doorknob. "You ready?"

Hadley gave an assertive nod. Was she ready to go

in and make pleasant chitchat with the parents of the woman whose head had been between her legs a few hours before? Sure. Sounded like fun.

Tyne opened the door, calling out, "Mom? Dad? Owen?"

An adorable sound that could only be Owen's giggle rang out from his playpen, and Hadley instantly found herself giggling along. It was impossible not to. There was something about walking into a home and hearing a happy baby, as if it was a special kind of magic she'd never known existed before.

"How was the drive?" Keith hugged his daughter and placed a hand on Hadley's shoulder, giving it a squeeze. Or was his meaty hand tightening more vise-like because he wanted to have a word with the not so good doctor?

Hadley let out a nervous laugh as she tried not to flinch. There was no way he suspected what she and his little girl had been getting up to the night before. Surely, this wasn't his way of subtly reminding Hadley he could snap her in half like a twig with those beastly paws, right? Her imagination was running wild?

"Getting out of Boston was a nightmare," Tyne said, swooping Owen into her arms as she spoke. "Every road we needed was under construction, and then the GPS tried to get us to turn right, going the wrong way down a one-way street."

"Ugh, Boston. You couldn't pay me enough to live in that city," Keith said. There was another precious giggle from Owen. "See? My grandson agrees with me."

Hadley bit her tongue to keep from reminding him there was every chance the boy would be a full-time resident of Beantown and that he would probably love it.

"What does your grandson agree with you about?" asked Michelle, who entered the living room slowly but with no obvious signs of distress. Hadley appraised her gait, encouraged to see it was not as stiff and halting as the time she'd been on the floor in over-whelming pain.

"Dad's being silly," Tyne said. Hadley wondered if that had been for her benefit, if she'd felt uncomfortable about what her father's words implied.

"How's your back?" Hadley asked. "Have you been keeping up with the exercises we discussed?"

"It's feeling much better, but the doctor still thinks I might need surgery if I'm not careful, so no heavy lifting. He'll reevaluate in the fall." Michelle waved Hadley to the couch, taking the seat next to her. "I'm doing the exercises every day and that really helps, but I think the biggest difference is the stress hanging over me was popped when we received that second letter from the lawyer, telling us not to worry about completing that financial disclosure."

Keith chimed in. "I swear, they wanted us to gather every piece of documentation since birth. Worse than a tax audit."

Hadley tried not to squirm. Her lawyer had told her it would be a nightmare. She cast a nervous glance at Tyne, hoping to find her too occupied with Owen to pay any attention to the conversation. Her heart plummeted when she saw the intense look of concentration on Tyne's face, like she was memorizing every word.

"When we got the first letter, it terrified me," Michelle confided. "This has been a hard year for the trucking company. Hauling's been down with the economy the way it is, and we've had payments to make from a new trailer we'd committed to right before everything went tits up. Foolish on our part, though we're recovering. But I wasn't too keen sharing all that with a lawyer."

"Me either, so thanks for calling off your attack dogs." Keith let out a hearty laugh even as Hadley wished she could disappear under the sofa.

"Oh, he's joking." Michelle put a hand on Hadley's arm, giving it a maternal pat. "We know this had nothing to do with you. Lawyers are the worst. They'd tie their own child to a railroad track to make a buck."

"It's a relief, though, that's for sure," Keith said. "An accountant was the last thing we wanted to spend money on with all the other expenses that have piled up."

"We don't have to tell you about unexpected expenses making money tight," Michelle said, her expression brimming with compassion. "You must know all about it after the issues your parents had with their house last year. First, it was the boiler. Then, the ice dam that leaked into the family room."

"A week later their dishwasher went kaput," Keith added.

"Right after Christmas, too." Michelle shook her head as though she couldn't believe the rotten timing. "What was that last thing? Back in February, I think?"

Hadley pretended like she was combing her memory, but in truth, she was in shock. She didn't know what Michelle was talking about. Of this laundry list of disasters, she hadn't heard about a single one.

"The roof," Tyne prompted. Hadley stared. How did Tyne know about these things and Hadley didn't?

"Oh, that's right. Poor Ryan." Michelle sighed in a way that was happy and sad at the same time, the way one often did when remembering something humorous about a person who had since passed. "He was up and down that ladder so many times he said he was thinking of challenging the fire department to a race."

Hadley chuckled because she knew Michelle expected her to, but inside it horrified her how much her baby sister had been managing all on her own. She'd had a husband and a new baby, yet had taken on all the work of caring for their ailing parents without a single complaint. Not only that, it had never crossed Hadley's mind to ask what was going on, except in that generic way that accepted an answer of *fine* as being sufficient. Hadley couldn't have been any more of an insensitive ass if she'd tried.

In Hadley's mind, her parents were still young and vibrant. Her mom was the one who could keep track of a dozen school activities at once, knew whose turn it was to drive in the car pool on any given day, and who could wrestle even the unruliest of hair into a bun for ballet class in under a minute. Her dad had been quick on his feet, eager for a game of catch in the backyard or a thrilling game of Horse with all the children on the block.

That had been decades ago.

"Would you mind if I used your bathroom?" Hadley needed to get out of the room to compose herself.

"Of course," Michelle replied, her tone saying Hadley was part of the family. "You know where it is."

And Hadley *should* have remembered where the bathroom was. After all, how many times had she been here? But as she fled down the hall, the first door she opened revealed a linen closet. It was only on the second guess she got it right. Just another example of how fucking oblivious she could be to everything around her.

Standing in front of the sink, Hadley turned on the faucet and splashed cold water on her face. She stared at herself in the bathroom mirror, water dripping down her face, and barely recognized the reflection as her own. When had she become this person? A daughter who paid no attention to her parents' frailties as they aged. A sister who never bothered to lend a hand. It was only after thoroughly chastising herself for these failings that Hadley let the morning's other disastrous discovery wash over her.

Tyne knew.

Not about her parents' troubles, though she was much more cognizant about those things. Tyne knew about the lawyer, about the demands Hadley had authorized her to make on Hadley's behalf that were the equivalent of a financial rectal exam. She hadn't shown the least inkling of surprise when Michelle and Keith were talking about it, which made sense because Tyne actually gave a shit about her family and listened when her parents had troubles. Tyne must have known this entire time.

When Hadley finally ventured out of the bathroom, Tyne and her family were shifting to the kitchen in search of iced tea. Keith was carrying Owen, which gave Hadley an opening to catch Tyne gently by the arm. "Can we talk for a second? In private?"

With a frown, Tyne cast a glance at the kitchen and nodded. "Let's step outside."

As soon as they were out, Hadley blurted, "I have to confess something."

"Oh?" Tyne's expression became guarded.

"That financial audit your parents got? It was my fault."

"I know," Tyne said quietly. "As soon as I opened the envelope and saw the letterhead, I knew it had to be from your lawyer and not a routine request from the court."

"You did?" Hadley swallowed as she processed the rest of Tyne's words. "Why were you the one opening your parents' letter?"

"I didn't open theirs. I opened mine."

"You mean you received yours, too?" The knowledge plunged into Hadley like a knife.

"It came to our house last weekend, right in the middle of the party." Tyne's voice was quiet, and there was no mistaking her pain.

"I'm so sorry." Hadley trembled. "So, so sorry. And, embarrassed. When the lawyer explained what her strategy was, I knew it was sleazy. You had to have been so mad."

"The correct word is livid."

Hadley winced. "She assured me it was normal, but that's not an excuse."

Tyne squeezed her hands together, her skin turning bright red. She looked about ready to be sick. "Hadley, I need to tell—"

"No, wait." Hadley held up a hand, knowing if she didn't say everything now, she might not get through it later. "Let me say one other thing first. I had a choice to say yes or no, and I signed off on it, which was a total betrayal of your trust. As soon as I came to my senses, I called it off. I foolishly thought I'd done it in time and the letters had never arrived or had been lost in the mail."

Tyne nodded, her eyes closed. "That's why you didn't say anything about it before?"

Hadley blinked back tears. "I know this must be impossible for you to understand because you would never do something so devious. I hope you can forgive me."

"I do. I understand, and I forgive you." Tyne's eyes darted away. "As for never doing something—"

"Tyne? Hadley?" Michelle called from the front door. "Oh, there you two are. Owen's getting fussy. I think he's going to want a bottle and a nap soon."

"We should get going," Hadley said. "I'll take care of getting him fed and to sleep when we get home."

"No, I'll do it." Tyne's tone hadn't been short, but something was off, nonetheless.

Hadley wanted to ask what was the matter, but she was already on such thin ice she didn't want to press. At least her confession and knowledge Tyne had forgiven the treacherous move had lifted a million tons from her shoulders, but Hadley vowed not to be oblivious this time and leave it at that. She would do everything she could to make up for what she had done and to continue to pull her weight, and then some, when it came to Owen. The last thing she wanted was to treat Tyne the way she'd been treating her parents and sister. She still had time to correct the situation with her parents, but she could never make things up to Kayleigh.

LATE THAT NIGHT, once Owen had gone to bed, Hadley dug through a closet in the room at their rental house that she and Tyne were using as an office. She was searching for a cardboard box of files that had come from her sister's apartment. They'd grabbed it because among the things were Owen's birth certificate and medical information. Hadley had a slight memory that it contained other papers, too.

When she found it, she slipped off the lid and flicked through the files, seeing one labeled Repairs for 2978. That was her parents' street address.

Hadley took the file to the desk and sorted through the invoices. Her head pounded as the extent of the issues her parents had faced, as well as the costs, became clear.

"Why didn't Kayleigh tell me?" Hadley whispered.

Tyne popped her head into the doorway. "I'm not a doctor, but I hear talking to yourself isn't usually a good sign."

"Yeah, probably not." Hadley massaged her temples.

"I'm going to make some sleepy time tea. Would you like some?" She appraised Hadley with a look of gentle concern. "Is everything okay?"

Hadley closed the file on the desk. "I'm realizing how awful I've been."

Tyne strode through the room, taking a seat on the

edge of the desk. With her index finger, she tilted Hadley's chin upward until their eyes met. "Don't say that. Don't even think it. Is this because of the dustup with the lawyer?"

"No. Not that, even though that's bad enough." Hadley had to fight back tears as she flicked the file full of receipts. "You knew about all the repairs at my parents' house?"

"Of course. I helped repaint the family room."

"Really?" Hadley buried her face in her hands. "So, I was the only one?"

"The only one to what?"

"I didn't have a clue about any of it." Hadley took in a deep breath, praying for calm. "Not the boiler, the ice dam, repainting."

"You were in Boston, and Kayleigh had it under control."

Hadley barely heard, her mind still whirling. "Oh, and, the roof. I forgot about the roof. How much did *that* cost? No, wait, I have all the receipts, so I can add it up myself."

As she whipped the folder open, Tyne put a hand on Hadley's arm to stop her. "You don't need to torture yourself. You had no way of knowing."

"I—I'm such a shitty daughter and sister."

Tyne reached for Hadley, putting her arms around her. "That's not true."

"It is." Hadley was stiff against Tyne's chest. "And

after the stunt I pulled with the lawyer, I can totally understand if you never want to speak to me again."

"I've known about that for a week. It didn't stop me from talking to you. Not to mention, you know, doing *other* things." Tyne trailed her fingers along Hadley's spine, melting her from the inside out. "Or have you forgotten about that?"

"Yeah, that." Hadley felt like she was burning up. "Do you think we should talk about *that*?"

"The immature part of me really doesn't want to." Tyne made a sound that was laughter mixed with a groan.

"I can get onboard with that," Hadley said quickly. "Maturity is overrated."

"But we probably should."

It was Hadley's turn to make a strangled, unhappy noise. "I was afraid you were going to say that. Where should we begin?"

"How about with what does it mean?"

"What does it mean that we slept together?" Hadley clarified. After so much miscommunication, the last thing they needed was to not be on the same page now.

Tyne nodded. "I mean, I know we have this thing with Owen hanging over us, but I can't ignore how I feel."

Hadley's heart pounded in her throat. "Which is...?"

"Oh, sure. Put me on the spot to say it first." For

an excruciatingly long second, it seemed like Tyne might be annoyed, but then she winked. "I would be lying if I said I wasn't developing feelings for you."

Hadley resisted the urge to perform a spontaneous interpretive dance, opting instead for a simple, "Me too."

Tyne's next breath sounded filled with relief. "Then I hope we can agree on this, too. I don't want us to keep letting our lawyers do the dirty work. No more nasty games. It's not who I am, and I have to tell you—"

"No, you're right," Hadley said quickly. "I fucked up on that front, and I broke a promise."

"Hadley, it wasn't just—"

Hadley placed a finger on Tyne's lips. "I can be better. I *need* to be better about so many things. You. Owen. My parents. It's funny. Kayleigh was so much younger, but she clearly soared past me in the adulting department."

"That's what happens when you get married and have a kid," Tyne soothed. "You grow up."

"Apparently." Hadley's eyes fell to the file again. "When we agreed to move into this house together, we said we'd make our cases and let the experts weigh the circumstances and decide what was best for Owen. Are you still up for that?"

"I wish I could say I believed we could come up with the perfect compromise on our own," Tyne replied, "but I think we're too close to it. We're both too passionate."

"I told you before, passion is a trait I admire."

"I do, too. Especially in you." Tyne looked at her steadily, her meaning clear, and Hadley felt her insides quake.

"So, we stick with the plan?"

"Not sure how to break this to you," Tyne said, her mouth twitching with humor, "but I think we may have thrown a little wrench into that plan last night."

"Not sure anything about last night can rightly be called *little*." Hadley pinched her lips together with her hand to keep from laughing.

"Should we take it day by day? See where the chips fall?"

"We make a good team. It's a lot easier having you to talk to and... you know." Hadley gave a suggestive shrug.

Tyne laughed. "That was the most loaded *you know* I've ever heard."

"Was it?" Hadley batted her eyelashes. "I didn't mean for it to be."

"Liar."

"About that, yes," Hadley admitted. "But nothing else. I promise. Please believe me."

"I know. I trust you." Tyne stuck out her hand. "Let's shake on it one more time."

Hadley took Tyne's hand. "To taking things slowly and no more dirty, rotten tricks."

After they'd shaken on it, their hands remained clasped, as if neither of them wanted to let go. Looking at the way their fingers twined, Hadley couldn't help wondering if perhaps a compromise wasn't so impossible after all. If things between her and Tyne went the way she was hoping they would, the courts wouldn't have to decide at all.

Everything seemed to be on its way to working out perfectly on its own.

CHAPTER EIGHTEEN

"Damn it!" Tyne's injured hand flew back from the pot, boiling water sloshing everywhere. It hit the stovetop with a sizzle that sounded uncomfortably like a soundtrack to accompany her burning flesh. This was the last thing she needed when Owen's social worker would be arriving any minute to perform their two-month evaluation.

Hadley rushed to her side as urgently as if someone had called a code blue. "Let me see."

"It's fine—"

"Listen, I won't tell you what colors to choose when painting a sunset as long as you admit I'm the expert for burns." Hadley inspected the angry red skin along Tyne's palm. "Does it hurt?"

"Nah," Tyne denied. It throbbed like hell, but this wasn't the time to dwell on such an idiotic move. "It startled me more than anything."

Hadley glanced into the steaming pot, clearly perplexed. "What were you trying to do? This looks like a witch's cauldron. Are you boiling sticks?"

"Cinnamon sticks," Tyne corrected. "And some cloves, star anise, and a dash of ginger. I read in an article somewhere it's even better than potpourri for making a house smell nice. They listed it as a realtor's trick to make a house more welcoming, along with baking cookies."

"Which you did an hour ago. Are you really this nervous about the social worker coming over?"

"Aren't you?" Tyne squeaked.

"It's only an evaluation of the physical environment, and we've gone through the checklist five times," Hadley pointed out, as if the prospect of having overlooked something wasn't terrifying. "We've got this in the bag."

"What if the social worker sees I burned my finger, and we lose points?"

"I don't think it works that way. This step is more of a formality than anything since we're Owen's blood relatives. You need to stay calm."

"Are you insane?" Tyne demanded, feeling more frantic each second. "A total stranger is about to come over to grade my ability to care for a baby, and I've maimed myself."

Taking hold of Tyne's hand, Hadley raised the injured spot to her lips, kissing it lightly. "There you go. All better."

"Is that a technique you use often in the ER?"

"Absolutely," Hadley said in a mock-serious tone. "Unless someone burns their ass, in which case I usually opt for an ice pack and some ointment. Ass-kissing is strictly reserved for the head of my department during yearly performance reviews."

"Is that right?" Tyne regarded Hadley with an evil smirk. "Because I've got this crystal clear memory from when you joined me in the shower the other day—"

Tyne giggled as Hadley gave her a playful swat. It wasn't like she could argue. In the month since their fateful trip to Boston, there were few spots left on either of them that hadn't been kissed.

"Has anyone ever come in to be treated for an ass burn?" Tyne asked, still breathy with laughter.

"Believe it or not, yes. There was this one kid—he must have been sixteen."

"How did it happen?"

"Classic case of being in the wrong place at the wrong time. Afraid I can't say more." Hadley winked, clearly enjoying herself. "HIPAA regulations, you know."

"Oh, no you don't." Tyne put a hand on her hip. "You can't leave a juicy story hanging like that, patient privacy be damned."

"Fine, but it's probably not as lurid as you think." Hadley chuckled. "He went to a vocational high school, like the one Mason attends, where they required students to try out a variety of trades. I got the impression he was great with car engines but a disaster in the culinary arts. He had a run-in, or I should say back-in, with a pizza oven. I sent him home with a note excusing him from cooking classes, along with a special cushion he needed to sit on for the rest of the semester."

"Did he do it? Because I don't know many boys who would sit on a hemorrhoid donut in high school. No way in hell."

Hadley shrugged. "That's what I love about my job. I fix them up and send them off. If they don't do what I say, I never know about it. I will say I *have* wondered how he'll explain those scars to anyone in the future who might get the chance to see them."

"Probably with something a little more badass than an old cooking school injury."

"No doubt," Hadley agreed. "How's your hand now?"

"What about it?" Tyne's mouth dropped open. "Wait. Did you tell me that story to get me to think about something else so I'd forget about my burn?"

"Did it work?"

They were grinning like fools at one another when the sound of the doorbell caused them both to freeze, their expressions morphing as if they expected to find Satan himself at the front door, asking them to come out and play.

Tyne pointed a finger at Hadley's face. "You *are* just as nervous as I am. Don't deny it."

Hadley blew a loose strand of hair out of her eyes. "Here goes nothing."

They stood shoulder to shoulder as they opened the door. If her hand wasn't still so tender, Tyne would've grabbed onto Hadley and not let go. They were about to invite a person into their house who had the power to decide Owen's future and who would spend the next several hours digging through every inch of their space with a fine-tooth comb. Tyne pictured someone with a Sherlock Holmes hat and a giant magnifying glass. Instead, the woman standing on the front step hardly looked old enough to have graduated from college, yet she wore the harried expression of a soldier in the trenches.

"Hi, I'm Zelda. I'm here to do the home study."

"Come on in." Hadley waved, smiling awkwardly.

"Would you like something to drink?" Tyne offered. "Coffee? Tea? We also have sparkling water, orange juice, some diet soda..." Realizing she sounded like a waitress reciting the beverage menu, Tyne's voice trailed off.

"I'd kill for a coffee." Zelda's smile said she'd experienced this type of nervous behavior, and pretty much everything else, before.

"Cookies? Muffins?" Tyne stopped herself before she recited the entire contents of the kitchen.

"I really shouldn't." Zelda sniffed the air with a hint of longing. "Are the cookies homemade?"

"They are," Tyne answered, shooting Hadley a look that said *I told you baking cookies was a good idea.* "Chocolate chip, with extra big chunks."

"In that case, yes, please." Zelda wore a guilty look. "I've gained five pounds since I started this job. Stress baking is a more common reaction to these visits than you might think, and on days when I have four or five homes with no time for lunch, I pretty much live on cookies."

"We have some fruit, too," Tyne offered. "And croissants."

"I'll go get everything," Hadley said, presumably jumping in before Tyne launched into the menu again. "Tyne, why don't you show Zelda to the living room and have a seat? I'll be right back."

"She's helpful," Zelda remarked. "Does she do dishes, too?"

"Uh, yes." Tyne went wide-eyed. Had the interview started, or was the social worker making chitchat? Better to answer as completely as possible, just in case. "We divide household tasks and childcare duties equitably between us."

"Nice." Zelda took a seat but didn't make a move to take notes, so Tyne suspected the answer she'd given would not be recorded in their permanent file. "I wish I knew how to get my boyfriend to do that."

Hadley entered the room, carrying a tray laden with

food, a carafe, and mugs. Relieved for a distraction, Tyne hopped up to clear a space on the coffee table. While Hadley poured the first steaming cup, handing it to Zelda, Tyne placed the milk and sugar closer to the woman so she could fix it however she liked.

Hadley poured two more cups. Tyne prepped one for herself, adding exactly the right amount of milk and sugar to the second before handing it to Hadley. Their fingers brushed, and Tyne felt a warm glow inside.

"This isn't your first time," Zelda said, digging into her overstuffed bag and pulling out a stack of file folders.

First time doing what? Tyne wasn't sure what Zelda was referring to. Brushing fingers? Doing a home study? Making coffee? So many options to choose from.

"We have coffee every day," Tyne went with, knowing there was a high probability what she'd said wouldn't make any sense.

"It's addictive." Zelda took a long sip from her mug.

Had that been a criticism? Was this a trick question about nutrition?

"We drink plenty of water, too," Tyne rushed to assure her. "Hadley's always pushing fluids."

Zelda chuckled. "Pushing fluids, that's funny."

Why was that funny? Tyne forced a laugh, but inside, it terrified her she'd either made it sound like

Hadley was a drug dealer or a control freak. How much longer was this visit going to last? Tyne wasn't sure she could make it.

Hadley sat on the couch next to Tyne, all calm, cool, and collected. "I can't help it. I'm a doctor, and hydration's important."

"Can I ask you something?" Zelda leaned forward, looking intently at Hadley. "I read the other day it's really important for your pee to be clear. Is that true? Because no matter what I do, mine's pretty yellow, and there's a history of bladder issues on my mother's side, so I don't know if I should worry or not."

Is this social worker seeking free medical advice from my—

She almost completed that thought with the word *girlfriend* but had enough presence of mind left to stop herself. Which was fortunate because Tyne didn't think her brain could deal with that plus trying to figure out if this conversation was actually real or if she was in the middle of another warped dream brought on by stress.

"That's a common misconception," Hadley replied in a good-natured way that suggested she was used to being pumped for diagnoses by strangers. "Clear can be a sign of drinking too much water. The healthy range is anywhere from light yellow to deep amber. Now, if it's orange or brown, you want to see a doctor, because that can indicate kidney or bladder disease."

Yes, this conversation was absolutely real. Of all the things Tyne had prepared for with this home visit, a discussion of the proper color of pee had never crossed her mind.

"That is so reassuring to hear." Zelda relaxed against the back sofa cushion with a sigh. "I guess that's why they say not to get your medical advice off the internet."

Amazing. Far from going down as a black mark in their file for worst coffee conversation ever, it appeared Hadley had scored them a few points with the social worker.

Her coffee finished, Zelda grabbed a cookie in one hand as she rifled through the mess of folders she'd placed on the couch beside her. She grabbed a blue folder, checked the name at the top, and then said, "Owen, right?"

"Yes." Tyne sat up straighter. Game time. "He's taking a nap. Should I wake him?"

"That's not necessary. I can wait until he's finished his nap to talk to him."

Talk to him?

It was only when Hadley laughed that Tyne realized Zelda had been making a joke. "Can I ask," Hadley said in a casual tone, "what exactly *are* you going to do today? You know, other than interviewing Owen?"

Tyne covered her mouth as she giggled at the mental image that conjured up. Some of the tension in her shoulders eased, and she shot a grateful look at Hadley, marveling at how easily the woman could take what felt to Tyne like a harrowing experience in stride.

Tyne doubted she could ever be so put-together herself and hoped it wouldn't count against her in the future when a judge had to decide between them in determining Owen's forever home.

"I'm doing a health and safety evaluation, but it's really not as scary as it might sound." Zelda's eyes traveled around the room above ground level. "For example, I see all the plugs are childproofed in here, so that's already a check in the right column. As soon as we're ready, we can start at the top floor of the house and work our way down. I need to go into each room, open all the cupboards and closets."

"To see if they're organized?" Tyne asked.

"No, we don't care about that. I'll be checking to make sure medicines and household chemicals are stored properly, along with weapons or the like."

"I guess we'll have to let you see the sex dungeon in the basement then," Hadley not so helpfully tossed out.

"Absolutely, I'll need to see that." Zelda stared at Hadley in shock as she started digging through her papers furiously. "Oh my. I may need to call my supervisor for a protocol on this."

"Hadley!" Tyne implored, clenching her hands to keep her from wringing Hadley's neck. What was she thinking, saying something like that? And so dead pan, too. Doctor Cool must've been more nervous than she let on.

"No, Zelda. That was a joke." Hadley's face was bright crimson. "Really, there's not... I swear."

Tyne had never seen Hadley so flustered. Her outrage evaporated, and instead Tyne felt strangely reassured that she wasn't the only one with jangling nerves today. As cool as Hadley had been trying to act, this slipup made it clear she was far less confident than she appeared beneath that serene exterior.

"Maybe we should start that house tour now," Tyne suggested, feeling better about this whole thing than she had all day.

It was surprisingly uneventful, as Zelda had tried to assure them, although Tyne did wonder a few times if the social worker was bracing for the discovery of an illicit sex dungeon as she opened a closet door.

When they arrived at Owen's room, Tyne opened the door with caution, holding a finger to her lips to urge quiet. As she'd suspected, the little tyke was fast asleep. They kept his bedroom as dark as possible with a thick blackout shade she and Hadley had added to the window when the lengthening days started interfering with his sleep.

"Still out like a light." Tyne eased the door shut but not before allowing Zelda a peek inside.

"Goodness," the social worker remarked. "He's small for his age."

"Is he?" Tyne exchanged looks with Hadley, who also seemed surprised by the comment. They'd taken him for a checkup, and the pediatrician hadn't said a word about that.

"How are his motor skills?" Zelda asked, making a note on her file as they returned to the living room to wrap up.

"He has a firm grasp," Hadley said, "and good hand-eye coordination."

"That's good to hear." Still, Zelda furrowed her brow.

Tyne recognized her tone as the one their doctors had used when examining her brother Mason in the early days, when they were starting to suspect he was developmentally delayed. Her heart pounded. What had the woman caught that she and Hadley had missed?

"He loves to reach out and grab me with one hand and Hadley with the other," Tyne explained, desperate to tell Zelda something that would reassure her everything was okay with the tot.

"Yeah, it's his thing. He loves to hold on to both of us." Hadley gave Tyne a look that soothed her worry more than anything the social worker could have said. "He's the glue in our little family."

Innocent as it was, it blew Tyne away to realize this was the closest Hadley had ever come to saying *I love you*. Coupled with that look, it pierced Tyne's heart with joy. Blinking so that she wouldn't start bawling, Tyne reached out and brushed Hadley's hand with her fingers.

"Aww, look at you two," Zelda said. "I'm pretty sure this paperwork is going to soar through the courts."

"Is that all you need?" Hadley asked.

"Yes, except for the interview with Owen, but I hate to wake him up. I can come back another day."

There wasn't a hint of humor in Zelda's statement, and Tyne was utterly perplexed. "How are you going to interview Owen?"

"Just a standard set of age-appropriate questions," Zelda said as though the answer wasn't ludicrous. "Completely routine."

"Age-appropriate?" Tyne looked from Hadley's dumbfounded face to Zelda, who looked increasingly uneasy.

"Our nephew doesn't even turn one until next week," Hadley added.

"No wonder he seemed so small." Zelda's hand flew to her mouth. "Did you say nephew?"

"Yes." Tyne exchanged another look with Hadley. "My brother was Owen's father, and Hadley's sister was his mom."

Zelda nodded slowly, like she was absorbing the details for the first time but unable to add everything up. "And you're trying to adopt him?"

Tyne furrowed her brows. "Is that what this home study is for? I thought we were still working on the co-guardianship thing."

"Why would you need that when you're already his foster parents?" Zelda seemed baffled.

"I don't think we are." Tyne's eyes darted to Hadley. "Are we?"

"Uh…" The twist in conversation appeared to have rendered Hadley speechless. "Not that I—"

"Wait, wait." Zelda sat on the couch and pulled out her stack of files again. "Owen Brisby, right?"

"No," Tyne corrected. "Owen Briggs."

It was a good thing Zelda was sitting down already because it looked like she might pass out. "You two aren't the married couple adopting your three-year-old foster son?"

"Us?" Tyne tittered nervously. "We're not married. We're barely dating." Did she say dating? That was the last thing they needed to reveal to an officer of the court.

Hadley rushed to jump in. "What she's trying to say is, we're supposed to be talking about Owen Briggs, age eleven months. Are you, or are you not, assigned to his case?"

"Hold on." Zelda shuffled a few files. "Okay, now I have the right folder. Sorry about that."

"Owen *Briggs*." Tyne emphasized the last name.

"Yes." Zelda's jaw tensed as she held up her mammoth stack of folders. "Do you have any idea how many visits I handle every week? We're so under-staffed; my workload has doubled since the beginning of the year. Twelve of my cases are in same-sex households, and I have four kids named *Owen* to evaluate this week alone. It's a very popular name."

For a brief second, Hadley looked as if she wanted to strangle the social worker, but then she regained control in that way Tyne admired so much. "I suppose it's an honest mistake. Sounds like there isn't much about us that's unique."

The social worker shook her head as she skimmed through the file she held open, definitely the correct one this time. "Actually, there is, and if I'm totally honest, that's part of what caused my confusion. Parents dying without a will, Boston attorneys, relatives from two different sides of the family locked in a custody battle and completely unable to reach a compromise."

As Zelda read through the exhaustive list of their shortcomings, Tyne felt like she'd shrunk to about an inch in height. "It sounds bad when you say it all together like that."

"When I read this file, I expected to walk into a war zone. Then I met you two. Is it any wonder I got confused?" Zelda waved her hand, encompassing them both, which was the first time Tyne fully realized she and Hadley had chosen to sit side by side on the loveseat, arms looped and fingers clasped. "Forgive me if I'm out of line here, but are you sure you two don't want to adopt?"

"Eventually," Tyne said, her voice small. "After a judge decides which one of us gets to."

"I meant together." Zelda pressed her lips together, looking like she was trying to decide whether to continue. "I know you're not the married couple I assumed you were, but I think it's fair to say you're also not the bitter old backstabbing aunts I expected you to be either. No offense."

"None taken," Hadley sounded as disconcerted as Tyne felt to discover the social worker had expected them to be a pair of acrimonious, double-crossing shrews.

"Everything I've seen today tells me you two are doing a fantastic job raising Owen together. You make a great team, better than many families I've seen, and I've seen a lot." Once again, the young woman's expression betrayed exactly how much she must have experienced in the course of doing her tough job. "Have you thought about adopting your nephew together?"

"How?" Tyne leaned in, confused but intrigued. "We already told you we're not married."

"You don't have to be," Zelda said. "The state allows unmarried couples to adopt."

"I didn't know that was possible," said Hadley, her face mirroring Tyne's own conflicting emotions.

"I assure you, it is. I've seen it before, and frankly, from what I've seen of you two, it's something you might want to give more thought." Zelda checked her watch and hopped to her feet. "I've gotta run. I'm going to be late for my next appointment. Mind if I take one for the road?" Zelda pointed to the tray of cookies.

"Sure," Tyne responded with a shrug. She had too much else on her mind now to give any thought to snacks.

"Thanks. They're delish." Zelda grabbed one from the tray and added a second for good measure.

Owen's cry came over the baby monitor.

Zelda laughed. "Look who's up. I guess I don't have to worry about that interview, though."

"I'll go get him," Hadley said, heading quickly to the stairs. "Thank you, Zelda."

"My pleasure. See you next time." The social worker lifted her hand in a wave and followed Tyne to the door. "As for my report from today, there's no cause for concern. It's all positive, no matter which way you two decide to proceed."

"Thank you for that." Tyne shook her hand.

Zelda held on for an extra second, giving Tyne's hand a pat. "Good luck. And I'm serious about the co-adoption idea. I have a feeling it would work out for you two really well."

"I'll think about it." Tyne watched the woman return to her car before shutting the door. Her insides were shaky, and she couldn't decide if it was bad or good.

She had a lot to think about all right.

CHAPTER NINETEEN

Hadley drove past the park in the center of the square where preparations for the upcoming Fourth of July festivities were already under way. American flags flapped in the wind and a stage for a live band was being set up. She did a quick memory check to ensure she knew what day it was. The holiday wasn't this weekend, right? The Briggs were hosting a big party on the fifth, and Tyne would kill her if she missed it. No, she was pretty sure she still had another week to go.

She parked in the staff lot at Pioneer Valley Hospital, enjoying the bright sunshine on her face as she walked across the hot asphalt toward the entrance to the emergency department. It still felt weird sometimes to work the day shift after so many years of vampire hours, but she had to admit there were benefits to it when you had a family waiting for you at home.

Family.

Her reaction to the word used to be one of ambivalence. Now the thought of Tyne greeting her at the door, Owen in her arms, after a long shift made Hadley break into a grin from ear to ear. And knowing how very temporary it all was kept her up many nights.

An ambulance pulled into the bay, and Hadley quickened her steps, putting all thoughts out of her head except what she needed to do her job. Most of the patients she had treated since her arrival at Pioneer Valley were exactly what one would expect at a small hospital. Lots of sprained ankles, broken bones, headaches, cuts, and stomach pains. The arrival of an ambulance by definition meant a more serious emergency, and Hadley wanted in on the action.

Almost as soon as she walked into the building and through the ER doors, Hadley could feel the frenetic energy. A nurse she recognized whizzed past her down the hall, and Hadley called after her. "Darla, what's going on? How can I help?"

"GSW on his way into trauma room two," the nurse said without breaking stride.

A gunshot wound? Hadley doubled her pace. "They brought him here?"

"This was the closest facility that could stabilize him. I heard they've sent for the helicopter."

"Jesus." That was some next-level excitement for this sleepy little place.

A cacophony at the end of the hall told Hadley they'd arrived at the right place. An EMT was performing chest compressions while Dr. Cassidy, two nurses, and several technicians surrounded the patient on the gurney.

A harried Dr. Cassidy waved her over as soon as Hadley entered the room. "Dr. Moore, I need you over here. Working in the city, I'm thinking you may have seen more bullet wounds than I have."

"Sadly so." Hadley shrugged on protective gear as she made a beeline for the patient. "What do we know?"

"Patient is a male, mid-twenties, with a gunshot wound to his chest. He coded as they were getting him out of the ambulance. We're getting the IVs going and preparing to intubate."

"Good start." Hadley flagged down one of the nurses. "Quick, let's cut these clothes off him. I need to see the extent of the damage."

As soon as the patient was naked, Hadley scanned his body for wounds. There was just the one, right near his heart. She made a quick calculation of the bullet's trajectory. "It's nicked his heart. I'm almost sure of it. How long until Dr. Greene arrives?"

"Mid-July," Dr. Cassidy replied. "He's on vacation."

"Shit." Dr. Greene was the most reliable of the hospital's very limited selection of surgeons. "He's going to need his chest opened. Is there a trauma or thoracic surgeon on call?"

"Dr. Chen. He's on his way in, but it could take another twenty minutes."

"This guy doesn't have twenty minutes. He needs a thoracotomy now." Hadley knew that after fifteen minutes without a pulse, the window for performing this potentially lifesaving technique to access and repair the damage to his heart would be shut. "Have you done them before?"

"An emergency thoracotomy?" Dr. Cassidy gave a hollow laugh. "Uh, no. I mean, it was in the curriculum, but I've never done one for real. How about you?"

Hadley cleared her throat. "Once."

"Well then," Dr. Cassidy said, "looks like he's all yours."

"Just so we're clear, there's not a single surgeon in the hospital right now we can call on to crack this guy open?"

"Afraid that's right."

Her heart hammered against her ribs. Shit was getting real.

This was the adrenaline rush Hadley lived for.

"Get the thoracotomy tray," Hadley directed, her voice strong and confident. "We've got a penetrating chest trauma and no pulse. We sure as hell can't make him any worse. Hopefully, by the time we get a look inside and find the damage, Dr. Chen will be here to stitch him up good as new."

After a quick splash of Betadine across the patient's chest, Hadley gripped the scalpel. "Hold compressions."

If she were back in Boston, no way would she be doing this. They would never ask an emergency physician to perform a procedure like this when there were always a dozen specialists on hand to take the lead. The one time in her life she'd been volunteering at an emergency field hospital and had to step in to perform the procedure herself, there'd been a qualified surgeon on standby to provide definitive treatment the moment the patient was stabilized. She would've considered it unthinkable to start cutting otherwise, but she simply didn't have any other choice this time.

Michael would hand me my ass for pulling a stunt like this.

But she was still going to do it, because if she didn't, well, the patient was dead already.

Trying not to think about how awkward the 10-blade scalpel felt in her hand, Hadley sliced along the curve of the ribs, through the skin and subcutaneous tissue, to the muscles that run between the ribs. These she cut through with heavy scissors, pushing two fingers into the incision to move the patient's lung out of the way. Next came the sternum, which the trauma shears made short work of.

"Rib spreaders." Hadley was moving at lightning speed, not because she was that confident in what she was doing but because she didn't have a choice. "I need this lung out of the way so I can see."

Dr. Cassidy's gloved hand quickly appeared with a retractor, and as soon as she'd moved it, Hadley could see the man's heart, purple and still. There was the hole, clear as day, such a tiny thing to have caused so much trouble.

"Where's Dr. Chen?" Hadley asked, debating how much more she should do.

"Still several minutes out," a voice answered.

Not close enough.

"Right. I can put a suture in there if I can reach it." Hadley carried through with this plan, drawing on techniques she hadn't practiced in years, but which mercifully returned to her at the moment she needed them most. "I'm going to give the heart a gentle squeeze, see if I can get some blood to his brain."

As she did this, Hadley examined the membrane surrounding the heart. "Huh. I see some blood clots in the pericardium."

She cleared away a few large clots before giving the heart another gentle squeeze. Suddenly, the man's heart leaped to life in her hand. "Oh, my God. It's beating."

"The helicopter has landed," someone announced, "and Dr. Chen's car just pulled up outside the entrance."

The news was most welcome, though Hadley wasn't sure who'd delivered it. She was too busy marveling at the rhythmic thumping of her patient's heart and the steady movement of his lungs as they inflated with air.

"Can I get a blood pressure?" Hadley called out. She felt a mix of shock and elation as the numbers came back astonishingly good. "Well, holy shit. Welcome back to the land of the living."

"Unbelievable," Dr. Cassidy said, her voice filled with awe. "What's next?"

"He's stable for the moment, and I'd rather not jeopardize that doing the wrong thing, so let's monitor the bleeding and keep him sedated until Dr. Chen can take over."

The surgeon dashed into the trauma room moments later. It surprised him how little he still needed to do, but Hadley was more than happy to let him take over. As soon as that heart had started to beat beneath her fingers, every ounce of fear she probably should've been experiencing the whole time had hit her like a proverbial ton of bricks.

The reason was simple. When her patient was dead, there wasn't much to lose. Once he had a pulse, he was alive again. The giant hole she'd cut in his chest and the blood smeared all over the place were stark reminders of how easily any mistake she made could kill him.

With the patient safely delivered to the expert, Hadley went into an adjacent room, stripped off her protective clothing, and scrubbed her hands. Finally, Hadley allowed herself to let out a relieved sigh.

Dr. Cassidy entered the room and stood beside her. "That was some impressive shit in there, Moore."

"I don't know. It kind of brings home how rusty I've gotten at so many of the things I learned during residency."

"If that's you being rusty, I'm pretty sure you're the best hire I've made in my entire career. I have to admit I'm not looking forward to you going back to Boston."

"It's funny because I would never have been allowed to do anything like this there. My hospital chief of staff would've demanded my head on a platter. He's not a fan of mavericks."

"I know it can be boring around here compared to a level one trauma center, but sometimes it can surprise you."

"That was a surprise all right." Now that the adrenaline was wearing off, Hadley trembled with a combination of exhaustion and anger. "What were the paramedics thinking, bringing a critical patient like that here? He could've died."

"Hadley," Dr. Cassidy's etched face was completely serious, "if you hadn't been here, he *would* have died. I don't think I could've done what you did, which as a doctor yourself, you know how hard that is for me to admit."

"But why didn't they bring the helicopter directly to

him at the scene and fly him straight to Springfield." The more Hadley thought of how close that patient had come to dying, the more shook up she became.

"Bad weather a little farther west kept them from being able to land," Dr. Cassidy explained, "so the next best option was an ambulance to the closest hospital with an emergency department and a helipad. This might be hard for a city person to grasp, but out here, sometimes we're all there is."

Hadley pondered this reality, and for the first time, it really struck her that if Kayleigh and Ryan's accident had happened somewhere else—or if there had been even one doctor around at that moment with the right knowledge—maybe the outcome would've been different. Not that she believed she could have saved them, she wasn't that arrogant, but in a setting like this, a single set of skilled hands could be the difference between living and dying. Dr. Cassidy studied her closely, the look in her eyes suggesting she knew what thoughts were racing through Hadley's head.

"I know things with your family and personal life are in flux right now, but there's something I've been mulling over." The doctor sounded cautious but hopeful. "Is there any chance you'd want to stay here and take a full-time, permanent position in this department?"

In her mind, Hadley had to admit today's experience had brought back all the reasons she'd gone into medicine in the first place. It had been exhilarating in a way she never expected, and if she was completely honest with herself, in a way her job in Boston would never be. As rewarding as it was to be one of many talented doctors in a top-notch urban hospital, she was only one small part of a machine that ran just as smoothly in her absence. It was a little like the wild west out here, which meant a cowboy doctor wasn't necessarily a bad thing. That held way more appeal than Hadley had ever realized.

My life's in Boston, she reasoned, but almost instantly, a different voice popped into her head, demanding, *Is it?* There was a time that had been true, but now Hadley wasn't so sure. When she closed her eyes and tried to picture what mattered to her most, it wasn't her Beacon Hill condo or the Boston skyline that sprang to mind. It was her family.

Owen.

Her parents.

And Tyne.

Hadley took a deep breath, almost feeling like she'd had the wind knocked out of her. This wasn't a possibility she'd ever considered, but maybe it was time to start. Would such an enormous change be something she could get used to for the rest of her life? It could solve so many issues, but would she be happy?

She was nowhere ready to commit, but she gave Dr. Cassidy a nod and said, "I'll give it some thought."

-\/\/\/\-

"YOU READY TO GO?" Hadley stood in the kitchen with her car keys in hand.

It was Saturday. Kayleigh used to take Owen to their parents' house every Saturday so they could visit with their grandson, and she could refill Mom's pills and look after things around the house. Now Hadley carried on the tradition.

"Just a minute." Tyne hollered down from the second level.

Hadley shook the keys in front of Owen. "Never fall in love with an artist, Owen. Nothing but frustration." She winked at him, and he burst into laughter. "You're a giggle machine, little man. I'd love to be as happy as you all the time."

The most shocking development, considering the reason she was there in the first place, was how much of the time Hadley was that happy. It was unexpected, and sometimes she wasn't sure if it was a sign of human resilience or a flaw in her character. It felt disloyal, or perhaps shallow, to feel as content as she did.

Her heart clenched, knowing Kayleigh should be the one raising Owen. Her sister had been a devoted mother. She would've cherished every minute of watching Owen grow up, which was happening at lightning speed. It was only a matter of days, if not hours, that the little man would take his first step. Just yesterday, Hadley was convinced he was going to do it. She hoped she would be there when he finally did, but

Kayleigh would miss every milestone, and it wasn't fair.

Hadley glanced upward, and not for the first time, she wondered whether her sister's spirit still existed. Hadley was no expert on God, but the human body was a marvel, and the more she'd learned about it, the more she believed it hadn't happened all on its own. Just about every civilization in human history had a theory about the afterlife. Hadley wasn't prepared to pick one of them above the others as being right, but neither was she keen to declare the entirety of humanity to be wrong. So, perhaps her sister was out there in some form, smiling down on her precious boy.

Hadley prayed that was the case.

"What are you doing?" Tyne nudged Hadley's shoulder, breaking her out of the trance she'd been in.

"Nothing," Hadley answered, embarrassed at the thoughts that had been swirling in her head. She was a scientist, pragmatic. Metaphysical stuff was for artsy types, like Tyne.

"You almost looked like you were praying." Tyne didn't say it to tease.

"Yes, well, you caught me." Although she basically had been, Hadley said it like the very idea was preposterous. "I was praying to all the powers that be for you to hurry so we wouldn't be late to my parents."

Tyne swatted Hadley's arm.

"Hey," Hadley pretended to scold, "no violence in front of the boy."

Tyne shook her head but couldn't help laughing. "Your auntie thinks she's so funny."

"If you asked any of my former residents, few would accuse me of having a sense of humor. But even fewer would accuse me of being late. So...?" Hadley looked hopeful.

"You're the one standing around chitchatting with God," Tyne said with a shrug. "I've been ready for days."

The drive to her childhood home was short. Too short. Hadley chastised herself for thinking that way, but these weekend visits took a lot out of her. After learning how much Kayleigh had been juggling on her own, Hadley had sworn to do better, but it didn't mean it was easy to achieve. While Hadley had come to love dropping in on the joyful chaos that was Tyne's family, every time they pulled up in front of her own parents' house, Hadley's body tensed for whatever new challenge the universe would throw at her. Her parents were not aging well, and even as a medical professional, it overwhelmed her. She didn't know how other people, those without her knowledge and resources, managed it at all.

The second Hadley walked through the front door, her nostrils recoiled, triggering a gag reflex. "Dad, what is that stench?"

Hadley's father sat in his recliner, his feet up, looking mildly perplexed. "Is it still bad? I thought it was starting to clear."

Joining her in the living room, Tyne covered her mouth with a palm. "Oh, wow."

"Are you telling me you don't notice it?" Hadley flipped through her mental index of conditions that caused a loss of smell. Diabetes. High blood pressure medication. Simply growing old. Her father checked off multiple boxes.

"Kayleigh, is that you?" Though it was in the upper eighties and the air was thick with humidity, Hadley's mom was wearing a heavy sweater.

Hadley's heart clenched when she heard her sister's name. "Mom, it's Hadley."

Did she need to say more, remind her mother that Kayleigh was dead? It seemed impossible she could've forgotten, but if she had, maybe reminding her would be unnecessarily cruel.

"Yes, of course." The confusion slowly dissipated from her mother's eyes, replaced by pain. She'd remembered on her own, letting Hadley off the hook. This time. "And there's my baby Owen."

"What a lovely sweater, Nancy," Tyne said, helping the older woman to the couch and keeping a firm grasp on the baby even as she let Hadley's mom feel like she was holding him on her own. "Are you sure you don't want something cooler?"

"No, I'm okay." Hadley's mom sniffed, her nose wrinkling. "Do you smell something?"

"Yeah, definitely." Hadley's eyes stung from how terrible it smelled in the house. How long had it been like this? Hadley gave Tyne a questioning look, asking if she was okay with her parents. When Tyne nodded, Hadley announced, "I'm going to hunt down the smell."

"I thought it might be a dead mouse in the kitchen, but I couldn't bend far enough to check under the radiators and the refrigerator." Her dad struggled to get out of his chair as if to join her in the hunt, but Hadley quickly put a stop to it.

"Leave it to me, Dad."

The closer she got to the kitchen, the more she agreed with her father that this was the source of the stench. It was nearly overwhelming, getting stronger the closer she got to the oven. She studied the dark area beneath the appliance with distaste, grabbing a broom.

"It's just a dead mouse," she muttered as she swept into the small space, fighting a wave of nausea brought on in part by the rotten odor but also by the thought of pulling the dead thing into the light. "If you can cut into bodies, you can handle this."

Aside from a few dust bunnies, the broom came out empty. There was nothing on the burners. Even the counters were devoid of dishes, and the few items in the refrigerator looked fresh.

Where could it be?

Her eyes landed on the oven. It was the only place left to check. Her fingers wrapped around the metal handle. The slightest crack of the door released a cloud of noxious fumes into the air. Gagging, Hadley used oven mitts to pull out the contents, an aluminum casserole dish still covered with foil. She didn't bother to remove the covering before tossing the entire container into a plastic garbage bag, tying several knots to contain the disgustingness, and then carrying it directly to the trash can on the side of the house.

"Did you find it?" Hadley's dad asked when she finally came back into the room.

"I sure did." She shuddered. Of all the truly gross smells she had encountered in the emergency room, this one was still near the top of the list.

"Was it a mouse?" Tyne's expression was filled with sympathy for the poor, dead creature.

"No. My guess is a tuna casserole."

Hadley's mom put a hand over her mouth, her expression like that of a kid who just realized they forgot to do their homework. "Oh dear. I think I pulled a tuna casserole out of the freezer the other day and set it in the oven to let it thaw. Paul, did we ever have it for dinner?"

"Not sure," her dad replied. "All those casseroles seem alike."

Were they for real? Her parents were acting like this was an everyday occurrence. It wasn't. This was the beginning of the end.

"Mom. Dad." As Hadley raised her voice, her parents stopped trying to remember which casseroles they'd eaten and turned to her with matching shocked expressions.

"What is it, Hadley?" She couldn't put her finger on why, but her mom sounded angry.

"I can't let you two continue to live like this." Hadley emphasized her words with her hands.

"Young lady"—her dad sat forward, his voice deep and stern—"you are not in a position to *let* us do anything. We are your parents, and believe it or not, we've been getting by just fine without you."

"Not that we had a choice about that," her mom added, like a spear between Hadley's ribs. "You were too busy to make time for us before. Don't think you get to make decisions for us now because Kayleigh's gone."

"I..." Hadley fell silent. There was nothing left to say.

A little while later, while Owen kept her parents occupied, Hadley and Tyne slipped into the kitchen, which finally smelled better thanks to every window being open and the ceiling fan running full speed.

Hadley leaned against the counter. "What am I going to do? My mom isn't capable of heating up a prepared dish. My dad's feet are so bad he can barely walk. Kayleigh swore to them they'd never have to go into a nursing home, but with my job and Owen, I'm not sure that's a promise I can keep. I don't want to let them down, but you heard them in there. They're too angry with me to listen to reason."

"I know." Tyne ran her hand up and down Hadley's arm. "They can't continue like this, no matter what they say, but maybe it doesn't have to be as bad as you all think. Didn't Rebecca Porter mention her mom works at a new assisted living facility?"

"I think so. But how do I talk them into going?"

"You don't." Tyne's hand stilled, heat soaking into Hadley's arm like it was a sponge. "You get them to think it's their idea. Just like with kids."

Hadley looked at Tyne askance. "You think they'd fall for it?"

Tyne chuckled. "It works on my brothers. It will with them, too. Maybe we should give Rebecca a call to see what that place is all about. If it's right for them, we'll proceed. But with a gentle touch. I'll walk you through it."

"You're way better at this family stuff than I am," Hadley admitted. As distressing as the situation was, Tyne's use of the word *we* made Hadley feel stronger. "Actually, there might be another reason for me to call Rebecca soon."

"Oh?" Tyne's face prepared for the worst, making Hadley grateful she didn't have bad news.

"What would you think if I accepted an offer to work at Pioneer Valley Hospital?" Hadley's heart raced as she tried to interpret the look on Tyne's face. She'd half expected the woman to dance a jig at the prospect of such a straightforward solution to their issues, but

Tyne's expression remained guarded as she chewed her lower lip.

"You already do work there." Tyne's expression was searching as she looked into Hadley's eyes. "Are you talking about giving up your life in Boston and moving here for good?"

"I'm not sure, but maybe." Hadley rubbed her hands together, squeezing her fingers. "It would make certain decisions easier."

"You mean with Owen," Tyne said.

"And my parents, too." *And you*, Hadley added silently, knowing that was the biggest draw of all.

Tyne took a deep breath. "But is it what you want? Your whole life is in Boston. You have a condo to die for, and you work at one of the preeminent hospitals not just in Massachusetts but in the entire country. You'd be giving up a lot."

Hadley nodded slowly. "I would. But maybe I'd be gaining in other ways. I thought you'd be all for it."

Tyne placed her hand on Hadley's arm. "I would love to think this is the answer to everything, that you could be happy living in this little world with Owen and me. But I worry it won't be enough for you. I can't bear the thought of you being miserable because you made a choice you thought I wanted you to make, not the one your heart is telling you to choose."

"This is all so much to think about." Hadley waved her hand as if to encompass her parents, Owen, Tyne, and maybe the rest of the universe, too. She felt like she was drowning and grabbed Tyne's hand to stay afloat. "I'm not sure if I know what to do."

"We'll figure it out together," Tyne assured her. "Whatever you decide, we'll make it work. Your happiness is worth more than taking an easy way out."

Assurance washed over her, filling Hadley with calm. Just yesterday she'd held onto an actual beating heart, but it was becoming increasingly clear that when it came to her own heart, it was completely in Tyne's hands.

CHAPTER TWENTY

"Sleep tight, baby Owen." Tyne kissed her fingertips and gently placed them on the baby's head, relieved he'd finally fallen asleep. This latest round of teething had been rough, and sleep had been scarce for everyone.

She tiptoed down the stairs, doing her best to avoid the fifth step, which groaned no matter the amount of weight. It was one of the house's many quirks, not that she was complaining. In fact, Tyne had grown to love living here so much she could hardly bear to think of moving. It wasn't just the house she would miss. Then again, there were so many unknowns in her future, Tyne avoided thinking about it as much as she could. The furthest ahead she dared to look was the middle of the week, when Sheila from the art gallery was sending her guy to pick up Tyne's painting.

In the kitchen, Tyne's eyes darted from the electric

kettle to the wine rack, weighing her options. Despite being known all over town as the paint and sip lady, she was usually more of an herbal tea in the evening kind of girl. On the other hand, Owen had spent most of the day crying from his sore gums, and her nerves were shot. She chose a bottle at random, digging the corkscrew out of the drawer and filling one of the bulbous glasses a bit past the halfway point.

"It's a celebration," she said out loud, though it wasn't like the house cared how much she imbibed. And if Ryan's spirit was watching over her, as she liked to imagine sometimes it was, she knew her brother would've been the first to raise his glass on this momentous occasion. It wasn't every day an artist made a gallery sale.

Opening the sliding door, she stepped onto the deck, her heart expanding at the sight of the backyard art studio. What a godsend that place had been. Tyne was incredibly proud of her painting. Her creativity had rocketed to a whole new level, and she knew without a doubt she had that amazing space to thank for it.

And Hadley, who was the reason she was here.

Stubborn woman, she thought with a smile, not like she was much different. It was the one thing keeping them from coming to a compromise, although if Hadley would listen, Tyne had come up with the most brilliant solution. With a little bit of luck, they could enjoy the best of city and small-town living, and do it without spending a single night apart. At least it turned out the past few long, sleepless nights had been good for something. She had done a bit of thinking and couldn't wait for Hadley to get home so she could share her idea in detail.

The sound of a car coming up the driveway alerted Tyne to Hadley's return. The kitchen door squeaked open just as Tyne slipped back inside the house. She was about to say great timing, but when her eyes landed on Hadley's devastated face, the first thing out of her mouth was, "Did someone die?"

"I wish." Anger flashed in Hadley's eyes.

A twinge of nervousness set Tyne on edge. It was unlike Hadley even to joke about that. "What happened?"

Instead of answering, Hadley crossed to the counter where the open wine bottle sat, and poured a glass. She didn't sip it slowly but drank down several gulps without stopping to breathe.

Tyne's pulse raced. Something was very wrong. "Please, tell me what's going on."

"Like you don't already know," Hadley snapped.

"I'm not following." Tyne's brow scrunched. "You're not making any sense."

Hadley sat heavily on one of the barstools, tracing the rim of the almost empty wineglass with her index finger. "I'm being fired."

"What?" Tyne cringed over her screech. She placed a finger to her lips and then pointed upstairs to the nursery to explain why they should be quiet. "I don't understand. They love you at Pioneer Valley, besides which, they're perpetually short-staffed."

"I'm not talking about PVH, although they're probably next." Hadley was struggling to get the words out since she was speaking through gritted teeth. "I'm talking about Boston."

"Oh, Hadley, no! Are they making cuts?" Tyne's brain swirled. Poor Hadley. No wonder she was so upset. "This doesn't make sense. I thought your job was protected because of the family leave laws."

"Yeah, it is. Until Friday, when my twelve weeks expire."

"But after that you're going on an unpaid leave of absence. They wouldn't save a dime by letting you go right now." Tyne was starting to shake. "This makes no sense. You must've made a mistake."

"I've made a lot of mistakes," Hadley muttered. "This isn't about money, Tyne. One of the first-year residents filed a complaint against me, claiming a hostile work environment."

"You can't be serious." Hand pressed against her chest, Tyne lowered herself onto one of the other bar stools. "Surely it's not true."

"Of course, it's not true," Hadley barked, causing Tyne to pull back like she was afraid of being bitten by an unfriendly dog. "I only worked with her one night, the night of the accident, ironically enough. She made a lazy mistake that nearly killed a patient. I lectured her about it, which is part of my job. Any other doctor would've done the same."

"I know I'm not an HR expert," Tyne said, her voice as soothing as she could make it, "but I don't think they can terminate your employment based on nothing but the word of one disgruntled underling with an ax to grind. Won't they need to have an investigation?"

"If they intended to fire me officially, yes. But they found a loophole. The hospital's arrogant horse's ass of a chief of staff—"

"You've mentioned him before and how you two have butted heads."

"He's had it in for me from the start. Now he's claiming they have no record of my official request for a leave of absence, even though I filed the paperwork in person. He's telling everyone I informed management I'd started working at PVH—which I did, on the same day I filed the fucking paperwork he says I didn't do—and as a result, he assumed I simply wasn't planning to come back. Ever so conveniently, it's a week past the deadline to ask for a leave of absence, so I'm shit out of luck."

"He can't do that, can he?"

"Apparently, he can, at least according to Marcy." Hadley shut her eyes, looking like her head might explode at any second. "She's not even supposed to be talking to me about any of this since she represents the hospital, but she cleared up a thing or two once I promised not to use her name."

"What else did she tell you?"

"That the real reason the hospital administration is shitting bricks over Amanda is because of the lawyer she's got representing her."

"I can't believe this. It figures someone like her would hire a bloodsucker. Who is it?"

"Does the name Robert Atkinson ring a bell?" Hadley's expression turned to pure venom. "You don't have to pretend anymore."

All of Tyne's blood turned to ice at the mention of the attorney's name, but this couldn't have anything to do with her. It had to be a sick, terrible coincidence and nothing more. "What are you talking about?"

"I have to hand it to you. The way you've been playing it so cool until now. You're getting everything you wanted." Hadley clapped her hands slowly. "Bravo."

"I didn't want any of this." Tyne's words came out as a shriek. The room was closing in on her. It was impossible. She'd called and told him not to do anything. And this went beyond anything she'd imagined. She would never have agreed to anything like this. There'd been a mistake.

"I have to admit when I first heard the news, I figured Michael was the evil genius, but no. He's capitalizing on what you put into motion. He probably couldn't believe his good luck. Of course, when PVH finds out—and that will only be a matter of time—I know exactly how it will play out. Dr. Cassidy may want me, but management will act like they don't know me. There's no reason for them to get tangled up with a slime ball like Atkinson. The man's a fucking shark, but you already know that."

"Me?" Tyne placed a hand on her chest.

"Seriously," Hadley's volume increased to just under a shout. "Stop. You don't have to keep up the pretense. It's over. I know what you did. You hired him to do this."

Tyne was trembling so badly she had to press her hands against the counter to keep them still. "No. I mean, yes, I went to see Atkinson, but, I only did it after you got the dirty-tricks ball rolling."

"So, this is my fault? I ask for a few tax returns, and you arrange for me to never work again. That's what you'd call tit for tat?"

"Stop putting words in my mouth." Tyne balled her fists, digging them into her thighs. "For one thing, you know it was *way* more than a few tax returns. When I got that letter from your lawyer, demanding all those insane financial disclosures, I was scared. And, yes, mad. I went to see Atkinson, but less than twenty-four hours passed before I called him and said I didn't want to do it. He must not have gotten my message."

"He might not have, but I'm getting the message loud and clear." The muscles in Hadley's jaw tensed. "The kicker is, at first, I thought it had to be a mistake, too. Marcy told me Atkinson never takes on a client unless he's met them face-to-face. I told her it was impossible for you to be involved, because I couldn't think of a time when you could've snuck off to Boston on your own. Then it dawned on me. I've been such an idiot."

Tyne's stomach plummeted. "Hadley, I can explain."

"I drove you to Boston so you could stab me in the back." Hadley's eyes were glassy with tears. "You fucked me over. And if that wasn't bad enough, later that night, you literally fucked me. Did you think it was funny? A sick joke?"

"That wasn't—" Tyne choked, unable to continue.

"How could you? You promised I could trust you, and I did, and now look where it got me. Was it not enough to lie and cheat to take Owen? You needed to destroy me on every level? That's cold."

"It wasn't like that." Tyne's words were barely more than a pathetic whimper.

"Which part?" Hadley folded her hands on the kitchen island, leaning back as if daring her to speak.

"All of it!" Tyne clasped her hands, willing Hadley to believe her. "I knew Atkinson played rough, but I had no idea going after your career was part of the plan. I swear. He never said a thing about it."

"Uh-huh." Hadley's eyes burrowed into her, unblinking. "What *was* the plan, exactly? I'm really dying to know how he could've gotten things so wrong."

"Uh, we didn't talk about specifics." Tyne knew

how weak an excuse that was. She'd never buy it, either.

"Yeah, right. When I met with my lawyer, she spelled out everything. The paperwork trick was totally legitimate, and I thought *that* felt dirty and couldn't stomach it. You and Atkinson took it to a whole new level. If you wanted Owen this bad—"

"I didn't," Tyne sobbed. "This wasn't supposed to happen."

"My career is dead. There's no way I'll recover from this." Hadley massaged her forehead. "You've won."

"Please, let me fix it."

"You can't, and I can't do this anymore." Hadley unsteadily got to her feet. "I'm going."

"Where?"

"Home."

Before Tyne could regain the ability to speak, Hadley stormed out the door. A minute later, a car engine roared to life outside and tore out of the driveway. Tyne crumpled, laying her head on the cold countertop and closing her eyes as if she could shut out the world.

She wasn't sure how much time passed before she was able to move, able to think. When she finally could form a coherent thought, she reached for her phone and punched in the number for her lawyer. It was after seven o'clock by then, but she was sure he'd be working late. Guys like him usually did. By the time his assistant patched Tyne through, she was seeing red.

"Atkinson," he barked.

"What the *fuck* did you do?" Tyne screamed.

"Who is this?" he asked, his tone so calm it was clearly not the first time someone he didn't know had called and screamed obscenities at him.

"Tyne Briggs."

"Tyne Briggs. Tyne Briggs," he drawled as if waiting for his memory to click. "Oh, the nephew case. Yeah, I think that went pretty well."

"You think it went *well*?"

"Sure. We've got her right where we need her now."

"It's a lie!"

"It's an allegation. One that will evaporate as soon as she agrees to the custody terms we set forth."

"*We*? No, no. This is all you. How could you do this? I left a message—"

"Ah, that's right. I remember now."

For a moment, Tyne stopped breathing. "You mean to say you got my message, and you still went after her *job*?"

"Listen, sweetheart, we established on day one that I'm in charge. The buck stops with me. I've been in this business long enough to know when a client calls at the crack of dawn and leaves some rambling message because they suddenly grew a damn conscience overnight, it's bullshit."

"It wasn't bullshit," Tyne spat.

"Then you should've fired me. I told you, as long as we had a contract, you did it my way."

"You also told me the retainer was nonrefundable," Tyne pointed out. "If I fired you outright, I couldn't afford anyone else for all the paperwork."

"Then you made your choice. Look, lady. You'll thank me once the shock has worn off. From what I've heard, that Dr. Moore is in a world of pain." He chuckled, sounding worse than any villain she'd watched in a movie. "She'll give you whatever you want to make it go away."

That wasn't true. It wasn't even possible. What Tyne wanted was Hadley, and thanks to this demented stunt, that was the one thing she was certain to never, ever have.

"I'll tell you what I want, and this time I'll say it in words you'll understand. You're fired!" Tyne ended the call, glaring at the dark screen.

Finally, she slammed the phone onto the counter. Then she picked it up and did it again. Sheila at the art gallery had been right. Sometimes when you were mad enough, there was nothing more satisfying in the world.

What was she going to do now? How could she get Hadley to believe her? One moment of weakness had destroyed every ounce of trust they'd built between them. She wanted to take it all back, but it was impossible. Tyne's only recourse was to build a time machine. Hadley loved being a doctor, and Tyne had taken that away. Hadley would never forgive that. She'd said Tyne had won, but that wasn't the case. She'd lost everything.

Tyne had fallen completely, desperately in love with Hadley, and now she had lost her. At the speed Hadley had been driving, she was probably already halfway to Boston. And Tyne would never see her again.

A tear rolled down her cheek.

Followed by another.

She wanted to talk to Ryan so badly, but of course, that was impossible, and this time pretending to ask his ghost for advice wouldn't cut it. She needed real help.

Gingerly, Tyne picked up her phone, checking it over for cracks from her recent outburst before dialing the only other person she could think of who might understand.

"Hi, Mom. Can you come over? I've done something terrible, and I think I may have ruined my life."

CHAPTER TWENTY-ONE

Hadley woke with a start. Was that a baby crying?

Owen.

"Hold on, baby boy." She kicked off the covers, ready to spring into action, but when her feet hit the floor, she froze at the feel of carpet instead of a hardwood floor.

Where am I?

Straining to hear, she realized it wasn't a baby's cry that had torn her from her slumber but a particularly loudmouthed crow. When fully awake, the two sounds weren't all that similar, but this new nurturing instinct of hers seemed to intensify every single day.

Not that it matters now.

Hadley rubbed her face, but she didn't cry. She was all done with that, having soaked her pillow into the wee hours before finally falling into a fitful sleep. Her tears were gone, all used up, leaving an empty hollowness inside her chest.

Crying was pointless. Everything seemed pointless.

She was still exhausted, but she wouldn't be able to fall back asleep. The sun was already up, giving her a clear view of her mom's jumbled craft room. When she'd gotten in her car the night before, her parents' house was the only place she could think of to go. Blinking red numbers on an old clock radio told her it was six minutes after six. She'd slept in her clothes, so she was already dressed, though not exactly looking forward to facing the day.

"Might as well get it over with," she mumbled to herself.

In the front room, her dad was manning his usual post, seated in his recliner with his swollen feet propped up, a hole in the toe of one sock. Her mother was knitting. It was oddly refreshing, considering Hadley's world had been turned upside down, to know that here at her childhood home, her parents were doing exactly what they would normally do. The world kept spinning.

"Couldn't you sleep?" Her mom tucked her knitting away in the basket by the couch.

"Crow."

"What?" Her dad's face twisted into confusion.

"A crow, as in the big black bird, was outside my window making a racket."

"Let me get you a cup of coffee." Her mom made a

move to get up, but Hadley waved for her to sit back down.

"I got it. Does anyone need a refill?"

They handed over their empty mugs with looks of gratitude. In the kitchen, the coffee maker was already making those funny burbling noises that told her a fresh pot was almost done. When she returned with coffee in hand, her mom was back to knitting and her dad had dozed off in his chair with a gentle snore. Lucky guy. Unfortunately, Hadley got her restlessness from her mother, who filled every hour doing something useful.

"Whatcha knitting?" Hadley sat down on the couch near her mom.

"A sweater for Owen." She motioned to a sheet of cryptic letters and numbers she could somehow turn into three-dimensional objects, though Hadley had never figured out how. Her mother's knitting knowledge was so ingrained it seemed to be untouched by her lapses in memory, at least for now. She held the half-finished garment up to show Hadley. "He's getting so big."

"He's almost walking." Any day now, her sweet baby nephew was sure to take his first step, and she would miss it. She'd miss it all. Hadley swallowed her coffee, forcing down a sob.

"What are you doing home again?" The question had nothing to do with memory. Her mom's inquiry was pointed, much like the knitting needles that clicked and clacked in her hands. "You didn't really say when you got here last night. Just ran down the hall and closed the door."

"Sorry about that." Hadley shut her eyes, awash in a wave of embarrassment. Her parents must have thought she was nuts. Or she'd scared the hell out of them. Either way, it hadn't been her finest moment. "It's complicated."

"This has to do with Tyne." It was a statement, not a question, and Hadley could tell from her mom's tone this was one of her lucid days, when all the synapses in her brain were firing at full speed. That could be either good or bad for Hadley, depending what the woman had to say. "You don't have to pretend, honey. Your dad and I know you two have been dating, or whatever the term for it is these days."

"I'm not sure a term exists for what's been going on between us." Hadley hoped there was no dictionary entry for it, because that would mean it was a frequent enough occurrence to merit its own word. Hadley wouldn't wish the experience she was going through on another living soul.

"That doesn't sound good." The clicking of needles slowed. "I don't think I've ever seen you as happy as you've been since you and Tyne moved in together and started taking care of Owen. I was positive things were going well."

"They were, but—that's over."

"Just like that? The daughter I know and love has never been one to quit." Her mom didn't meet Hadley's eye, but she didn't have to.

"It isn't like that."

"What is it like then?" The needles stilled, and her mom gave Hadley the stare, the one that said to give it to her straight, and don't even think of trying to con her. *Good ol' Mom.* That look used to strike terror into Hadley when she was a teenager, but it relieved her almost to the point of tears to see it now when she needed her mother so badly.

"Tyne hired a lawyer to represent her in the custody dispute."

"Of course, she did. So did you. Surely, you must have expected her to do the same?"

"It's not the fact she hired one that's the issue. The guy's as shady as they come, and he's put a dirty trick in motion that's threatening to wreck my career."

"Can you fill in the blanks?" Her mom was back to knitting, but Hadley knew she was listening intently and would take in the details.

As much as Hadley didn't want to go into the particulars, because it still hurt like hell, she needed to talk about it. She explained the leave of absence paperwork, the made-up allegations, and how it could impact her shot at a permanent position at PVH. When she reached the end, Hadley's tone hardened. "And Tyne let him do it."

She'd finished her story, but her mom leveled her eyes at Hadley as if to say she knew there was more. "And, what did you do to force Tyne into a corner?"

"You've always done that," Hadley defended. "Even when I was a kid. If I said Patrick down the block hit me, you asked what *I* did to deserve it. You've never been on my side."

"I've always been on your side, but I also know my daughter. You never like to lose. And while it's possible I've read her wrong, I really don't think Tyne is the type to resort to nasty tricks out of the blue."

Hadley tried to stay firm, but her mom's unrelenting gaze made Hadley feel like that little kid trying to say her hand wasn't in the cookie jar when it was. "It's possible I hired a lawyer who put some things in motion that were less than kind."

"Uh-huh." While her mom's tone was smug at being right, it was clear she wasn't passing judgement, at least not until she heard everything. "What might those things have been?"

"The lawyer filed a request for full, detailed financial disclosures, both business and personal, for Tyne and also her parents."

"Beyond what the court would normally require?"

"Way beyond." Hadley's chin drooped toward her chest. She didn't want to admit everything, but she knew she had to. "Technically, it was within my rights to ask for them, but I knew the real purpose was to make her jump through enough hoops that she'd get overwhelmed and give up."

"Hadley." Shit, that was her mom's *I'm disappointed in you, young lady* tone. "How could you do such a thing?"

"I know, Mom. I know." Hadley squirmed, wishing she could disappear. Even if what Tyne's lawyer had done was way worse, it didn't negate the fact Hadley had fucked up. "I called it off, but it was too late. I foolishly thought because none of them ever mentioned it, the lawyer hadn't gotten around to filing the request. But that wasn't the case. Tyne was mad, and she had every right to be, and that's when she hired her own attack dog to come rip my throat out."

Her mom flinched, her eyes displaying a mixture of disappointment and disbelief. "That doesn't sound like Tyne. She's one of the sweetest people I've ever met. In fact, she painted this room for us."

Hadley's gaze flitted to the walls, noting the line of stenciled roses near the ceiling. Of course, Tyne wouldn't think it was good enough to slap on a fresh coat of paint and call it done. She'd gone above and beyond to make it as pretty and cheerful as she could. It was exactly what Hadley would've expected from the Tyne she thought she knew. Hadley let out an anguished sigh.

"Tyne claims she didn't know what her lawyer would do, but..." Hadley swiped away a tear. "Even if that's true, how do I go on as if it never happened? I feel completely betrayed. It hurts so much because I think I was falling in love with her."

As soon as the words were out, Hadley knew there was no doubt about it. She loved Tyne in a way she'd never experienced before or suspected she ever would again. The only other person she loved with the same all-encompassing intensity was Owen. And now they both were gone. Her heart shattered at the realization of all she'd lost.

Her mom set her knitting aside, scooted closer, and put a hand on Hadley's shoulder. "Can't the two of you reach a compromise without lawyers?"

"After all of this?"

"*Because* of all this." Her mom's tone hinted at a lecture to come, one that no doubt would be right on the money but Hadley probably wouldn't like. "This isn't about hurt feelings, pride, or anything else. It's about Owen, an innocent baby who is parentless through no fault of his own. The two of you need to stop playing games and put that sweet child first. If you really think you have what it takes to be a parent, you need to learn that everything from this point forward is about *him*. Everything else comes second, including you."

Deep inside, Hadley began to shake, and not only because she knew her mother was right. She also fully realized for the first time the love her mother described was exactly what she felt for her own daughters. Had Kayleigh known? She probably had. In a lot of ways, her baby sister had been a lot smarter than Hadley. Not in school, but in the stuff that really counted.

Her mind went to the lecture she'd given Amanda, the same one she'd given so many residents throughout the years, and that was now being used against her. It was basically the doctor's version of what her mom had just said. A good doctor puts the patient's life first over everything else. How was it Hadley could do that on a professional level but was utterly failing when applying the rule to her private life?

"You're right. I'll fix it." Hadley got up, not sure where she was going but knowing she needed to move her body in order to clear her mind. "Mom, I..."

"What is it?" Her mom, who had just begun to reach for her knitting, paused and looked at her expectantly.

"I love you." Hadley's heart lurched. Life was uncertain. Her mom might forget someday that she'd said it, or might not even know who she was, but Hadley would always remember, and that counted for something. From now on, she would do all she could to make sure her parents always knew how much she loved them and appreciated everything they'd done for her.

-⎰⎱⎰⎱-

THE NONDESCRIPT DINER was quiet as Hadley waited, somewhere in MetroWest Boston, not far from the turnpike. She was scanning the day's news on her phone with halfhearted interest, but looked up as a shadow fell across her. Marcy, still dressed in a suit from the office, slipped into the red and white vinyl booth and folded her hands on the white Formica table. "You know I'm not supposed to talk to you."

"Yet, you came anyway," Hadley pointed out.

"It was on my way home from work, and I hear they have good coffee." Marcy raised a hand, signaling the server to bring her a cup.

The woman came over with a full pot, and Hadley nodded toward her own half-empty cup when it was her turn. She'd lost track of how much she'd already had, but considering her lousy sleep the night before, not to mention the long drive ahead of her to get back to her parents' house, what she really needed was caffeine on an IV drip. "I appreciate you coming. I have a question for you, and I knew it wasn't a good idea to talk over the phone."

"It's not a great idea for me to talk to you in person, either, but to hell with it. What management's trying to do to you is wrong."

"Why is this happening?" Hadley set her white ceramic mug down on the table in a motion that came just short of slamming. "Amanda's complaint is as see-through as a white T-shirt in the rain. They can't possibly be giving it any real weight."

Marcy sighed. "I am unable to comment on an ongoing—"

"I know. I know." Hadley's head drooped. Calling Marcy had been a real Hail Mary, but she'd hoped as a friend, the woman might offer her a crumb or two.

Marcy held up her hand. "I wasn't done. Given my position, I can't comment on your current predicament vis-à-vis hospital management. I can, however, tell you a fascinating true story of a good friend of mine. We'll call her... *Padley*."

Hadley smiled, leaning forward. "I'm all ears. Was this Padley person a doctor?"

"No, she worked at an ice cream stand."

Hadley pretended to give a serious nod. "I see. So definitely nothing at all like me."

"Exactly." Marcy's mouth twitched. "Totally different scenario. In Padley's case, she had a boss who was a grade-A turd—"

"Let me guess. Was his name Tichael?"

"As a matter of fact, yes. Like I said, he was a turd, but it wasn't completely his fault because a much bigger ice cream conglomerate had recently bought the stand and was putting a lot of pressure on everyone to cut costs and increase ROI, along with a bunch of other acronyms that business people care about."

"And getting rid of a highly paid... *ice cream scooper* was a convenient way to meet his goal?"

"Precisely, especially because he has an inferiority complex and doesn't like that Padley is better at scooping ice cream than he is. So, when he got a letter from a big shot law firm representing an obnoxious junior employee who is almost universally disliked for being a pain in the ass who does not take her ice cream scooping career seriously enough, Tichael sensed an opportunity."

"Because no one's going to ask questions about missing leave of absence paperwork for someone who's facing legal action, even if it's nothing more than a nuisance suit?"

"That's it in a nutshell."

Hadley rested her chin against her palm, feeling like the universe was pressing down on her. "What can I do to make my problem go away?"

"As I see it, there are a few things you could try," Marcy replied, dropping any pretense they weren't discussing Hadley's case. "Legally, federal law protects your job through Friday. If you were to return to work before then, it makes Michael's little stunt a lot harder to pull off."

"I'm not on the schedule."

"Friday kicks off Fourth of July weekend. I'm sure you could find someone who'd jump at the chance to make a last-minute trade."

Hadley laughed faintly as she pictured what Michael's face would look like if she showed up for work on Friday. "But what about the other thing? The

Amanda issue?"

"The only reason anyone gave her so much as a minute of their time was because she waltzed in with Robert Atkinson backing her up. He's... well-known. Which is why when the stupid girl started telling everyone who would listen that he was helping her pro bono, as if that would prove how strong a case she had, I knew something was up."

"A guy like that doesn't help his grandmother across the street without there being something in it for him," Hadley scoffed. "You were right, by the way. He's representing Tyne. She admitted it herself, even if she denied giving him the go-ahead for what he did."

"That means the only thing he cares about is the custody case."

"Meaning?"

"Meaning if that gets resolved, he'll make any excuse to drop Amanda like a hot potato. There's no money in it, and as soon as that happens, she's gone. There's no end to the list of people she's pissed off as she's made her way through the rotations."

Hadley considered her friend's advice with a heavy heart. "I honestly don't know how Tyne and I can reach a compromise with everything that's gone on between us."

"There's another option, though I know you won't like it." Marcy's expression was grim. "You can take yourself out of the equation."

It took a second for that to sink in. "You're suggesting I withdraw my petition for custody."

"I'm not officially suggesting anything because this conversation never happened. But you know that saying about it taking two to tango? The same goes for legal battles."

"What happens if I refuse to cave?"

"Atkinson's the type of guy who gets his kicks from being a sadistic fuck." Marcy's face twisted with obvious revulsion. "Truth's on your side, and I like to believe that still matters in the end, but until then, it won't be pretty."

"I appreciate the advice, Marcy. I really do." Standing, Hadley pulled out her wallet, dropping a twenty-dollar bill on the table for the waitress. "I think I know what I need to do."

Marcy gave Hadley's shoulder a pat. "Hang in there, my friend. Never forget you're not only a good person but a damn fine doctor. This will work out. Have faith."

Hadley promised to do so, though it would've been easier to have faith if she hadn't so recently had everything she believed in torn to shreds. Still, between talking with her mother this morning and now Marcy, Hadley had come to a vital decision. She could not, would not, use her nephew as a pawn. She would do what was best for Owen, even though it was going to hurt like hell.

What made it worse was after all of this, she was still in love with Tyne.

Hadley wanted Owen. She wanted Tyne. And more than anything, she wanted both of them in her life every day. But she had to face the truth. What she wanted was impossible.

The only way to put Owen first so he could have the life he deserved was for her to walk away.

CHAPTER TWENTY-TWO

"There you go, buddy. All clean." Tyne set the towel on the counter and lifted Owen out of the high chair. She tickled his belly. "Until you figure out how to get the spoon to your mouth a little more consistently, I think what we really need is a device to run you through like an automatic carwash. Would you like that?"

He giggled, wrapping his arms around her neck. She pressed him close against her chest, her fingertips sinking into his soft baby rolls. It was one of the best feelings on earth, but still wasn't enough to raise her spirits this morning.

Tyne looked at the kitchen door with a desperate longing. She could picture Hadley opening it wide, striding in, and saying, "Good morning!" like she always did when she came home after an overnight shift. Only that wasn't going to happen, because she wasn't at work right now.

She was just *gone*.

It had been over twenty-four hours, and there'd been no word from her. Tyne looked down at the baby in her arms, her heart a lead weight. She held the baby tighter to her chest, and he rested against her just right so the spattering of blond fuzz on top of his head tickled her chin.

Tyne's phone buzzed, and her breath caught in her chest as she fumbled to retrieve the device from her pocket with one hand while holding Owen with the other. Her spirits plummeted when she saw it was her mother calling and not Hadley, but she did her best to keep the disappointment out of her tone.

"Hi, Mom."

"Still no word from her?" Obviously, no matter how much she tried, there was no fooling her mother.

"Not even a text. I've left so many messages I've lost track, but I can't get her to respond."

"Have you checked with her parents?"

"I didn't want to worry them, but Owen and I took a drive past their house yesterday afternoon, and there was no sign of her car." Tyne shut her eyes, feeling a fresh stab of pain as she remembered the empty driveway.

"Don't give up hope, honey," her mom urged.

Easier said than done.

"I want her to come home." Except, this wasn't

Hadley's home, and if she hadn't come back by now, it was unlikely she intended to. "I've gotta go, but I'll call you if I hear anything."

Hanging up the phone, Tyne wanted to cry, but Owen didn't need that from her.

He needed his family to put him first, and that was what she intended to do.

Even if it cleaved her heart into pieces that might never mend.

Tyne set Owen in his playpen as she sat on the couch in the living room to rummage through a pile of paperwork she'd asked her mom to bring over the day before. The information she needed was sure to be there somewhere.

Here it is.

Tyne plucked the emergency guardianship paperwork from the middle of the stack and scanned toward the bottom. William Thatcher was the name of the judge who had signed off on it, the same judge who had finalized her and Hadley's co-guardianship agreement. That was the man she needed to see.

She scooped Owen from his playpen and found his shoes.

"How about we go on an adventure?" she asked in an excited voice as she got him ready. It took every ounce of will she had to keep her tone cheery. "Would you like that, Owen? Adventure!"

The baby squealed, raising his chubby arms. He was so adorable Tyne nearly lost it. Sometimes it seemed like it was this kid's purpose on Earth to be as cute as possible.

Tyne got him buckled into his car seat and slid behind the wheel. Once the key was in the ignition, she paused. Did she really have to do this? She knew she did. This mess was her fault, and she would be the one to fix it.

She started the car, turning on Owen's favorite collection of sing-along songs for the ride to the courthouse. The street outside the formidable brick building was mostly deserted, making parking a breeze. Tyne took Owen from his car seat and hoisted him onto her hip, recalling from their previous visits that the metal detector at the entrance was nearly impossible to navigate with a stroller. Never in her life had Tyne expected to become a pro at going to court.

"Put your bag through the X-ray machine," the security guard directed as they entered the lobby. "Loose articles go in the plastic dish."

Tyne did as directed, fishing her phone and keys from the pocket of her jeans. "That should be everything. What about shoes?"

"This isn't an airport," he told her, chuckling as if he'd told a joke. "Shoes can stay on."

"Oh, okay." She remembered him saying the same thing last time. "Should I walk through?"

The guard squinted at Owen. "Does he walk on his own?"

"Afraid not."

"Well, then carry him through. Don't put him on the X-ray belt." There wasn't a hint of joking this time, and Tyne's eyes widened as she realized someone must've actually tried that before.

She walked through, tensing for the dreaded buzz of an alarm, even though she was certain there wasn't a scrap of metal on her. What was it about a security line that instantly made her feel irrationally guilty? The sensation intensified when the guard opened her diaper bag and rummaged through the main pocket. Even though Tyne knew there was nothing in it to worry about, she trembled inside as if there was a chance an unknown criminal had filled it with illicit substances without her noticing.

"Here you go."

Tyne took the bag without a word, her heart beating against her ribcage like a bird wanting to break free.

"Where are you headed today?" the guard asked, eyeing her shaking hands with a look that said he was of half a mind to check her bag one more time.

Tyne sputtered, "Thatcher."

"What?" He gave her a look that could only be translated as *Are you on drugs*?

She cleared her throat and attempted to channel that inner confidence Hadley always managed so well. No one ever questioned things when Hadley said them. "I need to speak to Judge Thatcher."

The guard's eyes narrowed. He wasn't buying it. "Do you have an appointment?"

"Not exactly. I have a family emergency."

He shot her a *get real* look. "Listen, sister. Everyone who comes through these doors has a family emergency. You can't waltz into a judge's chambers. Reception is that way." He motioned to his right. "They can give you instructions for obtaining legal counsel who can interact with the judge on your behalf."

Tyne, who'd finally grasped why there were so many mean jokes about lawyers, did not want legal counsel. She was about to say as much when the front door opened, and a man and woman tumbled inside, screaming at each other. From the sound of it, they, too, were experiencing a family emergency and had no qualms about letting half the Commonwealth in on the airing of their dirty laundry.

Turning his attention away from Tyne, the security guard hurried toward the couple, waving his arms. "Whoa. No yelling. This is a *no yelling* zone."

Tearing her attention away from the commotion, Tyne looked to the right, where she had been told to go, and then to the left, where a gray door led to what appeared to be a stairwell. If she were a betting woman, she'd place a hefty wager the judge's chambers were through there. It was worth a closer inspection.

She shot a last look at the guard, who was now

yelling that this was a *no yelling* zone at the top of his lungs.

Was it wrong to ignore the guard's instructions and, as he'd put it, go waltzing in to see the judge unannounced? Probably. No doubt it broke more protocols than Tyne could fathom. But this was her last resort. She had to speak to Judge Thatcher right away, and she had to do it alone. No more lawyers. They'd caused enough trouble for one lifetime.

She wanted to do the right thing, and she needed to do it before she lost her nerve.

"Come on, kiddo," she whispered to Owen as they darted through the door. "Adventure time."

Owen put his arms in the air. His baby cries of "Weee!" echoed all the way down the stairs as they descended. Any minute now, they'd probably get arrested.

"Shh!" Tyne placed her index finger over her lips as she nudged the door open at the bottom of the stairs. Owen quieted down, and a moment later, they stepped out into a long hallway lined with doors. "Let's see if one of these has the judge's name on it."

Unfortunately, the only markings on the doors were letters and numbers that meant nothing to her, and as far as Tyne could see, there wasn't a directory. Of course. Why would they need to post a directory when they didn't want people like her down here in the first place?

The only plan that sprang to mind was to start on

one end and work her way to the other, knocking on each door along the way. It was a terrible plan, but she was about to enact it anyway when Tyne spotted a slender gentleman with gray hair exiting a door with a sign above it marking it as the men's room. Even without his black robes, Tyne recognized him as Judge Thatcher.

"Your Honor?" Tyne scurried down the hall as the man turned, wearing a startled expression. "Please wait!"

"Weee!" cried Owen.

"What's the meaning of this?" the judge asked. "Are you supposed to be down here, young lady?"

Breathing heavily, Tyne said, "My name is Tyne Briggs. It's very important I speak to you about my nephew, Owen."

"I don't know what's going on, but it's like a revolving door up there today," the judge muttered at the ceiling, not paying her any attention. "I've half a mind to march upstairs right now and have that nitwit at security fired."

"Please, don't do that," Tyne begged. "I'm sorry. I know I shouldn't have come down here without an appointment, but I'm desperate. You're the only person who can help. Please, sir. I only need a minute to explain."

Owen gurgled, and the judge's face softened a bit at the edges. "My chambers are this way. Follow me."

"Thank you. Thank you so much," Tyne gushed,

quickening her pace to keep up with the man's wide gait. "You won't regret it."

"I already do," he grumbled. "This is highly irregular, miss. Possibly unethical. *Ex parte* communications are strictly prohibited, so depending on the nature of your business, I may have to stop you immediately."

"I understand."

"Furthermore"—Judge Thatcher opened a door and motioned for her to step through—"I'm leaving early for the Cape, so you'll need to make this quick. Do you have any idea how backed up traffic over the Bourne Bridge gets before a holiday weekend?"

"Pretty bad, I imagine," Tyne replied. "I'll get right to the point. I want to withdraw my petition for custody of Owen Briggs."

"You what?"

Tyne lifted Owen higher on her hip. "Withdraw—"

The judge held up a hand to stop her. "I heard you the first time, but you can't do that."

Tyne frowned. "I thought it would be simple. Are there not forms I can fill out or something you can sign?"

"Forms?" Shaking his head, the judge lowered himself into the leather chair behind his desk. "I remember you. You and this little fella's other auntie were ready to fight to the death over who got to keep him. Isn't that right?"

"Yes," Tyne whispered, shame and remorse flooding her. "But, I need to do this."

"I need. *I need.*" Anger flashed in the man's eyes. "Seems to me both of you ladies need to be giving more thought to what *he* needs right now."

"Yes, sir. I am. I'm not doing this lightly." Tears spilled down Tyne's cheeks.

Looking like he'd rather be anywhere else, including stuck in traffic on the Bourne Bridge, the judge slid a box of tissues across his desk toward her. "Take a seat, and pull yourself together. Once you've calmed down, I think you'd better tell me exactly what's going on."

Tyne nodded, dabbing her eyes before blowing her nose and crumpling the tissue into a ball. "You're right that Hadley and I—Hadley Moore, that's Owen's other aunt—were in your courtroom before. You granted us temporary co-guardianship."

"As I recall, I also urged you to come to a compromise on permanent custody or else the court would decide for you."

"We tried. Well, actually, I'm not sure if trying is really the right word. You see, we both hired lawyers, only it turned out mine was a despicable human being. Hers wasn't much better. But mine pulled a rotten trick." Tyne took a breath, knowing she should end her story there but feeling compelled to continue. "I love Owen. So much. But, I also love Hadley. We were sharing the house and taking care of Owen. Then one thing led to another, and I honestly thought everything would work out like a fairy tale. Now it's terrible, and I don't want to hurt her. This is the only way."

The judge threw his pen onto his desk. "Well, that causes a big problem."

"I didn't realize." Tyne bounced Owen on her knee, grateful for a way to expend her nervous energy. "Is it a lot harder than I thought?"

"It's the start of the Fourth of July weekend, and aside from not beating the traffic, it will be nearly impossible to find him suitable foster care at such short notice when everyone and their uncle is on vacation."

"He can't go into foster care!" Tyne clapped her hand to her mouth as her screech echoed. "I grew up in foster care. I know what it's like. Besides, there's no need for that."

The judge fixed her with a stern stare. "Neither set of grandparents are able to take him. Where else do you expect him to go?"

"Not foster care." Panic was rising, leaving Tyne short of breath. "Why wouldn't he go live with Hadley?"

The judge threw his hands into the air. "Because Hadley Moore is in my assistant's office this very second, filling out the same paperwork you just asked for."

Tyne's head spun. "I don't understand."

"Apparently, today is my lucky day. I've had not one but two frantic women come crashing into my office, sobbing about evil lawyers and dirty tricks and falling in love. I've heard the whole story before, right down to that elusive quest for a fairy tale ending. If I wasn't positive this is real life, I'd swear I was watching a rerun." He folded his hands together on the desk. "I have to ask, why didn't you and Miss Moore take my advice and talk this out with each other before barreling toward the worst-case scenario at a hundred miles an hour?"

"I..." Tyne blinked, praying her head would clear. "Wait. She's actually still here? You weren't exaggerating?"

The judge pressed a button on his desk. "Susan, is Miss Moore still here?"

"She's in the conference room," a woman's voice replied through the intercom speaker.

"There you have it." The judge's voice was gruff, but there was kindness in his eyes. He got to his feet and walked around his desk. "Now, if you'll please come with me, Miss Briggs."

Tyne stood, dazed, and followed the judge into the hallway. "Where are we going?"

"To the conference room. I don't want to put Owen in foster care, which means I am going to need one of you two women to rethink withdrawing your petition. Otherwise, I'll have no choice, which would be a tragedy considering he clearly has a family who loves him." The judge stopped in front of a closed door and placed his hand on the knob. "Remember communication is critical for healthy families."

As soon as he opened the door, Tyne saw Hadley seated at the far end of a long conference table. She was holding a pen in her right hand as she flipped to the last page of a thick document.

"Don't do it!" Tyne shouted.

Hadley looked up, her face a perfect picture of surprise. "What are you doing here?"

Tyne held out Owen to the judge. "Here. Hold him for a moment."

"I'm not a babysitter, Ms. Briggs!" he argued but took the boy anyway.

Tyne ran toward Hadley as the judge made cooing sounds, and Owen giggled.

"I can't let you do this."

"You left me no choice." Hadley gripped her pen. "We're never going to agree."

"There's always room for compromise," said the judge, who, despite his earlier protests, rocked Owen in his arms like a seasoned grandfather.

"I wish I could believe he's right," Hadley said softly, "but we're never going to agree, and arguing over Owen is wrong. I need to do what's best for him."

"No, *we* do. Please, Hadley," Tyne begged, "set the pen down, and listen."

"What could you possibly have to say that hasn't already been said before?"

"I love you."

The pen slipped from Hadley's fingers and clattered onto the floor. "Huh?"

"I said I love you." Strangely, as soon as she'd admitted it, all of Tyne's nervousness evaporated. She'd never felt such calm. "If you'll hear me out, I came up with a plan. You just have to trust me. Before you say anything, I know I'm on thin ice in the trust department, and I'm so sorry for that, but I'm also convinced this will work."

"I'm listening."

Before Tyne could launch into her idea, they were interrupted.

"Whoa," the judge said. "Careful there, buddy."

Tyne and Hadley both turned in time to see Owen squirm from the judge's arms, sliding down his leg and onto the floor with a gentle plop. He rocked to his knees and crawled to the leg of the conference table, where he pulled himself up until he was standing on his feet.

He let go of the table leg, wobbled, and for a moment, it seemed he would fall flat on his face.

"Owen," Tyne and Hadley cried out at the same time, their voices filled with alarm.

Owen steadied himself, still standing on his own.

Tyne and Hadley locked eyes briefly, and then they watched in hushed anticipation as Owen lifted one little foot and set it down. He did the same with the other.

Hadley clutched Tyne's arm. "Did you see that?"

Owen swayed, bending his knees and straightening again. He took a step and then another.

Tyne gasped, putting her hand on top of Hadley's and squeezing. "He's doing it!"

Giggling, Owen toddled another two steps, then fell onto his butt with a plop. Hadley and Tyne jumped from their seats at the same time and ran toward him. As soon as they were close enough, Owen reached out with both his hands, grasping Hadley's in one and Tyne's in the other as he pulled himself back onto his feet. Laughing, their eyes sparkling with tears, they scooped him up and returned with him to their seats, where they sat down and balanced him between them on their laps.

"You see. Even the baby understands how this is supposed to work." Walking over to them, the judge snatched the as-yet unsigned document from the table and folded it in two like it was a piece of garbage destined for the nearest bin. "He seems to want both of you, so I suggest you figure out how to make that happen. I have my own family to get to."

Shaking his head, he left the office, and from somewhere down the hallway, Tyne thought she could hear him exclaim, "Women!"

Now that they were alone, Tyne took a moment to soak in the joy that came simply from being in the presence of the two people she loved most in the world.

Her family. Or at least she hoped so.

"Can I tell you my idea now?" Tyne asked.

"Yes, but there's something I need to say first, if that's okay."

"Okay." Tyne's belly fluttered as she waited for Hadley to speak.

"I love you, too."

Breaking into a grin, Tyne wrapped her arms around Hadley, wanting nothing more than to aim her mouth straight at Hadley's lips. Only the need to avoid squishing Owen in the process slowed her down, though not by much. The kiss was passionate and sweet, like a fine dark chocolate with a hint of chili pepper, the type of kiss that left Tyne wanting more.

When they finally stopped, Hadley rested her forehead against Tyne's and sighed. "Why did we complicate the hell out of this?"

"I don't know." Tyne plunked a kiss on Owen's head so he wouldn't feel too left out. "But let's pinky swear we'll never do anything like this again."

"Deal." Hadley offered her pinky. "Now, let's beat it before security has to clear us out. I want to go home."

"Me, too," Tyne replied, but in so many ways, she felt like she was already there.

CHAPTER TWENTY-THREE

"Is he asleep?" Hadley wrapped an arm around Tyne's waist, fighting exhaustion. It wasn't even very late, but all the twists and turns of the emotional roller coaster she'd been on made it feel like the longest day of her life.

"It's like he didn't want the day to end." Tyne turned her head to stare deeply into Hadley's eyes. A shiver of longing raced along Hadley's spine and straight to her core, reminding her there were a few things left on her wish list before she was ready to see this day end as well.

They tiptoed out of the room and carefully made their way down the steps.

"Watch out for the fifth one," Tyne cautioned, but Hadley was already stepping around it. "I see you've learned that trick."

"I've learned a lot of things since I moved in with you."

"Not all of them good." Tyne led the way into the kitchen, heading straight for the wine rack. "Care to join me for a glass?"

"Please." Hadley watched in mild confusion as Tyne took a bottle from the rack and proceeded to open it. "Is there none from the other night?"

"Are you joking? After you left, I finished off the bottle and then some."

"Drinking alone?"

"My mom helped."

"I'm sorry I reacted the way I did." Hadley took the wineglass Tyne offered and held it without drinking. "I was so hurt and angry, but the mature response would have been to stay and talk it out."

"Which we wouldn't have needed if I'd confronted you about the financial disclosures instead of stewing and then trying to one-up you." Tyne set the wine bottle down and picked up her glass. "Want to go sit in the living room?"

"Time for a debrief?"

"Is that code for a heart-to-heart talk, or are you suggesting we take off each other's underwear? Debriefing, get it? Like the briefs you wear..." Tyne dissolved into a fit of giggles.

"What?" Startled, Hadley's internal temperature ticked higher. She hadn't been thinking along those lines, but now she was.

"Never mind. That was a terrible pun. I couldn't help it, though. Here I was planning to settle in with a glass of wine, maybe light a few candles, and have a serious discussion about our future. You sound like you're preparing for a staff meeting. Next you're going to want to leverage our paradigms."

"I don't know. Sounds kinda kinky." Hadley chuckled.

"Only if you do it right," Tyne teased, making Hadley blush even more.

"I'm realizing how rusty I am when it comes to my personal life."

"My track record as of late isn't so stellar, either." Tyne curled up on the couch, tucking her feet beneath her. "I feel terrible about what Robert Atkinson did. It was completely unacceptable. I may not have known the specifics of what he was going to do, but the guy made my skin crawl, which should've been enough to make me run the other way, and I didn't."

"From what I hear, the man has no soul." Joining Tyne on the couch, Hadley reached for a throw blanket and draped it across her lap. The night was pleasant, but the thought of that creep sent shivers throughout her entire body. "Not that mine was any better. I'm truly ashamed of the role I played in all of this."

"I am, too." Tyne sipped her wine and set the glass on the coffee table. "It was easy to pretend everything was fantastic, and we didn't have a care in the world with our lawyers as proxies to do the dirty work."

Hadley clasped her hands, clenching her fingers together until the skin on her pinkies glowed red. "Are you saying you don't think we'll make a good team now that the buffer's been removed?"

"Not at all." Tyne inched closer, reaching for Hadley's hands. "I'm saying we need to be one hundred percent honest from now on about what we want. Starting tonight."

"What we want for…" Hadley let her thought trail off for Tyne to fill in the blank.

"Everything. Our relationship. Owen. All of it." Tyne slid closer still, resting her hand on Hadley's shoulder in a half embrace. "We're in love. It's a whole new world, and I don't want to face it apart. I want us to be together as a family, you, me, and Owen."

"So do I, more than anything. Back at the courthouse, you said you had an idea, a compromise of sorts." Hadley struggled to concentrate. Tyne's hand on her shoulder, innocent as the touch was, set all her nerve endings zinging.

"Right." Tyne cleared her throat, touching her tongue to her lips as if her mouth had gone dry. "The other night, I was going to propose—"

"Propose?" Hadley pressed her palm to her chest as her breathing quickened.

"No!" Tyne's eyes bulged. "I didn't mean it like that. I was going to *suggest* we spend a few days here and a few days in Boston."

"For the holiday weekend?" Hadley couldn't see how Tyne thought this would solve their problem.

"No, permanently. Or at least until Owen's old enough to make us both slaves to his playdate calendar and soccer practice schedule."

Hadley blinked several times in rapid succession. "I'm not understanding."

"Ryan loved soccer when he was a kid. I'm sure Owen will want to play."

"That wasn't what I meant. Are you saying you'd be willing to live in Boston?"

"Yes. Part-time, at least. I know you like being here with Owen and me, and this pace in life suits me fine, but I'm no fool. Boston is a world-class city. Your career would take a hit, and you'd resent us for it."

"There are benefits to a smaller hospital I never realized," Hadley argued. "Did you know a man is alive right now thanks to me? I'm not being arrogant. It's true. Last week, a guy came in with a gunshot wound, and I was the only one in the department who was comfortable performing the procedure that saved his life."

"You didn't tell me about that." For a moment, the admiration in Tyne's eyes stopped Hadley's breath. After how close they'd come to disaster, could she really be this lucky?

"I didn't have a chance to mention it before, and I think I was still trying to make sense of what it meant." Remembering the incident now filled Hadley with awe. "There are so many skilled doctors in a big hospital, so I'm nothing special. But having just one person with my knowledge at a hospital like PVH could be the difference between life and death. If I could be the reason another family doesn't have to go through what we have, could anything be more fulfilling? I won't resent you if I leave Boston behind."

"In that case, can I admit something?" Tyne shifted on the couch. "There might be a little part of me that isn't as thrilled with the pace of life here as I let on. When you took me out for dinner by the waterfront, it was the most amazing night of my life."

"Is that right?" Hadley raised an eyebrow, unable to hold back a smirk. "It was a good night for me, too."

"Your condo is incredible and surprisingly roomy. Maybe we could find a little place to live around here, too. Then I can schedule my art classes on the nights we're here, and you can work at PVH, but you could still put in shifts in Boston while I take Owen out for some big city culture."

Hadley warmed to the idea. "I know you were saving up to open a second studio. What about one in Boston?"

Tyne cringed. "It's possible I handed that money over as a retainer for a certain barracuda lawyer. Nonrefundable, naturally."

Hadley groaned. "I'm so sorry. If I hadn't put the ball in motion—"

"I didn't have to do it." Tyne closed her eyes,

massaging her temples. "Seriously. Swear to me, going forward, we'll talk before going off the deep end. Hopefully, talking will prevent the latter. It hit me, with the judge today, that all of this resulted from us not acting like rational adults. So much pain and suffering all because we were scared to say *I like you* and *do you want to try being a family*."

"Yes." Hadley's lips twitched as Tyne tilted her head to one side.

"How did you mean that? Yes, you agree we acted like idiots?"

"Yes, I like you. And yes, I want us to make this work. With us and with Owen." Hadley pointed toward the ceiling. "That little boy deserves happiness, and I think he's been trying to play matchmaker this whole time, always latching onto both of us as if saying, *You two belong together. Stop fighting it.*"

Tyne grinned. "He's done a magnificent job of it."

It was Hadley's turn to gaze with open admiration. "This compromise of yours isn't too shabby, either. Best of both worlds. I like it."

"It really is. When I think about having my painting on display at a real art gallery, I—" Tyne choked, her eyes filling with panic. "Oh, shit. Is today Wednesday?"

"Yes." Hadley's heart rate accelerated. "What's wrong?"

"The guy from the gallery. He was supposed to pick up the painting today, and I forgot all about it." Tyne swept up her phone. As soon as she looked at the screen, she fell back against the couch. "Twelve missed calls, all from the 617 area code. This is a disaster. My one shot, and I blew it."

"No, I refuse to believe that." Hadley jumped into action to save Tyne's career opportunity the same way she would save a critical patient. "We'll call Sheila first thing in the morning, explain the entire story, and drive it directly to the gallery ourselves."

"The entire story?" Tyne looked aghast. "You want me to confess to a gallery owner I barely know all the terrible shit we've done to each other over the past few months?"

"Maybe we should go with a family emergency and leave out the particulars."

"Good thinking." Tyne rested her head on Hadley's shoulder. "I'm sorry. I hate to make you drive us all the way to Boston at the start of a holiday weekend."

"I kinda had to go anyway," Hadley admitted.

"Why?"

"That job we're counting on me having in Boston? If I want to keep it, I have about forty-eight hours to show up to work and foil my chief of staff's evil plan to get rid of me."

"That alone will be worth the drive. I hope you can ask someone to get a video of his face when you walk through the door." They both laughed, and Tyne added, "I hear the fireworks at the Esplanade are fantastic."

"They are, and you can see them from my—" Hadley shook her head. "You can see them from our condo."

"Perfect. As long as we make it back for the big Briggs cookout on Monday."

"Wouldn't have it any other way. Now that the future looks so bright, I'd hate for your parents to have to kill me."

"It would be such a waste." Tyne threaded her fingers through Hadley's.

Hadley lifted Tyne's hand to her mouth, giving it a kiss. A moment later, she yawned.

"Time for bed?" Tyne asked.

"Yes." Hadley rose from the couch, reaching for Tyne's hands to pull her to her feet. "But first, we need a debriefing."

"I thought we agreed to call them heart-to-heart talks," Tyne corrected. "But what else could we possibly need to discuss tonight?"

"Absolutely nothing." Hadley flashed a sly smile. "I meant the other kind of debriefing."

Tyne grinned. "Race you upstairs."

WHEN THEY CRAWLED INTO BED, Hadley pulled Tyne into her arms, her naked front against the silky skin of Tyne's bare back. The woman's body reacted to the slightest touch as she let out a moan that dispelled any notion she was in the mood for sleep. They hadn't bothered with pajamas. The agenda for the evening made it clear there was no need.

Hadley kissed the back of Tyne's head, trailing her fingers through short waves of hair. Though it was too dark to see, Hadley pictured its pale-yellow color, with the single streak of pink, her signature color that perfectly expressed her artistic soul.

Hadley grazed her lips along Tyne's neck, massaging her shoulders at the same time with thumbs pressing deep, slow circles. Tyne whimpered, such a vulnerable sound, and Hadley's eyes stung with unexpected tears.

This week had shown Hadley a different type of grief, a loss that was impossible to mourn, so pointless and self-inflicted. There had been moments when total darkness had threatened to engulf her, and she'd feared if it went out, the light would never shine again. After all the trust that had been broken between them, it seemed like a miracle they were here now, rebuilding with each caress and kiss.

Hadley let out a ragged breath, unable to stop the teardrops from flowing down her cheeks.

"What's wrong?" Tyne turned to face her, capturing her in a close embrace.

Hadley nuzzled the hollow of Tyne's neck. "I honestly thought we would never do this again. When I left the other night, I thought it was over."

"Never," Tyne whispered. "No way was I going to

let that be the end. I'm a determined woman when I want to be, and not being able to do this again would be too cruel."

"Of all the thoughts that kept plaguing me, the knowledge of it being over between us was the worst. Weren't you afraid that was true?"

"Terrified. But the worst part for me was knowing you believed I was that callous person, capable of—I don't know the word for it. Depravity, maybe?" Tyne shuddered, clasping Hadley even tighter as if afraid she would slip away. "A person would have to be, to do what you thought I did. Tell me the truth. Did you honestly believe when I made love to you in Boston I was anything but sincere, that I could've used you like that?"

"All my senses told me what we shared was real. But then I wondered if I was wearing blinders, reluctant to see the ugly truth because of how much I wanted to believe I meant something to you." As she spoke, Hadley's hands roamed across soft, warm flesh. After days of hell, she'd found paradise. "I shouldn't have doubted, not even a tiny bit. If I'd stopped to think about it, I would've realized there was more to the story. I should've trusted you."

"I gave you no reason to," Tyne murmured, peppering Hadley's forehead with gentle kisses. "I may not have behaved as badly as you assumed, but I can't make excuses, either. I was far from innocent, and the things I *did* hire that awful attorney to do in my name were bad enough."

"Shh." Hadley placed her index finger against Tyne's lips, so soft and plump. "Let's not talk about it anymore."

Tyne's tongue poked between her lips, swiping along Hadley's finger. The next moment she captured Hadley's hand, pulling it away from her mouth as her other hand slid behind Hadley's head, bringing her close enough their mouths could meet. There was to be no gentle teasing this time, no tentative grazing. Tyne dove in with complete abandon, devouring her mouth with the same enthusiasm a starving person would show a ribeye steak. Hadley was equally famished.

Tyne made a move as if to straddle her, but Hadley had other ideas and rolled Tyne onto her back instead, stretching out across the length of her. When her desperate craving had subsided enough for Hadley to register her mouth and jaw aching, she slowed the pace. Finally, she pushed back, sitting astride Tyne's pelvis while supporting her weight on her knees, and studied her lover's body in the dim light that shone from a trio of electric candles on the nightstand.

Now that Tyne's breasts were on full display, the urge to suck one of the pert round nipples into her mouth was nearly overwhelming. She kept herself in check, barely, and instead lunged, catlike, to place a hand on either side of Tyne's shoulders. Hadley's back formed a deep arch as she placed the softest, gentlest of kisses on Tyne's lips. She inched down to Tyne's chin, delighting in making her way downward to the hollow of Tyne's throat. Only after all this did she succumb to temptation, latching her mouth firmly around the much longed-for nipple.

Tyne let out a gasp, arching her back. Her legs pushed against Hadley's thighs as they sought to spread wide but couldn't escape. Hadley remained in place, each brush of Tyne's wriggling body against her most sensitive region intensifying her arousal. After a very long time, possibly days, Hadley moved to the other nipple but continued rolling the other between two fingers, pinching and tweaking enough to offer assurance it hadn't been forgotten.

She inhaled the light scent of peaches, nearly choking on how sweet, how perfect it smelled. Every detail held Hadley spellbound, from the rise and fall of Tyne's chest to the way she dug her fingers into the sheets at her side.

In this moment, it was so clear they belonged together.

How had she—had *they*—nearly messed up everything?

Even the strongest love was fragile, too easy to destroy with carelessness.

Never again.

As if in tune with Hadley's thoughts, Tyne

entwined her fingers with Hadley's free hand and gave it a squeeze.

Calm engulfed her, but Hadley could sense Tyne's need gathering strength like a stormfront on the horizon, urging her to continue her downward trek. Channeling every emotion she struggled to put into words, Hadley focused on transforming them into action, demonstrating for Tyne the depths of her devotion in a way that could never be misunderstood.

Hadley kissed and licked as she progressed on the journey, occasionally moving to the side, delighted to discover a ticklish spot that had escaped detection before. Tyne reacted by squirming underneath her, sparking new urgency.

As she passed Tyne's belly button, the woman writhed with abandon. Each kiss and touch seeming to drive her to the brink of madness.

Hadley arrived at Tyne's V and veered to the inside of her thigh. Hadley's nose filled with the aroma of Tyne's wanting, and she inhaled deeply. Once. Twice. On the third inhalation, Hadley flicked Tyne's clit with the tip of her tongue. Tyne bucked, her knees falling to the sides as she landed back on the mattress, giving Hadley all the access she could desire.

With her finger, Hadley caressed Tyne's slit. It was slick with wetness, nearly dripping. Slowly Hadley separated the swollen folds, seeking entrance, all the while continuing to circle her tongue around Tyne's pulsing clit.

Starting slowly and then gaining speed, Hadley's tongue and fingers moved in tandem.

In and out.

Around and around.

Over and over again.

Tyne's fingers dug into Hadley's shoulders, kneading as if keeping tempo with Hadley's rhythm.

A second finger joined the first, plunging unrelentingly as Tyne panted with desire, begging for release without uttering a word. At that moment, Hadley's existence had no greater purpose than to grant this wish. She doubled her efforts, each thrust of her fingers, each swipe of her tongue driving Tyne closer to that moment of pure abandon.

Hadley wanted to bring her to the edge and beyond.

Finally, Tyne succumbed, surrendering as her body quivered and shook. Hadley thought it might never end, and if the only thing she experienced for the rest of her life was that single moment, it would be enough.

Eventually the spasms quieted. Hadley rested her cheek on Tyne's pelvis, her fingers remaining deep inside her until the very last tremor had passed.

Silence descended on them.

Time stood still.

"I love you." Tyne could barely get the words out, her breathing still ragged.

Her voice may have been unsteady, but Hadley

trusted completely the sentiment was true, that Tyne's love for Hadley would prove as solid and enduring as Hadley's for her.

Hadley snaked her way upward, pulling Tyne into an embrace, nuzzling her head in the crook of Tyne's neck. "I adore you more than I ever thought possible."

CHAPTER TWENTY-FOUR

Tyne stepped back to appraise her handy work. "You're all set for the day, little man."

Owen, standing with his hand on his favorite wooden rocking horse, jutted out his chin, clearly pleased with his new jeans, plaid shirt, and puffy vest with a fox on the front. Though it was only early October and the leaves in Boston were barely changing yet, a cold front had ushered in a week of below average temperatures. After a sweltering summer, Tyne was ready for sweater weather.

Dressed in fresh scrubs and a pristine white coat, Hadley popped her head into the nursery. "Check you out, GQ." She produced her phone from one of her pockets and snapped a photo. "Mom and Dad are going to love this shot. I'll send it to your parents, too, if you want."

"Please. He looks like a mini-version of Ryan." Tyne

gave a wistful sigh. It'd been six months since the accident that had cut short the lives of their siblings, but grief was a wound that took a lifetime to heal.

"Ry!" Owen parroted, not quite mastering the second syllable. That didn't stop him from looking so proud of himself. "Ry!"

"That's right, sweetie. Ryan," Tyne said through the lump in her throat. "That's your daddy."

"Da!"

Entering the room, Hadley hunched down and pointed to his vest. "What animal is that?"

Owen peered down, his tongue sticking out as he concentrated.

"Is it a fox?" Hadley prodded.

"Pffft!"

"Close enough." Hadley held up her hand for a high five then straightened with a grunt. "These weather changes are wreaking havoc on my joints. Why is it so cold?"

"Quit your complaining," Tyne scolded. "While I am grateful that both the condo and the house have central air-conditioning, I've had more than enough of boob sweat every time I go outside."

"Didn't I tell you the best cure for that is to go topless?" Hadley shook her head in pretend disappointment. "You need to stop disregarding my expert medical opinion on these matters."

"Expert medical opinion, my ass," Tyne shot back, rolling her eyes.

"Yes, come to think of it, you should leave that uncovered, as well. Strictly for health reasons, of course." Unable to keep a straight face any longer, Hadley broke into a grin. "And, you need to put a dollar in the swear jar."

Tyne put her hands on her hips. "For what?"

"You said the A-word."

"The he—*hello* I did."

"Nice save." Hadley's eyes twinkled. "You were the one who said you didn't want Owen starting preschool with the vocabulary of a sailor on shore leave. I'm just making sure the rule gets enforced equally."

"Fine, but I don't have cash," Tyne grumbled.

"Millennials." Shaking her head, Hadley pulled out her phone. "No worries."

Tyne jumped as her own phone vibrated. She'd just received a payment request of one dollar on her Venmo account with a note that read *swear jar*. "Are you fu—ndamentally kidding me with this? When did you even set it up? I didn't think you had an account."

"I made one after the last time you claimed not to have cash for the jar. This is going into Owen's college fund, so you better believe I intend to ride your ass about it."

"Busted!" Tyne did a dance of glee.

"God damn it!" Hadley clamped a hand over her mouth as Tyne squealed.

"That will be two dollars, Dr. Moore."

"Maybe I should pay five dollars so I can tell you what I'm really thinking right now."

"Hear that, my precious boy?" Tyne said to Owen. "You better study hard in school because at this rate, we'll have enough for Harvard by the time you graduate high school."

"Harvard?" Hadley pretended she was about to faint. "I guess I'd better get to work. Off to the salt mines with me."

"I'd feel bad for you, except I know for a fact now that Michael's gone, it's a nonstop fiesta in that ER of yours."

"I'm not sure I'd go that far, but the new chief of staff is an all-around improvement."

As for Amanda, she'd done them the favor of getting herself kicked out of the residency program all on her own. If her spurious complaints about Hadley hadn't been quite enough to do it, screwing over the entire surgical department by scheduling a two-week vacation for the middle of her rotation had sealed the deal. According to Hadley, absolutely no one had been sorry to see her go.

Hadley kissed Tyne's cheek. "Seriously, though, I've got to run."

"Okay." Tyne pressed her lips together as if to hold on to the kiss a little longer. "Don't forget to ask for the week off at Thanksgiving."

"That's more than a month away," Hadley argued.

"I know you're excited to host dinner, but take it down a notch, will ya?"

"I can't help it." Tyne threw her hands in the air for emphasis, wondering how Hadley could remain so calm. "It's our first big event in the new house."

"What are you talking about?" Hadley held up fingers as she counted. "We had the cookout, Owen's birthday party, that water park themed thing for Labor Day, Connor's graduation. Between yours and mine, our families are literally at the house all the time."

"Yes, but we were still renting when we had those parties. It doesn't count." Sometimes Tyne couldn't believe their good luck that the owners of the house decided to sell at just the right time. Her dreams of Owen growing up there were coming true after all. "Now that it truly belongs to us, it's different."

"It's the same bloody house." Hadley pointed a finger at Tyne. "Before you try to charge me for that swear, remember we agreed dirty words from outside America don't count."

"I'm aware. You've compiled so many British obscenities our house is starting to sound like a very foul-mouthed version of *Downton Abbey*."

Hadley shrugged, grinning broadly. "I didn't make the rules. I just follow them."

"Oh, yeah? Since when?"

"Come here, Owen. Give me a kiss goodbye." Ignoring Tyne's question, Hadley hunched down in time for Owen to launch himself at her at full speed.

"Ba ba!" He wrapped his little arms around her neck, holding on tight.

"Yes, bye-bye." Hadley stood, a little wobbly from Owen's exuberance. "I'll be back for dinner, hopefully. I love you both."

"We love you, too. Fingers crossed for a slow day for you." Tyne crossed hers to be safe.

"It makes the day crawl, but it means people aren't dying or sick, so..." With that, Hadley left the nursery.

Tyne took a second to allow the warm fuzzy feeling of their lives to wash over her. Once they'd put their minds to it and started working toward a common goal, everything had fallen into place. It felt like a dream, and Tyne pinched herself regularly to make sure it wasn't.

"You ready for our walk?" Tyne asked Owen. "Let's get your monkey backpack on."

"Ta!"

Owen knew the drill and stuck his arms through the straps of the stuffed plush monkey whose long tail allowed Tyne to keep their budding daredevil from darting into traffic. Finally, Tyne circled a piece of blue painter's tape around his wrist, sticky part out. Now they were ready to go.

Outside on the brick sidewalk, it took Owen less than five seconds to pick up his first slightly yellowed leaf from the ground. He placed it on the tape and raised his arm up for Tyne to admire.

"Great job. We have to keep moving so we can find some more things for your bracelet."

Owen took a step—backward, but Tyne had grown accustomed to their walks taking five times longer than necessary. Sometimes, it felt like she was trying to navigate a drunk friend home, but with Owen, it was his curiosity to see and touch everything that slowed them down. Tyne could live with that, as long as she was able to stop him from picking up the truly disgusting objects from the ground. Like the time he tried to scoop up some dog poo. He was learning what he could and couldn't touch, and Tyne was learning to never leave the house without hand sanitizer and wipes for bigger emergencies.

By the time they'd reached Charles Street, Owen's bracelet was nearly complete.

Grasping Owen's monkey tail leash, Tyne reached for the door of the gallery. She paused for a moment to look at her paintings in the front window—three of them this month—overwhelmed with a sense of wonder. Was her art really on display at a Beacon Hill art gallery? It was almost impossible to believe.

"I need my Owen hug for the day," Sheila called out from the back of the shop, approaching with a hunched back and a giant smile, her arms held wide.

Owen threw himself into the grandmotherly woman's arms.

"I swear when you guys are out of town, my life feels emptier." Sheila tousled the little boy's hair. She pointed to the blue band on his wrist. "Did you make this, my talented young man?"

"Show Sheila your bracelet, Owen," Tyne coaxed.

"Baa!" He lifted his arm.

"These are lovely. Just wait a couple more weeks, and the colors will be even more vibrant." Sheila turned to Tyne. "Did you see the new display?"

"Yes, but I thought you said you were going to use the blue one." Tyne picked up Owen as he edged closer and closer to a display of blown glass.

"It already sold." Sheila opened the door for the three of them to step outside. "You see your mommy's masterpieces, Owen?"

Tyne adored how everyone who interacted with Owen on a regular basis loved the sweet little boy.

"I can't believe it." Tyne's eyes wandered the latest paintings she'd created. "I can barely keep up."

Sheila laughed. "Please try. It won't be long before we need another one, especially after our inaugural paint and sip event."

The trio re-entered the shop.

"Is there anything you need me to do?" Tyne asked.

"Other than show up and teach, everything's set. There'll be a cash bar over there." Sheila pointed to the spot. "Appetizers are being catered by that new place down the block. And, Joseph has agreed to play the violin during the breaks."

Tyne listened, wide-eyed, to every detail.

"This is so much fancier than anything I've ever

done back home. Most people pick up a bottle of wine from the packie," she joked, using the Massachusetts slang word for a liquor store.

"Boston Brahmins don't buy their vino from a package store, my dear, and it's their deep pockets we need to attract," Sheila said with a chuckle. "But with my expertise in hosting gallery openings and your ability to teach, we can't go wrong."

"We'll see," Tyne said with caution. "We haven't hosted the first one yet."

"And we already have a waiting list for the next." Sheila gave her a motherly pat on the back. "This paint and sip series is the talk of the town. That's the power of—what do the marketing people call it, buzz?"

"I hope everyone has a good time and gets their money's worth." Considering how much they'd been able to charge for tickets, Tyne was determined to bring her A game. It was a little scary, but this collaboration with Sheila had the ability to move her career higher on almost every level.

One of the leaves from Owen's bracelet fell, and he squirmed in her arms to retrieve it. Never missing a beat, Sheila swept it up and put it back in place.

Sheila patted Owen's head. "What's your plan today?"

"Going to the park. I want to tire Owen out as much as possible before Evan arrives to babysit him."

"How is your brother getting along now that he's transferred to Boston University?"

"He's liking his degree program so much better at BU. It helps that we're here a few days most weeks. He likes to think he's independent, but he needs his family just as much as we need him."

"Families are like that." Sheila's eyes shone. "And speaking of, now that I've found such a reliable partner to keep the wheels turning at the gallery while I'm away, I'm counting the days to my first winter in Arizona where I'll get unlimited visits with my new granddaughter."

"You've more than earned your retirement."

"*Semi*retirement," Sheila corrected. "Don't count me out completely yet."

A customer came in requiring the woman's full attention, so Tyne and Owen waved goodbye.

Back out on Charles Street, Tyne put Owen down, grasped his monkey tail, and turned toward Boston Common. "Come on, buddy. Let's see what this big, beautiful world has to offer us today!"

EPILOGUE

"Hold on, Owen." Hadley tried to reel in the two-year-old, but he was a force to be reckoned with, slipping from her grasp like a wiggly ball of slime. "Remind me again why we didn't put him in Mr. Monkey today."

"Because a stuffed monkey on his back doesn't really go with his toddler tux," Tyne said, catching the boy by his sleeve before he could run down the hall. Her tone implied the *like we've already discussed a hundred times* part she left unsaid.

"Jug!" Owen shouted, trying to make a break for it. Fortunately, Tyne was more skilled at keeping hold of him than Hadley was.

"We're not seeing Judge Thatcher today, little man." Tyne had to laugh at his dramatic pout. How many other little kids got this upset about not getting to see a family court judge? "He really is taken with the man."

"That's because the judge spoils him with lollipops every time we come to the courthouse for something."

"I suppose since he was there for Owen's first steps, the judge feels like an honorary grandfather."

"I don't know who's worse, the judge with his candy or Sheila with all those cookies she gives him." Hadley pretended to be grumpier about it than she really was, considering she was just as bad about giving in to his begging for sweets. He was too cute to say no to. "At this rate, all of his teeth are going to rot out of his head before he's eighteen."

"You know he's going to get another set, right?" Tyne gave her a suspicious look. "Are you sure you went to medical school?"

As Owen tugged free of Tyne's grasp, Hadley reached out to grab him by the shoulders with both hands. "He's determined to go that way, and once he gets his mind set on something, it's easier to move a mountain."

"He gets it from both sides of the family." Tyne took matters into her own hands, hoisting Owen and plopping him on her hip. "Hey, bud. Adoption day is next month. We're going somewhere else today."

"Destination forever land." Hadley chuckled as Tyne looked askance at her. "I'm guessing you think I need to workshop that title some more."

Tyne tried not to roll her eyes but failed. "It sounds

like one of those cartoons Owen would watch where two dinosaurs go on a quest to find a mythical land so they can stop climate change."

Hadley's eyebrows scrunched. "Why would dinosaurs want to stop climate change? They're cold-blooded."

"I don't know," Tyne shot back. "Why does a doctor know what type of blood dinosaurs had but doesn't realize kids lose their baby teeth?"

"Pretty sure that's a wedding day foul." Hadley kissed her cheek.

Tyne offered a bemused smile. "What is?"

"Making fun. You can't mock me until we seal the deal."

"Seal the deal?" Tyne clicked her tongue. "You have such a way with words. That's about as romantic a phrase as debriefing."

"I don't remember you complaining about my debriefing techniques last night. That's all I'm saying." Hadley bopped Owen on the nose with her index finger. "Remember this, my boy. Haters are going to hate."

They rounded the corner, heading toward a sign at the far end of a long hallway that marked the justice of the peace's office. Both sets of parents, plus Tyne's three brothers, were already standing outside the door.

"Are we late?" Tyne asked.

"We're always late." Hadley let out an exaggerated sigh. "I haven't been on time for anything in a year."

"That's because we have a toddler," Tyne said, giving the same excuse she always did.

Hadley had learned there was as little point in arguing about it as there was in trying to get her soon-to-be wife out of the house on time. For about three weeks around Christmas, she'd thought she'd won when it occurred to her to set all the clocks ahead by fifteen minutes. But then Tyne had caught on, and there'd been *H-E-double hockey sticks* to pay. Now she told everyone to expect them to be fashionably late. The only exception was Tyne's art classes, which somehow, she managed to begin and end on time. It was one of the woman's many surprising and inexplicable talents.

"Do you think I can put him down now?" Tyne's face was turning red. "He's getting so big."

"Might as well. We've got the whole crew to round him up." Hadley waved, as much to acknowledge the family as to alert them that Owen would probably try to make a break for it.

As soon as his feet hit the floor, Owen immediately made a U-turn, heading the way he wanted to go. "Jug!"

"Owen," Michelle called out, cupping her hands around her mouth. "Come to Grammy, and you can have cake."

The boy stopped in his tracks but didn't turn around.

"Chocolate cake," Tyne coaxed.

"It's not chocolate," Hadley corrected. "We went for the carrot cake. And it's back at the house."

Tyne put a finger to her lips, her eyes shouting *stop talking*. "Are you trying to make this harder?"

"Geez Louise, are you guys getting cold feet down there?" Evan shouted.

"Talk to your nephew about it." Tyne pointed to Owen.

"Owen, my man. Come hang out with the boys." Evan, who had a special touch with Owen, crouched down to his level and gave an encouraging smile. Sure enough, Owen went running, this time in the correct direction and into Evan's outstretched arms.

Hadley and Tyne strolled hand in hand at a leisurely pace that was more suitable for their grown-up status, although Hadley knew if she let go, Tyne was just as likely to go skipping all the way to the Justice of the Peace's office. She was unpredictable that way, which it turned out was a big part of why Hadley adored her.

"Why does there always have to be a production with this family?" Conner barely looked up from his phone, his fingers flying as he continued whatever text conversation he was engaged in.

Keith swatted the back of his son's head. "Your sister's getting married. You can put the phone away for half an hour."

"Clock's ticking, then. Are we going to do this or not?" Connor stood from the wooden bench, full of late-teen attitude but stuffing the phone in his pocket as his dad had asked. "I've got plans later."

"With a girl," Mason added.

"You have a date?" Tyne smirked at Connor as his cheeks burned red and then shifted her attention to Mason. "You gotta fill me in on every juicy detail later on today, buddy, okay?"

"If you give me cake," Mason said with the impeccable comedic timing that never failed to take Hadley by surprise. He might have an intellectual disability, but anyone who thought the boy wasn't smart wasn't paying close enough attention.

"Cake!" Owen parroted, and everyone laughed.

"It's like everyone only came for cake." Hadley puffed out her bottom lip.

"Not true." Hadley's mom gave her daughter a hug. "I came to make sure this goes through. Your father and I have been waiting for this day for a very long time, and we don't want you to mess it up. Then we'll have cake."

Hadley's phone buzzed, and she read a text from her father that consisted of two brides and a wedge of cake. She showed it to Tyne. "Even my own father. And let me take this chance to thank you again for teaching Dad how emojis work."

"Someone had to," Tyne argued, clearly choosing to ignore the heavy sarcasm. "It seemed cruel to leave such important skills training to a Gen-Xer like you."

"Now that he can speak in emojis, I'm afraid he'll never talk again," Hadley said.

"Just as well." Her mom's eyes narrowed as she pointed at her husband. "The less he says to those cougars in the Pioneer Acres recreation room, the better. As much as I'm enjoying the perks of retirement living, if I catch Agnes trying to draw you into one of her canasta games again when she thinks I'm not looking, we're moving."

"It's not my fault," he defended with a sheepish smile. "Those poor widows are lonely, and there aren't many men there."

"Because women live longer than men," her mom pointed out.

"Because you nag us to an early grave," he said, crossing his arms.

"Are you sure you want to do this?" Tyne raised an eyebrow at Hadley. "You may have had a point before when you said marriage was an outdated institution. Perhaps we should discuss it some more."

"Nope." Even though she knew Tyne was joking, Hadley's heart beat faster at the mere mention of not going through with it. They'd been through way too much to back out now. "Outdated or not, I refuse to be the one to make Owen explain to the other kids when he gets older why his mommies aren't married."

"Scientists." Tyne shook her head as if inviting everyone to feel pity for her choice of life partner. "Always so practical."

Practical, yes. That, along with not wanting to be the center of attention in a room full of people she barely knew, was why they were holding their no-frills nuptials at the courthouse, followed by an intimate reception at the house for family and close friends. But what Hadley didn't say was now that Tyne had helped her learn the true importance of family, nothing was going to keep her from building her own, with all the bells and whistles, starting with matching gold bands.

Of course, knowing Tyne's brothers, they had brought actual bells and whistles with them and would use them to draw the attention of every stranger on the street to the two white-clad brides as soon as they got outside. Even that she could live with, as long as it meant she and Tyne had officially tied the knot.

"Looks like they're ready for you inside," Tyne's mom announced, putting an arm around both Hadley and Tyne. "You look so beautiful."

"Thanks, Michelle," Hadley said.

"She was talking to me," Tyne said in an exaggerated stage whisper.

"I was talking about *both* of you."

Hadley stuck her tongue out at Tyne.

"Mature."

Hadley shrugged. "You make me feel younger. Plus, it's really too late for you to change your mind now."

"Not until I sign on the dotted line." Tyne tapped Hadley lovingly on the tip of her nose. "Lucky for you, I made up my mind quite some time ago."

Lucky, indeed.

Tyne's father started to usher everyone inside. "You two coming?"

"In just a minute," Hadley said. He disappeared inside, leaving Hadley and Tyne out in the hallway for a private moment.

"What's with the delay?" Tyne asked. "I thought you said it was too late to change our minds."

"I wanted to do something before we went in." Hadley made a coughing noise as she tried to clear the lump in her throat.

"Not a debriefing, I hope." Tyne's nervousness came through in her laugh, whether from the fact they were minutes from getting married or because of Hadley's uncharacteristic seriousness, it was hard to tell. "I told you that's happening later tonight, after all our friends and family go home from the reception."

"No, not that." Hadley grinned wickedly. "Although now that's all I'll be able to think about while we're exchanging vows."

"Happy to help."

Hadley reached into the pocket of her white linen jacket—which some might consider a fashion faux pas since it was a week after Labor Day, but as far as she was concerned, it suited the occasion. She pulled out a velvet box and opened the lid. "I got you this."

Her stomach fluttered as she watched Tyne pull the simple locket out by its silver chain. When Tyne opened it, displaying a tiny picture of Ryan, Kayleigh, and a newborn Owen on one side, with a similar one of them and the rambunctious toddler he'd become on the other side, tears welled in her eyes. "It's beautiful."

"Let me help you put it on." Hadley reached for the necklace, clasping it behind Tyne's neck.

Tyne tucked it into her lacy white sundress and gave it a pat as if to press it close to her heart. She rested her forehead against Hadley's. "I wish Ryan and Kayleigh were here."

"They are." Hadley's eyes darted upward, technically looking at the ceiling but imagining all the bigger mysteries that remained unseen.

"It's hard not to feel guilty sometimes. Here it is, the happiest day of my life, but"—Tyne bit her lip—"part of me knows if they hadn't died, if you hadn't come back home for your parents and Owen, we wouldn't be here."

Hadley brushed a tear from Tyne's cheek. Her heart clenched. "I don't know. Maybe we would be. I'm sure I would've come home for Christmas at some point, and you're hard not to notice."

"It's the pink hair." Tyne pointed to the single, chunky streak. "Even so, you didn't remember my name. You called me Tina."

"What's in a name? That's Shakespeare, you know. Direct quote, so remember *that* the next time you try to accuse me of not being romantic enough. I quoted Shakespeare on our wedding day." Hadley's expression grew serious as she looked deep into the eyes of the woman who was about to become her wife. "I was an idiot. However, I have a feeling my little sister wouldn't have let me be an idiot forever. I'll never believe that losing them was meant to be, but as for us? No one can convince me otherwise."

Tyne sucked in a breath, her mouth trembling as she pressed her fingers to the corners of her eyes to remove any last traces of crying. "Okay, Dr. Moore. You ready to make an honest woman out of me?"

"I'm ready to fall more in love with you every day. Tina."

Tyne giggled, the joy returning to her face, as Hadley had hoped to accomplish.

Hadley threaded her fingers through Tyne's. "Come on. Let's get this over with so we can have some cake."

THANK YOU FOR READING!

Hi there!

Miranda here. I can't thank you enough for deciding to read my book today. There is nothing more amazing to me as an author than knowing people like you are out there reading and enjoying my books.

Here are just a few things you might want to know about Hadley and Tyne's story. The setting is a small town in western Massachusetts. While the exact location is fictional, it is based on Turners Falls and Montague, home of the famous Montague Bookmill, a bookstore that offers books you don't need in a place you can't find!

I owe a great debt of gratitude to Vicki Harris who provided so much useful information and insight into the custody and adoption process.

I love to do hands on research for my books, and this one was no exception. If you want to hear about the paint and sip classes I attended and see photos of my "masterpieces," be sure to sign up for my newsletter.

You'll be alerted to my latest new releases and special offers, plus get your free copy of my debut novel, *Telling Lies Online*, not to mention keep up with my mischievous kittens, the Sisters of Chaos. I'd really like to stay in touch!

Finally, if you enjoyed *Hearts in Motion*, would you consider leaving a review or recommending it to other readers on social media? As an independent author, even a short review or rating can really help.

Happy reading!

Miranda

Made in the USA
Middletown, DE
15 July 2021

44161429R10246